D1149528

LOVERS AND STRANGERS

LOVERS AND STRANGERS
Two Novellas

David Grossman

Translated from the Hebrew
by Jessica Cohen

BLOOMSBURY

First published in Great Britain 2005

Copyright © 2002 by David Grossman

Translation copyright © 2005 by Jessica Cohen

The moral right of the author has been asserted

A CIP catalogue record for this book is available from the British Library

ISBN 0 7475 8025 1
ISBN-13 9780747580256

10 9 8 7 6 5 4 3 2 1

Printed in Great Britain by Clays Ltd, St Ives plc

All papers used by Bloomsbury Publishing are natural recyclable products made
from wood grown in well-managed forests. The manufacturing processes conform
to the environmental regualtions of the country of origin

Frenzy

How does she do it? he wonders. Over and over again, the meticulous rituals she must perform and the nervous scurrying through rooms before leaving, slamming closet doors, opening and closing drawers. An impenetrable expression grips her lovely face during those moments—God forbid she should forget a comb or a book or a bottle of shampoo, or everything might collapse. He sits at his empty desk with his head in his hands as she tosses him a quick goodbye from the door, and his heart sinks: she didn't even come near him to take her leave. Something special is going to happen there today, and she's already rushing out into the street, looking down so as not to make eye contact with anyone and get entangled in a needless conversation. How does she keep it up? Where does she find the strength to go through with it every day?

Then, after this momentary lapse of watchfulness, he shuts his eyes and hurries to accompany her as she gets into her car, a little green Polo. He had bought it for her as a surprise. She was horrified by the color and the extravagance, but he wanted her to have her own car. So you can come and go as you wish, he had said. So we won't keep fighting over the car. And he wanted her to have a very green car. He pictured it as a shiny microchip inserted into her veins so a camera could monitor her. Slowly he lowers his head against the back of the chair, and she drives away. Her face is strained and held too close to the windshield. It will take her about eight or nine minutes to get there. Allow for any unforeseen delays (traffic, a broken stoplight, the man waiting for her there at the apartment mislaying the

3

keys and taking a while to open the door), and already another four or five precious minutes are lost. "Elisheva," he slowly says out loud, enunciating each syllable.

Then he says it again, for that man.

The man who does not want to have to waste any time later undressing—time is short—so that while she navigates the car through the braids of tiny streets connecting this house to that one, he already begins to undress in the bedroom, or perhaps by the door, taking off his baggy brown corduroys and large faded shirt. It used to be orange or brown, or even pink—he was certainly capable of wearing a pink shirt, what did he care what people thought? That's what's great about him, Shaul thinks: that he doesn't care about anything, unconcerned by what people might think or say. That is his strength, his healthy internal perfection; that is what she must be attracted to.

She drives to him, charges toward him, her eyes pinned on the road, her mouth pulled taut. Soon that mouth will be kissed and it will soften and swell and burn. Lips will slide over it, first only flitting, barely touching, then a tongue will come and trace the outline of her lips over and over and she will try not to smile as he grumbles, Don't move while I'm drawing. She will let out a moan of consent; then his lips will rest on hers with all of their rough, masculine force, they will swallow them, wallow in them, and leave them for a moment. A warm breath will pass over them, then they will slowly be sucked with the solemnity of truly great desire, tongues will intertwine with each other like creatures with a life of their own, and she will open her eyes briefly with a weak sigh, her eyeballs will roll up a little, fade, disappear. Half-closed eyelids will reveal an empty, frightening whiteness.

She is a large woman, Elisheva, her generosity extending to her body too. She's even a little too large for such a small car, and perhaps this was why she had been angry that he'd bought her the Polo, of all things. This also may have been precisely the reason he had chosen it—this thought has only just occurred to him—for the sense of her practically bursting through its shell on her way there, erupting toward the waiting man as she tries to keep her mind on the road, delighting in her guess that he and she are thinking the same exact thoughts. That way we gain another few minutes together, she once told him.

She charges ahead, the green car dances through the network of arteries that spreads from here all the way to him, and when Shaul emerges from the wave of pain, she's already there with him. He can see them dimly, a large wide blur of warmth, solid arms, and her brisk movements as she holds on to his shoulder with one hand and bends over to pull off her shoes without unbuckling them. Her fingers stiff with longing, she touches his naked body; his clothes are already at his feet, and hers fall on top of them, and Shaul shuts his eyes and absorbs the blow embodied in this intermingling of fabric, and it hurts so much that he has to look away from the man's clothes, because, for a moment, even the man himself is less painful than the clothes shed on top of one another. This man who had undressed early to save a few more precious seconds, had waited for her anxiously as he walked around the house naked and burning with excitement, thrilling himself with thoughts of the large, beautiful, decisive woman who was pressing on toward him in the green, *sexy* car—that was how the grinning, dark-skinned salesman had tried to sell it to Shaul; that word had left Shaul no choice but to buy it. The naked man had rushed around the tiny apartment, even though he is a fairly slow man by nature, and Shaul can actually see every single one of his motions, the way he walks and his slightly plodding, authoritative speech. But now his excitement builds because she is already hurrying up the steps; she is really coming now and he opens the door and carefully selects the position in which he will appear to her, because his nudity is, to put it delicately, perhaps not likely to awaken any joy in Elisheva, particularly when he stands, especially in daylight, which certainly does not flatter the many moles that dot his stomach and chest or his large, masterful male breasts and ample gray hair. As she runs up the stairs today, he opens the door just a crack and hurries to the bed in a carefully darkened room, where he lies down in a flattering pose on his stomach, one knee slightly bent, as if he had dozed off into a pleasant snooze as soon as he had opened the door for her, sleeping with the carelessness of a thoroughly healthy man who has no problems with digestion or conscience, so that the first thing she sees when she enters is his back, which looks strong—and probably is strong—then his buttocks and his legs, which look almost youthful in this position. She stands there for a moment, watching, smiling to herself, then she walks to the bed and with calculated gentleness runs one finger along his back, from his neck to his buttocks, then leans over and runs her tongue slowly, reservedly, over his neck from side to side, just the tip of her tongue, just a hint of her mouth's moisture, and he shudders with a restrained moan into the pillow as if he were about to be beheaded—

Later, two or maybe three days later—when Elisheva was gone, time became a round prison cell—Shaul lay sprawled on the backseat of a large Volvo. The windshield wipers intermittently smeared then erased the chilly, misty October night. Next to him on the car floor lay a pair of crutches. His left leg, fractured from ankle to knee, rested on a frayed old cushion, and he stared at the whiteness of the cast moving this way and that, as if struggling to understand how it concerned him. Esti, his brother Micah's wife, was driving, and they had been driving for almost half an hour without managing to strike up a real conversation; every sentence they uttered stirred in him a sense of dejection. She was five years younger than him, maybe six, he couldn't remember for sure, and he always felt even drier and more shriveled up than normal around her. His long, thin limbs, his sharp face, even his prominent Adam's apple, all seemed exaggerated when she was near him, with her full body and her dark, broad face. Every time she looked at him in the rearview mirror, he reminded himself of one of those old wooden rulers his father used to have, a grooved yellow yardstick that folded up into thin segments. As she had helped him into the backseat, there was a moment when almost his

6

entire body had rested on her shoulders, and she didn't even grumble. If his weight had been hard for her to bear, she probably thought it was just because of the cast; he knew he had no weight in her view, and that her body was making the inevitable comparison between him and his brother. She glanced in the mirror, alarmed by his sigh: she had never heard him this way.

His brother was supposed to drive him, but at the last minute he was called away to handle an acetone spill on the Coastal Highway, and Esti had turned up at his door. She stood with her arms at her sides, apologizing for not being Micah, and bothered by a vague sense that she and Shaul were staring at each other as if looking into a funhouse mirror. She took a deep breath and unconsciously hunched her shoulders in anticipation of the approaching storm, and at first he seemed not to understand who she was. Then he was taken aback: No, no, thank you, I need Micah, only Micah. But as he spoke he took a step forward, as if to push his way outside to leave, then went back inside and grasped the door handle and stood with his head down, trying to recall something.

But where is Elisheva? she asked urgently, as if wanting to know why his mother wasn't looking after him. She had always thought he seemed lost without her, and even more so now, with his bruised face and one leg in a cast. He did not answer but just stood and stared at her, at her nomadic features, suddenly sharper now. This was exactly how she had first arrived in the family years ago, standing next to Micah in this posture with the same frightened, wild expression. "From the slums," his mother had decreed at the time, and Esti knew perfectly well what he was seeing now. She planted her feet firmly. Inside, she searched frantically for her ore of survival skills, for the unloved but stubborn little girl who had known how to turn herself, when necessary, into a tiny fistful of a human being, one who comes along and joins in precisely where she is unwanted, then stands there and slows her pulse down to a standstill, until somehow everyone becomes accustomed to her presence and to what little she has to offer, and finally cannot manage without her—

She had risen above all that, with all her years and all her children and Micah and the fullness of her flesh, and she crossed her arms beneath her chest and said perhaps he shouldn't go in this condition, just hours after such a bad accident, and she cautiously asked just how it had happened. He withdrew again, retreated into the house, and almost collapsed, still unskilled with the crutches, seeming not to have heard her at all. His eyes were red, from crying or from lack of sleep, and from something else that burned in them and that she did not recognize. He whispered hoarsely that he had to go and that she couldn't possibly drive him. Skirting his unconcealed hostility, she asked where exactly he wanted to go, and he said, South. Then all at once he waved a crutch in the air with a ludicrous birdlike motion and said, All right, we're going. He tried to fake a merry laugh and announced that the whole situation was completely crazy but he had to be there tonight, it was a case of *force majeure*, he enunciated in an accent which sounded to her under the circumstances like the rustle of a ruined nobleman's silk robe. Explaining the obvious, he told her he simply could not get there on his own in his condition, and that this was why he had asked Micah to take him. She tried again to understand where exactly he expected her to drive him in the middle of the night on such short notice, but he did not answer, and she silently fumed at him, but even more so at Micah, who had sent her on this mission only to please his brother, who would never do such a thing for him, much less for her. Shaul sobered for a moment, as if her silent anger had managed to trickle through the chaos within him, and he glanced at her with a look that almost shattered her with its misery and said, I know this is hard for you, but I really don't have any choice. She nodded, confused and slightly alarmed at what she saw. On the way, he said, I'll explain on the way.

Sometimes they have calm days over there, truly peaceful, Shaul reminds himself as he lies feverishly in the back of the old Volvo, trying with all his might to rid himself of the presence of the silent driver and the swarms of invisible ants crawling along his leg beneath the cast. Like the day before yesterday, for example—or was it four days ago?—when Elisheva walks into that apartment through the door left ajar for her, saunters with her shoulders tilted provocatively (who knew she still had this sense of playfulness in her?), and smiles with relief at being back there, where she is free from pretending and faking, from the endless effort of her other life. She pauses for a minute to get her breath back, and wonders how many more years she'll be able to run up the four flights of stairs like that. Perhaps it will not be long now until they have to look for another place again; they had already had to change apartments six or seven times, they were unlucky with real estate, but perhaps you could not be lucky with everything. She puts down her blue gym bag and quietly clicks the front door shut and is filled with new joy, because she knows that he, her man, can hear even this soft sound, and that his eyes are squeezed shut as if they could no longer contain anything more, and that his flesh is straining toward her like the needle of a compass. But he doesn't know she has other plans today.

She slowly walks down the hallway, wondering how to convince him to let it go today, unaware of the effect of her slow walk, which seems deliberately feline to him, twisting the tendons of his passion until it hurts. She stops when she reaches the room and leans against the doorway and looks at him tenderly. I'm here, she says quietly. He turns around slowly, as if surprised by her presence, carefully holding in his gut. Here you are, he says, unable to hide his happiness, his face actually opening up and shining, and she still does not move as she inhales the scene, absorbing and carefully distributing it to every cell in her body, provisions that must last her for a long time, for another whole day of hunger and thirst. She envelops his entirety with her gaze, from the soles of his large and venerable-looking feet, with toes splayed out, to his luminous face, and smiles as she whispers again, Here I am. The man does not think there is anything superfluous in her utterance; on the contrary, he expands his chest to take in everything contained in those three words. Here I am, here is all of me for you, here I am as I truly am, here I am—unpeel me. His face says yes, his body says yes, and his heart and eyes and breath, everything says yes, and for the thousandth time he marvels at how even when she says something simple and obvious, as she often does, it is always followed by an echo of wonder. After all, Shaul thinks, that is precisely it: everything she says there is somehow composed of these two elements, the obvious and the wondrous. In the corner of her tired smile, a rosy freshness now glitters, and the man smiles too. His entire face changes when he smiles at her, and Shaul's face unwittingly forms the same smile. As she drives, Esti, troubled by Shaul's continuing silence, turns to him for a moment and recoils from what she sees, as if she had opened someone else's letter. She looks back at the road with large, dark eyes, and realizes that is exactly how he used to look at Elisheva, years ago, and almost unconsciously she readjusts the rearview mirror and uses it to frame his face, his closed eyes still covered with the same hypnotically foreign expression, a mixture of happiness and loneliness and supplication.

Shaul had been in such a hurry to leave that he forgot to lock the door, and only realized it when they were standing by the car. Esti said, Wait, I'll go, but before she locked the door she went inside and darted through the rooms as if looking for something. She hadn't been to visit for three or four years, even had trouble remembering the last time they had invited the family over; Elisheva may have wanted to, but Shaul probably objected. She noticed how the house had changed—the spaces between the objects seemed much larger, the furniture was arranged with a kind of violent precision—and the thought slowed her movements. She trod carefully, turning away with a strange feeling, as if only a moment ago someone had cracked a whip in the air and every piece of furniture had snapped into place and frozen. It's him, she thought, it can't be her, because Elisheva always had a charming sloppiness about her, and everywhere she went she left a trail of forgotten objects—keys, a purse, a comb, a scarf—

and whenever she spent time in a room she left a soft imprint of scat- teredness. Where are you? Esti thought. You've grown so distant—

She locked the door and, vaguely distressed, walked through the garden, which in the dark seemed neglected and amazingly wild. She could see Shaul waiting for her by the car, talking to himself as he nervously rocked on one crutch, never suspecting her little invasion. The streetlamp coated him with a velvety wax, and his entire be- ing was focused on something unseen by her. Esti still thought he shouldn't be moved around in his condition, and could not imagine what was so pressing. He himself knew he should not go there, cer- tainly not with her—what was she to him and how would he explain it to her and what story would he tell her? It was years since they'd exchanged more than a few polite, evasive words at family events. There was something about her that always unsteadied him slightly and he did not know what it was. Perhaps because she completely refused to acknowledge his status, his reputation, the professional admiration he commanded everywhere. She always seemed to be de- manding a completely different type of proof from him, one that he was not at all capable of providing—

Shaul, she said softly, in a tone that had never existed between them, as if declaring an immediate and total truce. But he shook his head angrily. Off we go, he announced. Help me in.

And Elisheva still stands where he had left off briefly, her gaze enveloping the face of the man in the bed as she distractedly bites her lower lip. She used to have that fleeting, unconscious habit at the be- ginning, when Shaul had met her, but then she stopped biting her lip in anticipation of him. Motionless, she whispers, I love your face so much. He makes a face. Me? My frog face? She slowly approaches the bed with her wonderful walk, thighs whispering, sits on the edge of the bed and holds out her hand and runs it from shoulder to thumb along his quivering arm. Yes, that face, she says with a sud- den sadness as her body crumples and flows next to him, still not touching him, and he grumbles that she's wearing too many clothes for his taste, and she closes her eyes and says, Not today, today we'll just lie here and slowly caress each other. He is disappointed—after all, he has already fantasized and pumped warm blood through his body and undressed and arranged himself in a flattering position. But he obeys her, as always; every one of her desires immediately becomes his too; even now, in his passion, he obeys her, astounded at his enchantment, and for some reason he greatly enjoys feeling weak and devoid of his own desires beside her. He closes his eyes and feels the thin stream of his will running out as hers flows in, sculpting a hidden soul in him, new and unknown, and he turns over lazily, because if they're only going to caress each other there's no need for him to maintain his careful pose. He exposes his bearish chest hair, but she turns her back to him, cuddling and pushing against his stomach, rounding her body into a question mark opposite the exclamation point of his flesh as it straightens and gropes behind her through her dress. She takes his large, warm hand and rubs it over her face with a slow, dreamy motion, over and over again, tightening her face into his palm, clinging, emptying her visage into his hand, and now he finally feels what Shaul had already noticed before him, long before him—that she is giving him something the likes of which they have not yet had, creating a new combination out of familiar body signs, and at once his soul fills with gratitude and joy, as does his body, of course. But Elisheva herself looks unhappy, her expression is tense and pained, and she buries herself in his palm with a kind of determined desperation, leaving a souvenir, as if her face were a farewell letter meant only for his hand. Sometimes she writes a long, curly line on his back with her wet tongue or with a finger she has moistened down there, and refuses to tell him what it says. Read it through your skin, she tells him. Now she holds his fingers with both hands and walks them fervently over the arc of her forehead, then on her translucent eyebrows and over a slender eyelid and down her long, shapely face, and from there briefly to her mouth, her wide mouth, and inside, and she bites down hard on his fingers. He restrains himself and does not even sigh: amazingly tolerant, he knows very well that she is testing him to see if he can withstand her, and she places two of his fingers on her bottom teeth and presses them against each of her fillings, presses and bites and shudders with an emotion he does not comprehend. She's dismantling her face, he thinks, she is presenting me with her fragmented face, and he burns with an indistinct apprehension, one of those vague fears she often arouses in him, which leave their residue on the inner walls of his body.

Shaul thinks perhaps he does not always completely understand her either, but he, in contrast, knows how to expand his palm at these moments to contain her entire face and all its conflicts, and with patience and wisdom he suppresses the frightened motions until she is silent, breathing warm air into his hand, and then, slowly, he begins to give her face back to her, restoring each feature to its proper place, redrawing its boundaries, smoothing it over and feeling her clenched body loosen and relax, and his heart fills— What happened to her? Where had she taken him without his comprehending? How is she able continually to surprise and excite him, as if a nervous wing fluttered constantly inside her? Even after all their years together, he still cannot understand how such a small wing can move all of him, rock and stir all two hundred pounds of him and melt away his cynical sobriety. Shaul thinks and swallows; he opens his eyes, which he had screwed shut as if to violently crush the drops of these scenes out of them, and now he lies drained.

Just another moment, not yet, it's hard to let go. Now Elisheva turns around and faces him, curling up to his chest, exhausted by what had shaken her a moment ago. Her eyes close and she almost falls asleep, but the man does not let her, he props himself up on his elbow and leans over her and demands to know what that was before, what had frightened her so much. She replies: I don't know, I suddenly got very scared. And he, somewhat critically: But of what? She, wearily: I really don't know. And he, almost hurt: Then why didn't you say anything? Why do you always turn inward like that without telling me how I can help? And she whispers, with a smile, that he knows exactly how to help, that no one in the world can help as well as he does, that she was simply incapable of speaking. You know, she says later, how sometimes when you're making love, you reach a state that you simply can't contain? When you just can't say anything more? Well, that's what happened to me now, but the grief . . . I don't know, something scared me suddenly, made me shrink away, I don't know. And the man nods in astonishment, believing that she doesn't know and that she cannot give a more detailed explanation now, and this too makes him love her even more, her inarticulateness at such moments. She rests her head on his chest again, light now. She has suffered and disconnected herself, and now she is purring with soft delight, Shaul thinks, and says to himself carefully, as if reciting: This is a pleasure I do not know, a pleasure awakened in her only when she is with him. There is a substance expressed into the heart only in the presence of one particular person and never in the presence of another, he thinks, and Elisheva's eyes are still closed as she breathes lightly. You remember I'm going away tomorrow, she mumbles into his chest, drugged by the sweetness.

Mmm . . . he confirms.

Silence.

Four days? He checks again. That's a long time.

To be alone, she daydreams. Four days all by myself.

Wouldn't you like me to come?

Her eyes open. He feels her eyelashes moving on his chest hairs and knows the look without seeing it.

He sighs, and they both curl into themselves, carrying together for a moment the burden of the impossible complication of her life. The duplicity which divides her. The never-ending noise inside her head. A hive of secrets and lies. Sometimes she can't understand how she's even capable of feeling anything toward either one of them.

He smiles. Maybe you'll meet someone there, you never know.

She prods his shoulder with her nose. Now you're starting too?

The man wrinkles his forehead. Is he already losing his temper?

He's going out of his mind, she says. Every year I think, Enough, this time he'll take it easy, get used to it, it's only four days, I don't—

He presses her to the side of his body, mending with his big hand what Shaul breaks. He sighs deeply.

She struggles not to tell him everything. Tries to maintain Shaul's dignity. Inside her burns the internal wire she stretches out anew every minute, the borderline between her two men. The man listens with his eyes shut. Every so often he nods his head sorrowfully.

This morning when I started packing, she finally bursts out, he came up close to me like this—she hesitates, then touches her lips to his big ear and whispers. Shaul cannot hear her, though he knows only too well what happened that morning and what he threw into her open suitcase, and yet his soul stands on its tiptoes, straining to hear what exactly is being whispered about him there, how and with which words he is described, between her mouth and his ear.

Silence. The man's quiet eyes fill with violent darkness. Elisheva places a calming hand on his chest.

They had already left the Tel Aviv road and were heading south, and Shaul hesitated to tell her where she was taking him; there was never a right time, and when he thought about what he'd say and how he'd explain it all, it seemed groundless, an utter delusion. Finally he leaned his head against the window and closed his eyes with the surrender of a trapped animal, but every time he opened them he saw her profile in front of him, and the memory came back to him with a piercing sense as if for the first time. Their silence now held an explicit, almost rude declaration of animosity as they tried, unconsciously, to pretend they were two distinct species, with no affinity of genus or of prey between them, and after a half hour of driving they were exhausted.

Her jaw ached from her increasing exasperation at him and at Micah, at the way Micah fawned over Shaul, which was the reason for her being here. But if once in a blue moon he asks me for something . . . Micah had mumbled, rendered almost mute by the fact that Shaul had even made contact with him, that he even knew their number. Esti, hanging laundry up on the porch, heard only Micah's side of the conversation, his exclamations of sorrow and shock at something terrible that had happened to Shaul the day before (but you always hear only one side, she thought). Micah kept asking questions, in his characteristic way—he always interrupted any story he was told with a series of questions meant to prove to the narrator his level of interest and sympathy and, above all, his boundless loyalty. But Shaul never allowed himself to be interrupted, and with a few short words he had stemmed the flood of emotion even as it rushed at him; she saw Micah stymied, shrinking, tongue-tied, and she already felt insulted on his behalf and furious at Shaul, though despite herself she was somewhat excited by his ability to be so aggressive. Two minutes after Micah put the phone down, the call came from Environmental Control.

She sucked in dense air through her pursed lips. How would she have the energy to drive after such a long day? Who knew how long this would take? And then she'd probably have to take him back from wherever-they-were-going to Jerusalem, then back home to Kfar-Saba. Why was she even playing along with this idiotic mystery? She wondered hazily whether they might go through Beersheba, her hometown, and Shaul breathed heavily, absorbing the blow of a new wave of pain. He hoped something would happen to him soon, that he'd faint or lose consciousness before they reached the end of the road, but he didn't even dare to sleep in her presence, in the shadow of her Indian profile, its heavy chin and ample black hair. She had once brought them a painting, when Tom was born— he couldn't say whether she'd painted it or cooked it or baked it; it was made with paprika and cumin and curry powder on rough recycled paper and depicted a mother and child who resembled her far more than Elisheva and Tom. He also recalled that for years her scent wafted out from the painting every time he got near it, because sometimes, though not tonight, she had a clear, strong body odor that she did not bother to mask. Shaul wondered how his brother could be undisturbed by it, and remembered what his mother had said about it when Micah announced he was marrying her—she'd even spoken of her scent, that's how far she had gone! Now he grew even angrier at Esti because of this nonsense flitting around in his mind and breaking his concentration, and Esti hummed to herself quietly, briskly. Shira's uniform was waiting for her on the ironing board, she had to sew ranks onto three shirts, the twins' knight costumes had to be ready for kindergarten tomorrow; she still had not grasped that in front of her lay a long, open road, that she did not even know their destination. She had not yet sensed the pea beneath the pile of mattresses, the pea that belonged to the little brown-skinned girl who used to make up stories to keep her soul pinned down inside her or, at times, to let it fly—stories whose most exciting element was the word "suddenly" at the beginning of every sentence and before each description: Suddenly, suddenly, her heart would leap when she whispered to herself, *suddenly*.

And where was Elisheva? she thought. Why wouldn't he say where she was? Maybe he'd done something to her. She glanced in the mirror, dimly saw the red bruise beneath his right eye, and as always when their eyes met in the mirror, they drew back from each other as if at the touch of a stranger's fingernail. He really looks as if he's murdered someone, she thought. The idea had crossed her mind when she'd been in their house, grounds for her invasion of the rooms. Because if not—she raised an eyebrow—why was he being so secretive? She stretched out and clicked her tongue. She gave him a long look. Just the day before yesterday she had seen him on television, giving an interview about the budget cuts for science education. He was sharp and witty, utterly persuasive in the venomous dryness with which he tore the Treasury people to shreds. The subject matter itself was of no interest to her, but as always when she caught him on screen, she followed his expressions closely, on the lookout for what he was so wonderful at concealing in public. Calm down, she thought, and rubbed her tense neck, he didn't murder her. He can't move an inch without her. And he's too much of a coward. Her pupils lengthened like cat eyes in the greenish light coming from the instrument panel. She liked to imagine spousal murders, it was a little trick she employed to spark some curiosity and even affection toward couples she was otherwise unable to warm to: she would imagine them creeping up on each other silently, lying in wait and prowling through the thickets of their domestic savannas. Sometimes during boring evenings at friends' houses, she'd sit with the contemplative determination of a worm in a juicy apple and slowly examine possible murder weapons: a heavy Murano glass fruit bowl, a cheese knife with a Delft china handle, nutcrackers, bottle openers . . . Shaul saw her strange, scheming smile. His scattered look lingered on it for a moment, and they experienced a brief, clear encounter, of which they were unaware. As if he had wasted precious time, he shut his eyes and removed himself from everything, focusing inward, on one murky shaft of light, and in the dark, damp window in front of him his face was reflected, revealing a shimmering image of Elisheva

Running on a white hillside, running fast, her movements sharp, cutting through the dark, her light pants torn at the hems—perhaps they had caught on a thorn. He almost yells in amazement at the sight of her there, but summons all his strength to keep quiet so the driver won't see her. Because now there is a man driving. At midnight the phone had rung and a voice had informed him that his wife was missing. Gone. No one knew where or why. The voice even had a vaguely accusatory tone, as if Shaul were to blame for her disappearance. He listened quietly. The man said they were sending someone to bring him. He didn't even ask where to. There must be a search party, he thought foggily. He reached a sleepy hand out to her side of the bed and found it vacant, and only then seemed to comprehend and sat up quickly. The man told him to get ready, then hung up, and he sat and stared. Since when do the police notify a family that someone is missing? Usually it's the other way around, isn't it? A moment later there was a knock at the door: a fat, thick man with smooth, short, dolphin-like hands. Like the hands of the man who installed the intercom that connects Elisheva's day-care center on the ground floor to his study. He followed him silently to a filthy, battered Subaru, not even a police car, and got into the backseat and huddled there without saying a word. That was how they drove south for a long time, until he suddenly saw her running on the hill opposite him, light, swallowed up in the darkness and then emerging a moment later on another hill, so quick, rushing with thin, brisk motions like a fingerling in a night ocean, and around her were dozens of eyes she did not notice—red, sparkling, lighting up as she passed them. Now her thin blouse catches on the branch of a low tree and is torn away, and she is left wearing his favorite white bra, from which she knows how to seductively remove a pure, warm breast for him, longing to be sucked by his mouth. Why doesn't she turn around and see him and be rescued? All she has to do is just look at him and he'll reach out and save her, but she doesn't, she must not want to, she wants to go on running—that much is clear—she doesn't even feel she needs to be saved from anything, she enjoys being alone, moving rapidly . . . Her legs move up and down, her face leans forward, her body suddenly so strong—who knew she had this kind of strength in her? Running almost naked, peeled away, soon the bra too, but she doesn't stop, doesn't tire, glimmers in the shadows that lurk around her as if the tips of her exposed nerves were producing electricity. She floats with incomprehensible ease, light of body, but also with a certain lightheadedness, and then, precisely at that moment, a new shadow, elongated, silently emerges from behind one of the rocks and a large, supple, alert body starts running after her

Shaul let out a moan of amazement and shook his head: Not yet, there's still time, get out of here, get yourself out, quickly. He glanced at Esti and wondered if he'd made any suspicious sounds, but she was lost in her own thoughts as she drove, nodding at some reflection, and he thought distractedly that from here, from this angle, she definitely had an impressive face—not beautiful but strong, a hardworking face, which led him to notice a tiny, round earring he had not observed before, like the cheap jewelry a girl would wear, he thought vaguely, a girl playing by herself on the sidewalk; he went on staring at the glittering gold in her earlobe, drawn to it with a strange sense of emptying out, and slowly but surely he relaxed.

Then, for no reason, their conversation flowed with ease for a few moments. Shaul asked her about the kids. He said the names of Shira and Eran, and added Na'ama's name with a certain effort. He can't remember the twins' names, Esti thought, and she knew that five kids must be a sign of vulgarity for him, a kind of bad taste, like someone putting five spoonfuls of sugar in their coffee. But the thought that he couldn't remember the names of his brother's children also aroused a certain flutter of compassion toward him, and she decided to try to stop fighting him, at least for the duration of the journey, to stop constantly settling scores with him in her heart and being insulted by his alienation from the family. This night was already a lost cause anyway, she thought, might as well get some good out of it. So she answered his hesitant questions and expanded with stories about the kids, repeating their names over and over to help him connect the names with the children. She also threw in something of each child's personality, spending a little more time on her Ido, the smaller twin, perhaps because he sometimes reminded her of Shaul, although he looked nothing like him—he was the only one of them who had some of her coloring—but even so, in the fragility, the distance, the thread of dejected absentmindedness that lingered in him, which sometimes pinched her heart with a vague sense of guilt.

And she asked about Tom—she had always thought something bad might one day emerge from that boy—and Shaul told her about the math studies at the Sorbonne and the grants Tom was collecting there, sifting any hint of pride or satisfaction out of his voice. As he spoke, she could see Tom sitting in some gloomy library, his too-large head weighing down on his thin neck, and she wanted to ask something but thought better of it.

And does Eran have a girlfriend already? Shaul inquired, and Esti, though she suspected he was just trying to distract her from Tom, or rushing so he could sink back into that stormy internal mumbling, was happy to talk about Eran's sweet young girl. She joked about how they had already set up a family room in the house, up in the attic, and how Micah was of course nervous about it, he thought seventeen was too early, but nowadays everyone starts everything early. Then she caught herself and said, Well, not everyone, of course, everyone has their own pace. Shaul nodded, touched by her understanding. He said he kept hoping it was only his lousy long-bachelorhood genes, and that eventually someone would move in on Tom too, the way Elisheva had on him. Esti smiled and said she had those genes too, in fact, and Shaul said, So what are you saying—that someone like Micah may end up moving in on him? And it was a joke, but it wasn't, because they both knew that Tom might have that in him too. Their eyes met in the mirror, which for a fleeting moment displayed possibilities, his and hers, and wishes and longings and complications that had long ago been covered with thick layers of life's dust, and Esti blinked first and looked away, sensing that in his current situation he was actually capable of seeing more, even seeing too much. She slid him a quick, misleading smile in the mirror, teeth shining, and Shaul again recalled the first time his brother had introduced her to him: It's been a long time, hasn't it? Twenty years, Esti noted, I was almost twenty-nine when we met. Shaul was amazed and said feebly that she had hardly changed, and she threw her head back and laughed from the bottom of her heart, knowing that he sincerely believed she had gone through all those years and all those kids without changing. He saw only general concepts, she once explained to Micah, only silhouettes. But now, with his gaze surrounding her, it seemed to her that he'd already completely given up the possibility of breaking through his shell and truly knowing anything outside himself. But your hair was braided then, wasn't it? he suddenly exclaimed, and she was touched that he remembered. My beautiful braid, she said, and slid her hand down her neck and shoulder. Shaul looked enchanted at the soft motion of her hand, and it was the same thing every time he remembered any concrete detail from the distant past: a strange sense of gratitude spread through him, melting, as if he had managed to acquire further evidence that might help him one day, in some future debate, when he would be required to prove that there had been moments of fertilization between him and life itself. Sure, he said, you had a long braid, kind of thick. He latched onto this memory and refused to let go, and Esti guessed what he was going through—she, who was unable to forget anything, who remembered every word anyone said to her, and gestures and voices and smells—and she drew him into the conversation and reminded him how nervous Micah had been at that first meeting, how afraid she was of Shaul's stern judgment; I felt as if he were presenting me to a Supreme Court judge. She suddenly turned serious: You know, your parents' house was a true refuge for me, an absolute salvation. She hesitated over whether she could even tell him that only when she got to his parents' house did she truly understand what a home and a family were, but Shaul was thinking of his mother's shout-and-whisper performance when it transpired that Micah was uncharacteristically determined to marry "that woman of his," and for a moment he wondered how Esti had in fact overcome his mother's deep, almost pagan, animosity. If he had not been embarrassed, he would have asked her what magic she had worked on her to make his mother so devoted to her now, and Esti smiled to herself and thought perhaps it was a good thing after all that she had agreed to take this trip.

They went on talking with the newfound playfulness of two people who have somehow managed to avoid an unpleasant confrontation, although Esti noticed that even when he was laughing with her and seemingly swept up in the memories of his parents' house, Shaul still held them both back from completely giving in to the sweetness of the small details, cautious not to let the conversation go beyond the small talk of two acquaintances who had once been, say, to summer camp together. Or to a concentration camp, Shaul thought, and Esti saw his long, tortured face in the mirror, and for a moment was unable to look away from it and from his lips, which moved constantly as if he were conducting another stormy conversation within himself, one that existed independently of the conversation with her. At once she was struck by a sense of sorrow, and she wondered whether he was truly close to anyone, whether there was anyone in the world who coincided with him on some parallel line.

Apart from Elisheva, of course, she later thought with some effort.

She reached out and rummaged quickly through the large handbag on the passenger seat, and offered Shaul the sandwiches she had made and wrapped before leaving; she also had fruit and vegetables and hard-boiled brown eggs, two vanilla puddings, and a wedge of Camembert in a little cooler, and a tin full of her famous sesame cookies. Shaul looked on in wonderment as she fumbled in the bag and produced one piece of food after another, while still driving in a perfectly straight line, and he remembered the instant of last night's accident and complained that he had no appetite. Esti used her teeth to unwrap a sandwich for herself and hesitated for a moment, knowing how she would feel when she chewed and the sound was magnified in her head, but she shrugged her shoulders and ate it anyway, with enjoyment, then picked out some black olives and drank coffee from a flask. Shaul inhaled the smells of the food and the coffee aroma, and although his appetite was aroused, he decided not to ask for anything, imposing a little fine on himself for not accepting when she had first offered. Esti wiped her lips and asked for the third or fourth time how he could even travel with such a new fracture, and he assured her the Tramadol was already kicking in, only the itching was driving him crazy, the ants, and he hissed that even the worst pain in the world would not be punishment enough for such a stupid accident. She asked again where exactly it had happened, and he said, I can hardly remember, I was driving, I was driving home, I ran into a sidewalk—she felt compelled to flick the radio on to disperse the burden of his lie.

They listened quietly to the nine o'clock news. At the end, to Shaul's astonishment, the newswoman adopted the amused tone of voice that always signifies trivial anecdotes or minor catastrophes befalling other nations to report on a senior police officer in Spain, a well-known and respected man: only after he had passed away this week had it been revealed that he had two families living in different suburbs of Madrid, who knew nothing of one another. He had two wives, the newswoman said cheerfully, and six children with each of them, and he had given them all the same names, in parallel. Oh! Esti laughed. Two identical sets—just imagine! Shaul said, Imagine what, and his voice was too quick, like a snakebite. Hesitating, she said, Imagine such a thing, and he said gloomily, *That* I can actually imagine. She said nothing for a moment, then asked cautiously, Is something wrong, Shaul? He looked up heavily and stared at her with torn eyes, and suddenly moaned with such pain that Esti slammed the brakes and drove onto the shoulder and stopped. Shaul mumbled, No, no, go on, it's only my leg. But she didn't move, she sat very erect and waited as Shaul lay there, shriveled. A familiar storm began to brew inside him, wails and bitter whinnies interwoven into a roar that sucked his insides and threatened to slam him against the wall, any wall—after all, there must be a wall at the edge—or the bottom of a pit. How unbearably pleasurable it will be when everything is uprooted right in front of her eyes, he bitterly mocked his own misfortune. In front of her eyes would be best, he rejoiced, and then the thing inside him was cut off and sealed, and he pulled his unfractured leg to his stomach and thought, That was it, that must be what was decreed.

At the office, he said after a while with a hollow voice, there's a similar story.

Similar to what? she asked.

Like that guy in Madrid, the police officer.

I'm not following, she said, someone who's also married to two wives?

Something like that, he said, more or less. One day he discovered that his wife . . . that she was seeing someone.

Well, okay, she said, that happens all the time. But some hidden womanly gauge had awakened in her and slowly began to flicker.

No, he explained, not just someone on the side, not the usual story either, you know. He wondered if she was one of those people who said "fuck" easily. There's something much more serious going on there. In fact—he smiled, and she heard the smile and its complicated process of production—it's been going on for years, to this day.

You hear that kind of thing all the time, she said, confused. There was a light, strange breeze in his voice, an oblivion creeping down her spine on soft paws.

Then it grew quiet. A long silence, full of whispers. A light rainfall enveloped them in a thick screen. Every so often a car or truck passed them by and the Volvo rocked. Esti dimmed the headlights and stared at the side of the road. She saw blown shrubs and an old road sign lying on its side. Two white plastic cups blew around in the breeze. Shaul was still trying to save himself, straining to think what would happen after this, what would happen tomorrow morning, what she would do with what he was telling her, whether he could ever show his face to the family again, and how she herself would look at him. He kept pulling himself up straight, but his body would collapse again, and he wanted to ask her to take him home now, before disaster could strike, but he couldn't articulate the words, he so needed her to keep driving. The end of the road was drawing him away from the semblance of his life, the way you blow a raw egg out through a tiny hole in its shell. He told himself that his catastrophe had already begun from the moment he asked someone to drive him there. How had he even had the audacity to ask someone to drive him? What had he been thinking when he called Micah? How had he thought to explain this journey to anyone? He knew that he had not been thinking at all, that he did not have the strength to postpone what was coming, that he was prey.

But the thing here, with this couple—don't ask . . . He laughed softly, and she knew that laugh of his, a sharp spurt of bitterness, self-deprecating, ominous. It's something that's been going on for eight, nine, maybe ten years . . .

And he didn't sense anything, the husband? she asked. Shaul said, The husband knows. In fact, it turns out he's known about it for a very long time. Right from the beginning, probably.

She shifted in her seat, felt she should say something just to break the silence that congealed after each of his sentences.

Yes, absolutely, he said, though Esti was sure she hadn't had time to ask anything. He acquiesces, the husband, but with them it's even more complicated.

Now she could actually feel the sharp, familiar fingernails being drawn out one after the other from a soft paw, and she was hypnotized by their movement, and asked weakly, What could be more complicated than that?

He didn't answer, and it seemed to her that in between sentences he was sinking into himself as if he had to search for an appropriate answer that would both reveal and conceal, in the correct proportion.

I don't get it, she whispered. Tell me.

Then everything slowed down in him. His eyeballs grew heavy and seemed to harden. I'm telling it now, he thought with a strange calm—the tranquillity of the inevitable—and I'm telling it to her, of all people. Of all people, her. The terrible mistake spread like a sweet narcotic through the twisted innards of his thoughts, and he stared at the ceiling of the car and for a long moment did not breathe at all, until he felt a delicate shudder through his entire body, from the tip of his head to his toes, and he leaned his head against the cool window and closed his eyes, and slowly but surely his face relaxed and he focused inward, as if in anticipation of a naked pleasure.

He even knows, he mumbled, every time she goes to see the

other guy. He even *wants* to know. And he sighed. He—how can I put this—he must know, everything.

She swallowed. Asked feebly if he wanted something to drink. He didn't answer and she didn't dare turn to face him. They sat this way for a long time, lost in themselves, slightly shocked, as in the moment between a blow and the pain that follows, until Shaul turned his head with immense exhaustion and met her large black eyes in the mirror, eyes that were always surrounded with shadows, and whispered that she should keep driving, there was no time to lose.

Warmth radiated from him and enveloped the back of her neck and flowed beneath her dress. Even the plaster cast suddenly emitted fresh ripples of smell. She drove the Volvo onto the road and proceeded slowly, in a daze, and felt that she was filling up with a dust of floury stupidity that rendered her incapable of thought. She only vaguely guessed that the fact that he was even telling her these things was somehow connected to the injury; his talking reminded her of the children's babble when they got hurt, when they would pour forth a flow of hysterical chatter. She remembered Micah telling her that Shaul never got hit and never hit anyone, even as a boy. He never fought, never broke a hand or sprained an ankle, Micah said with wonder and a hint of admiration, as if Shaul were an exquisite museum piece. Esti now imagined how in an instant yesterday his skin and flesh were torn and his bones broken. Perhaps he's not really in control of himself now, she thought. She wanted to tell him to be careful not to say things he would regret tomorrow. But she waited, silenced, for what emerged from him, and was repelled and drawn, like eyes to a disaster.

He sits at home and waits for her, Shaul continued; he seemed serene, but every tendon in his body was rigid. He knows exactly how long it takes her to get to his house, to the second, and he sits and accompanies her on her journey until she arrives, and knows where she parks outside the house, and how she goes up the stairs, and knows exactly how many floors (four) and how many steps—

Esti waited for a moment, on the edge of her seat. He didn't say the number of steps, and only this allowed her to breathe again. Because if he had said the number of steps, she would have screamed.

So he . . . follows her? she asked when it was no longer possible to allow this distorted silence between them, but that was not the question she wanted to ask. Other things washed over her, and from the margins of her body, her elbow or her ankle, there also came a slight sigh of relief for Elisheva, that she had such a story in her life and that she was apparently not sick, as everyone had started to fear.

Shaul said, What? No, he doesn't follow her, of course not, and Esti thought he seemed angry at the question, or not at the question itself, but that another voice had intruded and prevented him from settling into his story. He doesn't have to follow her, he mumbled: he knows. He said these words softly but with decisive confidence, like someone placing a winning card on the dark red velvet of the table.

But how . . . she whispered and glanced over her shoulder, and was amazed to see in the darkness the change that had occurred in him during the last few minutes: his white face, with eyes shut, was strained and pulled forward as if seized by bold, merciless fingers. It's not true, she thought, it can't be, not Elisheva. He's not talking about him and her at all, that's just you and your screwed-up imagination. But why not, she argued—is anyone immune to it? And maybe that's why she's always been so sad and quiet for years now, ten years, he said. Maybe she's hiding a huge secret like this from the whole world. She sniffled, and Shaul furrowed his brow at the sound and begged himself as if pleading with a tyrant, Shut up now, shut up, you've done enough damage, you won't even be able to repair what you've already done.

And what's amazing, he continued, is that they have very little time to be together, the couple, because she leaves the house for an hour every day, an hour and ten minutes, no more, but every single day, supposedly to go to the pool, that's the official story, seven days a week, three hundred and sixty-five days a year—

The pool, she thought, Elisheva's sacred daily swim. Why is he telling me this? Why hasn't he ever told Micah? Would he even tell Micah if he were here with him instead of me? She opened the window a crack and breathed in the damp air and closed it again, as if she had done something forbidden, and asked herself if he might be flirting with her, because that was also a strange potential that now hovered around them in circles of heat. It occurred to her that this had always been there among the array of his many possibilities. There were evasive hints, stolen looks, moist and slightly surrendered—never at her, of course (it took a heart far wiser and more insightful than his to discover her, she thought as she exhaled lightly), but certainly at other women. Even so, it seemed to her that in the last few moments he had plucked some new string in her and in himself, and the image of two animals who had previously been indifferent and foreign to each other passed through her mind. They shook themselves, stomped their feet, and exhaled, as if a spark had lit up something that had been completely extinguished in them.

And listen to something funny—he leaned forward a bit, as far as his pain and the cast would allow him, and there was no smile on his quivering face—if you deduct the time it takes for her to get there and back from the hour-and-a-bit, even though he doesn't live far, quite close in fact, and then she has to look for parking, and climb up the stairs, and all the rest of it, before and after—how much time are we left with? Forty minutes? Fifty?

She examined him intently for a moment and knew he was not flirting with her. She was not having that bristling reaction. But even so, there was a flirtation here, slithering like a rattlesnake, but not with her. With whom, then? she thought, upset. With whom or with what was he flirting this way? She drove without seeing the road, and once in a while she opened her mouth to ask, then closed it and swallowed. Suddenly, as if a spear aimed at her from a great distance, years ago, had finally caught up with her, she groaned with a sharp pain, and for a second or two she clasped the wheel with both hands to stick to the road, then felt the sorrow and longing spread inside her. But Shaul, she thought with alarm, as if she had abandoned him, and she looked and saw him lost in himself, cramped and twisted like a crooked hieroglyph or a damaged chromosome—

And she loves them both, he went on, but apparently—he hesitated, searching for the words—there is, after all, a difference between the way she loves her husband and her love for him. It's hard to explain, he sighed, it's something different, two completely different dimensions. She seems to need them both, together, but it's actually more complicated for her with the husband, somehow with him she always takes it less for granted . . .

His mouth was dry and his forehead burned, and for the first time since they left he felt he had managed to capture the longed-for thread of emotion, and knew he had to make every effort to safeguard its purity, its pure opacity, and he groped for it and attached himself to it the way he sometimes attached himself—when he slept with Elisheva—to an evasive, dying firebrand of desire.

Esti had still not said a word. This sudden new talk of his, she thought, his talk, as if he's reading to me from a book he's been hiding. Who would have thought he was capable of articulating these words out loud, or even thinking them? She smelled the sweat on him and inhaled curiously, because even after all the years of knowing him she always avoided, for some reason, imagining his body completely, as if the very thought that he had a body was an intolerable invasion of his privacy. But now his pungent odor, of all things, softened something in her toward him, and of course she thought of Micah, who certainly did have a body and who, like all the men in the Kraus family, had become heavyset at a very young age, right after their wedding. He swelled up even more with each of her pregnancies, and went bald quickly, and his face and body became covered with large round beauty spots like nipples sprouting up everywhere. Something flashed in her, how sometimes in the rare family meetings imposed on Shaul, his shin would be exposed, between his sock and trouser leg, a white, smooth shin, and she would peek at it and tremble.

Her prolonged silence misled him. For a moment he believed he had somehow managed to defrost her doubtful, resolute presence, and he hoped he would be able to keep talking like this, unload the whole story that was buried alive inside him in one stream of vomit, just as he needed to and without any disturbances, by the time they arrived—

What you . . . what you said, Esti blurted uneasily, it's not . . . not by any chance you and Elisheva?

Yes, he said immediately, surprised like a sleepwalker who awakes to find himself on the edge of a rooftop. To his astonishment he felt immense relief, as if he'd paid a heavy tax and had managed to cross an impassable border, and now he was there, beyond. But how, he asked with absolute innocence, how did you know?

Were she not so distraught she would have laughed at his touching astonishment, his lack of street smarts. Come on, Shaul.

That's it, then, he said, and loosened his aching body and closed his eyes. Enough, he thought, you've ruined everything. You've defiled Elisheva and yourself, now you can tell her to go back.

I just can't see how . . . Esti said softly. No, no, no.

It really is hard to believe, he whispered.

She was quiet. She fixed her eyes on the yellow stripe along the shoulder of the road and let it pull her into the darkness. She gradually sat taller, filled up without realizing it. Her tongue ran over her lips, around and around. There was something there that opened up to her.

And I must ask, Shaul said softly.

She nodded, still distracted. Too many echoes were breaking inside her head.

Not even to Micah, he said.

I don't tell Micah everything. She thought she saw him shaking his head doubtfully. We're not Siamese twins, she said, surprised at the sharpness and aggression in her voice.

Look, his voice almost breaking, I told you because I was simply—and he stopped, and she finished his sentence herself: I was simply bursting, I would have lost my mind if I hadn't talked now, right this minute, with someone. Not just anyone. It's lucky you were here.

It's good that you told me, she said.

And a moment later, as if to herself: Thank you.

She knew it would take her weeks to become accustomed to what had happened here, to the strange sense that he was now pulling her toward him and out of herself, out of the domain of the family, and in the fog inside her head, the image of a sick, starving wolf flickered, howling in the valley and attracting a heavy domesticated bitch, weary and slightly tattered. Every so often she wondered, in a disjointed sort of way, how Elisheva had the courage to fall in love so powerfully that she could no longer hide it and had to share it with Shaul. It must be an enormous love for her to fight for it like this and maintain this relationship for so many years despite the pain it caused Shaul. How could he tolerate it? Where was he leading his terrible loneliness? She thought of Elisheva's breasts, which might have been the most beautiful she had ever seen. On the few occasions when she had seen them, she had actually gasped, and she once told an embarrassed Micah that they were Shaul's great hope and that if he suckled on them perhaps the toxins would evaporate from within him. But now she thought of the pain they must cause him, and Elisheva, how could she stand the never-ending longings of a life such as this, a life torn. She sighed softly, and a strange sweetness gathered beneath her tongue.

As always when she heard something new, she was quiet for a long time. She preferred not to hear too many details at first, just tried to see it in her mind's eye. Sometimes she would dive into herself like that even after hearing a joke, trying to imagine what the characters in the joke did after it was over, after the people on the outside had laughed. She tried to guess how this open and long-awaited talk was made possible, between Elisheva and Shaul, about everything she does with the other man, with her lover, her boyfriend—

Her boyfriend—

That stung. Even more than "lover."

Perhaps he forced her to tell him, she thought, and another globule of grudge against him rose to the surface. Yes, that was possible too. Much more logical than the invention that had rippled through her before, whereby Elisheva, in her absolute forthrightness, simply told him everything. She turned the picture over, and now Elisheva was sitting on a chair, a chair with a high back, and Shaul was standing over her wagging his finger. Perhaps this is the tax he levies on her in return for his consent? Yes, that seemed even more fitting, that he would torture her and himself every day by exacting precise, detailed descriptions. She pursed her lips, recalling how he had once interrogated her, years ago, about the religious school she went to in Beersheba; she was willing to bet he'd already forgotten that encounter. He was waging a private war against religious education at the time, one of those principled battles he used to conduct in the name of science, and he needed any possible information about the treatment of female students. She fell into his lap, as they say, from the empty skies above. As soon as she saw that he was equipped with a little black tape recorder and a yellow legal pad, she wanted to get up and leave, but she couldn't disappoint Micah, and a moment later she could no longer escape. He didn't just ask, he attacked and bombarded her with questions from every angle, digging out of her things she had preferred to bury, and she sat there answering all his questions with clenched teeth, paralyzed because of something primal, insulting, in some way related to status, which grew and swelled in her toward him like a poisonous cloud. And when she stupidly revealed some needless old story about something the teachers and the headmistress had done to her there, he fell upon the trivial anecdote almost gleefully and wanted to know all the hows and the whys, and who had determined and who had decreed, and she became confused and stuttered—even Micah didn't know about that affair—and though she squirmed he would not let up, opening up scars and churning the shame they bled, and every time she searched for his eyes she found a magnifying glass. Now she tried to imagine

33

how it must occur between him and Elisheva, how Elisheva sits and tells him, in the kitchen, say, or in any other room within the brutal order imposed in that house, which words she uses in her descriptions, whether she runs her fingers through her thick graying hair with that embarrassed, touching gesture. She couldn't summon up the image, even the thought of it was intolerable, so she escaped and tried to imagine Elisheva's boyfriend, tried to guess whether he was dark or light, younger or older than Elisheva, but she couldn't see, because another man kept cutting in front of him. In some side pocket of her soul, she was also annoyed because she had never imagined that something so exciting was occurring right before her eyes, between two people she knew, and she was even more surprised at having been so wrong about them, because they both seemed so drained, especially in recent years. She knew very well why she had failed to see it, and of course she did not spare herself from the conclusion, she even spent a long time immersed in it—after all, the sin had been committed, now she could linger over the punishment— because somewhere, sometime, who knew where or when it had happened, she had given up even the will to imagine such things. The imagination itself pained her, there was an ache in the part of her brain where she once had incessantly hallucinated little, mischievous fantasies, much as the whole body can sometimes hurt at the sensation of a missing hug, especially in the morning, right before opening one's eyes. Especially at night, at the last moment of sleepy wanderings. And perhaps because of this, without noticing, she had almost stopped fighting and had started to accept the simpler version of reality, without trying to save it from itself. Now she stared at the road as it was swallowed up beneath her, and her shoulders drooped a little, then the corners of her mouth and of her eyes.

The silence was insufferable, and Esti asked gingerly if he had ever asked Elisheva to stop seeing the man, but this wasn't the question she wanted to ask either, and a dull sourness filled her mouth. She thought to herself that she was already submerged in the viscous oil—the cholesterol of the soul, someone had once called it, a guy she knew long ago—and her body could tangibly sense the oil surrounding her heart, filling its chambers with thick, creeping layers.

And if I asked? Shaul sighed. Even if, let's say, I gave her some kind of ultimatum, would she stop loving him?

She turned around to face him almost completely; she wanted to see him, but not in the mirror, with his long face, elderly for his fifty-five years, the sad clown wrinkles around his mouth, the empty space, too large, between his nose and upper lip, and his unlovely skin, withered a little and translucent, which always seemed like a snakeskin ready to be shed, a kind of dry membrane that stored all his theoretical knowledge. She knew it would be a long time before she was able to truly comprehend, because that was the way she did things, slowly and in waves, the way her dead mother's face had suddenly emerged, years later, in an omelet burning in the frying pan, with her precise mouth that looked as if it were blowing her a kiss, the kiss she held back during her life. Or the way the humpbacked kid who had once molested her in the lot behind the bowling alley had come to apologize thirty-five years later, not in a dream but in a salad—Quasimodo showing through a crooked piece of red pepper. Even the children made fun of her sudden brooding disappearances— "space cadet," "flake," Shira would mock in her army-speak. "Estheronaut," Eran wrote in a limerick for her birthday. How could she even comprehend that Elisheva had such a hidden, full life? And what was this vicious pang at the bottom of her stomach? It had been going on for so many years, ten years of this, a whole decade of love, of life without compromise, in absolute honesty and without hiding. How could Shaul live with it? she wondered again. How great his love for Elisheva must be. Suddenly, in the same swing and in mid-motion, she veered and thought maybe he was lying, simply lying, because it was so implausible to think of innocent, transparent Elisheva as someone capable of tolerating even for one day the burden of such complications, or as someone capable of causing any person— especially Shaul—such suffering. For a moment she oscillated between the possibilities, but then the scales were tipped because of his previous explanation, the way he'd said, "And if I asked, would she stop loving him?" with complete simplicity and wisdom she never imagined he possessed. He sometimes seemed so obtuse when it came to human beings. All his titles and the research he had published in physics and education, all the senior offices he had held at the university and now in the Ministry of Education, had never made an impression on her. I don't care if he has an education as broad as a peacock's tail, she would say bombastically to Micah when he tried to defend him, if that's how he treats you and your parents. While she relived that anger for a moment, even clung to it a little, Shaul sank his head between his shoulders and, completely swept up within himself, muttered, What can I do? After all, I have no ownership of her emotions. She's entitled to love whomever she wants, isn't she?

She moistened her dry lips and took a deep breath. From one moment to the next, his body seemed to be presenting her with a newer, wider space, as if until now she had not understood or known anything about Shaul, and now she had to re-create him from scratch. When had he found the time to learn these things? she wondered. Maybe he really did need to distance himself from everyone, from the family, she thought warmly, because he had something to protect and he could not under any condition let them see inside him. She knew only too well how his story would have been related by them had they found out, how it would have been chewed and shredded and digested and ruminated. With lucid clarity she saw the looks exchanged around the dinner table, the head shaking of Grandma Hava, her mother-in-law, with her small, suspicious, bitter face, and her look, a flash of blue that burned and classified and defined and sentenced at the speed of light—and with the force of a spell, Esti sometimes felt, if not of mutilation.

She was already alert and upset, knowing as always that it was all signs, all hints and clues left for solitary spies, and she wished the night would not be over too soon; this night was very important to her. She inhaled into a spot deep inside her that was a glowing ember, carefully covered with heaps of cold ashes, and felt it blushing and flaring into a tiny flame. She looked in the mirror and adjusted it so she could stare straight into his eyes and said, Tell me, Shaul.

He twittered in surprise. But how? he asked. How can I tell someone a thing like this? And he added that ultimately a person was always alone in this kind of affair.

You can, she said with odd confidence, and when she did, she remembered the self she used to be, the one with whom you really could do anything. And I want you to know, she added excitedly, that everything stays here, just between the two of us. No matter what happens, it has nothing to do with anything or anyone, only me and you and only here.

He stopped her: But wait a minute. He was embarrassed and surprised at her outpouring. I'm still trying to grasp that I'm even . . .

She leaned back and rested the back of her neck on the seat, and her head pulsated with thoughts of suddenly, *suddenly*.

They sat in silence for a long while, breathing deeply, not believing this was happening. Shaul said, Look, Esther, I think I'll try to sleep a little, I haven't slept a wink since yesterday morning. And Esti said, Of course, sleep. She was disappointed, but also a little moved by the way he said her name: he had always avoided saying it, and now, of course, he chose the one name no one had called her for years and which was more precious to her than any of her nicknames. She slowed down so they wouldn't arrive, and as she passed by an avenue of wispy trees, her eyes lingered on a large road sign pointing to Beersheba. Whenever she went near there, she felt a little girl darkening inside her, and he said, If I don't wake up by the time we get to Kiryat Gat, wake me. He laced his fingers together tightly and closed his eyes, and his head shifted from side to side, searching for an invisible point in space

And immediately Elisheva surfaces on the bare hills in front of him, running, stripped of almost all her clothes, floating again with an odd lightness, defiant, and that same large shadow dislodges itself from behind one of the rocks, and she immediately hears the quiet, brisk beating of the stampede of large legs, or senses the pursuer, picks up his pulse in the open pores of her skin and the shivers running through her body. How can she sense him like that? He's still so far away from her. But suddenly the whites of her eyes start to glow—who would have guessed she still had such bold luster? Why does it seem to him as if this running is a form of conversing between herself and the pursuer, as if they are conducting an entire complex conversation, in a language and grammar to which he is not privy, and which no one in the world apart from them can understand. That's it, she's no longer mine, he admits with quick acquiescence, almost excitement. She belongs to this chase now, to the hunter, to the laws of predator and prey. If only he could see the pursuer, finally see his face for once, but the pursuer is hidden from him, always. He can divine his presence only from Elisheva, from the way the hairs on her skin stand on end and her pupils widen, the terrifying size of his arms and the imprint of his bare feet in the earth, the long, fleshy thumbs. He can also guess how those thumbs must bend to grasp the rocks with a kind of natural wisdom, like the talons of a wild beast, and in front of his torn eyes Elisheva sheds all the wrappings of their shared life as she runs—twenty-five years shed away one by one, they linger in midair for a moment and drop, and now she is truly naked; the body of his wife is naked, at night, on the hillsides along an unfamiliar road, his wife's magnificent body moves in the dark of night with determination and a wildness he has never known in her. But she has no chance, he can clearly see. Her steps are too small and she's too heavy, that much is clear. She's lost, it's over, and her breasts burden her too, of course, jiggling, hitting her ribs with a thud, and here, now, this is it, this is the end: a shadow falls on her calves from behind, her fair skin, her soft flesh, her flesh which was once so contained within the palm of the house—Why did you go out? Why did you even go out?—and the shadow floats above her back, a very large head with frizzy hair is displayed on her back, and two bony, massive arms reach out in midstride toward her waist, and only now does she finally turn to face

Shaul, and all her expressions are revealed to him. Save me, she begs with her eyes, and this is the last moment he can save her, but he doesn't, not now, not with the wail which emerges inside him and tears him apart as the two huge twisted arms grasp her hips from behind and wrap and crush and flail in the air. A foreign flesh is now becoming acquainted with her soft, round touch, a foreign flesh is learning her, and her flesh tenses toward him for a stolen, infinite instant, and a force unfamiliar to her flings her on the ground—as it should, a voice in his throbbing head rejoices with parched desperation—such a force that she had not even imagined could exist in a man, and a double, hoarse roar knifes the desert in half, the roar of two beasts, male and female

How could she be feeling the very same streams that rushed around within him? she thought, as they overflowed and lapped inside her too. She had never felt the inside of another person this way, and she sensed a new fear, that he was traveling to hurt Elisheva. Or her and the man. Before she had time to hesitate, she asked if Elisheva was there with him, in the place they were going to.

With him? . . . No, not with him, he said as he tore himself from the scene with all his remaining energy, and buried his face in his hands and pressed hard on his eyeballs. What was the matter with him? It was too early to be seeing such things, they still had almost two hours to go, and he'd lose his mind if he gave in to them this early. I don't think she's there with him, she goes there to be alone.

Alone? Her voice trailed off at the end of the word, and her heart shrank again, like before, when she had thought "her boyfriend." Shaul mistook her yearning for surprise. Yes, he said, what's wrong with that? She's entitled to be alone once a year, isn't she?

In fact, he was quoting Elisheva, who went on a four-day vacation every year, to a different place in Israel each time, and was not willing under any circumstances to give up these days; they were as essential to her as the air she breathed, she said quietly and with unusual force. And every year she had to have the argument with Shaul, who would be driven insane by the mere thought of it, months before. But now he spoke as if Micah or his parents were there. He knew exactly what they thought with their petty, provincial, ignorant views about these vacations and about what went on during them, and he arrogantly demonstrated to Esti how wholeheartedly he agreed with Elisheva and how he understood her need to be alone for a few days a year, and thus seemed to decree some moral superiority, a hierarchy of emotional development and enlightenment as compared to Micah, his parents, and the entire Kraus tribe. Because still, in everything he did and thought, both large and small, he had never stopped wrestling with them in his mind and taunting them in any way he could. What, he added generously, don't you sometimes feel like being alone? Just you, without Micah and the kids?

She heard all the streams churning in his voice and was not taken aback this time, and with a sudden urge she felt around and switched on the little ceiling lamp, flooding the space with light; they both squinted and Shaul did not protest or ask why she had done it, and she encountered his distorted, conflicted look and then turned off the light, and her eyes grew accustomed to the dark and the road again. For a moment she could not comprehend why they had avoided and deterred one another all those years, almost from the first, and had jabbed each other continually, without anyone else noticing, with a look that only the two of them knew how to conjure up and where exactly to aim it.

I spend a lot of time alone, she said, and when he looked up, she heard the echo that surrounded the word and immediately gave him another of her light, glossy, misleading smiles. Look, when you work at home you spend a lot of time alone.

But she knew very well that Shaul was not talking about that kind of alone, not her alone, which was crowded to the brim and buzzing with a drone that erupted from her even at nights now. Not the alone of always lying in wait, alert among the reeds, to ensure, for example, the routine of the refrigerator that filled up and emptied out with large, rapid breaths—even though she would never admit the almost physical pleasure she derived from the resuscitation and the whisper of its regular respirations: they are eating well, growing up nicely—and not the alone from which she leaped up in the blink of an eye with ridiculous fervor, she knew, to find a lost sock or a baseball cap or a bicycle pump or last year's report card or a military ID card or keys or soy sauce or a fine-tooth comb for lice. Her alone was alert, she jumped out of it at the sound of their calls a hundred times a day: they couldn't find it themselves, wouldn't remember where, wouldn't know how much water to dilute the antibiotics in or how to wrap the fish in Saran wrap, or where exactly you added softener to the washing machine. Nor would they know the small pleasure that occurred even in the rhythmical life cycle of doing tax returns, making down payments, depositing monthly amounts in the savings account, servicing the car, changing the water filters twice a year, exchanging summer clothes for winter clothes and vice versa, the list of regular visits for each of them to the dental hygienist—even Ido's daily insulin shots, with all the tumult they entailed. And she hated all this with all her heart, and had not a drop of talent for it; but even so, it was her alone. She longingly breathed in the smell of breast-feeding that filled the air after her counseling work, the drops of sour breast milk on the chairs after the new mothers left, the large green fan of a garden, the fruit trees, the rows of vegetables and flowers and herbs, the mother-in-law apartment in the yard, for which she was also responsible, the seven rooms in her house, each containing—*hush, little baby*—a child playing an instrument or sitting at the computer or dreaming or doing homework or sulking. And there was Ido, her chocolate boy, her divided twin, with whom you always had to listen for the things he was quiet about, and at least one child was always sprawled on her and Micah's bed at any time of day or night, and someone always needed you to help study for an exam on the Weimar Republic or interpret a difficult dream. And there was Yoav, the big twin, too big, who had to be taken to a dietitian twice a week and fought with over every meal and in between meals, and Na'ama, with whom everything was red-headed and stormy and fluid, who would summon her now, right now, urgently, to the treehouse, to listen to selected excerpts from her very private diary. And for the last six months a telephone cable had been strung through one of the five umbilical cords to connect her to a child-soldier who rang almost hourly to talk about courses and guard duty and to sob and boast and be spoiled. And at least once a week someone strolled down from the main road into the yard, a boy or girl come to spend the night or a couple of weeks: friends, or friends of friends, they slept in the basement or on the lawn or on the mats out on the porch, or just in the living room. They raided the fridge at night, played music, smoked—bronzed, half-naked gods walking in on her in the shower by mistake, shaming her flesh with the exact same suspicious look with which they examined the expiration dates on a container of cheese or yogurt. And within all this there was Micah, who called five or ten times a day from work to chat with her, to pass the time on his long journeys, striking up soul-baring conversations (never his own soul, though), giving her live reports from the road and taking her with him to the sites where he fought gaseous clouds, polluted estuaries, and containers carrying toxins, which always seemed to turn up in the most respectable places. For years he had made her a partner in his daily inventory, huge piles of mundane crumbs which he poured forth at her feet, piled up around her, tamping softly, affectionately, thoroughly, quoting for her what they just said on the radio or the latest rumors on his possible promotion, telling her of the accident he saw just now on Gehah Highway and the argument the guys at the office had about the movie on TV, relentlessly reporting the excruciating details of every meal he ate, with a strange sense of loyalty, and in his endearing and devoted and modest way he constantly sketched and copied for her a portrait of himself with a thousand light brushstrokes, and handed her his events for safekeeping and remembering, thus also relieving himself of any responsibility for them, so he could forget everything immediately—faces, names, stories—as if he'd already made up his mind that he was only the conduit through which his life flowed on its way to her, that only upon reaching her did it become real—she even knew his childhood memories better than he did. And she resisted and yet surrendered to his transparent and ample minutiae, to the warmth he pooled every day between her hands like a huge ball of dough—a soft man, always being baked and risen, steaming in anticipation of her.

Sometimes before going to bed at night she stands on the porch for a few minutes, hands on the railing, the exhausted captain of a large ship that roars beneath her, and it's good, it is the abundance of life, and a salty happiness beats in her throat, and it is more wonderful than she had ever dared to dream of in the miserable nothing she came from, and then all of her is there, she is the core of the fruit, and there is nothing better than to feel her blood pulsing and to know that she, only she, is the power that, in its warmth and persistence, allows the billions of molecules of the home and the family to keep adhering to one another, that she is a sole warrior against the massive forces of destruction which lie waiting to pounce on her every distraction and neglect. (But this week, when she was playing with the twins in the park, a Russian nanny asked her innocently if she got paid double, and everything fell apart again.)

She often catches herself making petty calculations: the twins will leave home for the army only in another thirteen years, but by that time, one hopes, there will be grandchildren from the big kids, and she may never stop running up and down the steps and around the yard, picking up toys and paper and paints and half-eaten rolls and gnawed peaches and flea collars and sheet music and Pokémon cards and widowed socks and heavy diapers and receipts and zit cream and bottle tops for prize drawings and hair scrunchies and coins and dust bunnies and little bras. And a hundred times a day she'll check off every task she completes—"Life is like a check-off play," Hagai used to joke—and the buzz she produces will never stop, God forbid it should stop, she thought, and in the momentary internal quiet she heard the truth she could never forget: that since being born, since being who she was, she'd been pursuing the human race, wide-eyed, and that Micah and the kids were the closest she'd ever come, and that no mortal could reasonably be asked to give up such an accomplishment.

She knows that if they even picked up a hint of these thoughts—Micah may sense something but he'd never say a word, not even to himself—they would not be merely astonished and hurt, they would simply shatter into pieces, disappear, evaporate before her very eyes like soap bubbles. These children she had stealthily made for herself, stolen or smuggled out of nothingness, and whom she protects like a wild animal, reviving them over and over again with an infinite series of acts and thoughts and intentions and deeds, conjugated in a maternal list of verbs. Again and again she gathers them up in defense against the treacherous urge to crumble that she senses in them constantly as it lurks beneath their skin, waiting for the one and only moment when she will tire. But she won't, not ever, she won't tire, but will also not be able to give up that bitter thought. She thought Shaul would understand this, and glanced at him and discovered with surprise that he was looking at her deeply, as if he had been following her changing expressions for a long time. Without thinking, she said, You know, sometimes after everyone goes inside, I stay in the garden for a while, beneath the willow branches, and if I need something more solid, I go right inside the rosemary bush, and for a few moments I watch the house from there, with its lit-up windows, the silhouettes of Micah and the kids, and I have this thing where I go backwards until I disappear.

He was quiet; his eyes seemed wistful to her. Then he said, It's getting crowded in that rosemary bush. And from far away he mustered up a shy, shaky smile for her.

Then he sank back in his place and withdrew into himself, trying to overcome the waves of pain that throbbed through his leg, making it swell until he felt it would burst. He wondered whether to take another pill, but decided it was not yet time, better to wait awhile. Instead, as always, he slowly fused his aches into a completely different pain, nameless and sharp, and he cautiously walked it—according to a precise plan whose details he knew well—over his entire body and soul and right into his burning eyes, and now, here

He is somewhere else, somewhere new, a sprawling flatland at the foot of shadowy masses, bordered by desert and mountains. He is surrounded by people, dozens, perhaps hundreds of volunteers come to search for his Elisheva. Every year they come, every year when Elisheva goes off. He tries to follow one of them, but it's like tracking a single ant in an ants' nest, and he persists and catches sight of a well-built young man wearing blue overalls and sticks with him. This man looks slightly familiar, a bit like the guy who once helped Elisheva and him when their car got stuck on the way up north; he had smiled as he swiftly maneuvered and explained, and as an afterthought had also helped them dislodge a jammed cassette from the tape deck and fixed a crooked windshield wiper, and only after they said goodbye had they discovered that he'd left them in a bit of a jam because he'd slid the driver's seat back to accommodate his long legs, and they couldn't get it forward again, and then Shaul had to drive all the way as if he were standing on tiptoe. The guy in the blue overalls rushes over to one of the parked trucks, climbs up on its back, and a moment later jumps down with a big, stuffed kit bag and runs over to a little water reservoir next to an acacia tree, his head thrust forward so he looks as if he is already in the midst of a furious search, lacking only his tongue sticking out of his mouth. He runs past another man, thicker and slower, and something about him vaguely recalls the Arab guy from the deli at the supermarket—Elisheva likes to quote the ambiguous idioms he produces as he tempts the customers to taste the goods, particularly the women, of course, but even with Shaul he jokes in amazing Hebrew about the salami and the quail eggs—he is also running here, carrying a kit bag; strange that even Arabs would come on this kind of search. He stops by another truck, and someone from inside it hands him a rifle, which is somewhat surprising—after all, he is an Arab—but this search must be beyond any national conflict, a clear humanitarian issue that unites all peoples, although it's unclear to Shaul why they even need weapons here. Who are they all going to fight, and over what, or whom? Not far from him a few men are quickly uncoiling huge rolls of barbed wire, setting up a fence and turning the site into a small, protected camp—but from whom? Two men who walk past him carry a large, sharpened wooden post. They shout to each other from either end, Where are you from? Netanya. I'm from Metulla, I was fast asleep, the first says. And me, I was in the middle of dinner, an omelet, and just the way I was, I got up and left. It just gets hold of you suddenly, the first one growls, just drops on you. They slow down and stop for a minute as if they've forgotten where they are headed; they lower their heads and a strange quiet surrounds them, a gloomy, intimate silence like the one that takes hold of your heart when twilight descends and the night becomes at once inevitable.

As he watches, a slight, feathery sense of worry emerges in him, and he brushes it off: they're here to help, to find her . . . Although of course, he concedes, ultimately it will be one, one of all these hundreds of men, who will find her, who will get to her first, who will stand in front of her alone and absorb her abundant gratefulness, the image of her chest swelling at him with excitement. And what will happen then? What will we do with that one? But it's too early to worry, he thinks. Before we can get to that one, we need the many, the multitudes. We need to filter them out slowly, propel them in their souls like a thousand grains of sand in a fine sieve to finally find within them the one golden grain for which Elisheva will sparkle, almost despite herself

There was a contradiction, she felt. There were facts that grated on one another. And in the days that followed she did not stop thinking of how she had wanted to be pulled after him into the story, and that was probably why she did not ask him how the two could be reconciled, Elisheva's explicit desire to be alone and his rushing toward her. Shaul opened his murky red eyes and seemed immediately to sense the doubt that had resurfaced in her, and he mumbled that it was something between himself and Elisheva. She asked if Elisheva knew about his visit, and he said no, and she cautiously remarked that Elisheva might be scared to death by his arrival in the middle of the night. He scratched around the edge of his cast and said very slowly, Please don't put pressure on me. Then he spat out, Well, it's really getting ridiculous that you don't even know where we're going. But at that very moment she almost interrupted him to ask him not to tell her yet, so she could keep going like this a little, driving with no borders and no purpose. He said, Have you heard of a place called Orcha, near the Ramon Crater? She breathed deeply, bade farewell to sweet ignorance, and told him she used to dream of going there alone to spend a few days in a cabin, to cleanse herself of all human contact. She always comes up with these godforsaken places, he said, and in his voice she heard something that reminded her that he was, after all, a Kraus—a vengeful tone, petty and calculating, and she thought of Elisheva, who was now in her own cabin in the heart of the desert, far and isolated from the other cabins, and she became concerned again. What would happen when he went into her cabin? What might he find there? And what was he intending to do? Shaul seemed unable to resist her thoughts, and immediately shrank and turned his face away like an escapee and moaned into the upholstery. Tell me, she said quickly, before he slipped away from her again. What is there to tell? he sighed. Tell me. Tell you what? About them, she ventured, surprised by the force that pushed her toward him unhindered. He must have sensed the slight tremor in her voice, and the tremor was familiar to him, because he smiled at it wearily and unhappily, the smile of a man who is lost, impure, who has corrupted a child.

Their most beautiful moments are when they are both calm, he thinks. His heart twinges and he longs to portray them for her as they are during those times, in all their beauty, to describe them in such a way that she will not be able to resist them—because they are irresistible, he repeats to himself—but how can he tell her?

During those moments of calm, he knows, they can imagine that they have time, that they do not have to give in at once to their urge, that urge which is so human and so understandable, he thinks with pursed lips, the urge to throw their bodies against and inside one another, to dig and burrow into each other, breathlessly rising and falling as they have done almost every day for ten years, with desperate dizziness, needing to squeeze every last drop out of their precious moments of closeness, every cell in their bodies an open mouth to kiss and suck and lick and bite.

He shuts his eyes, and as if he were pulling a book from a crowded shelf, he chooses one such day, when they are completely at ease. He holds the day in his hands and opens it up. He thinks of them relaxed, demilitarized. They are so different when they have time, when they're not tense and disappointed before they've even begun, because they know they'll have to rush. Their movements are different, their breaths, even their expressions. How can he tell her? How can he sneak across the border to the outside?

His hand lies softly on her bare stomach. For Shaul, this stomach represents the furnace of her femininity; he has no idea what it means to the other man. He sees the hand, the fingers, the ring, the stomach. He needs the picture to be slow and precise. And he wants to see it through Elisheva's eyes, from within her and using her words. "Lingering," for example, is a word of hers that fits here. She once knew how to linger, she often laments. She had great patience and the stillness to observe. Then she too became loaded with burdens and nuisances, and now she is like Shaul, like everyone, scampering around, constantly robbed. But when she is there, everything within her relaxes and protracts. Time—those fifty-something minutes—unfolds more and more hidden creases, the very same time which then freezes in Shaul's veins.

And you have to see where each and every finger is positioned, he thinks, the way his thick little finger rests on the evasive line between her hip and her thigh. Another brushes over her hairline. Touching this place always arouses her, and he too, her man, must know this, although of course he may use a completely different touch to arouse her, in places no other man could even imagine, and with acts no other man has dared commit even though the desire is great. Such a man might like, for example, to traverse her entire body with little kisses down to the soles of her feet, to wrap his lips around her plump white toes, one after the other, very slowly, sealing his lips over each of them and sucking gently but persistently, then to run his tongue around each toe, biting it lightly and sensing its feathery down bristle, things Shaul has been passionately longing to do for years but has never dared, because it is not for him—it is for her and her man, and deep in his heart he knows that it is far more appropriate for them than for himself and her. He no longer asks himself why this is or when it was decreed—there would be no point in pursuing that question. That is simply how things were decided in some distant place, in that way in which delicate matters such as these are normally determined and sealed: a man simply knows what belongs to him and what does not, and the act of slowly licking and sucking her toes does not belong to him, period. Much like the journey in the opposite direction, during which he might have sharply but gently bitten her ankles, still beautiful and refined, then ascended with those same nibbles up to her calves, where he could have made circles with his tongue around the pinkish dimples behind her knees. But he prefers not to think of that now, not today, because today they are relaxed, she and her man, completely still but for that one finger of his that traces light circles on her quivering skin. It's the finger with the silver ring she bought him on the fifth anniversary of their love. She bought two identical ones, and she wears hers only there, in the apartment. How can he tell her?

Esti looks for him in the mirror but does not find him, and for a moment she is alone in the car, in another time, and for a moment there is a strange silence and there is tranquillity, and a hidden door that opens just a crack. She takes a bottle of water from her bag and twists the cap off with her teeth, and then his voice comes from behind her again. He is here. Mumbling to himself with his bowed head rocking a little. But she doesn't listen. She gently disconnects from him as she would unravel her fingers from those of a sleeping child. Delicate feelers stir within her: her refugee senses pick up warmth, the scent of a beloved body, a deep, scorched voice, and loud heartbeats that she can still hear sometimes, even after twenty years, even in a crowded street, like a faraway drumming, and she starts to fervently search around herself, barely able to stop herself from calling out the name.

His finger now hovers over her sunken navel, Shaul can see, and his fleshy thumb sinks lightly into the soft pillow of her stomach. These delicate touches awaken whispers and currents above and beneath her skin, and she contains their motion within her as she lies still, her eyes closed and her pupils clinging to her translucent eyelids. He has only to simply flutter his finger from her navel down to her hairline, barely touching, for the fire to instantly consume her, and perhaps this is what he will do, because deep inside he has not yet completely accepted her desire to lie absolutely quietly beside each other today. Just be together, Elisheva says without opening her eyes. Just recharge, she mumbles, picturing an intravenous drip of quietude and solace—"solace" is such a lovely word for her, Shaul thinks—for both of them, he revises. How blissful for us to find fulfillment together in the power of mere closeness, in merely knowing that I am lying beside him, that my body is satiated—not from the satisfaction of passion, but simply from the sweetness of knowing that he is with me quietly, leisurely, belonging, in this pleasure that gushes up from the heart and boils over and spills onto the sheets, requiring almost no touch, no bodily division, with the silent knowledge that we are a mature man and woman, full of love.

Shaul moans to himself, and Esti hears the moan and perks up. He is sprawled with his face buried in the rough, slightly dusty upholstery, his chest rapidly rising and falling. It has taken him years of drilling down through his thoughts to be capable of reaching this stage, this stratum, where he can hold them together like this for almost a whole hour, an entire encounter, without having them lunge at each other. When he was finally able to do this, he realized he had lost her forever. It was difficult for him to explain this even to himself, but he vaguely sensed that if she and the man were capable of being in a state of utter calm, without passionately throwing themselves at each other, this must mean that he, Shaul, had lost her. And his pain is no duller even now, when he sees them like this, taut— but unlike a drawn bow with its arrow—floating in the warm fluids of illusion as if they had plenty of time for themselves, as if when these fifty minutes were over, another eternity of long hours would naturally follow, more days and nights would come—yes, surely, another whole night together, something he believes they have never had for almost the entire life of their love.

Perhaps at the beginning they did, he whispers suddenly into the seat. Perhaps at the beginning they did what? she asks. Perhaps—at the beginning—they—had—a night. He leaps suicidally into her arms as they open for him. An entire—night—together. He is excited to hear the words outside himself for the first time, and watches them full of wonder as they float like shimmering bubbles of poison. Perhaps when they first started, when I still used to do reserve duty in Julis, he says, and waits for his heart to calm down and thinks he won't be able to take it. Although even when I was on duty there, I almost always managed to get away and come home at night, he chokes, and Esti bites her lip, afraid to even look at him so as not to break the thin web. Just to get three or four hours of sleep at home next to her, he ruminates with a flooded heart. Just to lie close to her body and fill myself up with her breath. He shuts his eyes and his entire body clings to her womanly flesh, which even in sleep brings the promise that tomorrow, as if straight out of her body, the sun will shine. And don't forget Tom, he reminds Esti hoarsely. After all, she couldn't possibly have left him alone there for a whole night, you know what a crazy mother she is. No—he waves his hand—it's completely against her nature to do something like that. I mean, to wait until Tom falls asleep and then leave the house? No, she didn't do that, he determines. Although, on the other hand, she could have waited until the boy fell asleep and then phoned Paul to come over—

Paul? Esti asks quietly.

Yes, that's his name.

He's not Israeli?

Not really, it's a long story. He's Russian, but his family is from France.

Go on, I didn't mean to interrupt—

He falls quiet again and tries to understand how he can be saying these things, how it can be that his dark words are coming out into the light and yet he is still alive. At once he storms the doorway that has suddenly opened for him in the endless corridor in which he has been bumping around for years; words spill out, cut off, confused, ashamed, squeezing out. But it's so unlike Elisheva, he mumbles, to do something like that. I mean, to bring Paul into our house. What if Tom had woken up suddenly and come to the bedroom in tears? No, of this he absolved her almost completely, always, and it is important to him that Esti knows that even inside the chaos of their revealed and hidden lives, he knows that Elisheva is an honest person, the most honest person he knows, and that she is even loyal, in her own way. This is truly difficult to explain, and he finds it strange that Esti is quiet now and does not ask him anything about it, as if she understands on her own that such a contradiction is possible. And it's absolutely clear to me, he says, that a person less honest than Elisheva would not be so tormented by these transitions—

What transitions? she asks, confused.

The transitions, you know, between me and him, when she comes and goes, back and forth . . .

Yes, Esti pipes up, that is the most difficult part, the transitions . . .

That's the paradox, he continues, that because of her absolute honesty she probably has to pursue this lousy situation, because she just cannot be dishonest in her soul, you see, she cannot give up her great love . . . He stops and chokes down the gall of his words. Look, it's not easy for me to make peace with this, it's hard for me to even think of it, but this love must be worth all the suffering.

It's not suffering, says Esti softly, it's torture—think of how torn she is. Honestly, I can't understand how she takes it.

That's exactly what I'm saying: what she has with him must be worth the suffering for her. And maybe it's me who is the redundant one, he mumbles to himself. But you know her, he adds, she would never take a drastic step that might hurt me—how can I even use the word "hurt"? he sniggers, the bitterness in his mouth tasting like cyanide. It would destroy me. Annihilate me into dust.

In the dense space of the car she feels slightly dizzy, because of the warm streams emitted by the body lying behind her, and because of the inside of that body, which seems to be tearing apart and disgorging its burning contents, and she cannot follow all of Shaul's words. How difficult it must be, she thinks, to live with such a strain. And that is also why being with him always feels so oppressive. She's just so right for him, Shaul groans. Do you see what I'm up against? Esti nods, unable to utter a word—what could she say? What can one say? That's the thing, he whispers, there is something between them that cannot be canceled out or denied. It's as if she were born for him, he says with indescribable effort, and feels contaminated and miserable and yet freed in a way he has never felt before, and he extracts the words from within himself and places them one by one at her feet. Sometimes I think to myself that it was just their bad luck, or even a tragic error of some sort, that she and he did not— Esti lowers her head and silently begs him to take a break and let her breathe. How can he say such things? And how can she sit and listen to them as if nothing had happened? As if she didn't even recognize the words and the pangs and the sting of longing. She lets out a weak, crushed sigh. How could she be acting like Joseph, who denied knowing his brothers even as he yearned to get up and hug them and shout, *It's me!* And that voice, she listens, it's not at all his normal voice; this slightly reserved, ironic tone is something completely different, from another place . . . She is almost tempted to shut her eyes to the road: she has perfect pitch, not for music, but for human voices, and with the subtlety of a wine taster she can discern every nuance of tone. His voice is now replete and dark, as he paints for her a distant, wintry place, perhaps a forest covered with a thin layer of frost, a large tree trunk slowly burning in its midst, silently, occasionally making soft crackling sounds of pain.

She becomes more agitated toward him and against him and with him, and knows that she is opening up now in a new place, unfolding to him with the thirst of a student, and even if she does not understand exactly what he is teaching or what the topic of the lesson is, something inside her whispers that she is in the right place, faraway in a school basement, in a dark and vehemently denied little room; only a few believe in its existence, and only they can be drawn to it and are worthy of participating in the class always in session there, at all hours of the day and night, even when not a single student is present.

Tell me, how is it possible, he says—the thought always strikes him in the same way, from the same exact angle and always for the first time—how is it possible to grasp that this woman, my wife, my one and only true love, has not missed a single meeting with the man for the last ten years? Except maybe once or twice a year on her sick days or when there was a family event, a war here and there, trips abroad or out of town—days when she absolutely couldn't go out and maintain her life with him. Shaul deliberately uses that turn of phrase: "maintain her life with him." The words burn every time, but honesty forces him to say them even when he's talking with Esti. He has not believed for a long time that Elisheva was going out only "to meet with him." Because he knew very well that there was something far deeper between them than a mere "meeting," and certainly more than a fleeting sexual encounter—although that undoubtedly does occur almost every day, he notes diligently. After all, they are a normal man and woman, he snickers, and as he speaks those last words, a flame is ignited within him, and for the first time he directs its blaze at another person, and Esti feels it and rushes to protect herself from the sudden violent gust, the likes of which she has never known, as it lunges at her from the fluttering man behind her. She knows she must save herself, but does not know exactly from what, and is not even sure she really wants to be saved and banished this soon from the private master class. She fears that if she does not pull herself together at once, she may not have the strength later on to withstand the strange assault which now attacks her in waves with a kind of impersonal insistence, almost inhuman, or perhaps insufferably human. Practically yelling, she bursts out, I don't understand, Shaul, stop for a minute, I can't grasp anything anymore. I thought for a second that . . . No, you've got me completely confused. Start over, please.

And now it's a little easier for him. He doesn't know how it happened, but the path seems to have been paved, and all he has to do now is follow it over and over again until it is conquered, and for an instant he even contemplates the possibility that the pleasure of keeping a secret and the pleasure of revealing it are perhaps not so distant from each other. He explains that Elisheva, in her special circumstances, must be very efficient and businesslike because of those transitions. After all, she didn't use to be like that, he smiles forlornly, and Esti nods and sees the dreamy Elisheva of the past, frightened by large department stores, bungling tip calculations in restaurants, standing with a little street map, her brow furrowed, deliberating over which is her right hand; she is filled with longing for Elisheva again, for the days when everyone was still together. Even Shaul had been with them back then, in his own way, of course, kicking out now and then, but at least he was within kicking distance. As he continues talking, she recalls a distant sunny afternoon in her garden, when Tom was little and Shira and Eran were still babies. She sees Shaul and Micah playing ball with them, then forgetting about the little ones and horsing around with each other—Shaul happy as he dribbles the ball with a skill that surprises her and deceives Micah, Elisheva sprawling in a deck chair, full and soft and golden, smiling at him. She had huge sunglasses back then, Esti remembers, like Sophia Loren; she had asked her to go and buy them with her. When she smiles at Shaul, he seems to lose his balance for a second, then raises his arms and links his hands over his head in victory. He snatches up Tom and lifts him onto his shoulders and charges around the lawn with him. His parents and Micah watch Shaul and the boy with a longing that Esti did not understand at the time, and still cannot decipher in all its subtleties. They seemed to be praying for Tom to serve as a kind of appeals court, she now thinks, where they would win Shaul back, or perhaps gain him for the first time.

As if he had been listening to every word that passed through her mind, Shaul blurts out that everything has changed so much, and that you don't get used to something like this; that every time he thinks about it, it destroys him to comprehend that his wife—and here he stops and withdraws, *my wife*, he thinks, amazed, as if pronouncing the words for the first time, *my wife*, and for a moment he sees the words hover above him with his very own eyes, these words that enter the world gnawed, he feels, always surrounded by a ring of tooth marks— Where was I? he mutters, and Esti reminds him, and he whispers that he can never grasp that Elisheva has been maintaining an entire life with another man for at least ten years, fifty-odd minutes a day. These are fleeting moments, to be sure, but when I think about some of the couples I know, he says, there seem to be some who don't even have that daily time together, certainly not with a focus that is so . . . what's the word, so concentrated, and all the more so because Elisheva—and here a little smile lights up his face, making it almost beautiful for a moment—can be very intense with all her excitement and storminess and her moods and her enthusiasm. But here Esti disagrees, because her Elisheva was always remarkably tranquil, and that was also why she had so loved to be with her. No, no, he protests, as if all her thoughts are transparent to him, you can't imagine how stormy she can be, really pressurized, or at least she used to be when we were first together, before she started sharing her energies with another person. And when I think of it like that, he sighs, I can certainly see—I can imagine, I mean—how she in fact maintains her life with him. Esti, with limp and bloodless lips, asks how, and Shaul says dryly, as if slicing out thin and very crisp words, Listen, it's a life that has not even one moment of waste or boredom, or of fatigue, you know, because of tiredness or indifference, or just getting sick of each other. With them it's the opposite, he declares. Every moment of theirs is electrically charged and full of interest and passion. It's an intense life, he determines, and after a minute, as if a confession has been wrested from him, he adds, A full life.

Wait a minute, she said later, blinking. What did you say before? What did I say?

You said, she carefully reconstructed, that you can imagine.

Imagine what?

Her life with him.

He was quiet.

Because all this time I thought that you and she . . . that you—

She doesn't know that I know, he said. I thought you understood that. He started gnawing at his upper lip and did not look at her.

Esti felt the blood pulsing quickly in her knuckles as they grasped the wheel. The thought was so foreign that her tongue and lips moved with it in a slow chewing motion.

But how?

He nodded, defeated.

I don't understand. Her voice faded, lost. You just sit at home—

He wiped his face with both hands. His burning forehead, his temples.

Why? she practically yelled.

Why? He spoke into himself, sealed and dark. Why indeed?

Like a man shouting into a well, she thought.

It's been at least ten years that this thing of theirs has been going on, he said after a few moments. Don't you think I know her well enough?

And you never—

Never.

But how can you not? she whispered again, suddenly disbelieving him, recoiling, disgusted by him, and immediately also struck by a lightning bolt of loathsome pictures, soap operas and hidden cameras and people being paid to spy and rob other people of their intimacy and spoil their moments of sweetness. Secrets defiled in the light. She was horrified to think of innocent Elisheva, whose purse might contain a bug—for all she knew he had bugged every room in that apartment too, certainly the bedroom. Her stomach turned. Perhaps he just sits and watches her from the moment she leaves the house—

I've never followed her even once all these years, he said quietly, then almost whispered, But, Esther, please, she cannot know that I know.

Her pulse beat in her neck with crazed speed and her eyes became covered with a film. Only now, in rhythmic waves, was she struck by her stupidity, her blindness, her *estheronautiness*, and, above all, her longing, the insult of the power of her longing, and she knew very well that it was these shortcomings that had made her so eager to interweave in his story the threads of her secret dreams of candor and of painful, purifying honesty; of a generous togetherness in which everything was possible. For a moment, with all that had been spun and stabbed and defiled within her, her face took on the expression of a frightened, abandoned girl who lunges out to bite, who lives unimaginably close to the skin's surface, ready to be drawn out like a final plan of retreat.

His voice was tired, crushed. You know, I could drive after her when she says she's going to the pool, couldn't I? Any normal person in my situation would do it, wouldn't they? Maybe even you would.

Yes, she thought quickly. No, of course I wouldn't. Maybe just once, to see a different Micah—

Just follow her there and confront her, do it and be done with all this mess. And he laughed dully. You know, when Tom was injured on a school trip in the eleventh grade and they called me to the hospital, I didn't even phone the swimming pool for them to page her. I didn't want to embarrass her in any way, Esther.

And when he said it that way, simply, but also proudly, she saw inside him, and in a blinding flash, his insides were lit up for her like a drawing in an old nature book, a cross section of the soul, the secret soul, and for a moment she pulled back from this forbidden sight. Then she looked again, hypnotized, and knew he was giving her something that had no name, with a generosity that was also horrifying. She could see the negative image of her own reflection somewhere on the edge of his pupil, she had a place there, and with the instinct of a seed she held on and struck roots; only then, finally, did she extricate herself from the dullness that had enveloped her all evening and truly grasp the gift he was offering, his one-time invitation, and with both hands outstretched, she caught it quickly and resourcefully, with the same agility with which she catches the yolk of a broken egg. Then she sat and drove in a kind of hovering state, almost without touching the wheel, and wondered how an expanse could be made up of so many twisted damp crevices, because she suddenly felt an expanse, and drunkenness, and was amazed at how from misery and distortedness such as his, he had managed to lead her astray into this open space, a tortured and miserable place, but also uninhibited and possessed of a passion to destruct—a healthy passion to destruct, whose sharp, burning pleasure she had long ago forgotten. She thought he was mad, Shaul, and unbearable, and indefatigable, and that's what she told herself the next morning—that she had suddenly found one place in him where, in defiance of all logic, he was free.

He asked for some water and she passed him the bottle. He said the pain was returning, and she suggested he take two pills. He said, Yes, why not, and drank the water, and thanked her for it, and asked if she wanted the bottle next to her. She said, No, actually yes, and he gave it to her, and she drank and said he should raise the pillow under his leg a bit, and everything they said and did occurred outside them, in a kind of hollow practicality. They drove slowly along an almost empty road. Every so often they passed a semitrailer or a pickup truck loaded with crates. Esti suggested they stop along the side of the road so he could rest a little or change positions, and he said there was no need, that he was all right, but perhaps she had an apple. She did, and before passing it to him she polished it absentmindedly on her sleeve, as she did when she gave fruit to her children, and he held it in front of his slightly open mouth as if he had forgotten what to do with it

Out there in the shadows at the edge of the chaotic camp, one man stops running and turns to look back. Bewildered, he searches, guided toward a voice or a scent, or a slight tremble in the air. Next to the acacia tree another man slows down and freezes in mid-motion, and he too turns to look back and search. One after another, seemingly unconnected and unplanned, they all slow down and halt their movements, and silence descends and envelops them. Men stand in amazement all around the small camp, seeking out something in the air with their noses. Shaul grows excited: perhaps they can smell her, perhaps somehow, in some incomprehensible way, they are qualified to pick up every whiff of her scent; they must have all gone through special training. After a moment they begin to move, all of them, from all ends of the camp, with hesitant, cautious steps, their heads nodding like blind men's, and he realizes with a fright that they are walking toward him and getting nearer and closing in on him.

With unnatural slowness, their calves and thighs ascend and descend rhythmically, their eyes blink lazily, their tongues move and lick their lips with strange restraint, and he thinks perhaps he should start backing away from them a little, because he suddenly has an odd feeling, completely unfounded, that they will try to do something to him, although he has no idea what. But it would be ridiculous to flee them, these people who have come from all over the country to look for his wife. They did not respond to any public draft issued with some secret code word—rather, they hurried here as soon as they somehow found out about her, swept to this place even before he himself arrived. He scrutinizes their faces to discern their intentions as they storm him in a daze, and a nighttime breeze rises and ruffles his thin hair, which he immediately smooths down to cover his bald spot. They are already gathering around him, silent, grave, and he smiles with embarrassed politeness, nodding at this man or that, but not a single one of them responds, and soon a chilling fear rips through his innards, because in their eyes, in the eyes of each and every one of them, he reads something murky that cannot be translated into words, and that is difficult to even conceive . . .

Later, much later, he asked if she had something he could use to scratch his leg under the cast. She leaned over as she drove, rummaged in the glove compartment, and found a knitting needle—who knew how long it had been there waiting to be discovered at this very moment. He practically snatched it from her, and inserted it between the cast and his calf and scratched vigorously, addictively, and said he had no idea how he would survive with this cast for several weeks. She told him she'd once broken her arm when she was doing a back bend in school, and he said, Oh really, and after a minute he said, Do you remember how we talked a bit about that school once? She said she did, and he was quiet, and then he said, I was a nuisance, wasn't I? She said yes, and he said, Sometimes, when I latch onto an issue, I can be . . . And he sighed deeply, and she smiled and said, Yes, you certainly can. He said, It must have been torture for you, and she didn't know whether he meant the school or his interrogation, and she said, Yes, it was. After a moment he added that what stuck with him after that meeting was that she had told him how she'd been held back a year, and she choked and asked why that of all things, and he answered, I don't know, it's amazing that it even came to me, but I can clearly remember how hard it was for you to talk about it. To her surprise, she quickly told him that Micah didn't know about that to this day, that for some reason she hadn't been able to bring herself to tell him. She took a deep breath and said, smiling tensely, They thought I was retarded in that place, handicapped, that's why they held me back. Retarded or handicapped, she repeated, and her eyes brimmed over, and he, behind her, was quiet, and for an instant everything hung from a flimsy thread. He said, That's hard to believe, and the wonderment with which he said it filled her with quiet joy, as well as the fact that he said nothing else. She nodded to herself a few times, and found herself back in the morass of those years for a moment, back in the six-block radius of the neighborhood that had been her world then. With a toneless and quiet voice, she told him about the walk she had invented, and about the game she called "letter fasting," when she would say only words that didn't contain a certain letter, and as Shaul looked at her from his vantage point, he saw a small, thin girl hovering over a vast cement surface—

And who is he? she asked when she had calmed down. Tell me a little about him. And she silently tasted the name: Paul.

Shaul shook off her question. What is there to tell? Then he tittered softly. He's not me.

That's it, isn't it? she thought.

But sometimes, he said, I ask myself what there is in him. Not just "What does he have that I don't?" but really what is it about him that attracts her to him so strongly? Attracts her so much that . . . For a moment Esti felt that for some reason he was expecting her to validate what he was saying, to assure him assertively of this man's absolute superiority over him. Honestly, he continued when she said nothing, I suddenly realized what they mean when they talk of falling under someone's spell. He laughed and leaned his head back against the window. And then I realized that he is simply a person at peace with himself, you see, and that is why everything he does, no matter what, will always have flair, a kind of grace and style. Yes, something polished, nonchalant. She glanced back and saw that his eyes were closed again and his lips were pursed and slightly protruding, like the lips of someone pouring something out of a wide pitcher into a narrow bottle. People like him, he went on, people with such crystallized internal perfection, they just don't care what other people think about them or how others see them. Me, for example—he chuckled dismissively—at every step I wonder what people will think of me, what they'll say. But this guy just does exactly what he wants, he has no fears. If he wants something, he just does it. And everything within him is in harmony, you see. A man like him, he didn't even need to tell her he wanted her—I mean at the very beginning, when they had just met. She sensed it straightaway, on her own, from the inside. Because this perfection of his contains a kind of force of—how can I put it—necessity? Yes, yes, he has complete confidence in the fact that just wanting something turns his desire into an inevitability. It's simply *charisma*. Shaul sounded suddenly gleeful. That's the word I was looking for. Not style, forget style, charisma is what he has, and a man who has charisma, well . . . anything he wants immediately becomes the right thing, the inevitable thing. It's like a force of nature, charisma, like an act of God. His voice became louder and fuller: You see, he wanted her, and she got up and went to him. Well, obviously at this point it's her desire as well, but at the beginning? The moment he wanted her, at that very second, she could no longer resist his desire. She got up and went to him. But now still, when he suddenly wants something new from her—not something big, I'm not even talking about in bed, but let's say he suddenly wants her to, I don't know, make him some soup? He feels like soup, he wants it so badly that he's willing to waste their entire fifty minutes on it that day, and it's not because of the soup, believe me—after all, he knows she's not exactly the world's best cook. But he feels like seeing her standing in the kitchen and cooking, seeing her chopping vegetables, stirring, spicing, seeing those motions of her body, of a woman making soup for her man—

He went on in that same strange voice, alternately tense and relaxed, as if carried on some endless internal current, and Esti drove slowly and thought the Volvo was barely moving. It seemed as if it were only the huge hills around them that were stretching out into the darkness and changing into plains that slowly flattened backwards, only to be swallowed up by new plains, and she no longer knew whether Shaul was opening up to her with this sorrow that had been crammed and trapped inside him for so many years, or whether something completely different was going on here, on frequencies that her brain could not pick up but in which her soul was trembling with pain. Every few moments a question would come to her lips, an absolutely logical question, such as: *But how can you be certain that . . . ?* Or: *How can you hide from her?* And: *What would happen if you just told her you knew everything?* And even: *Why do you let it go on and torment the three of you like this?* But her tongue was heavy and thick, and she'd forget, and soon a new question would collect in her like a drop of water

They link to form rows around him, crowded, silent, breathless. Their eyes burn, almost red. He can smell their breath. A few of them look familiar, or almost familiar, or like the rough draft of someone familiar, but all their faces are distorted into one eager, wolfish expression. Tell us, a weak voice whispers from behind. Tell, another adds. Tell, tell, tell, they add one voice to another, spark whisper to whisper, and the dull grumble surrounds him and intertwines into a long, throaty growl mixed with crushed words, and he listens and tries to decipher word fragments, breaths, sighs. They want him to tell them about her, that must be it, that's all, and it certainly makes sense and is even legitimate—clearly the most important details are the ones given by the missing person's relatives. That must be what they are demanding from him with their warm, sour breaths, and it's probably worth their while to delay the search for another few moments so they can equip themselves—they breathlessly tell him as one—with information that only the husband can provide, and here they fall silent and gaze at him with tense expectation.

But how and what should he tell them? he wonders, and they lean in toward him even closer, as if they had heard his precise thought, and ready themselves to pounce, each and every one of them, to be the first to snatch every crumb of a thought that may pass through his mind. He decides he must focus, so he can finally be of some use, and he sucks his cheeks in as he always does when he thinks, and shifts from one foot to the other, and embarrassed by their penetrating looks, he lets out a silly twittering sound in a high squeaky voice and they quickly draw back and then lean in again. Then he realizes that they have already begun to "equip themselves" with information, that in fact they are already in the midst of the process and that even now, in the way he stands, in his hesitant shifting, his sudden screech, he is probably telling them something important about her, about his Elisheva, and perhaps about her uncontrollable urge to go off into the distance every so often and be alone.

Tell me—she could no longer bear what she thought he was doing to himself with a kind of tortured lust, so she dove into his silence and tore him out of it and brought him to the surface—that man, Paul, is he married? Does he have a family?

Shaul said, No, he isn't married. Because of her, I think. He sighed helplessly. I'm telling you, Esther, this is not just a fling. She is his great love. He paused, then sighed again with absolute sincerity. She is the love of his life— The Volvo suddenly rocked violently and leaped forward as she slammed on the brakes. What happened? Shaul shouted.

Nothing, Esti mumbled. It's these pedals, sorry, I got confused.

Shaul looked at her and straightened his broken leg a little. A crooked line formed between his eyebrows.

Every few weeks, he said after a few minutes—and now there was the trill of a newfound boldness in his voice—she offers to shave him. For no particular reason, just so he'll have a close shave, because he always misses a bit. He made an effort to smile as he explained, and saw Elisheva preparing a bowl with hot water and lathering his face with his ancient brush. Her tongue peeks out from between her lips as she concentrates on his upper lip, careful not to cut it, but even if she does, even if thick, dark red blood spurts out, she blots it so softly that it's hard to tell, then goes back to running the blade over his chin and cheeks, carving him. Her face is very close to his, and she gently pushes his hand away when it reaches out to her from below. She carefully washes his warm face, pats it, and holds it between her hands. At that moment, he said, she has a smile I'm not familiar with. In fact, he whispered, that's true of all her expressions there, when she's with him—those are expressions I've never seen in her—

Like what? she interrupted him, almost rudely.

I don't know, he said, but they're definitely sharper expressions of everything, of all the emotions. Passion, obviously, but also sadness, happiness, longing . . .

Esti said nothing.

That's the way it is, he explained what she knew in every cell of her body. Even when she's with him she misses him. Or misses being with him somewhere else, or in a different state. And he sighs: You know, I sometimes sit at home and count the minutes and think, Maybe today she'll be home five minutes earlier. Maybe today, for a change, they'll have had enough a little earlier, one minute earlier. And it's never yet happened, do you understand? Ten years, and it's never yet happened to them.

In an instant of enchanting illusion, her vision became blurred and she herself was Elisheva, driving to the man's house in her little Polo, sewing up the margins of the night with little bright green stitches. You know, she said after a while, I've never heard you talk like this.

I never do talk like this. And he gave her a long look and bit his lip with a tiny gesture of loneliness. I can't even comprehend yet that I'm really talking.

That's exactly how I feel, she murmured. As if I'm somehow reading your mind.

He nodded. They were quiet. That's it, she thought.

To tell you the truth? Her fingers tightened their grip on the wheel. I don't know how you have the courage.

Courage? He laughed in surprise. I don't think it has anything to do with courage. I may be a little drunk now, from talking, but what will I have tomorrow, when I'm hungover? Tell me that.

Call me, she said immediately. We'll talk in the daylight too.

Oh yeah? He shot her a playful, slanted look, almost charming for a moment. We'll have a support group?

No, she said. Yes, why not. Just the guys from the rosemary bush.

Sometimes, like when we eat, he said, after a minute, I look up at her when she's distracted and try to guess what that face looks like when she's with him, when his look alters her. And just in general I picture how her whole appearance changes—the aging and the little wrinkles and the tiredness—how when she's there they are smoothed over and refreshed, how she's illuminated there. That's the word, "illuminated."

And what then? she whispered.

And then it hurts, he said, and his voice broke. Then she's incredible.

Tell me.

Wait, he said, and held his hand up in front of his face. Wait. He spoke with the voice of someone excusing himself because he needs to be alone. And they had already tacitly agreed that every so often he needed to retire to another place, to take a different road, a side road, which was also—she guessed—part of the pleasure of his torment, just as she herself, it occurred to her, could retire and disappear into herself during these moments—

She shook herself abruptly before she could get carried away, and straightened up and coughed loudly and yawned exaggeratedly, but her body sank back again and delved softly into the seat, and she knew she had been there for many long moments, stripped of any determined decision and flooded with passion and longing and love. Sometimes she would even avoid thinking of him because of a vague sense that he became more and more absent with every thought, and besides, she decided she had no right to go back there out of the exile she had imposed on herself years ago, not even as a nostalgic tourist. But now it seemed that tentacles were being sent out from there to gather her in, and she no longer had the strength to resist. She dove into a whirlwind of smells and touches and wetness and fragments of pictures, the memory of the dreams that troubled her nights, and the new islands she discovered in her body, which had remained desolate ever since that time—

Shaul? she mumbled softly, as if asking him to come and draw her out of there. But he was gone

And he draws back, wanting to shout, to wake them up from the hypnotic and bothersome concentration with which they dig inside him, and he feels them sucking, or consuming something from him— but what? What are they sucking out of him without his knowledge, without his volition, completely against his will? As they burrow, he wakes to feel a vague fluttering deep inside, the flicker of the thing they are searching for within him, which moves inside him and tries to evade them like a smooth purse of skin, placental, damp, and engorged with shame. Their large fingers chase it through him, and he wants to scream, to uproot them from the violent silence and from what they are doing to him, from what they are humiliating and desecrating in him, and a moment before he suffocates, he manages to take control of the wave of alarm—panic will not help them find her, and he clears his throat and says in a choked but extremely civilized voice, Good evening, my name is—

A raucous choir of shouts of protest and barks of anger storms him, and a few men put their hands over their ears, and it occurs to him that now, at this stage of the search, he is forbidden to say his name. Apparently he must remain only "the husband." And Elisheva? He wonders to himself and does not dare to articulate, Am I allowed to say her name here? But the look coming from their eyes slams him with the answer, and a strange weakness spreads through his legs as he looks with terror from one man to the next and his lips begin to quiver. Who are you? he asks with no voice. Why have you come?

They do not bother to answer. Only a soft, wavy ripple flows back and forth between him and them. A few of them stand with their eyes closed, heads held back, their nostrils open at him, shamelessly inhaling him into themselves from head to toe, studying him, following him, looting. He straightens up with considerable effort and stands with his chest puffed out, although his knees threaten to fold in on themselves, and then he feels the belly of the earth growling. A very quiet, dull growl, and a humming tremble rises from the soles of his feet.

It's them, he thinks, horrified. It's the men. He listens with his body and distractedly presses his feet together, but to no avail—the tremble is already inside him and seems to be massaging his nerve centers and the mortar and pestle of every joint, and he does not resist it. How could one resist it? Every moment another of them adds his voice to the choir. At first the new voice sounds clear, slightly higher than the others, then it threads in with the rest, dives into them and thickens them, and he has to actually stop himself from adding his own voice in a quiet hum, but something in him guesses that his voice would not be welcomed.

The growl slowly dies down until finally a heavy silence descends all the way to the back rows. Then they stretch their arms up, stomp their feet a little, roll their heads around to loosen their necks. Undoubtedly, a certain stage has now concluded, and he breathes a sigh of relief. Maybe now they will begin searching in earnest.

A hand is raised somewhere in the back rows. A faceless voice asks him to describe her, the wife.

Where to begin? How do you describe a woman you've been living with for twenty-five years? It's a little like describing yourself, he thinks, like describing one of your internal organs, suddenly exposed. He clears his throat again and says she is fifty years old, even though she's forty-nine—he doesn't want to waste their time with nuances—but then he discovers that not a single sound is coming from his mouth. He has no voice.

He is gripped by terror. He tries to say something, tries to yell, but his vocal cords are unheard, and he is struck by the thought that perhaps with that continuous growl they had not only directed their voices together but had also taken his, as one confiscates the weapons of a treacherous soldier. I can't talk, he realizes with surrender, trying to rapidly assimilate all the novelties, to adapt himself precisely to what they need in order to find her. He is not allowed to talk and he is incapable of talking. Only thoughts are permitted here, and that's fine. But maybe not even thoughts—maybe only these currents which surge through the blood like bolts of lightning. He looks far beyond them and feels his desire and his life force running out of him, and that's it, he can no longer go on resisting, and with no remaining strength he finally gives himself over to the constitution that rules here, the constitution of the search, delivering himself into the hands of its emissaries, who have gathered here for the express purpose of leading him step by step and denying him any possibility of an appeal, so that he will perform, in the best possible way, the role he has always been destined for in this comedy

Sometimes, Shaul whispers, rousing Esti from her thoughts, sometimes—listen to this—in the middle of a hug, she says to him, Let's dance. And then he opens one eye, Paul, and laughs— Right now? But she's already up off the bed and hurrying to the record cabinet. Naked, Shaul adds silently, and sinks into a heavy, swampy meditation, then extracts himself and continues. She bought him a new stereo system, but he won't give up the records and phonograph he brought with him from Riga. And she likes that too, he explained, the way she likes the rotary phone he insists on keeping ("That way I can enjoy it for longer when I dial your number," he explains), and his heavy typewriter with the ink ribbons, his old pair of moccasins, the white undershirts and white underwear, and the shaving brush that Esti already knows about, and the old plaid shirts and his funny horn-rimmed glasses and the thick wool coat and the bookshelves piled high and the piles of books from floor to ceiling, and the cheap kitchenware he stubbornly refuses to replace. Although, he notes, they do have one set of fancy dishes, painted with a fruit motif, that Elisheva bought for their festive meals—

Shaul can see it: She leans over to browse through the albums. Paul straightens up in bed and looks at her as she bends over. She still doesn't sense it. She will in a minute.

He says nothing for a long time, and his eyelashes tremble with uncontrollable pain. Within the pod of pain, diving into eternity, floating alone in the empty depths, without relief—

He almost gets out of bed and walks over to her. Shaul sees it, and his blood, like the man's blood, screams for him to get up and go over and take hold of her from behind and grasp and spread and touch and wet and penetrate with massive force—and for one long moment he manages not to go, not to hold her—how does he manage? What incredible powers of restraint and self-control he must have. Elisheva, without looking, now feels his fervor, a huge furnace with swollen purple tendons, and Esti feels it too, even immersed in herself as she is, enraptured. It's been years since she has allowed herself this much. She remembers how almost everything used to be a sign, a secret private sign: colorful plastic bags blowing in the wind and catching on the branches of a tree opposite her house and filling up with rain at night so they looked like large tears hanging. Or a small item on the news about a stalactite in Absalom's Cave that had dripped into a stalagmite for thousands of years until finally they united. The world was incredibly garrulous.

Elisheva stops looking through the records and steals a glowing sideways look at him, and her passion sparks against his—

But no, no, she laughs, fighting him off, I wanted to dance now—

Wait a minute, Shaul says to Esti with a choking voice, I'll go on in a second.

He covers himself with a thin blanket that Esti had found for him in the trunk, and turns his face to the back of the seat and closes his eyes and goes back to that place of his. She can feel his body heat rise as soon as he gets there, and she wonders what he finds there, how much further he can go, and thinks it might be better if she does not understand exactly what she is collaborating with tonight, and what Elisheva would think of her, and what she herself will think of herself in the morning. But just tonight, she begs, and knows she is prepared to keep on driving him indefinitely, soaking up the heat he projects at her like a furnace

He tries to straighten up, but his head drops forward, and it seems he no longer has any will of his own, and this means that his volition has been taken from him along with his voice. That must be the procedure here. So everything's all right, everything is going according to their plan, and if so, he must think of her in his heart. He just doesn't know exactly how they want him to describe her in his thoughts, in what situation; in other words, what do they need for their search? But he soon understands exactly what they want. Their desire floods into him with a strong torrent: they want her without clothes, of course—naked, you idiot. But he refuses, and with his last remaining strength and dignity he tries to fight them, and the more he resists, the more their pressure increases, and he is surrounded by misty exhalations and hoarse sighs of anger as they sense immediately that he is trying to evade them, and he begs, Why is this necessary? Really, what does her naked body have to do with the search? It seems to him that even that thought sends a feverish chill through them, and that their eyes are now burning at him like dull embers. He quickly tries to wrap her with clothes, to hide her from them with his arms outspread, but what chance does he have opposite such an intense surge? He rocks and is shoved and tries to flee, but the waves of their desire easily subdue him, sweep him away and invade him, and his body falters on the field in front of them with none of his own desire, and he is tossed-from-side-to-side

Backwards-forwards
His-arms-thrown
And-his-feet-stomping
And-he-starts-dancing
And-dances-for-them
The-dance-of-the-husband
Telling-with-his-body
Telling-with-his-flesh
What Elisheva looks like
He goes Elisheva
And comes Elisheva
And laughs Elisheva
And blinks Elisheva
And dances Elisheva
And undresses Elisheva
And lusts for Elisheva
And Shaul Elisheva
From soles to head
Rounding curving
More beautiful
More delicate—

At once his arms drop to his sides and his body rocks some more, looking for the focal point of familiarity, which he has momentarily lost, and his eyes open again slowly, indulgently, with a loose straggling of the eyelashes. He believes something happened there while he was gone, but he doesn't have the strength to remember what it was. It was as if I were running here in front of them, he thinks, confused. As if someone were doing a dance. He rubs his hands together and looks at their foreign movement, the gesture of a cunning merchant offering a prized piece of merchandise to a customer, secretive and witty, and his tongue quickly licks his dry lips, and a thin circle of stolen, ashamed sweetness stirs within him, a small precise circle like a flower bed around the roots of his soul, and in complete surrender, like a eunuch fulfilling his duty at a harem, he undresses his wife for them . . .

Half an hour later, Elisheva gets out of bed again, slower and heavier, drenched with him. This time she makes sure to put something on—a T-shirt of his or a thin colorful dress that hangs in the closet—and slips her feet into his clumsy wool slippers, even though she keeps a pair of her own there, of course. Sometimes, when she's gone, Paul crouches next to the bed and holds one of her slippers in his hand—there is a special charm even in the way he holds her empty slipper, Shaul smiles to himself, and Esti leaves her train of thought for a moment and wonders where he is floating now—and he puts two fingers into the hollow of the slipper and twists them around to touch all its sides, then he lifts it to his face and inhales the smell of her foot, which is preserved in it, and imagines he is licking her toes and she is writhing with passion. He was the one who taught her how much pleasure is contained in one's toes, and that there is not a single limb in our body that has no longing for pleasure. And perhaps that is the reason, Shaul suddenly thinks, that I'm incapable of sleeping with her the way I used to at the beginning. Not just because of age and habitude, but because now each cell in her body is taut with the pleasure sensors he has revealed to her, and as soon as I touch her, they wake up and start looking for him. I feel them searching, he thought. That must also be why our sex has become rarer, and shorter. I don't make love to her anymore. You can't call it making love, certainly not like once. We had it so good once, before all this started. Over the last few years a silent arrangement has emerged between him and Elisheva. Shaul can't even remember when it began or how it became habit: they go to sleep as usual, with soft and concerned affection, read a little, say good night, and fall asleep. And in the middle of the night, at three or four, almost completely asleep, they press against each other with eyes shut, desperately twisting around each other, violently even, like two strangers meeting in a dream, plundering and being plundered in the dark. Hard and full of sharp passion, they moan and scratch and glisten with fresh sweat, and prey upon each other because of the foreignness, then disengage and fall into a heavy slumber. In the morning they do not say a word about it, perhaps only the flicker of a look of shame, as if they both see themselves there, two wolves fighting as they grunt and whine over which of them will grab the larger piece of pleasure, and there is always a little guilt at the corners of their eyes, as if it were not with each other that they had slept. Then come many more nights of nothing, and suddenly they are thrown against each other again in their sleep.

Meanwhile, Elisheva kneels—he had almost forgotten—by the record cabinet, leafing through his hundreds of albums, and now Shaul feels like seeing her in a long dress, homely but with a mischievous slit up to the knee, no higher—he always protects the varicose veins on her thighs from the other guy's look, as if they were one last secret, private and modest, between Shaul and her, and as if they also embodied the final chance that she would one day return and be only his, when she gets old, when she loses her beauty, when the other guy gets tired of her, if that is even possible. But all signs point to him loving her more and more as she gets older, as more wrinkles appear on her face and neck, and in truth, Shaul has long ago lost hope that Paul is a man who likes younger women. Perhaps he once was, but

75

she changed him, that's clear. She showed him the forgiving tenderness of growing old together, the shared relinquishing of the body that used to be, Shaul thinks, and his throat burns and he stops and stares for a moment, freezing her as she crouches by the record cabinet

He stands across from her, and out of all the hundreds of men waiting with their mouths wide open and strands of saliva glistening between their lips, he alone can see her and feel the warmth of her body and the slight shudder that passes through her. Without looking at her closed eyes, he slowly unbuttons her blouse and unfastens her belt and clasps, and realizes that until he began to undress her, he had not known she was dressed like this, wearing unfamiliar clothes—lace and embroidery and paper-thin muslin, appetizing garments of seduction—and he assumes she brought her clothes from there, from her other home; she must have wanted to look charming and wonderful. He kneels at her feet as she holds out one foot as if in her sleep, her head held up slightly like a sunflower to the moon, lips barely spread, and he pulls off a soft, velvety boot to reveal a white lace stocking, which he slowly rolls down her long golden leg. The shiver in her body intensifies, becoming a shudder now—why is she shaking so badly? Perhaps from cold, or from shame, or perhaps the looks coming from so many eager men are arousing and flustering her? To present her at her best, he softly pushes to turn her a little and hide her sweet little paunch from them. Then he displays her fully naked body to them, with the disdain they deserve, but as his finger points, he unwittingly adds an inviting little twirl, and against his will, a strange kind of belching utterance escapes his mouth: She's not bad, eh? And some devil pushes him to add: Look at those lips! See how long those legs are! He notices the shock that runs through their bodies when he says it, and he gulps down a smile and glances at them. He sees their eyelids closed tightly and many nostrils moving in front of him in damp shadowy pairs. All of a sudden the fear lets go of him and incomprehensible pleasure creeps into him and sprawls on the floor of his body, where it curls up lazily.

And she's a fairly tall woman, he tells them silently and feverishly, adding that she's even a little taller than him. And quite large, he emphasizes. But don't get me wrong—her body is still firm and supple. Even her chest, relatively. Slightly less perhaps in the last few years, but it certainly was until recently. Perhaps because as a girl she was a late bloomer, he says, carefully hiding the fact that he had always secretly believed it was him, with his caresses and his sucking, who had caused her hidden breasts to finally erupt into their present state. He falls silent with fright when a heavy, hoarse moan cleaves them at once as if with an ax. He takes a step back and titters. What is it? What have I said?

But they, the people—the soldiers, actually, because now he sees that they are all in uniform. He hadn't noticed that before, but now he sees identical dark clothing, camouflaged even. They bray at him to go on, and he cringes at the touch of a crude animal breeze that suddenly blows on him. When he steps back, they walk over and close in on him. When he tries to get away, the circle does not let up, it moves with him, around him, demanding with rhythmic brays that he tell more, that he continue to describe her. *Give it to us,* they yell, and he has no choice but to continue, and he hopes the little details he gives them honestly and forthrightly will somehow help the search, and that seems to be the case. It's hard to understand exactly how, but his words seem to somehow fan them in her direction, making her more tangible to them, even fleshy, because they look at him with yearning and complete self-oblivion, and he feels a desire to increase the stimulation even more, so they will be even more qualified for the search mission they face. Maybe that is in fact why they brought him here—yes, he finally understands—because now, indeed, it all depends on him, on the power of his description and his ability to impassion them, like a general energizing his troops for battle

———

Esther? he called out weakly, trying to calm his stubborn heart. Esther?

She did not answer. She drove very slowly, almost bending over the wheel as her strained eyes tried to penetrate the darkness, and he looked at her from the side, and something in the mirror at that moment looked familiar to him, and painful and beloved. Her body language, her mouth slightly open as if about to be kissed—

At nineteen she was a waitress in a banquet hall in Beersheba, and she was late for work that day. Just like that, running through the lobby, she pulled her sweater over her head, briefly exposing her stomach. Hagai gave her one glance and got up from his table and followed her into the kitchen and stayed with her for nine and a half years. He was a small, concentrated man, with an alert foxlike face and sharp features, and long hands, as if everything lacking in his body had flown into those fingers—

Shaul nodded slowly, distractedly, with rounding eyes, and through a veil of bewilderment he saw her almost erupting from her shell, sweetening.

We laughed so much together, she thought with a smile, and most of all we laughed at ourselves. Her eyes sparkled and she stretched out unknowingly, indulging her limbs. She had never been with a man so daring, in every way. (Men, Hagai used to joke. They call them that because they're a bad *omen*.) Together they delighted in his penis, which he thought was tiny, and her short legs, and his crooked fingers, and her ass, which developed nicely under his supervision and nurturing—"a fine posterior," he called it, and devotedly cultivated it—and his narrow girlish shoulders, and her Indian face.

She looked in the mirror, but Shaul was lost in himself. She grinned as she thought of how all her men always had to change her position when she stood in front of them, so that she faced them at a certain angle. They would actually take hold of her shoulders and shift her a little, as if casually—Micah did it to this day, without even realizing it—because she must seem very unbeautiful to them, grating even, unless she faced them with that good angle, the one

particular one. But Hagai was the only one who was always inter-
ested in all 360 degrees of her, and he would describe her from every
angle and with every nuance, the refractions of her beauty and odd-
ness through the prism of his gaze, never tiring and never repeating
himself. He excited her body and her mind because she saw how important it was for him to be precise about her, to be punctilious, with
the seriousness of a painter waiting for the moment at which Indian
red becomes purplish, Venetian, lilac and resin, just as her chin
changes when his look catches it—that round and heavy chin that,
from here, sometimes looks like a weight drawing her mouth slightly
open with an expression that used to drive her mother crazy, and because of which they probably thought what they had thought at
school. From one particular angle, that very same chin becomes a
concentrated, almost masculine fruit, eager to prove something to
someone—Why are you so combative, Esther?—and from a different
angle it's like a little fist, a kind of protesting block of spite. And
from this angle it softens into a virginal breast, tiny and tight—

They dance there sometimes, Shaul whispered to himself and to
her. His voice was soft and seemed to have been disrobed of all that
had stuck to it and twisted it over the years. You hear me? She and
he, they dance—

Tell me, she said, urging him. Tell . . .

Shaul thought it was Portuguese music. Elisheva had often said
she liked fado, had even mentioned some names of singers, and he
deliberately wondered out loud where she had heard of them, and Elisheva said, Oh, here and there. He made secret notes to himself—
there was one called Ramos, and another called Max, and of course
Amália Rodrigues—and decided to buy her a few CDs. He wanted to
make her happy, but then thought he would not be able to stand the
pain every time she listened to them at home. And that thought had
unintentionally led him to formulate the source of his never-ending
torment: everything she does with me, he told Esti, reminds her of
what she does there, or of what she doesn't do there. And I can't understand how she stands it, because Paul winks at her from every cup

of coffee we drink together, he sighed. From every smile she gives me, from every bowl of soup she serves me and every dinner we make together. His voice sank, mumbled, and melted. And every time we take a walk through the neighborhood after the news, he thought, and every time I hand her the phone to talk to someone, and when we undress for bed or brush our teeth together or change the sheets together, and when she rests her head on my shoulder at the movies—

He murmured, and Esti felt as if she were standing on tiptoe and glancing through their window, and she knew he was telling her everything as it was. For a moment she could not see how things could be reconciled, but she knew that it was possible, of course it was possible—there is a lot of human being in one couple, she thought, and felt consumed with longing and became even more despondent.

And when I read her the headlines from the paper in the morning, Shaul thought to himself, and when I squeeze her some orange juice or when she asks from the kitchen in her happy singsong voice which cake she should bake for Shabbat, and when we sometimes go down to the day care to clean up the mess from the morning, to rake the sand in the sandbox, to gather up toys, and when I cover her feet with a blanket when she falls asleep on the couch . . . His face softened and he smiled. When she helps me find my glasses, and when I make her laugh while she's on the phone, and just in general, he thought, every time she laughs or is happy, or forgets herself for a moment, or gets carried away or becomes alarmed at being carried away and not being on her guard, and of course, every time she sleeps with me and thinks of him, and every time she is careful not to touch me in some special way he taught her. And also every time I touch her, each part of her body I touch or am careful not to touch, because of him, and when I am careful not to kiss or suck and leave marks on her neck or breasts, so I won't have to sense her pulling away—not because of the pain but because of her inherent instinct to conceal. Shaul chokes up and holds his throbbing head. Oh, what a good life we could have had! What happiness there could have been. Simple happiness, without complications. The happiness I so wanted, which could have changed my entire life from one end to the other. I was so close to it . . .

He thought of what had happened to them a few weeks ago when they were sleeping together in their way—meaning, they had woken up from sleep and found themselves entwined in each other. For some reason Shaul was unable to maintain his determined slumber, instead arousing himself with thoughts of her man. And he knew with certainty—from her movements and her rhythm and her tightly shut eyes and her guardedness that was let down, and her lips that rounded and her body that clung to him with desperate addiction and her fingers, which suddenly touched him in a different way, at once daring and tender, as if plucking a tune on a completely different scale, and her hands, which suddenly pushed his head down to lick the tip of her pleasure until she cried out—he knew so absolutely and without any doubt that she was, in her entirety, having sex not with him, that when he finally managed to blind and stupefy himself enough to come, he almost called out Paul's name with a frightened moan.

She's really girlish when she dances with him, he said. I didn't know her as a girl, only from pictures, but he . . . he peels away all her years when they dance. And he strips her of the lie too, he thought to himself. What he's really peeling away is the thousands of lies that suffocate her. Something cold passed over his face, desperation or revulsion at himself, at letting her torment herself like this for years without telling her how transparent she was to him, and that he knew all her moves and acts, and even derived bitter satisfaction from her tortured twists every time she traveled from one man to the other, each time she was scanned at his secret customs station. He shut his eyes tightly, as if in prayer, and Elisheva danced, erect, light, all smiles, and Paul saw it too and let go of her and stepped back and opened the blinds up without thinking. They never opened the blinds there, so that no one would look in on them, but now at

81

once it was clear that this could not be hidden; it was a sin to hide such beauty.

The afternoon sun rushed in through the window that had always been forbidden. Elisheva danced, slowly lifting her arms over her head, and two fair, downy plumes nestled in her armpits. She turned her face up to bathe in the honeyed light, her eyes lightly shut, her fingers moving of their own accord, and her eyelashes and ankles and delicate knees and her hips . . . The sun in the window rebelled for a moment, sighed, and climbed back up a few degrees in the sky to see better, and clung to every limb of her body. All her limbs were curved, from the soles of her feet to her forehead, and the sun lingered like a handmaiden bathing her princess. Shaul was unable to move or breathe, and he consumed her with his gaze, and Paul did the same from his place, and between them, with herself, was Elisheva.

No, he's really something, he then declared with a bitter sigh. There's no doubt about that. Look, only an extraordinary man could justify what she has to go through to be with him. Feeling too exposed, he silently summoned up a distant flash of her to prick himself with quickly, from years ago when, as he says, they were still young and she was still beautiful. They had gone to see a movie about a grotesque hunchback hypnotist who mesmerized a woman from his audience. The woman got on stage, noble and restrained, but within minutes she was responding to all the hypnotist's disgusting advances, dancing and gyrating with him with a joyful smile on her face. Right in front of her husband and the entire audience, the hunchback kissed her on the mouth with his painted lips, a long and lustful kiss. Shaul looked away from the screen to glance sideways at Elisheva. As he looked at her face, at the very slight movement that passed through her lips, he knew with certainty that she too had a place in her soul where all her fairness and loyalty would be of no use to him, a place unruled by logic or even love, a kind of no-man's-land where any bastard could do as he wished. And he knew how easy it would be to penetrate that place, knew that there were people who could easily be there with one knock at the door—

Sometimes, he told Esti impetuously, when we're in bed, I think that if only I could take her body to the other room and question it, interrogate it, you know, get it to tell me everything it's learned there with him—Esti was shocked by the pain flowing from him in waves, like blood pulsating rhythmically—and forgive me for even letting you in on this, but you can already see where it leads me, because then I wonder how it can be possible that everything she hides—her life, her real life, I mean—everything is so close to me, behind perhaps one millimeter of skin, and yet I can't read it. It's all a total riddle to me.

But you do know everything, she whispered.

And their little customs, he went on as if he hadn't heard, their whole routine—that's the most difficult thing. Or words she only uses with him, he laughed: "ticklish," for example. What does that mean? Esti asked, momentarily lost in another place, in her own private dictionary. It's an English word. It means, let's say, a place that tickles if you touch it, and one day when we're in bed, she says to me about some spot on her waist that it's ticklish, and I tell you that's a word that was never even in our vocabulary—I never heard her say "ticklish"! Or once she described someone as being "seized with a frenzy." Can you hear her saying "seized with a frenzy"? Elisheva? But I suppose it's the same with me, he laughed. My lexicon has also changed, you must have noticed, because until all this happened to me I was half-mute, especially on these kinds of things. Really, even in my dreams I wasn't capable of being like this, like I am with you here.

He was quiet, and she was too, and he swallowed a hard lump and said, Yes, a whole dictionary has sprung up for me since then, and if Elisheva knew how I could speak, if she guessed I wasn't giving her any of it . . . He thought Esti asked why not, and even if she hadn't asked he replied immediately, firmly: Because words are his and her territory, that much is clear to me. But why is it so clear? Esti wondered. Oh, it's very clear, he answered. Maybe it's because they have so little time and opportunity for doing, so they talk. And therefore, he added, if she and he have words, I keep quiet. I—with all due respect—stay out of their domain! I don't step on his territory, get it? I don't get in their way and I don't invade their privacy. She pricked up her ears, perplexed by the dry argumentativeness that had suddenly taken hold of him, and even more so by his strange eagerness to be banished and exiled from that "territory" of theirs. She realized with surprise that he was practically forcing them to stand across from him with a flaming sword which turned every way, as if that were the deepest purpose of their love: to banish him from there.

A light fog covered the windows. They drove slowly, in a cloud. They did not see any other vehicles for a long while, and Esti thought maybe they should stop and wait for the fog to lift. But she too was being sucked in by the end, the end of the road, and she felt strips of heat on her skin as if she were jumping through his burning hoop again and again. Her whole body was different tonight. She suddenly felt heat in her shoulder, or her inner thigh, or felt she was being kissed fervently on her neck, or that a tongue was sliding over her ear—

More than anything, more than anything she had with him, she missed the language they had invented, the likes of which she had never had nor would again. The thoughts and ideas he had birthed in her, his golden touch, and the words that erupted from her and became sparks of light to him. They found they could multiply their pleasure, because every inch of the body had its own private name, every wrinkle and mole and freckle, every movement and touch and stroke and lick and tingle, and she could murmur in his ear how she wished he had a little tongue just above his penis, and hear him understanding and laughing softly in her ear. And she could call him, with a mouth full of yearning, My darling, my softness, my beloved, my endearment. Or leave him a note under his windshield wiper, with words that only he could understand: "This time tomorrow we'll be snuggling snugly." And together they could elevate a screw into lovemaking, a quickie to a flicker, climaxing to gushing. Look how beautiful you are, Esther, he would whisper to her in the middle of lovemaking, propping himself up on his arms over her and looking at her excitedly. Look. And she would smile and lift her head a little and look into his eyes to see.

Quiet in the car now. Shaul is in his circles, and she is distant, swiftly borne across great expanses, full of momentum, carrying Shaul like a burning torch above her head, stealing a few sparks of fire for herself from the hidden parts of their trail.

She thinks with surprise of how complete she was with him during those years, the first ones, so much so that she thoroughly loved his family too, and stealthily crept into it from outside, with self-effacement and childish excitement. And he, in his way, talked with her about everything, and shared with her everything he thought would not be too painful for her, even though she was gladly willing to pay the pain levy, which was sometimes unbearable, only so that he would not for a moment stop the flow of his talk with her, so he would not filter or protect her or think twice. With thirsty shyness and the gratitude of an illiterate, she learned from him the meaning of home and family, parents and children, and the wonderfully complex relationships between siblings. She adopted them all without their knowledge, and lived their eating disorders and their little illnesses and their parent-teacher meetings and their jazz classes and their nightmares, and clung to their minutiae with an enthusiasm that he might have found touching, but perhaps also embarrassing. She was certain back then, her bitter heart told her, that this was the greatest closeness to a family she would ever achieve, and during those years there was even some relief in that knowledge, and a feeling that it was precisely the right place for her. And when sometimes the light in the window went out and she was left in the dark, she also believed that it was what she deserved. Her eyes are almost closed to the road, her heart flinches to think of the girl she used to be, a kitten, not much older than Shira . . .

Because she and I always used simple language, he went on with a voice full of knots. We spoke without witticisms and euphemisms, and that's what she loved in me, once. Once, my scientific talk was fine for her. That's what she called it: functional language, rational, the language of human beings. And I always thought this language of ours was enough for her, and it was how we made Tom, and set up a decent home, and lived together, and you could even say we developed and grew together, she in her field and I in mine. But apparently she needed another language, he mumbled, and withdrew into himself again, and Esti watched briefly and thought about Elisheva's "field," and how surprised she had been when Elisheva had decided, years ago, to get up and leave her wonderful job at the Ministry of Immigrant Absorption and open a little day-care center in their backyard. How could Shaul agree to this? she had wondered then. How would he tolerate a day-care center right under his office window?

Perhaps they even have a different language between them, a third one. Shaul revived himself and Esti didn't answer. Something almost became clear to her, then fogged over again, a scene she had once seen: Elisheva at the day care, tired and gray-faced, surrounded on all sides by toddlers who clung to her happily and noisily, and above her, behind the window, Shaul's shadow.

It suddenly makes sense to me, he whispered with wonder. I can't believe I didn't think of it at the time: three years ago she got a bee in her bonnet and signed up for that Portuguese class, which was completely unnecessary—what use would Portuguese be for her in day care? Esti glanced and saw his face light up for an instant, viciously focused, as if he were a collector who had discovered a rare butterfly and was chasing it so he could pin it to one of his boards. Maybe they both decided to learn a language that would be theirs? Do you see? A language that would be clean of me, so they could listen to their fado together. Because that man, he hissed, has all the time in the world to spare. Twenty-three hours a day he does nothing but wait for her. I have no idea how he lives, what he lives on, who finances him, and if you ask me, the only thing he does all day is wait for her, prepare himself for her, fill himself up for her.

A swift, soulful impression passed through both travelers at once, of a creature-person who is nothing but a long tube of skin, pale and swollen, sprawled like a blind ant-king in the thick of the earth, in dank dimness, fed with the richest of foods; every day he discharges one white, round egg, and that is the course of his life and he cannot live without it. But Shaul was thinking of Elisheva's man, and Esti was thinking of Shaul, and she almost choked as she imagined the damp burrows. She practically shouted, Let's go back, Shaul! What do you need this for? It will only torture you even more to be there. But he said, No, no, I told you, she's not with him there, I'm almost certain she's without him. Esti was confused. Without him? Why would she be without him, when that's where they could . . .

Shaul took a deep breath and patiently explained again that Elisheva wanted to be there alone, had to be there alone. Without me and without him. She just wants quiet from both of us. He chuckled. But to tell you the truth, he later spat out, maybe she has someone there too, a third guy—who knows? Maybe he's the reason she insists on this trip. He closed his eyes as if he had just made a huge effort, and then apparently fell asleep. Every so often his head would fall forward and his body would shake, but still he continued to sleep as if he had to store up strength for the final and most difficult part of the journey.

She remembered how, during their first years together, he was happy with her like a child, and she was as happy as she knew how to be. Still, she was careful not to take too much, not to overdose. He was completely unable to understand why she held herself back, and she explained that she would gradually become more daring, but in the meantime he had to watch her like you watch a hungry survivor who mustn't be allowed to eat too much at first. You love me more than I'm capable of loving myself, she warned him. Even now, in the car, her fingers felt the touch of his small, pointed head, which she had held then between her hands. She had not known how to tell him that his loving whispers were always in her ears, like a story she'd been told, the story of a thing she did not deserve. But he understood. He called those thoughts "the baby teeth of a snake," and swore he would rip them out of her, and pledged to prove to her that the opposite was true. And he didn't even have to explain to her what he meant by "the opposite"; she knew it was the opposite of her.

Once in a while, he whispered, tugging a loose end out of his dream and threading it into the conversation, she surprises him by asking him to turn the TV on. Is there something special on? And she says, No, I just want us to be like this, the two of us sitting together on the couch, cuddling up, as if, as if . . . And when she says "as if," her voice cracks and she bursts into tears, and when she comes home she has to hide those tears and the puffy eyes, or at least excuse them—"Don't ask, they put loads of chlorine in the water today"—and the thought of having to do that humiliates her even more. As if, as if . . . she sobs. As if everything, as if we, as if happiness. And Paul says nothing, because there's nothing he can say. It's her decision to go on like this, in this duplicity, for years, without telling Shaul, so his innocent faith in her will not be damaged. Paul hugs her for a long time, fighting off the urges that the closeness of her body arouses in him. Then he gets up, Shaul said, and with a movement that is difficult to believe in a bear like him—but apparently there are many things you wouldn't believe about him, things that have enabled him to thrash me with such elegance for ten years at least . . . Where was I? And Esti, who could not follow the fragments of his thoughts, suddenly knew what he reminded her of: the scorpions in Beersheba, which the neighborhood children used to surround with a circle of burning rope, and they would make the circle smaller and smaller until the scorpion aimed its tail at its own head and stung itself. Then he gets up, Shaul recalled, and gets her up too, and with his hand on her back they go for a walk in the apartment, he and she;

it's a sad little joke they play sometimes. Let's go for a little walk, he says to her on days when he too is suffocating, and they walk the seven or eight steps down the hallway, arm in arm, then into his messy study, flooded with papers and piles of books—he whispered with the voice of someone trying to seduce, though it was mostly himself, and Esti wondered how he could be both the scorpion and the burner and the circle of fire—and then they turn around and go back into the hallway, three, four, six steps, trying not to trample all the stuff that's scattered there—it's an indescribable mess, Shaul noted disapprovingly, with clothes and books and newspapers and rags just lying everywhere; I can't understand how they live like that, how she, in that jungle—and continue to the bedroom, and turn around in front of their huge bed and go back to the hallway, and his hand is on her the whole time, and her hand is on his waist, and they walk very slowly. They're like a couple of elderly teenagers, Shaul thought, and Esti could sense with her whole being how Elisheva and Paul listened together to a sound that only they could hear, and that if they stopped hearing it they would become a joke even to themselves. Shaul closed his eyes and accompanied them to the kitchen, where they circle the table to gain another two or three steps, and Paul, said Shaul, leans over and whispers in her ear, You see, Sheva—that's what he calls her—don't say I never take you out, and Elisheva smiles, and her chin quivers slightly.

Then they do the whole path back again, Shaul saw, and his lips moved but he made no sound. And in the hallway, Paul stops to shake hands formally with the sleeve of his coat, which hangs there, and he chitchats with a neighbor and introduces him to Elisheva: Meet the woman in my life, this is the woman I've been waiting for here, twenty-three hours a day, for ten years. Elisheva puts her head on his shoulder, closes her eyes, and lets him walk her around. She would go anywhere in the world with him, blindfolded, because she trusts him, that's the thing—his voice suddenly lifted and extracted itself from the knot of his thoughts with a strange cheerfulness—here we are, Esther, it's a good thing we talked, because in the course of talking I've defined it for myself: there's something in him that gives her a sense of confidence, fills her with confidence, and that is something I have somehow been unable to give her. That's the thing, with me she is evidently never completely confident.

And perhaps because of his voice at that moment, or the look on his face, a thought flies through her, sudden, wounding—

Everything stops in her and sinks into silence. She drives slowly, foggy pictures painted in her mind. She has to open a window, but how will she withstand the rush of air? She can hardly breathe. She is frozen around a fragment embedded inside her. Only her heart is suddenly full of life, the only part of her that beats in excitement and goes out to Shaul, goes out limping, goes out hunchbacked, with Band-Aids stuck all over it, but goes out. How is it that her heart goes out to him? She should be angry at him now, should feel shocked and cheated, should disdain him, recoil from him . . . But she is at once utterly exhausted and also incapable of remembering where exactly one finds the conviction to be disdainful, or righteous, or to know something with any certainty. He has a singular obsession, she thinks. Or a singular genius. And the blood pulses hard, too hard, and some sweet internal assailant comes and quickly shreds the muscles of her shoulders and neck, and soon everything will fall and dissipate, nose and ears and the three gray cells she has left, and with all her strength she tries to calm down, she must stop this, but she is unable to give up these heartbeats, the forgotten, precise heartbeats which reply as an echo, and she remembers his hand upon the tablets of her heart, her hand on his chest—*feel it, our prisoners are corresponding.* But how? She is amazed. How did I let Shaul lead me on like this? Where have I been all evening? But she knows exactly how and where, what she was listening to and what her heart went out to. Look at you, she sighs. No, really, look at you, you and your reaching heart.

She feels for the bottle, and as she drives she pours some water into her palm and wets her forehead and then trickles a few drops down her nape, and stretches her legs and wiggles her toes in her shoes. Back to life, she commands, and for a start she tries to reconstruct their conversation since leaving. The announcer on the radio had talked about that police officer in Madrid, and since then almost nothing, she can't remember anything, only heat waves exchanging, growing hotter and dissipating, and it's as if that was the only thing. She takes a deep breath, finally breathing, like the first breath, and hears him mumbling to himself. How can he do it? How does he survive a whole life of this? She looks in the mirror and sees his face concentrating, trapped in the fiery ring of his hermetic torments. Tell me, she says in her heart, don't stop. She keeps asking against the backdrop of his whispers, and is carried away on his waves and hunches over, absorbed in herself, a little more, until she has to understand, to wake up.

What now? Shaul wonders, wanting to go back to sleep, to forget, to silence the voices, to subdue the flames which constantly demand new, richer burning material. Maybe I'll tell her to go back, he suggests to himself weakly. I'll tell her to turn around and go back at once, yes, before we get there, he says to himself, and swells up with a surge of power. I'll tell her to go back home. And deep in his mind a cold, mocking bolt of lightning strikes—who is he kidding? After all, even the supposed restraint of the present is an integral part of the complex and meticulous process of complete surrender, and besides, he knows that if something happens to her there, to Elisheva, it will happen tonight. It has to happen. Day one: acclimatization, checking out the field and filtering candidates. Day two: bonding with two or three of them. And on the last night, tonight, the implementation. The one. The speck of gold. What are you talking about? Elisheva smiles compassionately, with quiet desperation. Why are you torturing yourself with these thoughts? I really just go there to rest, to read, to clear my mind. In that case, he replies calmly, wrapping his voice with a falseness as it trembles with fury, in that case, you're just wasting your vacation and our money—what's the point of you even going every year if you don't find yourself someone there? Why all the bother? Why do you think people go to these kinds of places alone? Precisely for this, she replies, and her look smooths over his conflicted face. Why can't you believe that I just want to be with me, just me with myself, once a year?

Yesterday she rang in the afternoon, even though he had told her he didn't want to talk to her for the entire four days. She wanted to hear how he was. He spoke curtly. Asked if she'd met him. Met who? she asked wearily. I don't know his name, he rolled out a laugh. You want me to give you his name too? There was a long silence. Then Elisheva said, Shaul, really . . .

Listen, he said seriously, I love you, I even miss you, but I'm entitled not to be a part of what you're going through there. I'm entitled to protect myself from all that, aren't I?

What am I going through here? she asked tiredly, and he could see her grimacing. What do you think I'm going through?

No, no, he laughed bitterly, I don't want to hear about it.

They were quiet again together, and there was a shared tenderness or sadness. Their love escaped for an instant from the jaws of a large vise grip, relaxed between the two of them, searched for shelter. He held his breath for a moment, wanting Elisheva to yell at him, to scream, to hurl her fury at him. Perhaps all they needed was a few words from her to redeem them both.

He grumbled, Why did you even call?

I wanted to hear how you were. I suddenly had a bad feeling.

I feel wonderful.

Tell her now, without thinking, tell her everything: Listen, Elisheva, it's not just these seasonal attacks around your trip every year, it's more than that at this point. It's life itself, the way it gets dragged around everywhere. You have a right to know. I'm the sick one, but you're dying from it too. If only you knew. If only I could just sit down and tell you, talk with you the way I talk with myself, the way we used to be able to, about everything, maybe I could still get out of it somehow and wake up, go back to being a human being.

Look, all I need is one final, decisive piece of evidence to convince me that I'm wrong. I know I'm wrong, I'm almost a hundred percent certain that I'm wrong, so I'm willing to believe anything, even the feeblest, most unfounded proof, if you only give it to me with a truly pure heart, if you are still capable of that, if it's even possible to ask that of you anymore. Why are you so quiet? What do you have to be quiet about—

He said, Leah phoned for you about next year's program, and another young couple want to register their daughter who hasn't even been born yet. She smiled to herself with a certain sense of pride, and he heard her smile and couldn't help smiling with her. And again, for a fleeting instant, they were so close to relief, and he closed his eyes and saw her beloved face, but it was far above him, as if he were lying at the bottom of a well. If only she had the courage to descend, to bring him up with her. Why doesn't she come down? There's always a place where she stops. He knows the place where she shrinks back a little as if she'd met a ghost. They sighed together. For an instant they were both shown with biting tangibility how, for these past twenty-five years, the sediments of their sorrow and bitterness had crystallized, drop after drop, into a massive stalagmite of marriage.

Heavily, he put on his foreign voice again like a uniform, his robe of duress: We'll talk about the rest when you get home. Oh, Tom didn't call today either. And she said, He called me here. He's all right. He says hi to you. Shaul swallowed another small lump of insult and declared, That's it, I think that's it. Nothing else happened. Then he stopped and squeezed his eyelids as tight as he could to cap the lid on the unbearable simmering. He gave in, and having sworn to himself not to, he reminded her about the little package he'd thrown into her suitcase before she left. By now he was entirely consumed by that dark sweetness, its toxins seeping into its depths, the drug of an ancient lust for revenge—but on whom? he moaned when she hung up on him. On whom was he taking this revenge, always, all his life? On her? Why her? Why had it always been like this, from the first moment, ever since a great wave of love had come and washed him toward her, together with an unfamiliar rage that had also not dulled in him since the moment he knew she was the woman of his life, and which had caused him to first scorn her because she had settled for so little—settled for him

And his selfhood mounts all at once into a fierce erection. He is the living, pulsing seed of the faceless swarm that hums around him in its strange mating flight. All these people here, the soldiers, the men, are devoid of volition against what pours forth out of him—they are a thousandfold stronger than him and yet submissive and passive, pliable to him. He repels and retreats as if to taunt them, and they stay with him, move with him, guessing his next steps. Their senses open up to him: they see, listen, and inhale. Eyes dart over his body and face, scan his hands, his feet, the thinning hair on his head. Conclusions are gathered, important material collected, analyzed somewhere, but what is it? For a moment he is dazzled by the power of the presence of all these bodies, the smells, the pressure and force of so many wills and desires—

I find her beautiful, he quickly stresses. Some might disagree, but there are certain situations, he says, where she is truly beautiful. He grins at them defiantly from ear to ear, lips slightly quivering, and he knows that beyond the frozen masks of their faces they are smiling at this idiot—*idiot'e'le*, as his mother says—because while he was busy finding nice words to say, his wife ran away and left him with his dick in his hand and his tongue twirling. He is talking, naïvely, of her soft feet—an architectural wonder, he waxes poetic, apart from the second toe, of course, the one that climbs over the big toe on her left foot. It's hereditary—all the women in her family have it, he adds, and from this point on he continues talking and tells them everything, illustrates her entire body for them, every crease and wrinkle, every freckle and birthmark, and from one moment to the next he becomes more and more vibrant and stormy, giving them more and more. An indescribably dark transaction is occurring here tonight: he gives her to them so they can bring her back to him. And all this time their eyes are practically closed, their mouths open, they move with him in waves, they and their uniforms and their solidity and their field scent, spreading around him like a circular trail, the hem of a wide dress, as he twirls them around himself with a very slight movement of his hips, almost imperceptible, and proves to them without words that they are mistaken if they mean to judge him by the normal rules, by the acceptable regulations of human taxation, whereby he is nothing but an unyoung, unlovely man whose wife has decided to leave him ("to go away for four days and be alone, just me with myself, once a year, what's the big deal").

Tell me, Esti said with strange urgency. He pulled himself out of his depths and re-emerged in the car. There was almost begging in her voice, and they both pulsated now to the same heartbeat.

Tell me what you want to hear.

At first she thought he'd said "what you'd *like* to hear," like a salesman in the recesses of a dubious store, testing out a shy customer's preferences.

How they met, she said.

Oh . . . Well, it so happens that I don't exactly know the answer to that. In the darkness of the car he stared at her thoughtfully and seriously. Do you really want to hear?

Really. Really but not truly, she thought.

She met him when she still worked at the Ministry of Immigrant Absorption, he said, at least that's what she told me. She handled his case there. But one day he just came into our house . . .

How did she know to ask that? he wondered. How did she ask that question at precisely the right moment, the right point in his chain of thoughts and terrors? Because that is the thing that has remained fresh and new ever since things were first revealed to him in their true light. It is the point to which he can always return, even in his sleep, in the greatest desperation, when he needs to refuel his passion for her, and it is the minute that never ends, the eternal present that has been going on for ten years: Shaul and Elisheva are in the kitchen of their old house on Rachel Imenu Street, chopping vegetables for a salad, as they do every evening, chatting about how the day went and what will happen tomorrow and who paid what and who will take Tom to the dentist, when all of a sudden the door swings open to reveal a man Shaul has never seen before. He walks straight into the kitchen and says, with a heavy Russian accent, that he can't take it anymore.

No, no. Not so fast. Better to rewind and play it again, slowly and in the correct order. Shaul stands there wearing Elisheva's floral apron, holding a small bunch of dill ready to be chopped, and looks at Elisheva questioningly with a slightly amazed smile: Perhaps it's a prank or a joke? But why would she play a joke on him? Even so, he still tries to solve this nightmare in a positive way: maybe it's some aggressive marketing campaign for a vacation package to Izmir, or maybe the cable company is offering a new deal. But it seems pretty clear that that's not it. The man stands in their kitchen, filling it with his presence, with his quiet bearishness, and he is serious and somber, so somber that his tanned face is pale. Shaul also notices that his fingers are shaking a little, which must be a good sign, because it means the man is afraid of confronting him. Although, on the other hand, perhaps it says something about how acute his condition is. Meanwhile, the two of them, Shaul and he, do not move, and that's good too, because the stranger's element of surprise is becoming less of an advantage. Although, on the other hand, he is still in Shaul's kitchen rather than Shaul being in his kitchen. The man is slightly taller than him, but much more solid and broader, with a thick neck and a large face. He is not handsome but certainly powerful, no longer a young man, several years older than Shaul, ten at least, and he looks a little sad even, and here is where Shaul begins to sense that he's right for her. She likes the ones with sober and grave expressions.

And it is his graveness which is in fact most confusing, because you can tell just by looking at him that he deliberated a lot before taking this step, that he carefully evaluated the chances and the risks, and if he still decided to burst in here—the word "burst" is exaggerated; the truth is that he knocked on the door, so hesitantly in fact that they barely heard him, and Shaul went to open the door, and the guy said, Excuse me, and asked if Elisheva was home, and she called out from the kitchen, Yes, who is it? Come in, please, in a surprised and cheerful voice, the voice she had back then, and the man murmured something to Shaul and walked past him with a kind of apologetic bow and went into the kitchen—and if all that has happened, it must mean the man estimated he would get what he wanted, and that means Shaul will lose.

But what did "lose" mean? And how could he lose his life like this to a complete stranger? If indeed he is a complete stranger to Elisheva too, and this Shaul still cannot determine. But let's assume he really does lose, and that after the brief confrontation which will shortly occur—but how? Will they throw punches? Use knives? Like two deer locking antlers?—Shaul may have to leave this house. What would become of everything then? What would become of the house? And Elisheva? And the seven years of mortgage they still owe? And the large salad bowl and the silly apron Shaul is still wearing around his waist? Action must be taken now, immediately, and he surreptitiously grasps the edge of the table and clears his throat to restore his power of speech, and demands that the man explain what he is doing here. He already knows that this is a mistake, because he should have just gotten up and grabbed him by the shirt collar and thrown him down the stairs (although there were only two in that house), but instead, by the mere fact of his prolonged silence, it was as if he had already entered into negotiations over something, and had seemingly granted him what little legitimacy he needed as a stranger from the outside.

The man has still not moved. He sinks his head between his shoulders, and his entire posture is that of an overgrown foster child who has tired of being shifted around and uprooted and has come and planted himself down somewhere, with some family, wordlessly proclaiming that this is his final station, that he will not budge from here. Listen, he whispers to Elisheva without looking up, listen, I'm really sorry, but it's just no longer bearable. He falls silent and bows his head, and his lower jaw drops.

Slowly, almost stealthily, Shaul removes his apron. He regrets that he is not wearing shoes or something more solid than the brown plaid slippers. They were a gift from his parents for some anniversary, two matching pairs, his and hers, which his dad had gotten hold of in one of the barter transactions he advocated as a way of resisting income tax. But at least the slippers represent a silent, forceful declaration that they belong to each other, Elisheva and he, that they are far more like each other than Elisheva could ever be like a man with a heavy jaw and dark baggy eyes and a doglike and bitter look in his eyes, a man who makes a surprise infiltration into someone else's kitchen and demands Elisheva for himself. Shaul already realizes that he's not such a big hero, that he seems to have already used up most of his reserves of courage with his melodramatic bursting into the kitchen, and now he is trembling no less than Shaul, because most likely he has never been in such a situation either.

Out of embarrassment or weakness, the man leans against the fridge, but it seems to Shaul as if he has already taken this stance before, with this same fridge, as if he's used to standing there like that, among all the notes and the phone numbers and the pizza magnets. Shaul is amazed to think of how many times he himself has touched that same fridge without suspecting that perhaps an hour or two earlier, in his absence, another man had touched it for a minute. At once his mind becomes crowded with treacherous furniture, tables, bureaus, and couches that conspire against him, not to mention the double bed and even the air in the house—who knows how many times this man has touched them all and then left and closed the door behind him softly, without leaving any footprints? Elisheva herself walks in this space and breathes it inside her, and Shaul suddenly

understands the significance of her soft touch, the way she always caresses everything she touches, any item or furnishing, even mugs and
teaspoons that she holds with softly drawn fingers and a slight linger,
which until now has always secretly delighted him. The man, with a
mouth that looks torn from being stretched, says he doesn't have the
strength to wait any longer, that he's losing his mind.

And Elisheva? What is she going through? Shaul doesn't look at
her. Strange how he can't bring himself to turn his head to her, and
the man can't either, so neither of them knows what she is showing
them; they are both temporarily equal to each other in their inability
to turn their heads and look at her. Shaul resents the unfounded comparison with a stranger, with someone who is an immigrant in every
sense of the word, and he tosses a sighed question into the air: Does
Elisheva even know him? The stranger, for the first time since coming in, manages to turn his head with great effort, beating Shaul to
it, and looks straight at her. This causes Shaul to look too, and he sees
with surprise how from the weary Elisheva of 8 p.m., another woman
suddenly shines out from beneath her married skin. This is a woman
Shaul does not know. She is transparent and light, and her thin sil-
houette twitches inside his Elisheva like a dragonfly caught in a paper lantern, and all at once he is filled with an unknown strength and
is willing to fight for her and be killed and even kill. But then he
thinks perhaps this internal revelation of hers is not intended for him
but for the strange man, who is practically subdued by the image of
the illuminated dragonfly, his slightly crude face turning soft and
weak, the face of a man looking at a particularly beloved scene. Shaul
has no doubt of this, and Elisheva smiles softly and says yes, she
knows him.

You know him? Shaul lets out a deep groan. How? Where from?
For he, in his innocence, in his boundless stupidity, imagined at the
time that he knew every person in her life, and as far as he knew, she
had never mentioned this stranger, who looked as if he was about
to collapse on the floor, but for now was leaning over their dinner
table on both hands and looking at Elisheva with a huge face and

weighted, sagging cheeks. He is a sad-looking man, with silver stubble from a particularly sloppy shave, a pack of cigarettes crushed in his shirt pocket, dressed simply and almost neglectfully, like a Russian teacher from a lost generation, carrying a shopping bag from the neighborhood grocery. Shaul now thinks he looks like a work-weary family man, or perhaps a forlorn bachelor who lives a meticulous life, a kind of devoted workhorse who was suddenly stung by a wasp of madness and tore himself away from the furrow and started running amok, until he arrived here to tell Shaul's wife in a choked voice and for the third time, Elisheva, I can't go on like this anymore.

The fact that he knows her name. And the way he says it. Shaul's knees give in and he sits down, and the man stands, and the two of them breathe heavily, without looking at each other. The man's breath is heavy and wheezy and his face turns red. Elisheva whispers from her place by the sink, But you have to be patient, I keep telling you. In the end we'll find you a good place. Now go home, Paul. Come to the office tomorrow and we'll talk.

Shaul lowers his head and stares at the table. He slowly freezes and tightens on the chair. His feet barely reach the floor. His feet are swinging in the air. The man turns to him and says he is sorry. Shaul barely comprehends. The man's Hebrew is new but surprisingly fluent, and he explains to Shaul that it's already been a year and a half and they still haven't found a job for him. That he's not willing to make compromise— Is that how you say it? He turns to Elisheva questioningly, and she proudly confirms with a warm smile, Yes— with his art.

He's a cartoonist, Shaul explained to Esti with a Russian accent, mimicking Paul's speech with surprising mischief: "And I to know that Mrs. Elisheva making very much for that me have job, but year and a half I am inemployed, not employed, because is principle for me to work only art, only art!" Esti looked and saw his face change, become heavier and more daring. "And government here give to me—or office job, or guard job, or driving job! So what? Like that, no job, no art, and also no life!"

Shaul cannot understand what the stranger wants from him or what he's supposed to do now. Should I leave? he asks the man. No, Paul says, surprised. Why leave, sir? Is your house. Shaul smiles gratefully and looks around in a daze. Elisheva and Paul talk. There. He has put it into one sentence that doesn't immediately crack open: Elisheva and the-stranger-who-burst-into-their-kitchen talk. He hears the sounds of the stranger and Elisheva and does not comprehend. Maybe it's Hebrew, but he knows Hebrew. No, her stranger is talking with her in a language he does not know. And she's answering him. It's not Hungarian, of that Shaul is certain. He knows her Hungarian a little. And it's not Russian, or English or French; or Portuguese, he now adds to the list, or any civilized language. And when did she have time to learn another language? He listens with surprise to their strange dialect, full of breathing and soft consonants, and comprised mostly of gestures. He tries to follow, but cannot. Elisheva and the stranger even try to make it easier for him, slowing down their speech a little for his benefit. Sometimes they raise their voices, arguing. Elisheva seems to lose her patience. She is angry at something, and the man is sorry. God, Shaul thinks, so many shared emotions they have! And once in a while Shaul notices some pet name of hers, it seems, which the man repeats over and over again. It's unlike her name, and coming from him it sounds a little prolonged, seems foggy and melting at the edges: *belo . . . belo . . .* Shaul watches their lips attentively and devotedly. He has a vague feeling that if he is a good student they won't kick him out, that they'll let him stay in their house and abandon the idea of sending him to boarding school.

The stranger looks at Elisheva. A tortured look. Asking for mercy. He says something that even Shaul, who has not learned the language, understands is a huge request, something like: Teach me, Elisheva, teach me so I'll also know. Elisheva doesn't answer. Her head is bowed, her hair, still golden, hides her face. Shaul watches them both with his mouth open. They freeze that way, the three of them, for a long time. Then the man sighs, nods at Elisheva and Shaul without seeing them at all, mumbles "Sorry" to the air, and turns and leaves.

For the first time in several minutes, Shaul breathes a sigh of relief—at it all being over, with no blows exchanged or blood shed. Things like this can sometimes end in murder, after all. He is also relieved because in fact you could say that he beat the intruder, did he not? He managed this little conflict fairly wisely, did not lose his cool, and in the end he banished the man from his territory.

When the door shut behind the stranger, everything went back to normal at once. The radio came on, the neon light shone again, and Elisheva—as if everything that had happened hadn't—went on chatting and told Shaul about the man, an immigrant from the Soviet Union, the son of a French father and a Russian mother. She knew everything about him. He was a fairly well-known cartoonist in Riga, certainly an original artist, she said, but it had been a year and a half and she hadn't been able to find him a job in a suitable place, or even a newspaper to publish his cartoons or a gallery to show his famous creations. Who needs a cartoonist these days? She sighed. She'd already been through numerous job interviews with him, and begged curators and gallery owners and weekly editors, but nothing. Shaul did not look at her or listen to her words. His whole body trembled like a tiny animal cowering in a riverbed, listening to an oncoming torrent.

Then a calm fell upon him. The gushing began from all sorts of places, all over his body. He heard pleasurable little giggles on the outer edges of his mind, in the dark creases behind his thoughts. He felt good, better than he'd felt in years. As if he were inside a huge embrace. And he felt as if he had finally reached the right place, his home, his motherland. He realized that everything was beginning now. That up until now he must have been living only in the introduction. Elisheva said she wanted to go to sleep early, she had a crazy day ahead. Shaul nodded. She asked if he felt all right. Yes, he said. Yes, sure. She asked him not to be upset because of that Paul bursting in. Sometimes they can't take all the humiliations we put them through, she said, and with Paul it's somehow more complicated, it's really hard to find a place to match his talents and his principles. Shaul looked at the way her lips, when they said his name, rounded as if in a kiss. He imagined that her lips were cutting this strange name out of his own flesh: he was like a rolled-out ball of dough onto which she placed an upside-down cup, flattened it down tightly, and used it to cut circles of Paul out of him. She told him he'd already lost two of the jobs she'd managed to get him. He's a difficult one, she sighed. He's such an individualist, and he has such a special way of thinking. Shaul nodded obediently and threw her looks with eyes torn wide with amazement, as if he had never seen her like this. He said to himself, In fact, you've only just met her. You are only now meeting as you were really supposed to. And what was everything that came before? Perhaps just a preparatory meeting. Yes, a very long preparatory meeting between two slightly faded representatives of yourselves. You always sensed it and couldn't put a name to it, and now the real thing is starting. The battle, the game, the hunt.

He got up, slightly dizzy. Went to the bathroom, leaned both hands on the sink, and looked in the mirror. He suddenly understood that face of his, the elongated face with the sunken cheeks and the sad clown expression. Everything became clear. With complete simplicity he realized what his role in the play was, why he was designed this way, and what he had really been training for his entire life. Elisheva came in and asked if he was all right again. Shaul said yes. She asked if he needed the car the next evening, because "the girls" were meeting for one of their birthdays. It's okay, he said with pent-up cheer, I don't need the car tomorrow night. Beneath each of her words a small fire suddenly danced. Over and over he thought of how she had described Paul to him. An extreme individualist, a man of principle, and an idealist, a rare way of thinking . . . That was how she used to think of him, of Shaul, that's what drew her to him, but it turned out there was someone who offered her more. Strange, he always thought that if she found herself another man he would be completely different from him, someone physical and worldly in all his being, a farmer or a tour guide or an army man, certainly someone younger than him. To think that she had ended up going for someone of his ilk, only she had sought out a man who would be even more extreme than he was . . .

Later that night, when Elisheva undressed, he looked at her and immediately averted his eyes as if he had seen something forbidden. Every one of her movements was part of a dance that only now, apparently very late in the day, had revealed its complexity to him, its mystery. He looked at her with Paul's eyes, and she was attractive, ravishing. He stole looks at her. Her breasts fit Paul's large hands far better than his own. Maybe that's why they had grown after their marriage, not because of what he had always believed. He hugged his knees to his stomach, and like a lost and misguided bolt of lightning that had flashed in him years after the thunder had sounded, he felt what he had unknowingly expected, the cutting and painful snap of a huge and eternal whip—the law of nature itself. He closed his eyes and gloomily welcomed the sensation, the surrendered acceptance with which a crippled, damaged deer realizes that it must be shredded by the claws of a tiger.

She came and lay next to him with a sigh of relief, and clung to him as usual, and he flinched and withdrew and felt every hair on his body stand on end. What's going on? she asked, still tender. It's not because of that man, is it? Rubbish, someone squeaked from far away in the bends of his throat. That's your deal, not mine, please don't involve me in it. Elisheva propped herself up on one elbow and examined him closely: What do you mean, my deal? She laughed in surprise. It's your deal, he repeated, looking at the ceiling with a congealed smile, not mine. Just don't tell me about it. I don't want to know, he said. What I don't know won't hurt me. What are you talking about? she asked, and her forehead all at once became dark. What have you already been telling yourself? I'm not telling myself anything, he went on, rejoicing a little, light as a headless bird who no longer has to bear the weight of its own head. I really don't want to meddle in things that don't concern me, and the last thing I want is to ruin it for you, but I have one small request: don't ever, ever, from this moment on, tell me anything more about him and you. Don't mention his name, don't even hint at it, just leave me out of it. God, Elisheva sighed, I can't believe it, you're starting up again? Again with this talk? We had a break from all this for a while. I'm not starting up anything, he explained with frozen calmness, I respect your privacy and your needs. I'm certainly aware that a woman such as yourself can't be satisfied by one man, certainly not a man like me, and I only ask that you be fair and spare me from what I don't need to know. But there's nothing to spare you from! she shouted. What are you talking about? Why are you making a mountain out of a molehill? Whether there is or there isn't, he said, I really don't know, and you just remember my request not to tell me anything at all! He yelled suddenly and angrily beat the mattress, and Elisheva jumped out of bed and stood up, and he could see the hem of her flimsy nightdress quivering. She looked at him and shook her head. Look at how you're getting yourself into this again, she said. Shauli, she begged, and there was sorrow in her voice, don't fall into this same trap again. Let me help you. But he spread the widest possible grin on his face and repeated that everything was fine. There's no need for you to waste your energies on me, you need all your energy for him now, and he pointed out that he was happy to see that something good had finally come of her job, and that he seemed like a nice man and was certainly worthy of being her boyfriend. And when he said "boyfriend" he felt a long tongue of fire licking his innards, and added that he would advise her not to tire him out too much, because he didn't look all that young, but luckily for him, Elisheva no longer heard that—she had taken her pillow and stormed off to sleep in the other room.

Shaul tightened his body and cuddled up with himself, and for several very long moments he sucked in the thick black blood that must have been waiting concealed in his body for many years. He congratulated himself and his sharp intuition for calling Paul her "boyfriend," because the moment he had said that he had sensed how true it was, and how easily he could be her boyfriend—not just a lover, but a *boyfriend*. Because for all his—as she said—individualism and originality and idealism and brilliance and depth and rarity and uniqueness and devilish talent and genius and so forth, you could easily tell how much he and she were alike in the really essential and important things, in a kind of domestic tenderness, in the natural warmth that emanated from them both, in the humanity that flowed from them, and even in some simplicity of the body, the forgiveness they both showed toward their bodies. Shaul could easily picture them engaged in all sorts of pleasant, relaxed domestic scenes, whose space Paul began to fill with his complacent presence and with a quiet promise of continuity and sequence which encompassed his large body and his lanky movements, and with his tranquil authoritativeness, his complete and solid worldview, the massive self-confidence and ample personal charm, and his disposable charisma. Shaul felt a burning sensation in a new-old ulcer of the soul, and giggled to himself in surprise as he lay there stormily, ripped to shreds in a new and exciting way. Soon he also knew exactly what he had to do. He had almost no deliberations about whether or not he should spy on her, follow her, eavesdrop, snoop, because he felt it was beneath him, beneath the long worm that was putting down roots within him. He told himself that he believed in the slow, natural development of a relationship such as this, between him and her, because this kind of relationship must be gradually melded, with natural wisdom, like the ripening of a large and complex fruit, and for this sort of thing he has patience. More than that: he has respect for them, and he knows how to wait. He swore he would do anything, anything at all, so that she would not have to give up her real life, the place where she really existed in her entirety, in all her femininity and her vitality and her splendor, he thought, and his throat was tight and he didn't shout, didn't yell in a broken voice, but inhaled and told himself he would live from now on alongside this lovely, healthy relationship as one who is fighting a long and stubborn battle, of which no one else could know. He would sit in his place without moving and would look at the story of her and Paul unfolding, coming into being out of the thousands of tiny details and facts and memories and secrets and breaths of passion and longing, and little lies, thousands, multitudes of lies, which would slowly become the truth of his life. And all this he knew, or guessed with certainty, as early as that black night of nuptials, as he lay there tense, feeling his body changing and becoming another. Even his body. Because for all those years he had been immersed in the solution of her lie, loved only as an echo. As he should be, he thought. He was enchanted by his realization of how Elisheva had known to love him just the way he deserved, no more, while she herself must have contained a love that boiled and bubbled far beyond his narrow borders and meager strengths.

Just past Sde Boker, she saw a small roadside inn with lights on and stopped the car. Shaul didn't want to get out. How do you do it? she laughed. I have a bladder the size of a peanut. Oddly proud, he replied, I just do.

There were four men sitting inside, eating from steaming hot plates of meat and arguing about politics. The TV was tuned to the fashion channel. A matted old sack with a black snout was sprawled beneath one of the chairs. Esti quickly purchased a chocolate bar and some lemon candy, shifting from one foot to the other. She was hoarse as if she'd been shouting the whole way. The shopkeeper sized her up and lost interest. She went to pee and took a long time emptying her bladder. She imagined she could still hear the hum of Shaul's talk. Her eyes felt very heavy as she leaned her head back against the wall. She thought of how she had remained faithful to Hagai, in her own way, all these years. Had stayed at the same spot, with that ember that she had ignited for him and which remained his and hers alone, even at the high points of her love for Micah, whom she met six months after they broke up. Even though more than twenty years had passed, and five children had flown through her, and she hadn't seen him all that time and didn't even know whether he was alive. Even so, she had not been able to force herself to truly accept the thought that they would never be together again, in any of her realities and the branches of her life. And now too, as she did every time she thought this way, she felt as if she were driving the wrong way over spikes in a parking lot.

When she went out, she asked if she could use the phone. The shopkeeper blinked in the direction of the phone, and she called Micah's cell phone, which was turned off. He must have gotten home ages ago, she thought—but maybe not? She stopped herself and did not call home. For a long moment she stood and thought about what she would do if she found out he had a lover. There were times when she had almost hoped it would happen to him, wished it for him. Someone easier. Unequivocal. Happier. Still, she could not dial, and she stood with the receiver against her cheek, drawn to think of the woman she had designated for him: she had a clear and consistent quality, like a ray of light that is projected and reaches its destination—unlike me, she thought—without refractions, without internal subversions. She sensed the tiny serpents Shaul had planted inside her, writhing and mating with her own.

She dialed home, pausing after each digit, giving him time to get back, to sink deep into his and her daily sludge again. I can't be bothered with this now, she thought; she wished everything would remain exactly as it was, that Micah would remain Micah, that he would transport her home just by virtue of his Micah-ness.

He had been there for a long time and was waiting for her nervously; he could never fall asleep without her or without hearing her voice. He wanted to know how the trip was, how Shaul was, what this injury was all about, where they were going anyway, and where she was calling from. She listened to his voice and yearned for him. Micush, she said, I'll tell you everything tomorrow. He wouldn't let go: But are you talking with him? Is he telling you anything? Yes, she said, we're definitely talking. Are you really? And in his voice she heard a familiar tinge of pain. What are you talking about?

She made a note to herself that she would have to make up some story to tell him the next day, and the thought turned to metallic saliva in her mouth. More than usual, she needed Micah to be there with her, physically, if only for a minute, to hold her with all his great might, to cork her, or fling her, or suddenly turn her upside down and shake her hard until all the little thefts fell out of her pockets. She asked about the overturned container and he told her at length, in great detail and with sufficient modesty, but she knew that without him the container would still be out there spilling its toxins. When he finished, she asked what was going on at home, and he reported all the events, major and minor, and she listened with cursory attention, bathing herself in his warm, smiling voice as in a solution that would envelop and seal all her cracks, so her soul would not escape again. She thought of how his simplicity had won her over, slow and heavy, and still enabled him to tie her down to his earth with five strong cords, and for a moment she could almost not resist asking him what he thought about when he thought about her, and what he saw when he looked at her, and what he saw beyond her. From among his words came foundling memories and orphaned thoughts to scurry around inside her, and the four men sitting at the table yelled at each other, and anorexic girls walked down a narrow catwalk on the TV above her head, wearing clothes that revealed their unattractive bodies and vacant expressions, and Micah talked on and on, and she wearily wondered how, despite all the dreams she'd had, she had ended up being stuck for years in the only job she'd ever liked, as a lactation consultant, surrounded by women.

But something had gone irretrievably wrong—Shaul felt a twinge and looked worriedly at the door of the inn where Esti had disappeared a long time ago—some correct order had been disrupted tonight because of their conversation and her endless questions, and her presence in general. Not that her presence was so bad for him— on the contrary—but lots of time had been wasted on chatter and disturbances. And he had omitted quite a few essential details, as well as some scenes that should not, could not, be skipped. He quickly ran them through his mind: the bazaar, for example, the big market, the stalls that had been quickly set up in the search camp, the men hurrying with a strange glee of looting in their eyes, carrying racks filled with colorful clothes, hats, baskets laden with objects, a new colorfulness suddenly abounds . . . He tries to stop someone to find out what this place is now. And no one notices him. Everyone is hurrying, running around. Submissively, he walks among the stalls, trying to push his way through the people raiding the goods, but it's hard to reach, it's crowded and chaotic, a lot of money is changing hands. Suddenly he perks up: he thinks he recognizes something—a dress of hers! His heart leaps with joy. A flowery sundress, green and flimsy, with round wooden buttons down the front. What is her dress doing here? Maybe it's just a coincidence, he reassures his nay-saying heart, but very soon, on a nearby rack, he sees her white blouse with the high collar and the pattern of lemons, and in the nearby stall he finds the soft cotton shirt she bought on a trip to Venice, and above it hangs her loose purple dress, bursting with womanhood—

They're selling everything. There's a stall with her purses, a stall for glasses, one for jewelry and little knickknacks, another for combs and makeup, and one selling footwear, where he finds her sandals, almost new, and a pair of Palladium hiking boots she'd bought for the eleventh-grade camp at Kibbutz Mahanayim, and clumsy orthopedic shoes ("Golda shoes," he remembers they used to call them), and a pair of high heels she almost never wore because they made her taller than him, and green felt shoes, and sexy orange boots. The salesman waxes poetic: Every shoe still has her footprint in it. He fingers the shoes and feels the touch of her soles—they had always stayed smooth, always delightful; sometimes when he holds her foot in his sleep, he feels a rush of love for her and amazement that almost fifty years of walking and running and trampling through the world has left the soles of her feet as soft as a baby's. And they're selling her socks here, long ones and short ones, in all colors, a whole stall full of nylons from all ages, some stretched over shoe trees in risqué poses, some crumpled and torn, and here are two people haggling loudly over the pair of dark nylons she once agreed to rip for him right down the middle, when they were on their honeymoon in Amsterdam.

Men of every shape and color—tall, short, thick, supple, crude, neglected, handsome, elderly, refined, boyish, feminine, muscular, limp, chickenlike—a massive flow of masculinity in all its guises pours out toward him down the main street of the desert market. It is a hairy, sinewy, grumbling, throaty human throng, and the more he watches it, the more it loses its separate features and congeals into a mass of silt that fans out over a wide river, moving here and there, thick furrowed peels of skin with nervous looks darting around, excited and suspicious, and frizzy bushes of hair sprouting on the stump of a leg or a large arm, oversized lumps of mud from which reliefs of swollen arteries spring out, and sideburns and bald spots in a multitude of shapes, and sweat stains, and a convex skull and a molded forehead and a nervous muscle that tightens in the jaw, and throbbing biceps, and beneath the thick sludge a throng bubbles up toward him, like the permanent rumble of a river, the hum of covetousness and disquiet and short barks of deterrence, and also a deep comradeship, noisy, like in barracks or a stadium. Strange men and semi-familiar men, and men who look like men he knows, hurrying, rushing, touching, smelling the goods, haggling over a green wool glove, from which Elisheva's reddish fingers used to peek out during winter, or bickering over the gray-white pullover his mother knitted for her years ago, or holding up a thrilling little pair of underwear to the light, dancing drunkenly in the brilliance that shines through them, and in their brutalization they become beautiful for a moment through their contact with the splendor that enveloped her, refined as they touch the flimsy fabric—

When she had almost reached the door, after paying the guy at the counter for the phone call, she turned and went back to the phone and stood staring for a moment, as if wondering what she was doing there. Beyond two panes of glass she saw Shaul in the car, with his head leaning back, and she guessed that his lips were moving. Of their own accord, her fingers dialed the digits, and she knew the music the buttons produced from any telephone she'd ever been at. He lifted the receiver immediately, just as Micah had done before, and it was as if he'd been waiting for her by the phone all these years.

His voice was quick, even when he'd been sleeping: a low, penetrating "Hello." She froze. He was quiet for a long time, did not breathe, surrounded her with deep, dense quiet, then just said "Hello" again, a completely different one this time, almost defeated, and she hung up quickly and only then grasped what she had done. She stood with weak knees and didn't know what to do or where to go. She almost dialed the number again, her fingers seemed drawn to the buttons, but then she clutched the handset with both hands and pressed her mouth hard into the receiver, which stank from the saliva of strangers. Over the sound of the dial tone, she poured herself into him wordlessly. Unable to stop, she emptied her very core into him, and yelled and sobbed and laughed and promised and begged, and explained why and why not, and why they must and why they couldn't, and why there was no life without and how everything is always ripped in the same place and how she curses the moment and is resurrected over and over again endlessly

The most difficult times are when she comes home after being with him, Shaul said later, with a sigh, and Esti shook herself awake with fright and almost swallowed the candy she was sucking. It's not easy then, for me or for her, he said. She's always refreshed when she gets back, from the swim, of course, and her hair is a little damp, but she never looks me in the eye. It's not . . . and he laughed glumly, sliding pleasantly like a sleepwalker into their conversation, which was full of silences and deep valleys alongside each other, as in a prayer where everyone stands together but each person is on his own—and each of them, Esti thought, prays to a different God.

She was still quiet, barely holding her body up straight at the wheel. What had happened at the inn had exhausted her more than the long drive. She tried to guess what he was going through now. Saw him lying awake with his eyes open and sparkling in the dark, his tongue clicking between his cheeks, in his thinking position. She wondered whether he guessed it was her. Or perhaps he knew straightaway, as soon as he heard her silence. She kicked herself too, of course: maybe he thought it was someone else, a lover he had after her, whose call he had been waiting for. But she held her head up straight and shook it firmly: No.

Part of her brain repeatedly turned over his "hello," playing both instances of it again and again, the sigh and his voice, which was so old now, and the tiredness, which may not have been simply because it was late, and which sounded to her as if he were announcing that he was giving up something precious. How could he give up like that? she thought. He mustn't give up. And she answered herself, What gives you the right to even . . . ? She was frightened to think that he could be that way without her having known about it. Here you go again, she scolded herself, writing dissertations on the crumbs of his life. She drove around a bend and thought of how for years she had tried to imagine their reunion. It would be an accidental one, and she smiled because for some reason she was always convinced it would happen in a supermarket, that their eyes would rapidly scan the produce in each other's shopping carts, their families' tastes in breakfast cereals, dairy products, and meat. And more than that: the plenty and the abundance, which she always thought seemed a little defiant in her cart, a little too prepared for waving in front of his eyes. She knew she would be disoriented and stutter, that her legs would melt, and she knew how she would consume his face and his new wrinkles with her eyes, and try to guess which of them belonged to her.

She tormented herself with the memory of the one meeting she had agreed to after they broke up, at a little café on the banks of the Yarkon River. He looked ill, his fingers trembled, and he mumbled things that horrified her—that he had told her a thousand times she was the love of his life, but now it was clear to him that she was even more than that, that she was his life itself. He looked at her, frightened, and she alienated him with all her strength, with a cruelty she never imagined she possessed, so determined was she to finally start living her own life, unhidden. She sat opposite him, foreign and cold, trying to prove to him that there was no point, that he was completely wrong about her, and the more he begged, the more she hardened, like a heartless warden who keeps sending the wrong prisoner into a visitor's booth.

She still couldn't comprehend how it had even happened that she'd called him. How she had shattered years of restraint, of sometimes daily battles, and the regular torture of birthdays, his and hers, and their anniversaries, and when Shira went into the army, and when Na'ama was about to have surgery, and when there was a big terrorist attack on his street—she almost lost her mind that time, but she didn't call. She exhaled in amazement and a smile escaped, and she felt that perhaps even the dialing was enough for her, perhaps she did not need any more than that after so many years, because he raged within her now exactly as she remembered, with no partitions, just as it had always been, body and soul. She remembered with a smile how he had inquired euphorically as to whether he'd reached her pancreas yet; and again the breathless silence of them both, the electricity of mutual knowledge, and the sensation that never deadened in her that their love continued to exist as it was, in all its purity and fervor, just laid aside for a while, for an entire life even, on a shelf at a pawnbroker's, waiting for Esti to gather up the courage to reclaim it.

Startled, she leaned forward, her muscles tensing around the internal mouth that had let out the secret, but in her inner space a man and a woman flew around in colorful revelry; like cutouts of a Keith Haring drawing, they hugged, danced, laughed, tossed handfuls of their love-stamen into the air. Those moments of lovemaking, she thought longingly, where the more you gush the more you fill up; she inhaled with an excited sound, and her heart dug at the walls of her body, and she blushed and was hot and girlish, and again she awoke herself and reminded herself of vows and engraved on her mind in cuneiform script that there was no place for this, none, no place for this, for this there was no place . . . And how once, just before they broke up, she called him at home when she knew he was out, and the bright voice of a woman answered "Hello," and again and again, the voice of a woman that gradually became small and sad, and the voice was like a slap on her cheek that she had been wanting for a long time, and she put down the receiver and laid her heart down on the table and took a meat mallet and smashed it with all her merciless strength: there is a woman there and there are children, and what are you doing?

It's not easy for me when she gets back from there, Shaul said, and she turned to him eagerly. I'm listening, she said, begging, almost demanding. A few days ago she happened to hear on the radio that there was a way to cheat a polygraph: you put a thumbtack under your foot and step on it during the test, and the pain alters all your reactions.

Shaul told her that when she comes home, he hugs and kisses her, and he always thinks she tenses up for a moment, in her stomach and shoulders. But he does not always find the strength to go to her, because not every day, he admitted, is he capable of the exhausting effort of pretending. There are days when the anticipation of her drives him out of his mind to such an extent that he is unable to even get up and open the door for her. He pulls her head onto his shoulder and is repeatedly amazed at her professionalism and perfectionism, because her hair smells like chlorine. He holds her face back from his and looks into her eyes and smiles, and she nods with a kind of distant sadness, pained, as if she understands exactly what he is doing and yet does not stop him. Then she breaks away from him with an apologetic smile, releases herself from the embrace, and he manages to keep his smile and dam his lips against the torrent of filth which almost erupts when he thinks about where she's come from and what she did there. But she's already far away, Shaul sees, very active and busy, rushing around the rooms, tidying up, making calls, while he has to pretend to have just woken up from an afternoon slumber. I'm quite good at doing that, he told Esti with a crooked smile, I actually find it easy to masquerade as a husband turned silly from too much sleep. Over the years he discovered that even if he were a less convincing actor, she wouldn't have noticed, because she was so busy avoiding him, hiding the excitement that still colored her cheeks a vivid red. After a few minutes of hurrying around she is suddenly spent and collapses as if her last drop of energy has run out, and she lies down to rest. It's very difficult to catch the moment when this occurs: she disappears into her room—for some reason she does not take her siestas in their double bed but rather on the daybed in her little study—and instantly dives into an abyssal sleep, the sleep of a baby or an adolescent. He then—not out of nosiness, but out of amazement, out of true admiration for her thoroughness—quickly looks through her gym bag, and sees that the towel is wet as it should be, the bathing cap is damp, there is slightly less shampoo in the tube. He goes through this same routine every day, keeping his end of the bargain. He mustn't become sloppy and he will never give in, because, after all, these minute signs and tokens are, as he well knows, his one and only proof of her guilt.

Because, he thought, she has protected her secret perfectly over the years, and also with great elegance and professionalism, qualities which she has certainly picked up from her contact with Paul, who is an absolute perfectionist. It was this, in fact, which had eventually failed her and exposed her to Shaul, because it stands to reason—this was how he had formulated things a long time ago—that over the course of their twenty-five years together, there must have been at least a few cases, two, three, four, which should have aroused his suspicion. After all, she is not living in a bubble: she goes to the mall, to the bank, the garage, the clinic, lectures on all kinds of things, neighborhood committee meetings; every so often she takes part in professional conferences, sometimes out of town; she has meetings with the day-care parents, some of them men, and she and Shaul have three or four couples of friends, and in fact there are men everywhere. But she, in her determination to protect what she truly cherishes, has never once tripped up, never given anything away in her tone of voice or in a blush, or a choked-back gasp. Never has Shaul come home to catch her quickly hanging up the phone or covering a piece of paper on her desk with her hand. Never has he found a note with a suspicious phone number in her purse, or in the pockets of her clothes, and even when that man Paul burst into their kitchen, Elisheva was remarkably calm and businesslike, he has to admit, and she treated the incident as if it were a purely professional matter. She was generally so innocent and transparent and clear throughout that Shaul began to wonder what was going on and what she was hiding so perfectly.

Of course, he could not really believe that the moment a woman stepped out of her normal life, out of her trajectory, her furrow, she began to scatter—involuntarily, of course, without knowing it— some kind of chemical or biological substance which unconsciously affected every man around her, so that each one of them, every male Elisheva passed on her way from home to that "alone" of hers, was somehow influenced by this radiation, by the involuntary evaporation and percolation of primary essences, some sort of übermammal pheromones. But even so, was it really a stretch to assume that the first ones to be swept toward the stamen of this hidden radiation, during those four days of hers each year, would be those who come in daily contact with her? Even if that contact is minor and perfectly innocent? Shop clerks, supermarket employees, the bank teller, the gardener who worked for them until Shaul fired him not long ago, her hairdresser, the guy who delivers rolls in the morning . . . And without her or them knowing a thing, their pheromones were aroused to create a chain reaction whereby they both interpreted signals transmitted to them from their complementary genomes. And of course these messages are not only limited to the men who are close to her, because evolution, Shaul knows, cannot suffice with such a limited number of contacts. And so the pheromones spread with ever-widening ripples, and mate with the sensitive receptors of every man in their way, and these men too are swept after her without even understanding what is happening, without even knowing whom they are following. Because what attracts them, of course, is not one private Elisheva but the attractants she emits from the moment she is not within the circle of the man she lives with—or the two men, in her case. That is what they react to. That sexual gravitation, that horizontal gravity, all those men who experience a seemingly inexplicable, mysterious shockwave, the ones who are uprooted from their homes, their lives, or their dinners every time Elisheva leaves her life and goes off to be alone.

He sighed a deep "oh," and something sparked in Esti, the way the grin on the guy at the counter had suddenly changed after the second time she dialed. She smiled, because his eyes had followed her as she walked to the door and stayed on her through the window when she left.

And while she takes her afternoon nap, Shaul recounted, he sits on the porch drinking his coffee—that coffee, Esti thought, so solitary and bitter, while at her place they're all in the backyard enjoying Grandma Hava's tart—and tries to imagine what she talked about with Paul today, and hopes no one calls him during this hour, which is even more precious to him than the hour she spent with Paul, because now, when she is so close—he thought to himself—when her body is breathing beyond a thin wall, he feels he can know much more, that her substances are projected at him freely, and all he has to do is not resist them, allow himself to be invaded, be borderless. He can feel her and Paul and their day flowing and filling him up, slowly at first, like a thin trickle coming from far away, then becoming wild and frothy, and finally flooding him with hot torrents, in vibrant colors and scents and sounds. And I have these moments—Shaul laughed embarrassedly—which I would call, maybe, let's say, moments of inspiration. I have no illusions, of course—Esther mustn't think he has any such pretensions, because he doesn't, but sometimes, in these moments, he feels as if he could, for example, do something completely different with his life, be a sculptor, for instance, or draw or even write poetry—why not? He resisted telling her how his brain fills up and is compressed with warm blood and rich oxygen and dizziness, and his entire body sizzles with a cocktail of toxins and sweetness. But he could not stop himself from telling her that he himself barely exists at these moments, as do all the other elements of his being: the circumstances, the details, the facts that somehow stick to him day by day, even the worries for Tom, who can't find himself in Paris and is so lonely there that it breaks his heart, and the fight with the academic board that has been refusing to award him seniority for five years because of a dearth of publications, because of a complete lack of publications. I haven't even advanced one project all these years, did you know that? He sniggers. No, of course you didn't. I haven't had a single original idea. He tapped his head with his fingers. Ah! Empty. Completely emptied out. I don't know, sometimes I wonder how long they'll keep me on there. I've already heard talk of early retirement, and I'm not even fifty-five, you know? Esti listened in shock and wondered what would happen to them the next time they met with the whole family, how she would look at him, if he would evade her looks as usual, and how every word in the conversation would sound to him, and every laugh and sigh of Elisheva's, and if they would ever again enjoy another taste of this night's grace.

Shaul tensed his body as if trying to squeeze out a few more drops of the moments of elation during which everything sheds from him and he himself is everything and nothing, he is the stage and the play and the playwright and the director and the audience, and inside him a man and a woman rage in all their animalism and their beauty, she and he, grown adults, with developed emotions and ripe limbs, and the market is abuzz. Rows of stalls and tents and huts set up in minutes, in the blink of an eye. And it's all hers, it's all Elisheva. As if all the thousands of details that had ever made up her material life are spread out and itemized here in a wonderful kind of simultaneity. How did they get their hands on all this? When had they had time to plunder? Is it possible that the minute she "goes off to be alone," a temporary liquidator is appointed for everything that ties her to the mundane? Shocked and morose, he wanders through the crowds, turning down TEXTILE AVENUE, as the sign proclaims. A colorful whirl-wind rises up around him, composed of towels and coverlets and handkerchiefs and scarves and tablecloths and napkins and tapestries and rugs and sheets, his and her sheets—

In a back row of more modest stalls, he notices portraits of her in varying sizes here and there: Elisheva being thoughtful and Elisheva sleeping, Elisheva dancing, Elisheva dreaming, winking, Elisheva dressed, naked, breast-feeding.

There is a stall selling her own creations. Letters she wrote are displayed under a large glass pane. And lists of every kind—she is mad about lists, he smiles to himself—and work reports, and compositions she wrote as a child. He stands on tiptoe and glimpses at the titles over the broad shoulders of the crowds: "I Was a Little Raindrop," and "The Righteous Are Delivered Out of Trouble." There are papers from high school and university, birthday toasts, even shopping lists. There are also bundles of letters tied with red ribbons, and on the side there is a little sign telling buyers to ask the seller about special letters he keeps in a hidden drawer. And a special offer for collectors: highlights from her diary. Shaul didn't even know she kept a diary, although, on second thought, why not? He reads the price tags with astonishment: even if he wanted to, he couldn't afford to buy them!

But some people have money, and they make purchases, and offer to barter—one guy is willing to trade a diary excerpt from August 20 for one of her bras, any color, and another offers the May 4 page to the highest bidder. Apparently there are many takers, and a kind of public auction is held, and Shaul tries to push his way in, he has to know exactly what happened to her on August 20 and May 4, and where he was then. But there is such excitement over these two items that he is pushed out of the circle and watches brokenhearted as the bra changes hands—the thin, pure white bra, which he liked to open with two fingers when Elisheva was lying on her stomach; he would melt with passion at the sight of her lovely, long, smooth back and her round shoulders, and sink his tongue into the soft hairline on her nape, her hair, which had turned gray at some moment when Shaul must have been looking away—

The market stretches on and on into the horizon, dogs scurry between people's feet, and nimble peddlers sell hot corn on the cob and pink cotton candy and little candied apples, all the market trivialities which Elisheva actually likes. And there are a few crooks, of course. One of them is trying to make a fortune off one of her curls, which lies frizzy and innocent and impudent on a bed of velvet in a little box. Another offers miniature bottles, whose content he does not even disclose; he just waves this bottle or another in his hand and winks and blinks and snickers in the most disgusting and despicable manner. Shaul holds back from running over and strangling him with his own hands and taking over the whole inventory, opening the sealed bottles and dousing himself with her precious nectar. But he must hurry, skip along, he has no choice, because in a few minutes they will reach the hut where she resides and there are still things he has to see before he gets to her, still more loathsome blows to hit him with complete surprise on this haunted-house ride which he boards every year, a set course that cannot be changed. It seems that today he'll have to give up the public trial, with all its details and minutiae, a kind of field court-martial that is held for him to determine how he could allow such a thing to happen to his wife. But as it happens, there is a little more time, a couple of minutes, just to taste. The presiding judge uses an expedited procedure and asks if anyone in the crowd has a personal claim against him. After a long silence, a man steps forward, not a young man, heavy and sad—it is Paul, of course, he made it here after all, of course he did. He slowly makes his way until he is standing opposite Shaul, and a long and detailed debate ensues, right there in front of everyone, with examinations and cross-examinations that Paul conducts against him. It turns out that Paul knows all his secrets and all his little shames, knows exactly where to press and where to push and how to tear his life into shreds in front of everyone. Finally, the surprising verdict is handed down: a duel, in the nude, between him and the "public representative"—namely, Paul. But this will not be just a fistfight. That would be too easy—one man is hit and falls down, and that's the end of it. No, they must also hold an intellectual battle, that is the catch, and it must be in Shaul's fields of expertise. But it turns out that Paul knows more about these too, much more, always more, and Elisheva will suddenly emerge from one of the crevices on the mountain above, will stand with one leg slightly folded, like a doe, will look at them both, from Paul to him and back again, and her thin nostrils will suddenly widen with the tremble of decision

Esti slowed down. Little lights flickered far down the road. A roadblock. A tall, thin Ethiopian soldier with shiny eyes leaned in and asked for papers. He peered through the back window and noticed the figure lying there, huddled, covered with a blanket.

It's all right, Esti said, he's with me.

Have to see his face, the soldier said. Esti didn't understand. She looked back and saw that Shaul's hand was covering his face as he slept.

Leave him alone, she said angrily, he's sleeping. But she was surprised that Shaul had fallen asleep again, and that the flashlight and the strange voice hadn't woken him.

Have to see his face, the soldier insisted.

Shaul, she whispered softly.

He opened one eye and blinked at the light. There was a long silence. Esti tapped the wheel with her finger.

Oh, the soldier said, you came again today?

He handed the papers back to her, lightly patted the side of the car, and went back to his sandbag post. Esti closed the window slowly. Placed both hands on the wheel. They drove on.

And on and on.

Her left hand dropped to her thigh and pressed down hard. She felt her flesh being crushed. She pressed harder, then let go and concentrated entirely on the pain. But the pain passed and she remained. She stared at the dashboard. She would need to fill the car soon. The thought of the drive back troubled her. She was afraid she wouldn't be able to drive home alone after dropping him off. It takes two, she thought, to bear this weight. And again she saw how he had hidden his face with his hand, how he had blinked at the light. The hardest thing, she thought, is waking up someone who is pretending to be asleep.

When I got back—he finally ripped through the silence, unloading his confession impatiently, indifferently even—yesterday, you know, I was knocked out, it must have been 3 a.m. I drove into a telephone pole. We passed it earlier, just past Sde Boker—didn't you see? I took half a transformer with me.

She nodded. Some things took a while to sink in. And the day before yesterday you also went, she determined later, thoughtfully and very quietly.

He crossed his arms over his chest. Closed his eyes.

And every day Elisheva has been there, she thought, and every year when she goes to be alone. She could hear his breaths. She jostled her knees against each other a few times. Tell me, she said.

He opened a cloudy eye.

Yes, she said with sudden eagerness.

But I'm crazy, he mumbled, I'm a piece of shit.

You could say so, she said, but I want to hear.

Why?

Why? What could she say, where could she start? You ask as if there's only one reason.

Give me one.

When you talk about it, she said, I suddenly breathe differently.

Okay, that's a reason. He smiled pathetically.

I haven't told you about the wedding yet—he was barely audible, and she glanced in the mirror and saw him sinking further and further into himself, choking down his bleeding self—their wedding, which of course has no significance from a legal standpoint, but they did it anyway. The symbolic aspect, you see, was very important to them, it seems.

She shifted in her seat. Massaged her aching back against the seat. It was hard for her now, almost unbearable to go back there with him.

I think about it a lot, he said. I sometimes wonder when exactly they decided on it. Maybe it was the day Tom graduated from high school. That evening we were at the graduation with all the other students and their parents, and it was important to Elisheva to celebrate something meaningful with Paul too, at lunchtime. She listened. His voice, as usual, became stronger by the minute and filled with the blood of the story. Or did it happen after her mother died? Maybe she realized life was short and decided she wanted to finally take a real, uncompromising step.

His lips thickened as he pondered again, for the thousandth time, how and at what moment in life a person makes such a fateful decision. How one manages to hide from one's partner the difficulty of the decision making, the sighs of unease, the expansion of the heart when one suddenly feels it's the right thing to do and that one is in a place where laws and norms do not reign. Sometimes I think, he added, that perhaps I noticed a new expression on her face that day, the day she made the decision, but I didn't realize what it was. Or I try to remember a period of time, let's say a few days or a week, when she was unusually elated—a burst of happiness or something wild, irrational, maybe even a sense of vengeful glee toward me, over her finally being completely free of me, on a symbolic level, of course.

Then they deliberated over whether or not they should invite any friends, he went on, and even though they both knew right away that they didn't want any strangers at the ceremony—and for them, he snickered, a "stranger" is any human being at all—they still couldn't overcome the pleasure of amusing themselves with the thought that their close friends would be with them, you see, that for once they would be looked at lovingly from the outside too.

She nodded, eyes glazed over, trapped again and again in the burgeoning conversation that spread out for her within those two "hellos," in the silence, in the sigh. She thought: How can he still pull me out of my life like a hair from a ball of dough? Sighing, almost begging him to let her go, to release—

And just think, Shaul said from somewhere far away, how many of their days—I mean, their few hours—they wasted on planning the wedding. Although it's certainly possible that they didn't see it as a waste. He shrugged. Maybe dealing with it actually made them feel they were more, I don't know, real? Tangible? They definitely made lists. Or rather, Elisheva did. You know how fond she is of lists. He smiled, and Esti smiled dully with him, remembering the little yellow notes that always floated around Elisheva. And they wrote down for themselves all the pros and cons, whom to invite and whom not to, whom they could trust and who might blab, and tried to guess each person's reaction to the invitation, and I have to ask you—

She didn't even have to stop and think: Yes, I would have come.

He contemplated a little. She could tell he liked her answer. I don't blame you, he said.

Look, he sighed, this whole thing isn't easy for me. Sometimes I'm really enraged inside. I think, for example, of the wanderings my job has imposed on both of them. Over the past ten years we've been on two sabbaticals, one in Washington and one in Boston, and each time the sabbatical came up she didn't even try to protest, didn't look for excuses to get out of it, but just accepted it simply and even managed to seem happy. I remember how it amazed me then: she said it wouldn't be a bad thing for us to breathe some fresh air, for both of us to refresh ourselves a little together. She was really excited about it, even though I knew that such a long trip, for them, meant a huge, complicated, and completely unnecessary organizational effort. And think about him, about her Paul, who had to uproot himself from here and become an immigrant again in a strange country. He had to rent an apartment to be close to us, somewhere she could reach within her almost-hour of swimming, which she didn't give up anywhere, in any country on any day—his voice trembled—because she couldn't give it up, because without it she probably would die. It's as simple as that. Esti looked at him and for a moment he seemed even more exposed, almost naked in his clothes. And you have to understand, it's not easy for me to think that the second I announced the move she agreed immediately, and took it upon herself to get this whole trip off the ground, all the uprooting. Maybe she felt as if that way she was cleansing her sins somehow, I don't know. But sometimes the thought of her huge efforts, theirs, around those two trips, illuminates me in a rather unpleasant light, he said, as if they know something about me that I prefer not to know, not to think of. What? she asked feebly. What do you mean? As if I'm a person—he hesitated, his bottom lip trembling—whose grasp on life is tenuous, pathetic, like that of someone with a chronic illness, terminal even, or like one of those children who have to be kept in a sterile bubble their whole life.

Hypnotized, she hovers in the space of his sealed pod, a human flake carried this way and that on the current of a strong breeze. Thoughts pass through her, chills of consciousness, alien headlines, ridiculing, but she doesn't want them. Maybe later. Tomorrow. And she knows: as early as dawn. And she hopes she won't betray what she felt then either. And if she does, she hopes she at least knows that she is betraying. And that she remembers how excited she is now by this power of his to insist on keeping the ember that burns inside him alive, as if there is no one with him and he has no shame, no truth or lies, nothing forbidden or ugly. It excites her to think that he has, quite simply, shown her the cogwheels and levers and pistons of the abstract mechanism that generates—in his soul and in hers too—the dreams and nightmares and hallucinations and terrors and yearnings. They are all exposed to her, gaping generously in a way no one has ever given her before, and it is good for her there, she knows, it is so warm . . . She reaches back and feels around and finds his hand, envelops it with her fingers, squeezes, sending him strength, drawing it from him.

But they did have flowers, he laughs exaggeratedly, excited by her touch and not pulling his hand back. If there's one thing I know for sure, it's that Elisheva wanted the house to be full of flowers. Because when she's with him, in their home, flowers always give her a sense of space and freedom. You should see how she sniffs the bouquet she buys for Shabbat from the Yemenite guy by the post office—such a smiler, that one, with big lips, almost purple—and how she arranges the flowers in a vase, her seriousness, and how much time she spends on them, and the way suddenly, listen, as if she can't take it anymore, she leans over swiftly and puts her face in and inhales them as hard as she can—

He speaks quickly, grasping her hand as if trying to push away what will happen soon, what he will see in a few minutes. How did she manage not only, he says, to take off the veil she must have worn, not only the dress she bought for the ceremony and probably left in his closet among the other dresses, but how did she hide everything else? That's what I don't get: the excitement, the trembling knees when he lifted her veil to kiss her, the ring he bought her—after all, he put a ring on her finger, and then he had to take it off as soon as the ceremony was over, and that's the ring he puts on her finger every time she shows up at his door, and that way, every day they have a new little wedding ceremony. Maybe she even forgot to take the ring off that day, he thinks suddenly, and only when she left the apartment and stood at the steps to blow him one last kiss, only then did he notice it and, alarmed, whisper to her to return, and she didn't understand what for, but went up happily for another kiss, and he pulled the ring off and kissed her bare finger. Shaul chokes, and Esti sees his eyes glaze over in the mirror and his lips pucker for an imagined kiss, and her heart tears with compassion. That is the essence of his life, she thinks. These thoughts and fancies, they are more alive in him than anything else, they may even be more—something jolts in her—than what he has with Elisheva herself.

A few minutes later they drove past the entrance gate and into the cabin area. They saw no one. The headlights lit up a cabin wall every so often, or a tent, or a hut covered with palm fronds.

Straight and farther down, he said, no lights.

The car rocked heavily. Gravel flicked under the wheels.

Farther, farther down.

The path became a slope, twisted and more rocky.

Farther, all the way down.

Esti thought she'd never be able to get back up. It seemed to her as if the entire desert could hear the Volvo screeching and groaning.

That's it.

They were on the edge of a cliff.

Turn it off.

She killed the engine, straightened up a bit, and saw, on the plain beneath her, a small dark cabin. Bamboo walls, a roof of mats and branches.

The sudden silence filled up quickly with crickets and nocturnal rustles. She saw his face come and go in the mirror, and then settle there, a pale yellowish stain against the back window. They sat quietly. The mist had lifted and the sky over the desert was cloudless. Esti thought about Elisheva breathing beyond those thin walls. Asleep or awake. Maybe watching them.

Do you need help? she whispered.

What? Her voice had shocked him, and only then did she realize she was disturbing him.

I thought—should I help you out of the car?

No . . . I don't need anything.

His eyes were closed tight, and he bit his lower lip. Maybe he needs me to get out, she thought, maybe he wants to be left alone. But she didn't move, not wanting to disturb him. She leaned her head back and closed her eyes. And felt him erase her again. She did not exist, and for a long moment she delighted in the feeling.

She lost track of time. Years shed away from her. She might have slept. Maybe just hallucinated. When she opened her eyes once in a while, she saw his constricted face, and no longer tried to guess what was going through his mind. She was part of his imagination, an image flickering at the edge of his hallucinatory scene. She closed her eyes again and gave herself over to him and became the thing he saw, the back hiding the cabin in which Elisheva was writhing on her bed with a man, perhaps two, perhaps with all the men in the world.

Esther, he said later weakly, I think we can go back.

She found it hard to wake up. She started the engine and maneuvered the car clumsily onto the road and drove slowly, avoiding looking in the little mirror.

Stop for a minute, he said when they were some distance away, I want to move up front.

She stopped on the shoulder of the empty road. He opened the door and pushed himself out and stood leaning on the car with his leg slightly folded in midair. She got out and went to him and stood in front of him, enveloping herself in his arms, breathing the sharp air, rocking slowly. They stood together for a moment within the night's shell and did not know where to look. She extricated herself and hurried over to move the passenger seat back and lower the back down at an angle. She padded the floor with a coat and a blanket.

You can get in, she said, as he walked to the open door.

Wait, she murmured as he walked by her, and without thinking she pulled him in for an embrace.

What do you think? he said hesitantly when they were moving again and had been quiet for several miles. Maybe we can go through Beersheba? And she, alert at once, asked why. He said, I just thought maybe you'd show me your old places. She considered his offer. But it's nighttime, she said. And he said, Yes. She nodded slowly to herself a few times, thoughtfully, wondering where to begin.

February 2002

Her Body Knows

She interrupts me after the third sentence: "I saw something on TV yesterday and I thought of you."

I put down the pages. I can't believe she's cutting me off like that.

"I woke up and it was 3 a.m.," she says, "and I had nothing to do." She laboriously moves her swollen face on the pillow and turns to me. "It was something about a bunch of hippies in America. Saving birds that keep crashing into towers."

I wait. I can't see the connection.

"I thought you could have been with them."

"Me?"

Her hands make jittery fists on the blanket. Nervous flutters, a little like the ones you get after a nice dose of Haldol, although that's the one drug she isn't taking. I try to disassociate myself from those movements of hers, remind myself that they have nothing to do with me and that it's not a criticism of my story. Just jumpy little tics that will drive me insane in a few seconds.

"Every day at four in the morning, they walk past the skyscrapers." Then she explains: "That's because the birds migrate at night."

"Well, now it's clear," I say as I emphatically straighten my stack of papers. I'll never understand her way of taking in information or, even less, her way of spewing it out. It's taken me two months to prepare for this evening, and she just cuts me off like that.

"They collect the remains and put them in plastic bags," she continues, "and if there's a need, they treat them. I even saw them giving cortisone to one bird." Her common lot with the bird amuses her.

"Then they fling them back, set them free." She is astonished. "They look like normal people, they all have jobs, one's a lawyer, another one I saw was a librarian, but they're also, how should I put it, kind of *principled*."

"With that sort of self-righteous expression?" I ask slyly.

"What . . . yes," she admits, embarrassed. She herself probably didn't know why she had connected me with them.

I laugh, somewhat desperately. She is my mother, the ultimate seer, and yet she's a complete ignoramus when it comes to me. "I actually tend to side with the tower colliders," I tell her.

"No, no." She shakes her head heavily. "You're strong, very strong."

She says "strong." I hear "cruel." She dives a little deeper inside, where she may come across another crumb of memory to salvage. We are both quiet. I haven't seen her for two years, and there are moments when I can't reconcile her with the woman she used to be. Her lips move, mumbling thoughts, and I make sure not to read them. She turns her head and looks at me. *"Why do you think we have eyelids?"* I used to yell at her, and now I say nothing, dutifully taking what I deserve. It's one thing to sit at home in London and write the story, and feel shitty for half a day after our weekly phone calls because she doesn't even imagine what I'm doing to her in my writing, and it's a completely different thing to sit here and read it to her, word for word, as she suggested, as she demanded, as she compelled me to do with all the force of her dying.

"Okay," she sighs, "I interrupted you. From now on I'll be quiet. Read it again, from the beginning."

A small man with bulging eyes, crude lips, and large hands stands and looks at her. She senses him before she can see him. An ill breeze invades the circle that surrounds her. She opens her eyes and sees him upside down, leaning against the doorframe in shorts and a floral shirt, with very red lips, as if he has just consumed his prey. She calmly pushes her feet away from the wall and descends, one leg at a time, then gets up and stands tall. The man lets out a soft whistle of admiration that sounds like contempt.

"Once," he says, "when I was little, I could do that. Headstand too. The whole deal."

Nili makes no response. Maybe he just came into the wrong room. Must be looking for the gym.

"Well, then," he says with that same forced tone, tranquil and yet threatening. "Yoga, eh?"

She starts rolling up the mats left out from the morning. Three vacationing ladies had decided to refresh their bodies in her class. They hadn't stopped giggling and chattering, and couldn't even get one leg up in the air.

"Yes," she tells him with a "You got a problem with that?" voice. "Yoga."

"And yoga is what exactly, remind me." He takes out a pack of cheap Noblesse cigarettes, taps it a couple of times, and pulls one out.

"Yoga is— Would you mind not smoking in here?"

Their looks collide. He shakes his head slowly from one side to the other, as if reprimanding a very small child. His lips curl into a mocking kiss: "Anything for you, honey." She feels every inch of her body being surveyed in a brisk appraisal, and she is trapped, unable to move, and anger begins to ferment in her.

"So tell me—is yoga kind of like massage?"

"Massage is down the hall on the right." She can't resist adding, "The *medical* kind."

"And this, whatsitcalled, it's not medical?"

Okay, she thinks, I can be over and done with this in a flash. I have plenty of experience with these guys. She straightens up, a whole head taller than him, and crosses her arms over her chest. "No sir," she articulates clearly for him, "the kind of massage you want is not here." She flashes her matter-of-fact smile—broad, glowing, thirty-two splinters of contempt digging straight into his face.

But he's not all that impressed. On the contrary, he looks

amused. His tongue travels serenely around his mouth, under his lower lip, making little swellings that shift around, and Nili thinks of the wavelike motion of puppies in a pregnant tummy.

He snickers. "But I didn't ask you what it's not, I asked what it *is*."

Deep breath. Wait. Don't give him the satisfaction. Answer him from your quiet place. Let's see you when you're not sitting on top of a mountain, alone among the pale blue clouds. Do it here, with this.

"So you don't know what yoga is?" Again his tongue twists around in his lustful mouth. "Then how come the sign says 'Yoga Room'?"

"Because this is where we teach yoga, y-o-g-a, and for the massage you want"—she thrusts her head out, almost touching his forehead with her own, and her broad feline face bristles—"you can order someone over the phone. Ask them for the number at the front desk, there are girls around these hotels who would be happy to oblige. Now, please excuse me." She goes back to angrily rolling up the mats.

"But it's not for me," he slurs, and shifts from one foot to the other. "It's . . . to tell you the truth, it's for my son."

"Your son?" She slowly straightens up and plants her strong hands on her hips. "You want me to . . . for . . . What do you think I am?" She throws her head back, her cropped hair bristles with electricity. In New York and Calcutta that stance, along with her large, strong body, did wonders when problems came up or if someone was harassing her. Her girls would be amazed, she thinks, if they saw her like this, with the crudeness that slips out of her as swiftly as a switchblade. She herself is surprised at how easy it is for her to revert to that role.

The small man is impressed too. He takes half a step back, but still stares ahead with determination and seems to be forcing himself to deliver his message to completion. "He's . . . he's turning sixteen soon, on Passover, that's the situation. And he doesn't have a mother. I thought . . ."

"Yes? What did you think? That I would take your kid—and what? What exactly?" Her face turns red in disbelief at his insolence. But what can you expect when you agree to endure this humiliation for two weeks every year, with all the package tours and the union workers' vacations, employees from Hamashbir and Delek and who knows where else, to do the "yoga thing" for them.

From within her anger she observes: the crooked line that emerges and breaks under his mouth, the frequent blinking, the hand that starts to finger a thin gold chain on his chest; a rapid collapse, almost imperceptible, that suddenly occurs in him right in front of her eyes. His face becomes even more unsightly, more insidious and miserable. He must be on the workers' union board, she thinks, from the metal factories in Haifa or the warehouses in Lod. Mistreats his subordinates and flatters his superiors. Who do you think you're intimidating here? I can read you like an open book, with your taut little muscles, that swagger you picked up from the movies and, on top of everything else, your flat feet, lower back pain, and hemorrhoids.

He stands shriveled and shrunken beneath her gaze, and it only increases her desire for revenge, makes her feel like telling him sweetly what he really is. Or maybe I was just in the mood—she later thinks despondently—to patronize someone a little, to remember the taste of it. But then finally, something he said before penetrates her brain: what had he mumbled about the mother? (And what are you doing getting mixed up with him?) "And what am I supposed to do, in your opinion?" she asks, still preserving the frost in her voice. "With your son."

He looks at her with his rooster eyes. "He's a good kid. Look, he won't make any trouble, I guarantee it. The smallest problem, come straight to me."

"Problem?" She laughs despite herself. "What problem?"

"No, no, he's good, really. He just has . . . it's . . . he has ideas, he has bees in his bonnet"—the creases of anger and craftiness on his forehead loosen up a little, and between his eyes she sees a pained and

137

startled furrow of recognition—"and he's been with me since infancy, seeing as his mother died, bless her, when he was one month old, and I thought . . ."

He stops and gives her a look of stupidity and helplessness. She senses that he is a man with no echoes in his body. She crosses her arms and deliberates with herself. She has three girls, sixteen and a half, eleven, and eight, from three men, the last of whom left five years ago, and she knows what it's like, day by day, hour by hour. And this guy here, with his fleshy lips and crooked legs, with the "unloved" sign tacked to his back and chest. But who the hell is she to judge him?

"So what exactly were you thinking?"

He immediately senses her voice softening. A little hanger-on such as himself must be alert to any change. He quickly—too quickly for her taste—lets his shoulders relax, crosses his feet. "Well, I thought—now, don't get angry again, hear me out—I saw the sign here, yoga, so what did I think? That we're here for a week, me and the boy, and he's a good kid, honestly, but he doesn't have any friends. You see where I'm going with this?" And here he must sense that he's managed to cast an anchor in her, and he hurries to deepen it excitedly. "He's all alone. Nothing. He doesn't communicate. He can go a whole week—no communication!" He starts getting his confidence back, something about the goods he's selling her is going down well. "And he's a kid, believe me, you'll see him and you'll understand. You—you have a good eye. I could tell that about you as soon as I saw you." He leans forward slightly, lowering his voice. "The thing is that he's alone. No girls, girlfriends, that sort of thing. Nothing. So what did I think, what did I say to myself, I thought if you, if . . ."

"Come on already, spit it out!" Nili groans, growing tired of his transparent haggling, but possibly also tickled by hearing the words explicitly, like a scene from a B movie; after all, how many times in a lifetime do you get to hear a thing like this?

He swallows and tenses up. "I thought maybe you'd take him, take him privately, for money, make him a man."

He withdraws immediately and stretches out his small stature as tall as he can, and again he looks like a little rooster to her, feathers bristling, his fear making him dangerous. His narrow chest puffs up, he breathes rapidly, and one of his eyes starts to wander.

She stands with her arms crossed, nodding something to herself.

"Forget it," he suddenly bursts out. "Didn't happen. Never mind. Forget about it." And he turns to walk out of the room. He must have scared himself, Nili thinks. Must have been alarmed by his own proposal, by what his ears heard his mouth say. She doesn't know what's come over her—even later, when she reports the events to Leora, she finds it difficult to explain what happened, just that she suddenly knew it would be all right—more than all right, that it would be good. "It was like I guessed," she tells Leora, "like I guessed through him what was waiting for me there." She sighs deeply and her shoulders slouch. "And besides, me?" (*Who has done it all, with all sexes and all colors*, Leora silently completes her sentence.) "To be scared off by the idea of this kid?" Leora, on the phone at home, quickly wets her lips in preparation for an intense discussion, but Nili always knows when to simply close her eyes in enjoyment and hug herself. She laughs quietly. "So I thought to myself, Let the kid come, we'll have a little talk with him, give him the facts of life, and let him know what's what. What's the worst thing that could happen?" And so she hurries after the man who is now fleeing her, and once more she feels as if something was revealed when he said those things to her. When he turns to her, she sees shame in his red brimming eyes, and she says to him softly, deeply regretting what she had done to him thus far, "Send him over now, I'll wait for him."

"Okay, but I'm paying," he almost shouts.

"You're not paying anything, it's on the house." She laughs.

"But it's extra," he insists, sniffling.

"No need. Send the kid over."

He stands confused for a moment, suspicious, unable to comprehend the economic logic. But he still wants to thank her somehow, so he digs through the pockets of his too-tight pants and cannot find what he's looking for, doesn't even know what he's looking for. He finally tries to shake her hand, but their fingers miss each other. "Listen, if you ever need anything up north, at the quarries . . ."

I put down the pages, lunge for the cup, grab it with both hands, and drink huge gulps of water. I haven't dared to look at her until now. And I'm dying for a cigarette. Dying. How silent she was while I read. Abysmally silent. And I held the pages up between myself and her the whole time, with both hands, but the trembling only let up for the last few lines—

"Until this moment," she says softly, "I didn't know what it would be like."

"And now?" I force myself to look straight at her. Now the criticism will come. She'll say it's not her taste, it's too complicated for her now. "Smart aleck," she'll say, and she'll tell me to leave it. What does she know? What can she really make of all this, in her condition? And if you think about it honestly, when was the last time she held a book in her hand since high school?

"For a few months now, I've been lying here and thinking, What, she'll sit here next to me and read, and then what? What will happen to me?" Her voice is distant and stiff. It hadn't occurred to her to wonder what would happen to me. Old habits die hard. "So you wrote that story, after all," she says slowly.

I can't decipher her reaction. I have no idea whether what I've read up to now reminds her in any way of what happened there, if I'm even close. If that was how they spoke, she and his dad, if that was what went through her mind when he came to her with his proposition. I know so little, almost nothing. "Take him privately, make him a man"—that happened, she told me that as a kind of joke, I suppose, the day she came home. Maybe she thought it would entertain me, an amusing anecdote from her job; it had turned my stomach. There were another couple of details that trickled down to me, even though I tried hard not to let them, and of course I know the ending. But in the middle there was a black hole, the chasm of her silence that stretched out from then until today. And now too, in fact, what is she telling me? Nothing. She breathes heavily. Not because of me. I hope it's not because of me right now. Every breath costs her an effort. She's very large and bulky. Fills up the whole bed. I arrange my pages for the third time, not knowing whether I should go on reading or wait for her to say something, give me a sign, a direction. Nothing comes. The most exasperating thing for me is to discover how little I had imagined while I was writing at home in London, what I would feel here when I read to her. My pretension horrifies me, and my brilliant stupidity: did I really think I could sit here with my legs crossed and tell her a story I'd made up about her and him?

"And you made me seem so angry," she says.

"It's a story," I remind her dryly, but I suddenly feel a pang, as if I'd missed something.

"When have you ever seen me angry like that?"

"It's just a story, Nili," I say, annoyed. In my mouth I already feel the saliva of a foreknown failure. And really, where did I come up with her anger there? That righteous indignation I stuck on her is so unlike her—

"And you mention Leora by name."

"I didn't change any real names. Not Leora's, not yours, not mine either."

She contemplates at length, slowly absorbing. "You're in the story too?"

My heavy heart tramples over a particularly fragile joint on the way to her. "Yes, I'm in the story too."

But now she surprises me. I think I see a shadow of a smile, almost a satisfied expression. "Go on."

———

She sobers up, of course, the second he's gone. Have you lost your mind? What exactly are you going to do? This is a child we're talking about. How old did he say? Sixteen at Passover. Meaning he's now fifteen and a half. That's just great. A year younger than Rotem, and you're only three times his age. Congratulations. She walks around the room nervously, gathering up mats, laying them down again, regretting, standing, staring off into a bubble of the moment. What does this have to do with yoga? She sighs, and her heart starts sliding down the familiar slope. What does this have to do with the vows you once swore to yourself, when you were standing in the light? She sits down on a plastic chair in the corner. A slight chill seeps into her stomach, the coldness of a liar finally caught. And anyway, what is all that rubbish about standing in the light? she jabs at herself. When exactly have you truly stood in the light? She straightens her back, spreads out her hands on her hips, and searches for calmness inside, an indentation, even a small hollow of relief, of momentary forgetfulness. But a thick-necked little animal leaps out of there and expertly sinks its teeth into her. And let's assume that there was a time when you stood there, in your light—well, that simply means you were casting a shadow on someone else, weren't you? Isn't that the defective logic of "standing in the light"? She gets up, walks around the room, leans her back against the wall. And something else stings her from within: Why did he come to *her* with this proposal? What did he sense about her? What do people sense about her from the outside? She pushes herself away from the wall, the poison of the stupid, random insult already spreading through her. How do these twisted things always stick to you? No matter how far you run and how much you try to hide from them, it won't do any good, the magnet is working. She finds herself standing opposite the little mirror over the sink, her intense green eyes shooting sparks back at herself. She furiously freshens up her short-cropped hair, looks to the side, then back, and looks sideways at her impressive nose, slightly broken at the base. You thought it was safe for you here, didn't you, with all these vacationing families, a Mecca of boredom. She closely examines her large, beautiful teeth and licks her lips and hides a smile and is taken aback: wait a minute, what do you think you're doing?

She flees to the window. She opens it, chokes, and slams it shut. Her yoga room is located directly above the parking lot for the tour buses, and when she complained recently about the exhaust fumes and the noise, the activities manager smiled at her—she's at least five rungs above her on the food chain—and said, "The choice is yours, sweetie." Four buses spit out another cycle. The new arrivals stand for a minute, stunned and slowed down by the heat, looking like groups of refugees beginning to digest their catastrophe. Only one boy, who got off barefoot, hops crazily from one foot to the other. She reads the signs: NETANYA MUNICIPALITY EMPLOYEES, DEAD SEA VACATION. The heat vapors blur the mountains behind the buses. This is it, this is the last time. She'll buy new glasses for Inbal and then to hell with the money. Her arms hug her body tightly, but even it, the pride and joy of her life, seems suddenly a little strange and heavy, and when she walks, it moves with her in the room as if enclosed in a thick frame with a gilded caption beneath that says: *Woman's Body*. Maybe she'll call Leora, she thinks at first, because the moment she says it to someone out loud—especially to Leora—everything will cool down and dissipate. But the boy, she perks up, he may already be on his way here. Just think what's going through *his* mind. And Leora—oh yes, she's a real authority on these matters—stuck with the same Dovik since age seventeen. She is suddenly struck with horror: What did he mean, "doesn't communicate"? Could he be retarded? Think, Nili, think quickly, this is no joke, and it's certainly no joke for him, it's life or death.

With that phrase in her mind she finally realizes she is afraid, and she stands for a moment, trapped. She, who really has done it all, in lands near and far, and who has gladly and generously taught beloved men and women, and several students too, how to excite their partners and when to hold back and how to drive someone wild. Even when she gave classes in hospitals, even in old-age homes, she would pour forth her experience with deliberation and faith, teaching them

143

where to touch and how to caress and where only to flutter like eyelashes, because it would always keep them happy and fresh, always. But here, suddenly, something else entirely, and even if nothing happens—and it obviously won't, you fool—oh hell, what did I need this for.

"You're not taking any pity on me," she says when I stop to take a drink. But there is no complaint in her voice—quite the opposite.

"Should we stop?"

"No. The pillow."

I rearrange the pillow under her head. When I lean over her, it smothers me.

"I smell it too," she murmurs. "That's the way it always is at the end."

She would certainly know. She has accompanied so many men and women right up to the final gates. Taught them to say goodbye, to release their hold on life without anger or resentment. She was proud of this great talent of hers, her art.

"And the way you invent things. Where did you get such an imagination? Not from me, that's for sure."

I translate for myself: there's no resemblance, she means. No resemblance whatsoever to what went on there.

"And you know what else I remembered?" She laughs softly to herself. "While you were reading, I remembered how you used to make things up when you were little. You were such a fibber . . ."

When she says that, the shameful coil of dishonesty stretches out from the depths of my stomach to my tear ducts, and for a minute I delight in it, and think of Melanie, and how she is slowly but surely redeeming me, even from that.

"The bottom line is that I'm a person without a drop of imagination. That father of yours, too, I don't remember imagination being his strong suit."

Perhaps because of what she said before about lying, or just because of the unbearable contact that had been created inside me between her and Melanie, I pounce on her: "Did you ever think it might be something I didn't get from anyone? Maybe it happens to be something private of my own?"

"That really is what I think." She surprises me by circumventing the provocation, refusing to charge into our normal catfight. "I've been, you know, looking at you, since you came here the day before yesterday. I look at you and I think, That's it, I'm not in pain anymore, the birth is over."

"It's about time," I reply briskly. "Thirty-five years in the delivery room is certainly long enough." I stab at her some more and flash her a broad grin, but we both sense that I am suddenly talking like a character in a movie where the lip sync has gone wrong.

"The birth is over," she says.

She's different, I realize. She's different from the woman I knew, and not just because of the disease. There's something else about her, and I don't know what it is, and it annoys me and jolts my foot mercilessly.

She perks up. "What's the matter, what did you see?"

"What, nothing," I mumble, and she anxiously digs into my eyes.

"No, just now, when you looked—what did you see?"

We stare at each other for a minute. Scanning and being scanned without pity. Making sure neither one of us has used the forbidden weapon.

An hour later, when it's already obvious that the boy won't show up, she begins to calm down and even work it into a good story for anyone who may one day show an interest in her memoirs ("And then he says to me, I would really like you to help my son be . . ." No, wait a minute, how exactly had he put it? And the little pang of remorse comes, biting and familiar—shit, there goes another anecdote). She hears a gentle knock on the door and there he is, standing in the doorway, tall and thin, and Nili thinks, It can't be, his father isn't his father. *Egyptian prince* pops into her mind, and even the faint hint of a mustache doesn't give his face a stupid look—not that of his father or that of youth. He stands looking down, and because of his short black hair he somehow looks older than he is, and slightly gloomy.

"My dad said you'd give me something."

A closed, coiled voice that reminds her of her Rotem, who also recently adopted a nasal way of talking, as if to block off yet another opening to the outside. Nili stares and doesn't know what to do with him. She folds her arms in front, then behind, and he doesn't budge, letting her review him, and for a minute she is led astray by his limp arms and lowered head. He is so loose that there must be defiance in him. Yes, just like Rotem, who seems to enjoy projecting defiance from her bulky body. "*What a bummer,*" she always seems to be taunting, "*the yogini's daughter is a fish out of water.*" But at the same time her other senses are alerted, the more delicate ones. Her skin first begins to absorb his extraordinary heat—maybe he's ill, she thinks—and then she actually bangs into the thin, transparent wall that surrounds him, thrusting and deterring. At that moment something within him lunges at her, and Nili freezes, her nostrils turn black, and she inhales with a deep, animal concentration: hunger. Undoubtedly. The hunger of an orphan. She recognizes it, an old friend, and it's strong with him, and tyrannical like passion, and much older than his age. If it even has an age, that hunger, she thinks, and her mouth becomes suddenly dry. What's going on here? Who is he?

He still doesn't say a word, only shrinks a little when she approaches him with her hands held up with a dreamy motion. She slowly waves them in front of his face and around his shoulders and chest, then pulls back at once, amazed and also pained; it can't be, she thinks as she folds in her singed fingers. But it's a fact, you sensed it. She distractedly takes a few steps back. She feels as if her knees will give in, and she looks at him again from the side: just a fifteen-

and-a-half-year-old kid, wearing long pants—who wears pants in this heat wave?—and black shoes. Shoes? Here?

She makes an effort to smile. "Come on, please come in."

He walks in obediently, stiffly, with shoulders hunched up high. Even so, he is extremely handsome, she thinks as she looks with sweet shock at his sculpted nape. She shuts the door behind him, then leans against it and takes a deep breath: what now, what to do. He takes a few more steps, as if being pulled inside, and stops only when he's standing on the little Peruvian rug she brought with her, spread out exactly on her spot in the room. Then he turns his body a little, unaware, with the naturalness of a sunflower, and stands facing the high little window from which—if you stand on a chair—you can see a stripe of sea, and which is her spring of life and energy here. She watches his motions, cautious and surprised: how does he know? She decides he is a hunchback, like many adolescents, especially the tall ones—lots of pressure between the shoulder blades, weak knees, all the weight on the lower back. But those last three or four steps were completely different. He truly slid inside, and there was something soft, almost snakelike, in the flow of his limbs, but as soon as he stopped, he stiffened again and his shoulders crept up.

A dryness takes hold of her throat. "Um . . . what's your name?"

"Kobi."

"I'm Nili. Your father—did he tell you what I do?"

"Yoga."

"Do you know what yoga is?"

"No."

"And you want to learn yoga?"

"Whatever." He shrugs his shoulders, thrusting his neck down between them. "My dad, he said that I, that you'd give me . . ."

During those moments, with the uproar inside her, she thinks yoga might actually be very good for him. It might straighten his posture, for example, and increase his self-confidence, and even create a place for him that would be completely free of his father, a space of his own. She briefly considers that perhaps it's time she came up with new, fresher names for her usual formulas, the class mantras. She notices that he still has not looked at her since coming in, he just stands there with his dark eyes, tight and unbelonging, as if someone had played a magic trick on him, uprooting him from his natural place and throwing him into a forsaken land. At once she feels sad and insipid, over him being forced to come here by his father, and over herself having to be here in a bare and ugly room, with a strange boy, instead of spending the last week of summer vacation with the girls. But she pulls herself together and checks to see whether those vivid, confusing breezes are still swirling around him: there is nothing. Gone, as if a switch was turned off in him, as if they never existed.

She stretches up tall, sucking strength from the earth. There must have been some trickery here, maybe she herself caused it by being so tense about his coming. Yes, it must be just her and her imagination, and her infantile desires. She massages the joints of her fingers, cracks her knuckles, goes back to being a devoted craftsman preparing his tools; she doesn't even allow herself to revisit the strange moments when he had first entered the room, when she felt a sense of rejuvenation, because it was the hunger she had sensed in him that had brought back long-forgotten things in her. Strange, that hunger which for years had led her astray like a junkie, misguiding her toward any pair of open arms. Only recently—maybe she was getting old, maybe the fire was dying out—had the needy hunger, like a deceitful charmer, begun to loosen its grip on her a little. Where are you, my darling? she wondered, laughing to herself sadly.

"Come on, then," she says to the boy with forced cheer in her voice. "Let's find out if you can be a yogi."

"Wow," she says, and tries to raise herself up a little in bed. "I didn't imagine it would be so . . ."

"So what?" I shout. I have to get up, walk around, do something with my hands.

She sighs. "So . . . so uncomfortable, this pillow."

I rearrange the pillow again. "Improve" is the word, and I have another chance here to experience her with my own hands, but that's not what I seem to be doing, because once again I lament the special smell she has lost, a mixture of orange and jasmine and health, and she feels it, of course, and sees my face, and again I have improved nothing. Her few hairs are fine and fragile; for some reason they are drawn to my hand, and that tiny movement confuses me. What do they want from me, they must not have heard about me yet. Soft baby hairs, seemingly asking to be caressed. I stare at them and collapse on the chair in front of her, suddenly exhausted and emptied, and she too looks even sicker, as if a small private illness is emerging within the large disease. I feel as if it is only now becoming clear to both of us what we've gotten ourselves into and what is awaiting us.

"It's so true what you wrote about that hunger," she says later. "But I keep asking myself how you know."

"How I know what?" I tense up, unsure whether to laugh or cry.

She doesn't answer. I don't ask. It hits me again, how little she knows me. Or is even capable of knowing. On the other hand, I remind myself, I could see that as an accomplishment—more than an accomplishment, a little life's work. She looks at me and I at her, and suddenly, in silence, and with no demarcation of time, as if eighteen years have not gone by, the fat and troubled girl I was comes home and finds her sitting in the kitchen with her robe half open, with eyes completely dead, saying with a stony face, "Listen, Rotem, something has happened."

"You'd better not have taken any pity on me in the story," she says immediately. "I'll know right away if you did."

They start with some light stretching, gently bending knees into stomach, side twists, lengthening arms and legs. But a moment later she stops, remembering something. She sits him down. She tells him who her teachers were, where she comes from, where she studied. She listens to her own voice, to the gentle, prolonged names that erupt from her mouth. Names of teachers, regions, ashrams. Once, she used to begin every first class with a new student this way, weaving him into her dynasty. Now she hears the accumulations of her stress in the joints of the soft sounds, and looks nervously into the boy's eyes to see if he noticed anything. "Stand up," she says, and corrects the way he stands. She shows him how to make proper transitions from one position to another, and thinks, What's come over me? Why did I tell him about them? What does he care about them? She harshly admonishes herself: In fact, what do I care about them? What do all those names have to do with what I'm doing here? And how much longer can I keep brandishing these expired letters of reference?

There is a strange quiet in the room. Now she teaches with cautious restraint, not her usual way, and he cooperates unenthusiastically, as if caught in some forced experiment. The standing poses tire him out, and the twisting poses embarrass him, and every so often he loses concentration and starts to daydream. But when she asks if he wants to stop, he shrugs his shoulders and says, in that same dim, obstructed voice, that they can go on a little longer.

Nili grows impatient. Twice she glances at the alarm clock next to the sink, and both times he notices it. It's not just another usual-bad-class. There's something else here, something troubling, like a long gaze at an unfocused photograph. Everything is clumsy, his long, stiff pants prevent him from moving, he flinches at every touch of hers, and every time she talks about his body—when she describes for him, for example, how his thigh muscles stretch when he bends over—he giggles embarrassedly and disconnects again. "You're not here," she scolds him. "Where are you?" He doesn't answer, and she feels as if she's preventing him from concentrating on something, and resents him for the disappointment he caused her after what he had ostensibly promised when he came into the room. She is amazed that she could have been so mistaken about him, and at the pathetic longing that had inflamed her imagination and made her almost believe.

Again and again she jabs herself with that choice quote from Swami . . . oh, come on, what the hell is his name, with the names it's getting worst of all . . . "The dog that sucks a dry bone imagines that the blood oozing from its mouth is coming from the bone," or something like that. But when the hour is finally up, to her surprise, he asks with a muffled mumble if he can come again. Nili hesitates for a moment, for an instant, but of course cannot withstand the shrinking pain in his eyes, and more than that—the speed with which he is trained to hide that pain. She says, "Sure, why not? Come tomorrow, I'm here all the time." He looks at the floor and asks if it can be today, now. And Nili almost shouts, "Already? Where's the fire?" But again, she gives in to his expression, perhaps to the strange obligation she feels to arm him with something to use against his father.

It's dark outside now. Behind my back, beyond a heavy door, the guest room stretches out, massive and dim, padded with thick rugs, crowded with sculptures and heavy, ornate furniture. It's certainly the most opulent house she's ever lived in, and the moment I came in I knew: this house cannot revive her. I get up and close the electric blinds, and turn on the little iron lamp. It's sculpted in the shape of a man and woman embracing, their faces turned to the light, and I get stuck there for a minute. Where does she find the strength to stay so quiet, I wonder. How can she not say a word about the story? About the boy in my story. It is, after all, the first time he has had a voice between us. The first time he's talking, saying things. I ask myself whether she's even capable of grasping what it means to me to give him a voice and words. And a body. The body was the hardest. I tried all sorts of bodies and none of them was right. For weeks I walked around London looking for a body that would be right for him, and when I found one I started to vomit. I hadn't been that sick even in my worst times. For days and nights I wrote and vomited, and thought of how my body wasn't willing to let me give him a body. And one so beautiful, at that.

"And you gave yourself two sisters," she says. She must have only just realized.

"Yes, congratulations to us!"

She used to burst out laughing at every silly joke I made. It was the easiest thing in the world to make her laugh, like making a little girl giggle. In elevators with strangers or during grave discussions with my teachers, one quiet word of mine was enough to send her into uncontrollable fits of laughter. On Passover seder nights at Leora's she was completely taken hostage by me, begging with terrified looks for me not to use my influence over her. Now it was as if I'd touched a patch of dead skin, with no nerves or sensations.

"Me, I don't know from writing," she says in the slightly stammering talk, serious and strange, which the disease has enforced on her. "But I'm curious, why did you think you needed to?"

"I just . . . I don't know. The pair of them just leaped onto the page, like two peas in a pod: Inbal and Eden."

Her head moves slowly. Her eyes pierce me, a little dim and colorless, but not letting up.

"I really don't know." I titter, stupidly embarrassed. "Maybe I also thought . . ."

"What." Now, with the last of her strength, she's not always able to bend her words into questions.

I can tell I won't get out of this easily, so I try to reconstruct what really happened. "I guess I thought I needed another two around me. To be with me. Picture it"—I try to wake her up, to find some warmth in her—"you and me, and another two. Another two the whole time. Why not?"

"Poor things," she groans. It may only be a joke, but it still shocks me. The unwritten rule says only I am allowed to say things like that about us.

The second class goes exactly like the first one, and Nili makes a note to herself that the young man is somehow managing to set her off-balance. It's not clear how—he's not doing anything to annoy her intentionally, but he seems to be enveloping himself intensely in a coat of boredom and dreariness. Yet still not willing to give up. With a stiff and ungraceful kind of determination he attempts the exercises and poses she suggests, slowly shifting from one to the next, as if trying on shoes in a store, and every so often he grabs hold of one of them and sinks into a particular pose for several moments, closing his eyes in a way that prompts in her the crazy thought that maybe he is trying to remember something through this. But then, all at once, he turns off and covers himself again with his obtuseness.

Toward the end of the hour she explains to him about the benefits of blood flowing to the brain, and to demonstrate, she does a handstand. In fact, she does this to relax herself as well, and at the same time she tells him her favorite story, the one about Nehru—or was it Gandhi? Suddenly even the most secure facts are undermined, the anecdotes she's recited thousands of times, even they roll down with rapid erosion, sending cracks up and down her consciousness. Nehru, she decides, I'm sure it was Nehru. She used to have some kind of code for remembering it. His baldness, because of the headstands. But Gandhi was bald too. Oh dear.

"While he was in prison, he did headstands and handstands every day, because he discovered that those poses filled him with a sense of inner freedom." Even though her muscles are engaged, her words have a soft, prolonged sound. From her upside-down position she can see his expression change, as if someone had turned on a dusty lamp, and he asks if he can do it too.

Nili stands up on her feet again. A slight tension pulls through her body. "A handstand isn't as easy as it looks," she explains, "and it's usually best to build up to it after a year or two of practice. I suggest that . . ." But he isn't listening to her, he just asks if he can try, and his face is suddenly focused and intense. She spreads her hands out and doesn't know what to say. She has bad experience with newbies doing handstands, most of them don't have the courage to really kick up, they falter with one leg in the air and fall, or their hands give way, and others are so afraid that they toss their legs up wildly—one of them broke her nose once. But the boy, Kobi, repeats his request a second time, and Nili gives in. She leans against the wall and prepares to catch his legs, ready to have her face kicked in, and knows that she deserves anything she gets. She is amazed to see him lightly and gracefully propel his left leg up, then add the right leg, and reach her outstretched arms with the precision of an acrobat or a dancer.

He stands that way for a few seconds. She didn't believe he'd be capable of that, and even when his arms start shaking, he doesn't give up, seems to be waiting for the borderline to be clearly marked between his weak body and his willpower, and only then does he come down with precise motions, his legs straight and his feet held together. He sprawls on the floor between her legs, his forehead resting on his hands, and Nili quickly massages his back between the shoulder blades, among the vertebrae, to dissipate the strain. This time he doesn't flinch at her touch; she thinks he even enjoys it. But when he doesn't move for several more minutes, she becomes afraid for some reason and turns him over sharply and sees his eyes looking at her, clear and completely open, pleading.

"For what exactly?" Leora demands to know on the phone, refusing to be impressed by Nili's interpretations. "I have no idea," Nili mumbles, and immediately gathers into herself—why the hell did I tell her, why her of all people, why don't I ever learn?—"but it was as if he was asking me for something, I mean"—she gulps, oh God, we're not going to go through our ritual dance again—"something he can't ask for explicitly?"

Leora—three years her senior, her sister, and from the age of seven also her mother, and from the age of forty-two, because of a miserable embroilment with the bank, also a kind of forced custodian in financial matters—stretches out her gaunt, laconic body. "And the massages, what about those? Did you get to that?"

"No, no." Nili pulls back, as if something had been desecrated. "Look, a second after he came in I completely forgot that that's what . . . No, I'm really just teaching him yoga." She laughs with surprise, but then turns very serious. "In fact, I'm just reminding him."

"Ni-li," Leora sighs, and Nili can almost sense her sister leaning over her like an evil teacher waking up a snoozing student.

Nili unconsciously hunches her shoulders, puts a hand over her wide, expressive mouth. The large face, the freckled lioness face, becomes lost for a moment. "Lilush, what did you ask?"

I lower the page a little and look at her. She lies with open eyes, staring at the ceiling. "Does it bother you that I wrote about her like that?"

"No."

"No? I thought—I was sure you would actually—"

She turns her head with great effort and looks at me, surprised. "I don't care with Leora."

"Every time I tried to change the names," I explain to her, angry at myself for needing to justify my decision, "it somehow sounded like a lie to me, but maybe in the final draft I'll change them. I don't know."

"Don't change." She doesn't suggest. She orders. I've never heard that tone from her. She shuts her eyes painfully, or weakly. "Everything should be like in life."

Like in life?! I can barely prevent myself from shouting; for the last two months I've been begging her to tell me something, to give me a hint, a direction.

She hears my silences very clearly. With them she always had a good flow of communication. She purses her lips and sticks them out. I've noticed she has a new expression now, an indescribably irritating one. An air of rebellion that is at once childish and elderly. She didn't use to be like that with me. So assertive. And callous and unreasoning. Unhesitatingly employing the exclusive entitlement awarded to those facing death.

She takes hold of his shoulders and helps him up, and asks hesitantly if he'd ever done a handstand before. He says he hadn't.

"And what did you feel now when you did it?"

He stammers. "I don't know. Everything was upside down, I saw everything upside down . . ."

"And at school you never did it?"

"I'm not in school."

"Then where are you?"

"At boarding school." He buries his voice again, evading her.

"Boarding school? Which one?"

"Hessedavraham."

"What did you say?"

"Hessed Avraham."

"A religious school?"

"Yes."

"Are you religious?"

"No."

"Oh." She falls quiet, trying to digest. Too much information flowing at once. "Wait, but don't you have P.E. at the boarding school?"

"Yeah, but I cut class."

"I can't hear you, what did you say?"

"I said I skip class."

"Why do you skip class?"

He shifts his weight from one foot to the other. "I don't . . . I don't really like gym . . ." He stands tensed, without looking at her.

She shakes herself off and says, "You know what, let's try and repeat the things we did before, and we'll see how it goes."

She sits him on the mat with his legs stretched forward, and asks him to try to reach up and bring his whole body, length and width, over his legs. He slowly leans and stretches his arms, inch by inch, and his fingers finally touch his toes. Then there is quiet. Nili, in a restrained voice, asks him to try to stay like that for one moment longer, despite the prickling she senses in his shoulders and his short hamstrings. He stays, lingering inside the pain for a long time, much longer than she thought he'd be able to, until she feels, together with him, the pain slowly melting and disappearing, and she comes and sits next to him until its final echoes are gone.

"What do you think, maybe you can try a shoulder stand now?" In the last class he kept falling, and once he even tumbled backwards and hit himself. Now he lies on his back, concentrating on his body, and then—calves, knees, thighs—lifts easily as if something is pulling him up, and positions himself upright and precise, a vertical human line, and his hands don't slide down as they support his back. They are both quiet, both perusing him silently, and after nine breaths in that position she suggests he try lowering his left leg into a bridge pose. "Be careful," she says, "it's a powerful pose." She supports his back with her hand, but there is no need. He descends slowly, with an almost perfect motion, then brings his right leg down too and stays arched like that, his face with an expression of deep contemplation.

That is when their first lesson really starts, because now he's there, in full, responding with enthusiastic shyness to what she has to offer him, and even though he does not utter a word or smile even once, she feels his limbs learning to delight in their movements, stretching and moving and expanding like unborn chicks filling their shells. Time after time she reminds herself not to rush so much with him, he's a complete novice, be careful, tomorrow he won't be able to wiggle a finger, he'll be in so much pain. But she can't resist his innocent enthusiasm and her growing feeling that in each of his motions and twists he seems to be trying to reach deeper inside and massage within himself some hidden, tightly held kernel. That feeling also sends warm ripples through her own body, which become broader and broader until they touch the pleasurable spot that has no name in any language, deep down inside, on the border between tickling and longing. What's amazing, she thinks, is how he seems to be remembering something through his body alone. She also notices how supple he is, as if he'd been exercising his whole life, but he assures her, "No, I hate exercising." She decides not to push him for now—maybe later it will turn out that he does do some kind of sport or dance—no way he's a dancer, she laughs, you saw how he walks, completely frozen like a zombie. But what else could explain that smooth, musical movement, as if an entire secret life is preserved inside him, on ice. She keeps trying to understand what had occurred that had suddenly brought on the change; she cannot identify it, but every time she thinks he's about to slip through her fingers, she has him stand on his hands again, and he remembers at once, and they are carried away again, and the room fills with their breath, because she too has started working alongside him without even noticing. It's hard for her to resist, her body moves of its own accord, as if to a musical beat; it's been ages since something like this happened to her, here or anywhere. And time after time she scolds herself for going too far, for not protecting him. This is not yoga, she knows, this is not the way you studied, not how you taught, but she's a little intoxicated by now—no wonder, such sharp happiness on an empty stomach. With boundless passion she consumes the moments and tries to engrave them on her memory like a surprising answer she had found in a dream, a decisive and final resolution to an argument she thought she had lost long ago, and soon she will wake up and forget everything.

She inhales the bold new scent of his body, and at the same moment he—as if sensing each one of her sensations and every fragment of a thought—mumbles, "Sorry."

"Sorry for what?" she asks.

"For me, you know, sweating."

She is moved. "No, don't apologize, sweat is our body's oil, our body's good oil." And even that sentence, which she's said thousands of times to her students over two decades of teaching, now sounds light and novel to her. "Rub it hard, spread it all over your skin, enjoy it, delight in it, there simply is no better smell than the smell of our sweat."

He looks at her, confused, and hesitantly rubs the sweat on his arms into his skin. For a fleeting instant his face changes, becomes soft and exposed, and weak, and Nili sees for the first time the sadness concealed in the depth of his eyes, and thinks, Even yoga can't reach that deep. She stands opposite him with her legs spread wide, generously rubbing herself, and her wide face slowly opens up, expanding like a huge hot-air balloon that has been crumpled up in a warehouse all winter. Be careful, she says to herself. This is not a game, give him only what he needs, remember what we said, life or death.

"That hunger," she remembers again when I stop for a moment to breathe. "Of the orphans," she reminds me. Her thoughts, as usual, sail this way and that along different currents. I wonder what she's even heard during the last half hour, since I threw him down between us. "It's so true what you said there, how you described it." Her eyes dig into me, begging me to tell her how I know, to exonerate her from the suspicion that it's from her.

"Sometimes"—I wriggle—"you can even feel orphaned by yourself, can't you?"

"You?" She sounds surprised. "You were always so strong, never needed anyone. Even when you were a kid, I was jealous of you for that."

Silent and restrained, I suck in all the air the room has to offer. It surprises me how, still, every miss of hers hammers another nail into me. Then I ask her in no uncertain terms not to try and make any more sketches of my character. "My perverse character," I add with a sweet smile. I could have said "reprehensible" or "depraved." I could have said nothing. In "perverse" there is something different, something condescending, status-setting, that slices the air between us.

"We're not going to fight now, Rotem."

"Why would we?"

I look through the pages. Wait for it to sink in a little. I leaf back a few pages after all, to the place where I mentioned that hunger, which for years had led her astray like a junkie. On the plane coming here, I had erased the words that came next: "and had thrown her repeatedly into the rows of people who hit and used and abused her." Why did I erase them? I suppose I didn't want to hurt her too much. But why did I really erase them? Perhaps it occurred to me that I had stood there in those rows myself, more than once. And that it had led her to me, among other people. My mother's orphan hunger.

At four in the afternoon he suddenly remembers that his dad wanted him to come and cheer him on in the backgammon championship, and Nili goes up to her room, and in the shower she thanks God for not forgetting her even in this remote dump, and for sending her another gift from His lost-and-found collection; she prays that He will keep sending them to her, and that she will keep learning and growing and becoming more bountiful.

Then, to dry off, she walks around her little room in the nude, reflected in the closet door mirror and the mirror on the wall. It is her little rebellion against Rotem, who follows her from room to room when she walks around at home like this, closing the blinds and drapes as she goes, with the fanaticism and indignation of a harem eunuch. Nili stops, sits down with a sigh, and dials home, and hears the forty-nine seconds of violent music which Rotem recorded on the answering machine and her hostile, barking voice: "Leave a message if you must, but between you and me, you're better off managing on your own." She tries to plan out what to say and how not to be annoying and not to make a mistake that would force her to drive home to Rishon immediately and get there to erase the message before it's played. She's so busy thinking and licking her lips that she doesn't notice the beep, and then she is propelled from inside and says with a tense, reprimanding voice, "Roti? Roti, honey? Are you there? Girls? It's me, Mom. I hope everything's okay at home, that you're getting along and having fun on your vacation . . ." The words sound like gravel to her. Lines out of a phrase book for tourists. She has a feeling—no, she *knows*—that Rotem is there by the phone, listening to her with her mocking smile. She can see the mouth, slightly swollen with bitterness, peeking out between the curtains of long hair, lying in wait for her slightest slip, even a minor mistake in her Hebrew. The mouth of a supreme-court judge, Nili thinks, and her hand reaches out to smooth it over, to soften its tiny crevices and angles, and Rotem pulls back—God forbid she should touch her: there must be no contact between bodies. "Listen, sweeties, I have to run now, I have a ton of work here, but I'll call tomorrow and we'll talk, and on Friday I'll be home. It's only a few more days, easy as pie, and on Saturday we'll have a wild time." She finishes quickly, relieved, and puts on a new white cotton shirt, smooths both hands over her bust and stomach and legs, as if erasing the creases of her soul, ironing herself and being reborn. The two of them, he and she, get back to the yoga room at exactly the same time. They meet at the door twenty-five minutes before the time they had arranged, and she sees that he's changed into shorts and an orange T-shirt that dances in his charcoal eyes, and he's wearing flip-flops that expose long, graceful toes. Again the words "Egyptian prince" twinkle inside her. When she shuts the door behind them, she asks matter-of-factly why he wore long pants up till now in this heat.

He chuckles sharply and smoothly. "Because of my dad, it gets on his nerves."

They keep working, an hour-long class and a fifteen-minute break, and when evening falls, they go on without stopping, instead diving into a long relaxation after their prolonged effort, lying beside each other on their mats, looking at the ceiling, hazing over a little together.

"And don't you get tired out?" asks Leora, who calls again at eleven that night, worried after their first conversation.

"Tired out? But I'm recharging the whole time! I'm full of energy, I don't even think I'll be able to fall asleep tonight."

Leora, the sandbag of this hot-air balloon for the past forty-seven years, squints her eyes suspiciously. "Now concentrate," she says, as she employs the deft movements of a sidewalk cardsharp to fold the dozens of freshly laundered socks and underwear—Dovik's and Ofer's and Ronnie's and Shachar's—"and try to explain to me, without using any Sanskrit or any cauliflower, what his story is."

"That's the thing—I have no idea." Nili spreads her fingers out helplessly. "But he just *knows*, he knows his body from inside. How can I explain it to you? It's like his spirit can easily reach any part of him . . ." Her voice trails off. "Cauliflower" was the name Leora had given, years ago, to all of Nili's "spiritual dealings," and even Nili herself had become resigned to it, with a forced sense of self-derision. "And what's interesting, Lilush, is that the strengthening poses—all those push-ups and sit-ups and all that stuff that guys usually do like crazy and mess up their backs for the rest of their lives? All that's not for him, and the truth is that he's really weak for a boy of his age. He's a real weakling"—*as if he's deliberately let his body atrophy*, a strange, chilling thought enters her mind—"but he has such flexibility, such flow, it's amazing, a kind of rejoicing of the body. I rarely find such a thing even in people who have been doing yoga for ten years." (There's that voice, Leora thinks, and feels a stinging sensation all over, that veiled voice.) "But it's not just the body with him, see? It's from a completely different place with him, it's as if he"—and she stops, and through all the mountains that separate them she gives Leora a look that she can aim only at her sister, a look that seems not to have matured even a day since the age of seven, the stubborn and rebellious look of a little girl who had a hand placed over her mouth so she'd finally stop talking nonsense, but her eyes are very bright, shooting sparks of words. Then suddenly, in complete opposition to the rules of the dance, she stops herself, and with a cunning that she's very proud of, she sighs. "You know what, never mind. Maybe it really is all in my head. Tell me, Lilush, how are the kids?"

I glance sideways at her and see a smile. A full smile. The old Nili. And at once I become filled with pathetic and irreparable pride. It's unclear to me exactly what I'm proud of. Of the fact that she thinks I've finally written a good piece? About inserting a little revenge against Leora on her behalf? I don't know. I only know that it's not really my pride, it's her pride in me, which is almost the real thing, and I quickly bury my secondhand pride deep down, as deep as possible, with the other emergency supplies I've never used. The shelves there are laden with sealed jars full of preserved pride (and joy, and enthusiasm, and the purpose of life, and various other delicacies), and she mustn't know of them, and I mustn't either. Maybe one day, I don't know, maybe after, or when it's easier. Meaning never.

With closed eyes, she immediately responds to my molecular changes. "What can I say, I never thought I'd have a writer daughter."

There is tenderness in her voice, and I am quick to pounce on her. Don't be a bitch, I command myself, let her have her moment of pride. But there is provincial, illiterate satisfaction in her voice. It seems to be rising and arching toward me, and a large fleshy tongue pokes around inside me, searching for a crack. And the flames of age fifteen, the grumble in my stomach that calls out immediately: Stop her now! It doesn't matter what she wants, stop whatever you can! Annihilate the greasy waves of high tide and longing with a look or a comment or a scornful silence! For a long moment I actually fight myself, using both hands to secure my soul as it arches and trembles in reaction to that voice, to the price it exacts, even during phone calls to London—yes, that far away—when in mid-sentence she would stop, focus inward, and apparently incapable of restraining herself, she would emerge with the pronouncement, like some gullible prophet, with that hearty, fluttering voice: "Sweetie pie, you're getting your period soon." I would lose my temper, scream at her to stop pushing her way into my soul and get the hell out of my womb, and besides, it's not even my day—and of course, an hour later, like clockwork . . .

"You know," I say to my complete surprise—and it's clear to me that what I courageously sealed off in one place has immediately started leaking from another—"you never said anything to me about that book of mine that came out, the one I wrote, the *Troubled Tourist* one."

She doesn't answer. I decide to leave it and move on. But what about the cigarettes, I ask myself, how do I get through this night without a cigarette? "I asked you to read it," I remind her, knowing exactly how I sound.

She beats me off, of course, pouting. "But I told you. Don't you remember I told you?"

I do. I don't. What difference does it make? Why am I picking on her?

"I tried, Rotem, twice even. I just didn't get it. I don't . . . What can I tell you. I'm too old for that putz-modernist style."

"That's not exactly it, but never mind now. Let's go on."

"I felt," she sighs, "I felt as if . . . as if you didn't want me to understand." Then she corrects herself: "As if you wanted me not to understand."

I laugh. "I wanted you not to—? But why would I . . ." I fall silent, amazed. What is she talking about anyway. In the blink of an eye we both inhale and swell up. All the sighs of the past in our sails. I remember that later on, soon, there is a sentence that describes a ridiculous and slightly distorted face of hers, a sock-puppet face, and I wonder whether I should skip it, save her from it now, and more than anything, I think of her reading my book, I see her struggling with it line after line, I see the wrinkle deepening between her eyes.

Once she looked like Simone Signoret. People would come up to her on the street and tell her that. Now her large bald head moves slowly on the pillow and turns to me. "Rotem, enough. You can't go backwards to fix things."

But a friend of mine who works at the Steimatsky's branch in Rishon told me that when the book came out, Nili would go into the store twice a day, stealthily, with her transparent slyness, and make sure two copies were on the display tables, so they'd stand out.

———

His snickering when he had said "It gets on my dad's nerves" had distressed her. It had made him sound like his father, with his splinters of malice and pettiness. And so, toward the end of the class, she asks him to stand across from her and stretch his arms out to the sides. "Really open up," she urges him, and lifts his arms higher, higher. "Imagine you're yawning with your armpits. Now close your eyes. Now smile."

His eyes shoot open. "What for?"

"I want you to smile. What do you care? Just so you'll see what a smile does to us inside."

"But how, just like that?"

"Yeah. What's the big deal? Even just the beginning of a smile. See what happens."

He looks at her worried, almost suspicious. "I can't do it just like that, without . . ."

They stare at each other for a moment, their looks casting about over each other and pulling back like strangers, and Nili thinks sometimes he's a bit thick. "Maybe think about something funny, like something funny that happened to you." Then she grows alarmed. "You have had at least one funny experience in your life, haven't you?"

"Sure, what do you mean? Loads."

"Well, then."

"But I can't laugh at the same thing twice."

"I can laugh ten times at the same thing," she tosses out with clumsy cheerfulness. "But that's not saying much with me, I can also cry about the same thing ten times."

The joke, which isn't a joke at all, doesn't go down well, and even seems to cause him pain. Nili sees the slight tension in the shadow behind his eyes and falls quiet, and all at once what little they had starts to melt away. As he stands, his shoulders seem to hunch up of their own accord. She sees him getting further away, unattainable. Within the blink of an eye, he is a stranger, and she guesses that this instinct of foreignness is perhaps the essence of his life wisdom. For a long moment she freezes helplessly, and feels the pulsating of a scar that has reopened and rehealed in her countless times, in her abandoned, pained place, but then she shakes out of it, takes a deep breath, puts two long fingers in the sides of her mouth and pulls it out to the sides, rolls her eyes around rapidly, dances her eyebrows up and down, and flaps her ears charmingly.

He examines her, and his face widens in surprise, shock even. She sees his pupils darting around. A quick internal debate is occurring: Should I surrender to her or not? Can I believe in a woman who makes a fool of herself with such ease? Another long gaze, slightly confused, trying to resist her but being pulled toward her as she holds her clown face, and then he shuts his eyes, spreads his arms to the sides, dives into himself, and disappears. For a long time nothing happens, and Nili holds her expression, exaggerated, like a sock puppet stretched over a hand that's too fat. After an eternity—she has never failed at this little trick—a tiny smile sprouts at the corners of his lips, quivering a little, then increasing and opening up as if the smile is making itself laugh, delighting itself. His lips spread and his eyeballs flutter beneath his slender eyelids, and a tingle of pleasure rolls down from the back of Nili's neck to the edges of her buttocks.

"Well, what did you feel?" she asks when he opens his eyes.

"It's great!" He laughs and pulls his head up with a motion she had not yet seen and would not have expected in him, and his eyes narrow into cracks of glowing pleasure. "It's like I could see these kinds of little clouds inside my brain, with a purple color, I've never—"

But upon seeing the reflection of his joy in her eyes, he sharply purses his lips and stands quietly again. Very polite and differentiated. Well-groomed, with no frayed edges. For a moment he reminds her of herself at the bank after she realized she was overdrawn.

"To the wall, quickly!" she orders in a panic. "On your hands!"

"Rotem, I have a request."
"What?"

"Don't turn."

"What do you mean?"

"You keep turning away from me."

"Sorry." I straighten up embarrassedly, only now realizing that my whole body is stiff.

"I want to see your face."

"Oh, come on, what is there to see in my face?"

"That's not true." Veteran soldier that she is, she immediately enlists her last remaining strength to protect me from myself. "In fact, you've become much prettier since last time you were here. And with your short hair, you can finally see your face."

Before I can cancel out the compliment, ridicule her, make myself ugly, Melanie floats up and fills me. Nili must see it happen, because she turns her head away from me.

"But he has some issue with his stomach," she ponders out loud the next morning at six-fifteen, still half asleep, alarmed by the telephone ring that had unraveled her dream. "He has this kind of nervous tic, he keeps touching it, as if he's making sure it's there." As she talks, she knows she doesn't want to say any more, not to Leora. She doesn't want to let her get a foot in the door between them, but in the mornings she is always spineless. "And yesterday evening I showed him how I suck my stomach in and roll it"—and again she sees his eyes pulling back in fear at seeing the hard, vertical roll of her muscles, turning right and left along her stomach—"and he really started feeling ill."

Leora, at home in Jerusalem, standing opposite the open fridge, is putting together the day's shopping list as they talk; she absent-mindedly touches her little belly, the only drop of flaccidity in her body, and pulls it in, conquering a sigh.

"That's exactly it." Nili quickly picks up on the sigh, compelled to briefly wade with Leora into the same warm, sisterly blister of anguish. "Because with us, stomachs are always a big deal. I mean, ten

167

times a day I come across it at work"—she purposely emphasizes the word "work" to Leora—" 'My stomach is too big,' 'It sags,' 'It's like jelly' . . . And all the emotions, and the insults, and the pregnancies, and afterward, and empty stomachs. But for men? And a kid of his age?"

"Lovely." Leora throws her out of the niche she was trying to creep into. "So now you're his therapist too?"

Silence. Only her heavy respirations saw through the air. I can't take it anymore. I'm going to ask her about him, about the kid, the boy. He was no more than a boy. I take a deep breath. Her breathing stops. I ask her if they talked like that, or kind of like that, she and Leora.

"No," she says cautiously, closing but not locking. "Leora, she only knew at the end. Only after it all happened."

I try to understand what this new information says about my story. Or about my imagination. For some reason that possibility never entered my mind, and I think I'm actually relieved inside, re- lieved at having been so far off. As if a wing that was tied to me has been released.

"And let's say, the boy, in the story—does he even remind you in any way of . . . ?"

She thinks. It takes her a long time to think now. Why did I need to ask her that? So miserable of me, beggarly. For years I used to erase him, but he would crawl right back in. Changing shapes, changing states, appearing in the rain, in the earth, in a cup of black coffee, in tree trunks. And always stubborn, dark, with the desperation of some- one afraid to be forgotten. Later, when I discovered the potential he held, our relationship began to stabilize; I already knew where to find him whenever I needed a quick whirl, and at a more advanced stage I even knew how to produce him myself. A revolving door at the hard- ware store in Finchley that you had to spin through quickly a few times (it was the rapid motion coupled with the reflections); or bending down, supposedly to tie a shoelace, next to the exhaust pipe of a car whose engine has just been turned off (ten, fifteen quick breaths was all it took; European cars were preferable to American ones for this purpose). There was also an ivy bush in the garden of a church in Hendon, a huge one, diseased, maybe dead already, but still imperial and abundant with intricate dry branches that created an entire audience of almost-human faces. And there were these sores of a particular, terrible kind, which I saw only on the faces and arms of retarded kids taken out for walks on Primrose Hill; they would walk by, always at the same time, opposite the courier's office where I worked. And a few other hidden reconstruction methods that would take me out of context for a few seconds and let me gallop along a sideline with a sense of dizziness and rapid depletion, a unique and exclusive epileptic seizure, not entirely unpleasant, which I invented for myself—my own private high, my little creation, which grew more and more sophisticated every day.

"The boy. I'm getting used to him."

Getting used to? I try to understand what she's telling me. It doesn't sound good. It's not like getting Leora wrong. At once I'm desperately removed from reality again, as remote as I was back then, when it happened. I put the pages down on the coffee table nearby, take my glasses off, and rub my eyes, which are starting to sting. Again the familiar pinch, that the world is a kind of huge game of musical chairs and I can never get a chair, not even with her—especially not with her. I can already see so clearly that she's not even capable of entering my story. She's always just looking at it from the side, remembering what really happened and scorning my pathetic, limited imagination. She doesn't have to be a seer—she must tell herself after every piece of nonsense I utter—I gave up on that a long time ago, but at least a drop of intuition?

"When you read," she says in a slow, grating voice, lethargic from the disease and the medication, "I feel as if the things you're saying really happened."

My mouth is dry. My left foot is really going wild. I wait for details. Maybe she'll finally say something about what really happened.

She gestures for me to go on.

Sometimes, at the end of class, she puts him on a chair and teaches him the secret of correct sitting, how to lengthen his thigh muscles, his hands and calves, and she draws the root pulled down from his tailbone into the earth, sucking energy from it and discharging the toxins of body and soul into it. Then she kneels at his feet and checks to see if his long, brown bare feet are planted firmly on the ground. She plants them by pressing each toe separately. "Is this yoga too?" he asks, and she says it's her yoga, even though she's never sat a student as young as him on a chair in class, always on the floor, but perhaps of all the things she's teaching him, it will be the memory of this simple white plastic chair that he'll take with him when he leaves, she thinks. Like that man she read about once—she doesn't even try to remember where, no chance—who dreamed that he came to Paradise and was given a flower there, and when he awoke he was holding a flower. "The most important thing is to remember how to step properly," she says. "Spread your toes, hold on to the earth happily, delight in it with every step." She recites to him: "Death begins in the feet, that's where our self-neglect develops from, our surrender."

From one hour to the next, she starts to see his body from the inside, the colors of his different senses. His points of resistance, rough and dark. Thrills of amazement and happiness pass through him like rays of light, and they instantly ignite a spark in her. She opens her eyes, and he does too—perhaps he heard my eyelashes, or maybe he's just trained always to be on guard, she thinks—and she smiles her warm smile at him, the one she has recently been feeling on her face like the tattered grimace of a tired clown, a dried-up old Pollyanna. She asks what he'd like to do now, what he'd like to change, to fix, to learn.

"Whaddayoumean?" He raises his lovely eyebrows in wonder. "You can fix things with yoga?"

She smiles. "Of course you can. Yoga is—" Where to begin? she wonders. And how? We have so little time to be together, and anything I say will be superficial and cheap. She breathes deeply. "Yoga is a system, it's just a system that helps us increase our physical and spiritual strengths, and the connection between our soul and our—"

And she stops, because his pupils are lifting as if pulled by a string, and his eyes almost close with pleasure. Enchanted, she watches his fluttering eyelashes until his look returns.

"Say it again."

She says the words slowly, looks at his face with tense expectation: *open sesame*. And again she sees the magic work. Sensing an urge to bring it about again, she adds something else that used to hang on her studio wall in Jerusalem: "When my consciousness is clear and pure, reality will be precisely reflected in it." There were times when the meaning of that sentence was as real and lucid to her as a bodily sensation, as taste or scent. Now she feels only the bite of emptiness, but when she sounds the saying in his ears, word after word, she can feel his soil moistening. It's unbelievable, she thinks, and strains her brain to fish out something from her first teacher: "A mistaken thought is incorrect knowledge, which is not based on the shape of the thing." But this time he looks at her without any expression. There is a long and empty silence, and Nili becomes worried. "Do you understand what that means?"

"No. What's it mean?"

"I don't . . . Look, once, years ago . . ." She stops again, embarrassed, because even ten and twenty years ago, even when she recited it to her students, she didn't completely understand. In fact, it was always that way, not just where yoga was concerned. Always, when the air vibrates from the gong of a polished and determined sentence, or some hammered-out, echoing truism, Nili feels a kind of dull sting in her left temple, the singe of an already familiar insult, and she closes off and the words dissipate and float in her mind with a kind of weary surrender, turning into soft clouds of impressions that slowly evaporate. That's the way I take things in, everything with me is intuition, she explains to herself and to her loved ones, with a shrug of her shoulders. I'm a seer, not a knower . . .

"Listen, the truth is, I don't really go in for abstract things, and anyway, I'm not that great with theory," she bursts out with strange eagerness. "Or with facts, actually," she is somehow driven to add with a well-practiced, crooked little smile. "Facts somehow never really sink in with me. That's it, that's the situation." And she is quiet, amazed at herself.

Her confession confuses him. "But to teach yoga, don't you need to know these kinds of things? Quotes and all that?"

"Look," she says simply what she should have said instead of the whole speech, "when I do things, I understand. I understand through my body."

Almost before she's done speaking he gets up, hurries to the wall, and hurls himself on his hands, tossed like a luscious fruit ready to burst. He stands straight for one minute, then one more. His arms are already shaking, his forehead is wrinkled with effort, and he breathes laboriously, looking at her without seeing. Something catches her attention. The watch, which he forgot to take off. A clumsy old watch which he always wears the wrong way, so it covers the inside of his wrist, is now turned to her and showing the wrong time. Three hours fast.

He comes down one leg after the other and lies on the floor, relaxing. With his head between his hands he moans, "I want you to teach me, if there is such a thing in yoga, to make me not . . . like, how to not suffer from noise."

She whispers, "Explain to me a little. I think I understand, but—"

He straightens up. She already knows: as soon as she doesn't understand him, he loses his patience, immediately.

"There's noise the whole time, right? So how . . . how can you make it so you can, so in the noise—"

A little wave beats in her throat, still she checks carefully, he's only fifteen for God's sake—okay, and a half. "What noise exactly do you mean?" She remembers the quarries. "You live in a kind of noisy area, don't you?"

He gives her a look she'll never forget, a piercing look of disappointed rebuke. Almost desperate. She shrinks in. Stupid. What were you thinking? Wake up. Get with the picture.

She shakes it off. "You know what? We'll learn together. Sit on the mat, sit opposite me."

They both sit cross-legged. Erect. Nili shuts her eyes, focuses inside. "It's as if I have a place there, a quiet place, and I can reach it instantly, in any situation almost." Or at least I used to be able to, she thinks instantly. "Slowly but surely you'll also be able to find your place." She makes an effort to smile, and her hand pulls down an invisible thread opposite the center of his chest, and she can feel the thread trembling, can hear with her fingers the humming fluctuations in his body. She senses them constantly, as if there's another heart beating in him, but a distant, underground one. "And it's a matter of practice, years of practice, knowing where your quiet is located, and then you can get there from wherever you are, in the loudest noise, in the midst of filth and crudeness," she whispers, and her eyes are closed tight. "You can put yourself in there and be protected." She breathes slowly, the bitterness of the words seeping into her throat. What's left of that? Only talk, words, cauliflower. She doesn't even want to think of how many times she's really been able to go in and stay there since she left Jerusalem, since she was exiled from Jerusalem, from her beloved little apartment that was too expensive, from the students who stayed with her for years. From her glory days. Her hands tighten on her knees. Her fingers draw two zeros. All she had now was a tiny, insulting apartment in Rishon, and the misery of the girls, uprooted because of her, because of her criminal ineptness in managing her affairs. And more than anything, Rotem, the waste of Rotem, the hatred of Rotem, the terrible drawing Rotem hung in her room, which keeps presenting itself like a curse in almost all of Nili's contact with the world: *My family in the food chain.* For three years now, she's been running around with her yoga in a town where no one has even heard of it, haggling over every penny with treasurers of *moshavim* and community center directors. But he, Kobi, wants to know what it's like in there, when she's in her quiet place, and Nili shakes her head with closed eyes. What can she tell him? How can she describe her place that has become a den? What can she tell him of the little beast that lurks for her there?

Even so, again, as always, she closes her eyes, lifts her head a little, her face looks ready for a kiss, and to her surprise she is there in the blink of an eye, an unexpected and so attainable gift. And the place is vacant, waiting for her with a bright welcome, and she squeezes her eyelids and tightens, knowing that shortly the sharp little teeth will sink in—

Total silence. She breathes deeply, enveloped in a dense pink sensation. God, she thinks, and chokes up a little, where were you all this time? I almost lost you.

Only after a few minutes does she remember Kobi, and sadly forces herself to climb back into her pupils, and he is waiting, a little hurt at being left outside, but eager, like a man aboard a ship who sees the diver coming back up. "What's it like down there? What did you see?"

"I can't explain it with words." She smiles, refreshed, distributing herself around like the scent of peeled mandarins. "When you get there you'll know, you'll sense it yourself." And when she sees the disappointment on his face, she hurriedly adds, "But there's something that maybe you can feel: my hands get warmer when I'm there, a lot of energy builds up in them, sometimes my skin actually quivers. It truly does." She smiles as he purses his lips in amazement.

"Can I touch?" He hasn't asked to touch her until now; only she has touched him, carefully, correcting a pose, straightening a foot, and his skin always shrinks away a little, as if from a light electric shock, the skin of a child who wasn't touched enough.

"Of course, touch."

He reaches out and touches the edge of her open palm. He announces immediately: "I don't feel anything," and pulls his hand back.

"Give it a minute." She smiles, pressing his hand to hers, magnetizing inside, taking with her the touch of his marvelously soft fingers, and within a moment she becomes focused, brimming with warmth inside; long threads of glowing tenderness flow through her limbs, and she walks around inside her body, inside the beautiful city of Brahma, and she is full and generous with herself all the way to the edges of her fingers. "Here, feel now."

"Wow. Can I get that way too?"

"If you practice, it will be even stronger with you," she says gravely.

"Really? How do you know?" He giggles, and for a moment he exposes something childish, the sudden twittering of milk teeth.

"I know. See, that kind of thing I *do* know."

A phone rings in one of the distant rooms of the house. She blinks at me not to answer it. We sit and count the rings and guess who might be calling.

"No phone calls until we're done," she decrees.

"Maybe it's Walter?" His name tastes uncomfortable in my mouth.

"I told him not to call, and he won't."

Walter was the attaché for commercial affairs at the German embassy in Israel. At the end of his service here he had conducted a private little defection. He's a tall man, delicate and hesitant. A little frail for my taste, and somewhat short even by her standards. On top of everything else, he doesn't look you in the eye. He met her five years ago on the street and fell in love with her in an absolute Siegfried-like way; this was also, it later transpired, the first love of his life. They had one year of bliss. Then she got ill. She points out again and again that it was when she became ill that he began to love her even more. She finds it strange. "It's as if he loves my illness too," she says. "As if he would be willing to make a deal, you know, to actually be ill instead of me." And I know her voice and know what troubles her, and do not enter with her into the alliance she wants to create. But she can't let it go, looking askance at me: "Doesn't it strike you as an oddity?" I play innocent: "What's odd about it? He loves you. When you love someone it includes everything." "Even so," she murmurs, "what does he need this for?"

Silence. Something damp and murky in the air. I realize I'm sitting with my back to her again. Why am I drawn there like that, to the anger at her, over and over again, as to a yearned-for childhood memory that burns my throat? She sinks into herself too. I have no idea where she is, and for a minute I don't care either. I'm fighting against an ancient whirlwind, superfluous now, which still sucks me inside with glee. The thing is that she always knew how to protect herself from the torments of others.

People who know her wouldn't believe it, but she had built a fortress, and I had encountered it, really slammed into it. Sometimes crashed. It was like a transparent protection layer, spiritual of course, but very dense, ironclad, which surrounded her entirely; she would hunch behind it, and no thing or person was allowed to penetrate it. When I finally dared to ask, I was about twelve—just to think that I could once talk with her like that, just come to her and ask directly—and she explained that thanks to that defense, that barrier of hers, she could give of herself to more and more people, she could flow freely. Precisely because none of them could take any of the powers she held there. When I insisted, because that one time I did—I remember the vague and frightened sense of churning that rose from the bottom of my stomach, and how what she said suddenly congealed into a lump inside me, into words, into a verdict—she explained with total honesty, with her criminal innocence, that if she let anyone infiltrate it and take things from there, she would no longer be herself. And she wouldn't be pure, she added, and wouldn't be able to be the utterly clear vessel, the transparent conduit for the healing powers that passed through her.

I understood, and yet I didn't. How could I understand such a thing? She tried to explain. She told me about the ocean of nectar inside the heart. About the island made of precious stones. She said I also had a place like that inside me. I tried to feel it, but all I found was darkness. She went on talking and I saw her on her island like a round, perfect animal, a mythological circle-creature, smooth with closed eyes, sprawled in complete and eternal rest, with its tail in its mouth. But what will happen if I'm sick? I wanted to ask. What will happen if I need all your powers, even your powers *from there*? I didn't ask. One touch of the electrified fence was enough for me. And she, as usual, heard my silence, and instead of answering, she kept trying to teach me how to take care of myself, how not to let the sorrow of the world, or anything else, penetrate my private place. "Not even the love of your life," she used to emphasize again and again, and I had not a single soul in the world to love back then. "Even your most beloved love of all—don't let him in there." And then she would smile her most charming, tempting smile and say, "Don't even let me in there."

On the third day, at the end of an exhausting class during which she had tired him out with fifty-four consecutive "sun salutations," and after bringing him to the place where his brain simply emptied of all thoughts—and that is when it occurs, when she feels it spreading through him, throughout all of him, the shine, the quiet, the internal crystal—he lies on the mat, a pillow under his head and one beneath his knees, and she softly guides him to relaxation. In the silence that descends, she thinks it was worth coming to this awful hotel for six years, two weeks every year, and suffering the rudeness and the contempt and the ignorance, just so that she could improve him like this. And it's good for her too, she knows, to see him this way, opening up like a flower in her hands. Her voice sweetens with happiness and gratitude as she tells him about the soles of his feet relaxing, about his knees slowly sinking, about his hips loosening, his chest . . . "The body is so beautiful," she says with the newly found wonder she senses. "So good and so precious. Sweet, this body of ours is sweet." She whispers, "It gives us so much goodness and happiness if we're only good to it, if we only listen to it, because it is so wise. It always knows what we want before we know ourselves, and it knows what's really good for us." She relaxes, opens up. "If we only understand what it's trying to tell us, our precious body, if we only love it as it is, exactly as it is . . ."

The sound of gulping opens her eyes. His face is tensed like a tightly clenched fist. His shoulders are hunched up almost to his ears, and his legs twist and squeeze each other forcefully.

"What's the matter, Kobi?"

He opens his eyes. His look is dark, confused. "What? Why did you stop?"

"I thought you . . . Do you feel okay?"

"Yes, I don't know . . ." He gets up with a wild look. "Let's take a break. I'm hungry."

"Wait"—she hurries to the door after him, not willing for him to leave in this state. Not understanding what happened, she suspects herself, maybe when she surrendered to herself for a moment it went wrong.

But he's already rushing away, and when he reaches the hallway he starts running. She goes back and sits down. You're using him, the probes in her stomach tell her; you can't resist it, can you? From the minute he walked in here you've been using him, that's what you're doing, a piece of easy prey for your ravenous ego fell from the sky at your feet. Haven't you ever heard of "erasing the self"? Isn't that the essence of yoga? And what about canceling out individual will, pettiness, competition, endless settling of accounts with the world? Just look at how every cell in your body keeps shouting out *me me* . . . That's not true, she protests weakly, backed against an inner wall. But if she were to admit it, even a little . . . Why should she admit it, what is there to admit, goddammit, what crime has she committed here?

She gets up abruptly, extricates herself, and walks briskly around the room, pacing in truncated lines. "All these years," she mumbles to herself, and shakes her hands in front of her, "all these years, from the very first class, I always said I disagreed with yoga about this bit, and I said that I, personally, was not willing to erase myself for yoga. Didn't I say that all these years? And that yoga has to accept us as we are, with our stories and all our complications and our little screw-ups and our urges—our human story—did I or did I not say that?

"Because maybe according to the books and the theories, and according to everything you've heard until today, I may in fact not be teaching you yoga." She stops suddenly and announces with a soft voice to the empty walls, showering them with her warm, broad smile, her introductory smile: "But I'll certainly teach you my yoga. Yoga as I see it, as I believe in it." She keeps on talking calmly, in her saturated voice, linking her hands with humility and depositing all her little secrets, her hearty shortcomings. She will let them choose whether or not to accept her as she is, thus easily overcoming the evil voices of her colleagues, who always accused her of being a charlatan, an ignoramus, lacking any theoretical or philosophical basis. She summons up her goodness to come to her aid—her horn of plenty, which shuts up all the cowardly mouths. And she summons the dozens or even hundreds of admiring students to testify on her behalf, and the patients she has treated with infinitely enduring work, thousands of hours of exercises and poses and breaths and massages and guided imagery for a sprained ankle, a pulled muscle, blocked intestines, a broken heart. And the terminally ill, whom she compassionately and courageously accompanied to their deaths, who became more addicted to her than to sedatives and painkillers—to her voice, to the touch of her hands on their tortured bodies. There were those who wanted only her at their side during their final hours; one young woman, whom she treated in the last months of her life, begged her to adopt her son, a three-year-old. "Be a mother to him like you've been to me." She walks around the bare room for a long time, the mist of memory enveloping her sweetly. She smiles at this one, caresses that one, drawn in a kind of self-inhalation, until she stops where she is, tilts her head a little, and from inside, without even meaning to, she produces the old sparkle, almost forgotten, her sparkle of charm and seduction, which sprays out and dances like a ray of light over the four walls. And Nili stands, a slightly dreamy smile on her face, and looks at it.

She breathes heavily. Opens her eyes. Her look says, You're killing me, but with her hand she gestures for me to go on, quickly. I'm not sure I'll have the energy. It's getting harder from one page to the next. And it seems so pathetic to heap all those words and long sentences on the pages just to try to capture one live moment, or a spark of her emotion. I grab the pen and cross out the whole last section, and she says, "Don't you dare." There is sharpness in her voice, as if I've stolen something from her, and I loosen my grip on the pen and sit there, reprimanded, staring at the page. What does she really want and why is she being stubborn? As if punishing both of us together. Putting us both on trial.

"About the yoga," she groans after a minute. Completely ignoring, in her usual evasive, feline way, the heaviness that accumulated over the last few minutes.

I fake an apologetic laugh. "I know. I got everything from one book for beginners that I found in a London library. You'll have to help me with that a little."

A sentence with a future-tense verb. A crude mistake on my part. She tightens her eyelids in pain. I move my chair closer to her—how to comfort? How to compensate for what I'm doing to her in writing and in person?

"But listen. When I wrote it, I realized how much yoga I had absorbed after all, without even noticing it, just from hearing you talk, from watching you, from the millions of lessons when I was in the background in the studio and the apartment in Jerusalem—in fact, ever since I was born."

"You would lie there in your baby seat," she says, immediately tempted by me, by the warmth that had suddenly flickered in me. It's so easy for me to win her over, still, she's so thirsty for me, still, still. How has she not grown sick of me? "You'd lie there with your pacifier, with your eyes wide open, huge. People in the classes couldn't get over how quiet you were."

But I never took a class with you, I tell her silently.

Or a massage, she replies with her eyes, and shakes her head on the pillow. "It's a pity you wouldn't let me give you a massage. I gave the whole world massages, except you."

I reach out and touch her hand. I don't want to make a big deal out of it, but it's the first time I've touched her in years. Somehow I never adopted the habit of touching with her. When we met, the day before yesterday, I stood next to her bed amazed, trying to find Nili inside her. Walter had prepared me for it on the way from the airport, but I wasn't prepared. I stood for a few moments, unable to move a finger, barely breathing, until Walter let out a kind of sob behind me, almost comical, and left. And then I sat down and we started talking, untouched by human hands.

Now I somehow find my fingers and hers intertwined. Hers are huge, thick and swollen, and my red ones peek through them. Not a beautiful scene. I rub them for her a bit. Searching for the joints within the swollen flesh. I can't find them. My motions are clumsy, they don't help at all. I don't have it, there's nothing I can do about that. And besides, I don't seem to be a particularly compassionate person by nature. I'm afraid that if I give her a squeeze of encouragement it might hurt her, or she'll think for some reason that I want to hurt her.

But she does not let go, she holds on. All of a sudden I sense her fear. For the first time. There's no mistaking it. Like white jet streams splitting off and flowing into me, and there are cold stripes of whiteness quickly spreading throughout me, and it's as if she's already call-ing to me from there, from beyond the gates. For a moment it actually paralyzes me, sucks me back into a bad place, and I can clearly tell what it will be like when she's gone, and how much strength I will need to not be carried away there again. I quickly pull myself to-gether. I'm really not sure that what is occurring here is a good thing. Mainly, I'm afraid of the effect it has on her: she may think that if she and I have reached this state, it must mean the end is really near.

"Should we go on?" I ask.

Slowly and with an encouraging smile, I release her fingers from my own. Avoiding her look. Unbelievable how I can put on the exact, precise expression I encountered years ago on the face of a nurse at the mental ward in Homerton Hospital in Hackney. She would twist my arm back easily—I weighed barely ninety pounds then—and jab me with a needle full of Rohypnol containing at least five hours of sleep, and still smile at me with the serpentine smile of a member of some exclusive club: *"It's all right, love, we're almost there."* And now it's me, now it's my turn—how wonderful is the recycling of life in na-ture. From a great distance I can see my hand giving her arm two or three caring pats, and I hear myself laugh out loud. "Do you know what it meant to me to write about yoga?"

She lingers a little. Digesting what has just flowed between us. In her body, she is still perceptive and bright as always. Certainly more than I am. And perhaps not only in her body. I don't know. Some-times I think maybe I'm the one who doesn't get anything. And maybe it was me who, in my stupidity, screwed everything up for us. Because sometimes, like now, when she purses her lips like that and turns herself off, it pains me to see how disciplined she is, the way she has trained herself to stop so as not to know me completely. Because that's what I demand of her, those are the terms of the contract, and that is how I always wanted it. And then of course I scorn her, be-cause for a second she looks like a little lab animal, a mouse or a rat, trained never to enter one particular cell that she especially likes. But that's how I wanted it, I recite to myself what I can never forget even for a minute, that is exactly how I wanted it. In the meantime, it turns out that I've suddenly become witty, and I am cheerfully chatting with her about my short research into yoga, and how I got myself into it. I quote a playwright—I can't remember who it is, he was English or Irish, his name escapes me now; with names it really is the worst— who said that the most complicated thing for him, always, is writing about his enemy "from the inside."

"I hope you mean yoga," she murmurs.

Four or five times during their days together, someone registers for her class at the front desk or knocks on the door and asks if they can take a lesson, and Nili grits her teeth and signs them up for the lunch hour or the dinner hour. She never eats in the dining room anyway. And then, during the imposed lesson—if you can call it a lesson, those dollish limbs dangling and that pathetic displacement of fat—she keeps stealing looks at the little alarm clock and counting the minutes, amazed at her inner rudeness, and announcing to herself that she must have reached the end of her professional road if she is putting all her money on him, with the odds stacked against her as they are. She reminds herself constantly not to make comparisons, to give herself fully to anyone who needs her, but at the end of every disturbance, after the nuisance has left, she hears a soft knock on the door, not shy and not demanding, just *I'm here*. She bounds up off her mat, full of the sweetness of acquiescence.

"So you've just fallen in love with him a *little*," Leora says stingingly in her role as sobriety inducer, stabbing at Nili with the entire length of the word as if she's pinning down a butterfly. She is astonished again, for the thousandth time, at the unbelievable variety of her sister's talent for imbroglio, and wonders how she'll get her out of this one and how much it will cost.

But Nili knows with absolute certainty that no, it's not love, not even attraction. "And don't worry, he's not falling in love with me either." She chuckles. "I'm too old for him, and anyway, it's happening in a completely different place, it belongs to a different department. Lilush, what do you think, let's talk after he leaves?"

"I don't understand how he isn't falling in love with you." Leora spits out the words like a pit and laughs clumsily and accusingly, but Nili also hears a surprising little sigh slip through the words, and for a moment she thinks Leora, in her indirect way, seems to be making some admission here, finally. But even that doesn't really make her happy now, she just thinks of how two minutes of conversation with her sister exhausts her more than a whole day of work. Then Leora suddenly flares up, hissing at her that she's playing with fire again, and that as usual she thinks there will be someone to clean up after her. She brings up some of her past sins, and Nili listens to the list, and quite a few of the items actually raise a little smile of pleasure on her face. But she is depressed by the thought that it's been three years now since the sweet little Trinidadian who worked at the building across the street; he wrote her lovely poetry in English with chalk on the scaffolding, and left her penniless on the beach at Rosh Hanikra. Since that time, her CV has included no significant transgressions that you could really dig your teeth into. But Leora persists, spitting out chains of words, and Nili guesses how her gaze is wandering now, without seeing, over the walls of her home, objects and furniture and housewares, and as she talks she seems to inhale the strengths of the day-to-day from them with a joyless longing. Nili knows how Leora looks at this moment too—just as she did when she used to have hysterics as a little girl, and later as an adolescent, when she suspected that Nili was seducing and stealing away the few boys that dated her. In an instant she would go berserk, turn into an ugly old lady, and Nili, eyes closed in fear, would walk into the storm of limbs and screams and spitting as into a burning house, and wrap her arms around her, and Leora would freeze in mid-diatribe, afraid, as if someone had woken her out of a hypnotic state. She would stand like that for a long time, lost.

Later that evening, he's in a great mood. Nili is confused; she thought he might not even come back, that she must have touched some open wound when she spoke of his body. But here he is, refusing to talk about what happened, taking large strides around the room, waving his arms widely, demanding that she teach him everything she knows. "Everything?" She smiles. "Yes, everything." She laughs, telling him, "My best students—listen to this carefully now—if after ten years of studying they begin to understand that they know almost nothing, then I'm a truly fortunate teacher. But you still want to know everything now, do you?" "Yes, yes," he enthuses, and she stops for a moment as a cold hand touches her, because perhaps he, in his strange rawness, feels that he doesn't have much time. But he seems so alive and blossoming to her now that she immediately erases her fear, and with a flood of pleasure she encounters within her that forgotten motion, where she tips the vase of her soul toward him.

"Come here," she orders cheerfully, and places a hand on his back and a hand on his chest, and shows him how to stand, how to bend over to pick something up off the floor. She hints at something about yin and yang, and gives practical little tips: which exercises for massaging the internal organs you can do while you brush your teeth in the morning, and how important it is to brush your tongue too, to clean the night's germs away—her modest treasure of knowledge—and in between she tells him carefully, so as not to scare him, about the sun nostril and the moon nostril, and about the two halves of the body, which are two separate and different entities. He listens with grave alertness and his lips repeat her words, reciting, swallowing. "And that thing you said yesterday, the chakras?" She points to each one of them and touches the tip of his head with its short buzz cut, amazingly soft. "From this chakra you can connect to the infinite cosmic," she says, and makes sure he's not pulling away yet—after all, Leora isn't the only one who makes a sour face when she starts flowing toward the universe, and Rotem just puts her hands over her ears and starts singing loudly. But he has the opposite reaction: every such idea excites him and stirs him, and awakens in her the desire to give him more, to empty her knowledge out into him.

How little time they have! In two or three days he'll disappear and she'll never see him again. But wait, why must that be? Why don't you ask him for his address? No, that can't be done. But why not? You can send him books and tapes about all sorts of things, not just yoga, give him some enrichment, put together a personal survival kit for his disaster areas. Stop, you fishwife, down! Why don't you find out his contact information from the front desk? At least so you'll have it just in case . . . Because no, she presses herself between two strong fingers, because something within him dissuades her, because she knows that the secret of their encounter is in its nonrecurrence. But more than anything, because perhaps it's best for him, perhaps she shouldn't burden him with everything she contains. She knows exactly what she's talking about, there's no need to go into detail, but for example, when she's here in the hotel, far away from the girls, she might ultimately be doing them some good. In other words, it's very possible that in her absence, yes, she is doing them more good than—take a deep breath—in other words . . .

"Should we take a break?" I ask hoarsely. I can't do it, I have to get some different air. Preferably smoke.

She is quiet. Her face is strained with pain.

When I can no longer bear the silence, I say, "To be honest, there were at least twenty times when I thought you'd stop me."

"Why?" Her voice comes from very far away.

Oh God, I think, what have I done? What have I written here and how deeply have I hurt her now? If I had children, I remind myself, maybe I would know how to behave in these situations. If I knew how to behave in these situations, I answer myself, great wit that I am, maybe I would have children. I attempt to refresh my voice after all, to find a warm tone that will not sound as if I had just killed her. "I thought you'd at least say what's going through your mind when you hear all these . . . these hallucinations of mine."

"Rotem," she says, as if in that word she has summed up the discussion.

I remain quiet. Any further questions would sound idiotic, would sound hungry, and there is no power in this world that could make me ask her about him and her. But for example, I think of her in my heart, for example, when I described the singe you feel in your brain every time you miss some fact, every time you expose your ignorance and stupidity, how is it that you don't ask me where I, your genius, your walking encyclopedia, the prodigy of your hometown, learned to describe that so precisely?

"I have to know, Nili," I finally blurt out. "It's enough. I have to hear now if anything I've been babbling here for the last two hours is even a little bit close to reality."

"But it is reality," she says slowly, with unexpected tenderness. Almost with compassion she says it. "It's exactly the reality I want to hear."

At 10 p.m., before they part, he suddenly remembers. "Listen," he says, and hesitantly takes two fifty-shekel bills out of his pocket, looking aside. "My dad said to give you this."

"I don't want money from you." But she lingers for a moment, sadly contemplating her nominal value as a woman to his father.

He pushes it into her hands. "Take it, you should."

"Why should I?"

"You know, for the yoga . . . for us . . . so we can go on."

And he explains to her, squirming and embarrassed. "He"—he usually refers to his father as just *he*—"doesn't understand this kind of thing."

"What kind of thing?"

"This. Doing something without money." And he giggles. "He has this saying, that there's no such thing as a free lunch."

Nili hesitates for a moment, caressing herself with these words: "for us to" (or maybe it was "for the two of us to"? What was it exactly? Never mind. The point is . . .). "Tell me, do you tell him what we do?"

He shoots her a sly look that encompasses everything, and she grasps that he tells his father, or at least hints at, exactly what his father wants to hear.

She takes the bills from him with a conspiratorial smile. After he leaves, she shoves them into her bra, laughing in the face of the bespectacled income tax inspector who has been hounding her for three years. Sorry, gifts are exempt.

A thin whistling sound, almost a whinny. She laughs softly with her eyes closed, and warm circles spread inside me.

She asks for a cup of tea. Just hot water and mint leaves. It's the only thing I've seen her consume these past two days, other than pills and yogurt. In the kitchen I scan the set of polished dishes. There are dishes and implements in there I don't even recognize, that could furnish any institution from a beauty parlor to a torture den. For some reason this fills me with joy. I take piece after piece into Nili's room, and she squints at them and proclaims: "Lettuce spinner," "melon scoop," "apple corer."

"Well, what do you expect," she says, teased, when I wave something made out of stainless steel and rubber that looks like an enema for birds. "I'm not going to change him now."

Walter, she means. She always had a rare talent, shameless and boundless, for attracting men and turning them into patrons. It always made me sick, even as a child, her ingratiating feminine game, and so did the men themselves, of course. But Walter, for a change, didn't take off at the moment of truth, and for that I am indebted to him. "Your mother is a wonderful woman," he said to me when he picked me up at the airport early the other morning. And he paid for my ticket. Every time he tried to talk about her, his eyes filled with tears and he choked up (I recognized it the second I saw him for the first time: a certified orphan. From birth). "She really is something," I said, and concentrated on the road blurring in front of his eyes. Then we kept on driving in silence, and I fought off the temptation to turn his wheel around and catch the first plane home. Ever since I was born, all my life, people who had met her would come up to me and recite these phrases to me, as if someone had dictated them from the concise dictionary of clichés: Larger than life. Straight out of the movies. Mother Earth.

Now she explains in a cautious voice that she's fairly used to him and to his habits, and to his tears when he steals a look at her. "And to his taste in art," she adds dryly. "All these statuettes. So maybe he has a few drawbacks, Walter," and we both agree with a silent nod of the head, but he promised her he would keep her at home until the last minute. She motions at the crowded rooms which spread into each other in the gloom and says, "At least I'll die against a nice backdrop."

"You'll die?"

Just like that, suddenly, stupidly, helplessly, with the voice of a three-year-old. It just popped out of my mouth.

The next morning he shows up looking pale and green, and apologizes. "It's my stomach, it really hurts. I didn't sleep all night."

"I knew it."

"What did you know?"

"That you weren't feeling well."

"How did you know?"

"I knew, I just knew." She walks around him worriedly. "At night I felt it too, and now, before you came in, it was really strong."

"But how did you know?" he demands, and she explains distractedly that every time before he comes, she sits quietly for a few minutes and tries to feel what he feels. His mouth opens wide, his pain seemingly letting up for a minute. "Even when I'm not here you sit here and think about me?"

"Tell me, do you have a lot of stomachaches?"

"Yeah, sometimes . . . But yesterday was the worst, I really didn't sleep."

"So do you want to leave it for today?"

"No, I don't know, it really hurts." As he talks, his pain seems to increase, or perhaps the talking incites the pain, and the wretchedness.

"Show me where it hurts." But her hand is already reaching out to touch the exact spot, beneath the rounding of his left ribs, deep inside.

He groans. "How did you know where—" He grabs her wrist hard, his eyes digging wildly into hers, with that hunger of orphans. But with suspicion too. "How did you know?"

"Lie down now. Don't speak." He obeys her and lies down. Every movement hurts him. She kneels by his mat, her buttocks resting on her heels. She passes her right hand over the core of the pain. Starts pulling into herself, drawing from him. A long time goes by. She doesn't move. She plays a quiet, monotonous tune to herself. She asks herself who raised him—certainly not that father of his; maybe some grandmother or an aunt. Or no one. He falls in and out of sleep. His body is limp, his forehead perspires. She wipes the sweat off with her hand and notices that he follows her with his gaze to see if she wipes her hand off on the mat. As he does so, she checks his wristwatch out of the corner of her eye, the one he wears on his right hand and obstinately refuses to take off. Now it's set five hours ahead. Maybe Thailand? Korea? Is New York ahead of us or behind us? He groans weakly. Opens miserable eyes, then falls into a brief slumber. She hears the hum, his two hearts beating, one large one, heavy, and one little one, straggling behind. If only she knew what he was really going through, who was wrestling inside him. She massages him tenderly and wonders if he himself knows; sometimes she thinks he's completely ignorant of everything that goes on inside him, and sometimes she's convinced that he knows very well. At this moment, for instance, even though he is giving himself over to her hands, she guesses that he'll allow her only to help him bear his heavy baggage, just for a few days, on condition that she never try to glimpse inside him even once.

His abdomen rises and falls. His stomach and intestines almost turn over, and sink and create whirlwinds on his velvety, perspiring skin. "Now, slowly, try to breathe into it."

"Into what?" He is alarmed.

"Into your pain." Her voice is soft and sweet, she refuses to get caught up in his alarm, she can't recall seeing such panic in any of the boys she's treated. "Now exhale it into my hands." He holds on to her arm, his head stretches back, and his fingers pinch her skin with a twitch. She steadies her kneeling position again. Her body is uncomfortable, and she soon knows something is wrong. There is some deceit here. The pain has already melted, she is certain, but it seems to be having trouble leaving his body. She touches, presses, and releases, listens with her fingers. Strange—as if it is the body which is now clinging with all its might to the pain, unwilling to give it up. "I'm here," she tells Kobi when she finally understands. "Let it go, you don't need it. I'm staying." And after a moment's hesitation she adds, "And I'll stay."

Over and over, reassuring, promising, repeating with pangs of guilt the promises she must not make. And slowly, like a tight fist painfully opening up, finger by finger, the pain breaks free. She feels the truncated billows absorbed in her palms dissolving. The face on the mat becomes calmer, consoled. She rounds her hands over his stomach, using wide, slow circles, and does this for several minutes, until his head falls to one side and his mouth opens slightly with a slight snore, tranquil.

Two hours later, she wakes up. She sees him sitting in a corner of the room with his knees folded into his chest, looking at her. She gets up slowly, sits, rubs her scalp. "Was I asleep?"

He celebrates his little victory. "When I woke up I saw you sleeping."

She yawns, opening her huge mouth wide, remembering too late to cover it. ("Even Einstein didn't look all that intelligent when he yawned," Rotem once explained to her sweetly.) "Wow, are you crazy? It's already lunchtime! We've missed half a day. Help me up."

He reaches out his hand, helps her stand up, but she sits down again. She collapses, scattering embarrassed smiles, and he stands above her, smiling at her confusion. There is a certain tender, cowlike grace to her slow heaviness right now. She holds her gaze on the two mats, realizes that she and he were sleeping here, side by side. She wonders what he thought when he saw her lying there like that, exposed to him.

"You know what I remembered?" he says, as if answering her thought. "Once, when I was three or four, more than four, at the water park this one time, my dad took me there once, and I got totally freaked out."

"From the water slides?" Nili asks supportively, recalling herself with the girls in that watery hell, guessing what a child like him must have felt there.

"No. All of a sudden I started"—he laughs to himself—"I had this idea: what if everyone in the whole world except me was dolls? Like, not real people."

She laughs. "That's quite an idea. And what did your dad say about that?" (He's talking, a little wheel in her head starts spinning faster than the others. Listen, he's telling you something.)

He gets down on one knee next to her, speaking with a strange, foreign satisfaction that frightens her a little. "My dad, he grabbed hold of me here with his hand"—he grasps the thin skin on the back of his forearm as he speaks—"and pinched me, and twisted his fingers around like this until I cried, and he kept laughing and asking me, Is this real? If this is real, then everything's real!"

As her eyes clear, she sees. A large scythe shape lightens on his dark skin, then disappears. She rubs her face and thinks vaguely, The fact that I slept here, the fact that he saw me asleep, it's as if it opened him up more than anything I've done or said.

"Wanna know the truth?" He smiles to himself. "To this day I sometimes think that, about people. Like dolls. Except now I don't care."

"And what about me," she asks, regretting it immediately, "am I real?"

He looks at her from a few inches away. Unseen fingers move inside her, leaving little indentations at the bottom. Finally, not with any ease, he says, "You are."

Then, with a sudden urge, she grasps his hand above the watch and quickly unfastens the thick leather strap; microscopic quivers of fear and refusal and imploring scurry between their hands, but he doesn't pull his hand away. She takes off the watch and turns his wrist over to see, fearfully, and she sees, and somehow she is not surprised, as if she had known all along.

His lips turn white. His look is wild, warning her not to ask anything. Not to dare. She drops his hand. Thinks dimly, It's still fresh, as if the skin there is still brittle, as if he's just been pinched; this happened not long ago, six months, a year, no more. She takes his hand again and lays it exactly over her left wrist, on the inside, and carefully and gently rubs the soft skin of her hand on his, absorbing into it, massaging and absorbing, absorbing and softening. She thinks, This child has been to hell and back, this child knows the way. She shuts her eyes and sees in front of her, for some reason, the showers at his boarding school, an iron pipe coming from the ceiling, a pink soap dispenser, torn around the edges, and a gray cement floor with thick drops of rust dripping onto it.

"We're getting closer," she says. Or asks—it's hard to tell.

"Don't be afraid," I say, compelled to protect her. "I haven't hurt you in there."

193

"No, it's not that." She looks surprised to discover how poorly I comprehend what is really worrying her now.

I drink some more tea. As I look at her from the side, stealthily, it flashes through my head that she's mature. That's it. That's the change. Perhaps even more than the illness. She is simply a mature person. She is, finally, more mature than I am.

That thought undermines me a little. I sink down for a minute, entangled in myself. Where does this place me now? And it's a little unfair, I think, for it to happen at this point, when there's no time left for me to get used to it and reorganize. How can I relearn, at my age, how to walk, talk, and be?

Suddenly, a memory: When I used to wake up in the mornings, she would already be doing a headstand. Her vest would fall down and cover her face, and her large breasts, which looked so soft, would drop and lengthen toward her neck. I would stand and stare at them as in a continuation of the night's dream—

A sweet drop of memory. Who sent it? And why now?

I serve her the day's last battery of pills. Twenty-one, I count. Almost every pill has a counterpill, intended to cancel out its side effects. "If only," she laughs. "If only it canceled them out, but it doesn't cancel anything. The only thing they're canceling out is me, slowly and thoroughly, but when I die—poof! That'll close down their playground." She whistles her new laugh, delighting in the revenge. Once, she wouldn't even swallow an aspirin, not even when she had a migraine. She would beat any pain she had on her own, through meditation and relaxation.

I give her the pills and glance at the piles in the drawer. There are a few there that I remember from here and there, them and their creative richness of expression: the worms that would crawl deep inside my throat from the Anafranil, or the messed-up feeling in the morning after spending a stormy night with Elavil, and various other episodes. But she doesn't know anything about that chapter of my life, and I am

194

careful, of course, not to demonstrate any knowledge. But my poisoned brain starts investigating the option of whisking away a few of her pills for use in times of trouble, and makes loathsome calculations about the quantities she'll still need and what they'll do with the scandalous leftovers. No matter how hard I try, I can't control these thoughts, and I console myself that this too is one of those survival habits that troubled tourists are apparently unable to be weaned from, but it's clear that I'd never be a good character witness for myself, in all honesty.

"Rotem," she moans softly, "shut the drawer already."

She asks me to moisten her lips with a damp cloth. Then she dozes off for a while. Or sinks into her thoughts. I have no way of knowing. She now has long disappearances when she simply is not there. Whisked away. I sit and watch her, and try to recover from the little class reunion I've had here. I see her breaths relaxing, and I breathe along with her, the way she used to relax me when I was little. I try to engrave her on my memory that way, to store up supplies. I know how people get erased from my mind after a while. Even now, a second after we spoke, I can't remember what it's like when her eyes are open and looking at me. And no matter how hard I try, I keep getting pushed out of that look, and that in and of itself is starting to annoy me so much that I almost make the mistake of waking her. But then her breaths do start working on me, and I sit and slowly manage to enjoy the situation, even becoming addicted to some suspicious tranquillity, as if all at once a true calm has prevailed inside. Perhaps it's because when she's sleeping I don't keep feeling as if particles of me are being sucked toward her without any control, and there is a somewhat stolen pleasantness about it, being near her like that, like watching the sun during an eclipse.

I think about what I just read to her, about the doll-people, about the watch she took off his wrist. I turn over my hands and look at the place that should have long ago developed a scar just from the thoughts I've transmitted to it. Nili sighs in her sleep, a thin sigh like a whimper, and I become uncalm again, pins and needles all over my body, and then the whole mess of my thoughts, and I don't seem able to rationally comprehend that in a short while, maybe weeks or days, she will not be. This person will be no more. There will be no such Nili in the world. This entity. My mother. I get up and leave the room, almost running.

In Walter's bathroom I try, unsuccessfully, to compose myself. I sit there on a padded wooden toilet seat, decorated with purple tassels of some sort, and marvel at the advances humanity has made in the field of toilet bowls and their accoutrements while I was wallowing in the latrines of my own income bracket. I think of what my life will be like very soon, after her. For example, a marginal matter—what connection will I have to this country? Will I ever want to come back here, even for a visit? Is it possible that this is my next-to-last time here? My chest starts to feel tight, but I don't leave. It looks as if my fingers have swollen a little on this visit. They look even redder than they normally do. Maybe it's just because of the bordello light in here. Their skin is peeling more than usual, my washerwoman's fingers. During the past few weeks I've gone back to biting my nails like a starved rabbit. I'll calm down soon. I rock myself back and forth, humming something to myself, and it doesn't help. A cigarette would help. A joint would be salvation. This house is driving me mad. With Walter, I don't even have to straighten the little pictures of shepherds hanging in the bathroom.

I think about things that won't exist anymore. There are things that exist only between me and her, and maybe I'll forget them when she's not around. I know I will. My heart suddenly turns sour at the thought that I have only a few times left, for example, to feel that breeze, the exhalation of the little lab animal passing in front of the forbidden cell. That occurrence, which lasts at most for a tenth of a second—her sorrowful sniffle, the little wave that rises in me when I sense her standing at my doorway and know she may take a wrong turn, and then the second wave that swells when she finally obeys and turns to leave submissively, like someone shrugging her shoulders and—what? Giving up? Abandoning? Deserting? A stupid thought goes through my mind: How will my body know how to create those materials on its own from now on? It may turn out that it needs them, that they're essential, that they are the only reason I am able to maintain some degree of balance. But I protest immediately: What is this nonsense? How can you just write yourself off like that as if you have no existence without her? You've been getting along without her for years. But the weakness persists, weakness of body and weakness of mind, and I sit and sob a little, to my surprise. I was hoping to avoid it; this must be a preview of the grief, the opening act for the great orphanhood, and it might actually be a good sign, like my happiness when I found my first gray hair and felt that I was part of their biology after all. But even that encouraging contemplation doesn't get me up off the toilet seat, and I sit there and cry silently, so she won't hear, and scratch my legs all down the back with ten open fingers. That takes me to exactly the right place, plowing me deep with pleasure until I bleed uncontrollably—because of her, and because of what will disappear with her, those materials that only she can produce in me, and also because even now it infuriates me to think of the secondhand things you get used to when you stand in the shade for too long, the way you become accustomed to getting secondhand light because someone else is standing in it, and to being silent and faded while she fills the room, any room, with her voice and her laughter and her colors. And the way you slowly turn this into ideology, espousing the shade, swearing by the faded, abstaining with stupid and pauperish pride from anything that is firsthand, and later—it happens very quickly—forgetting what you are allowed to ask for, forgetting that you even can ask, growing used to photosynthesizing by the light of the moon.

But that's enough now—what's the matter with you? It's time to go back. I wash the blood off my legs, stick some bits of toilet paper on them to dry and absorb the blood, clean the floor around me, calculate how many days I need for the sores to heal so Melanie won't find out. Let her find out, for all I care—I haven't done it for almost a year and I don't regret it. This is exactly what I needed now, like a good bout of masturbation. I wash my eyes with cold water and blink excessively, and restore my face, redesign the slightly bitter, hurt expression, so Nili won't be suspicious.

The night before coming here, when I had already been reduced to a state of ashes and dust, after packing and unpacking three times and announcing that that was it, I couldn't go, Melanie sat me down on a chair and started cutting my hair. Once every two months or so, when I quietly fall apart, she does it, and somehow, it's not clear why, it settles me, purifies me. Not the final result, which I don't particularly care about anyway, but just the feeling of her working on my head, tidying it for me, and the sense that for one whole hour that head isn't mine, not my responsibility, not my fault. Now, in the mirror, I try to see myself completely from the outside, and as usual, I decide I don't really like the woman I see. Not that I don't like her exactly, I just feel sorry for her. I know what I would think if I saw her passing on the street or if she squeezed past me on the Tube. "Lady," I would whisper to her, "relax, get the stick out of your ass."

I lean against the mirror and cool my forehead. I breathe warm vapors on the glass and write on it, *Melanie*. I like writing her name in Hebrew. I don't have many opportunities to do it. I like the way the spelling is similar to the Hebrew for *my angel*.

"And about that Melanie person," she asks the second I get back from the toilet, "have you written anything yet? Is she already in your stories too?"

I wait for a moment, counting to one million. "Not yet. But I'm gathering material about that Melanie person."

"Sorry."

We sit. Silent. A faint gurgling sound comes from somewhere beneath her. Her fluids are drained by means of a complex plumbing system which I was only just able to prevent her from explaining to me and demonstrating all its mysteries. I scan the walls around us with fascination.

"Were you crying?" she asks.

"A little."

"That's good. You should cry. Afterward too, don't hold it in. But remember always to bathe your eyes with chamomile."

She had never hidden her opinion of Melanie from me. She of all people, who had done everything with everyone and so forth, suddenly, when it came to me, her open-mindedness ran out. With surprising creativity she would pull out arguments and recite them sternly, with an assertion of responsibility I had never known in her: Melanie is an affair with no future and no continuity, meaning, no next generation, and in fact, Melanie is preventing you from finally finding true love, with all the perfection and depth that can exist only between a man and a woman, believe me. And there were all sorts of other dialectics hashed out in the darkest workshops of Rishon LeZion.

I deliberate for a while over whether this is the right time to open a debate. I suspect she has no grasp of where I've been and what I've done during my years in the Diaspora, while I was producing exciting material for my stories—the writings of a whacked-out tourist. I feel like simply telling her, without blaming and without whining, about all the years I lived without love for anyone. And how I looked at couples in love as if they were sick, crazy people, each consuming the other's soul through their lips. And how when I took a bath, I could convince myself to see a halo of bluish rot emanating from my body.

Or I could tell her the story of how I almost adopted a little girl because I thought that at least then I would have a girl with me, a living creature, verifiably alive. That through her I would be able to touch the artery that surely must pass through every human being. I'd already contracted with a lawyer who had deigned to mortgage all my assets in return for turning a blind eye when we came to the "medical history" section, ignoring the telling tremble of my fingers. But at the last moment I gave up, chickened out. And anyway, I knew I was only trying to fake my membership card in the human race. I still carry the picture of a one-year-old Filipina girl in my purse. She's seven and a half now, just this week. I have no idea where she is or what happened to her.

Maybe I'll just give her an abbreviated list of events, crashes, and wallowings; fortunately, I can't remember the details anymore anyway, only the names and the faces, and above all the various backs that were turned on me. And it's also true that sometimes I confuse what happened with what I invented around it later, in stories, in writing, but there's no doubt that I spent three or five years like that, being passed from hand to hand and broken up into small change. I scrubbed the bottom of the barrel really thoroughly, until one day I heard a voice next to me that said, "I think it's enough." And when I resisted and kicked and screamed, she said, "If you needed to prove something to someone, I think you've done that." And with complete serenity she added, "You've proven it so well, in fact, that you've almost refuted your own argument." And I barked, "Go away, get out of here, I'm incurable." She laughed and just hoisted me on her back like a sack, and carried me like a casualty through a few deserts, quietly absorbing the toxins I released, and explained to me the whole time that this was all because I was completely ignorant, I was like a child raised by wolves when it came to living together, living as a couple, and that it would gradually stop hurting me so badly, the kindness.

Then all of a sudden I give up. Regretting the harshness of my heart, I turn to her, extricating myself again from the twist I had unknowingly placed myself in. I put my papers aside and stretch out. Enough, I say to myself, and then to her too. "Enough already." She doesn't ask enough of what. I tell her about Melanie's dad's farm in Wales, with its green pastures where, as I told her family, "they maketh me lie down." And the creek that just runs innocently through the yard, and the sheep, which are the most sheeplike sheep in the world. I explain to her that when the cows sit down, it means it's going to rain, and if the sky is red like fire at dusk, that means it will rain, and if the sky is bright—it will also rain. From my purse I take out a stone I brought back from there; it is black and white and looks like half an apple, and in its center, like an open eye, is my birthstone. Melanie suggested I take it with me on the trip; I place it next to her on the nightstand. It warms my heart to say her name out loud. I'm less lonely when her name is in my mouth. I tell her how Melanie has already grown used to the way whenever she tells me something special, a story or a childhood memory, I pull out a pen and write it down. She even made up a saying: Telling secrets to a writer is like embracing a pickpocket.

Nili digests. Slowly and strenuously, the words pass through the cords that are gradually stopping up in her brain. But when she finally laughs, she laughs from the bottom of her heart, and a bright spark manages to burst through the haze of her eyes, and instead of being burned, I surprise myself by being flooded with happiness for them both.

She shows him the exercise they used to call "airplane" when she was a kid. She lies down on her back with her legs straight up in the air, and he puts his stomach on the soles of her feet and holds on to her hands. "Are you sure I can't fall like this?"

"Don't worry, I'm strong."

"But is this yoga too?"

"It's my yoga." She smiles, sparing him the whole speech. "Come on, get up."

And he does, surprising her with his lightness. His bones are so weightless, she thinks. But then he contorts his face in terrible pain and hisses through clenched teeth that his whole inside is tearing up from this.

"Do you want to come down?"

"No, not yet."

The soles of her feet can feel his stomach tightening against her. He groans and his face looks twisted and flushed, but still he stays up there a moment longer, and then, when the pain is almost intolerable, he suddenly gasps a first breath, then another, and another, and giggles, surprised. He tries a few bolder breaths, broader and deeper, and she smiles, and he hovers and breathes above her face with his eyes closed, focused on himself, and his stomach becomes soft and starts to flow, cradled in her feet. She tries to feel what he has in there, what the story is with his stomach, but she is unable to. He glides above her, then lets his hands and head drop, and smiles to himself as in a dream. She looks at him and sighs softly to herself.

Once, in Dharamsala, in a little market where she sold potatoes and Reiki lessons, with baby Rotem tied to her back with a large shawl like the local women did, she first heard the story of how the Dalai Lama was chosen at the age of four, when he could point to the set of false teeth that had belonged to the previous Dalai Lama. There, in Dharamsala, very far from home and from the man who had informed her that if she left she'd have nowhere to come back to, she often thought about the wonder of being chosen. She told herself hopefully that it must have something to do with the ability to choose correctly from among the multitude of possibilities. She had long ago given up the hope of, for once in her life, making the truly correct choice, one that time and life would not eventually disprove and make subject to mockery in some way or another. And of course she had already given up the foolish and pretentious wish that she would herself be chosen for something. But as she grew older, she often liked to fantasize about the happiness of the Tibetan monks at the moment they made the correct choice: how they laughed and glowed at each other, and the relief they must have felt when they realized they had once again been redeemed from loneliness, from barrenness, from the fear of living in a world with no such child.

She breathes deeply, her feet spreading out in his stomach as in a pair of slippers, familiar guests. His arms float over her, their joints so thin and delicate. He is incredibly beautiful right now, permitting himself to loosen up, to forget, to mist over. And out of the relaxation a speck of saliva drops from his mouth onto her, and he stiffens up at once. His eyes open wide, she can actually hear the alarm sounding inside him, alerting him to a dangerous leakage, and he leaps off her and kneels at her side and quickly wipes her with his hands, just a tiny drop of saliva on her forehead, but Nili sees his expression as she lies there, dejected, and she feels a cold metallic touch.

Fifteen minutes later he is happy again. For the first time he is able to fold his legs into an almost perfect lotus position, and he bravely withstands the pain in his foot muscles as they stretch unbearably, then undoes his legs and lies on his back, slowly letting go of the pain. Suddenly—she doesn't know why, perhaps out of gratitude for having kept quiet about other things—he tells her that his greatest dream is that one day he'll own a restaurant. "A restaurant?" she repeats, astonished. Why a restaurant? What would he have to do with a restaurant? Yes, but first he has to study. Prepare himself. Next year he's already going to start waiting tables. "And what about school?" He waves his hand dismissively, he's planning on leaving the boarding school. They're a bunch of religious fanatics over there, and he doesn't even believe in God. "You don't believe in—" She straightens up and looks at him. "Then what are you doing there?!"

"*He* makes me go, but starting next year I'm only doing what I feel like."

"Wait, wait." She perks up, recognizing the edge of a thread, trying to undo the knot. "Explain to me why you don't believe in God."

But he has no interest whatsoever in conducting a theological debate. "There's this guy in the neighborhood, he used to work at Greenberg's, and he just opened a Chinese restaurant and he's willing to take me on for a trial period starting in April, and I'm already memorizing the menu and the dishes and the prices." He smiles sheepishly. "Wanna hear something funny? When you said yin and yang, at first I thought they were names of dishes."

At once she feels space inside, because he's planning a future for himself. She breathes as if he had held her hand and helped her jump over the chasm of that scar.

He gets up. "Could you do me a favor?"

"Whatever you want."

"Hang on a sec, don't leave."

He runs out. She stays there, lying on the floor, a little confused, then laughs quietly. She basks in the pride every adult in the world must feel when an adolescent places his trust in them. Especially me, she recalls jarringly. "And what are you thinking of doing when you grow up, Nili?" Rotem had inquired with a poisonous smile a few days ago when Nili tried to have a simple, normal, mother-daughter conversation with her. Nili tenses around the acidic thread twisting through her stomach. She's lost count of the number of times she has asked and demanded that Rotem stop calling her by her name; now the little ones are starting to experiment with it too, and when she corrects them, she feels like an impostor, unworthy of her title.

Fortunately he returns soon, cutting off the sword dance. He's holding a long menu, bound in fake leather, with clumsy imitations of Chinese script. "Okay, test me."

She laughs. "What should I do?"

"Ask me. I'm worst at remembering the numbers of the dishes."

She peruses the menu gravely. "Six," she declares.

He responds immediately. "Shark-fin soup."

"Hmmm . . . nice. Twenty-one."

"Chow mein. Those ones are easy, do the expensive ones."

She dives in again, and surfaces victoriously: "Forty-nine!"

"Forty-nine . . ." He furrows his brow. "Wait a minute, wait a minute—yes! Duck with bean sprats, portion for two."

Nili laughs. "Great job, but it's bean *sprouts*, not bean sprats."

He shrugs his shoulders. "How should I know?"

"Well, haven't you ever had Chinese food?"

He smiles. "Ask me the wines now."

She tests him on each dish, reciting with him and correcting his mistakes. She comes up with funny mnemonics to help him remember, giving him all her secret tricks for memorizing tricky facts, wondering where all this educational talent of hers has been hiding, and why in fact she didn't use it at home when she was helping the girls study for exams.

I find myself talking, orating with a zeal that surprises me. "I'm not blaming you, I'm absolutely not blaming you for what happened anymore. And I don't want you to be in suspense until the end of the story. You'll see by the way I ended it, the exact point I chose to end it, and from my perspective this is really what I'm saying to you here . . ." I'm so nervous that my glass starts jolting around in my hand, drops of water fly onto the page, and I stare at my hand and finally grasp that something is approaching, my reliable date is coming, it will happen soon. It must have been the scratching before in the bathroom that brought it on. "And it's not just in the story that it's like that." I'm almost yelling now, trying to get it out before it paralyzes me. "It's not like that in life either. This is it, Nili, it's over and done with. I've thought about it a lot, it's the main thing I thought about while I was writing, and today I'm so sure that you gave yourself to him with abundance and generosity, because you're like that, that's what you are and you just couldn't do it any other way—" My words are becoming garbled, clambering over one another. My voice is hoarse as if I've been screaming for hours, and I don't know how much of all this is actually getting through, because my jaw is locked now, and soon the burping noises will start, and I have to get it out because we've never talked about this, even when she wanted to at first, after the incident, I wouldn't let her, I shut her up, I would throw tantrums, call her a murderer. Now the trembling is already climbing up from my feet with its pincerlike movements, swinging from my neck. "Because maybe it's your generosity, in fact," I shout, "and the power of your touch, the touch, your power, maybe because of that he maybe didn't maybe he couldn't bear . . ."

I can still see her terrified look. I think I somehow manage to tell her not to worry, but I'm already at the flamenco climax, just trying not to fall off my chair, not to fall, it keeps slipping out from under me,

I don't have any hands to grab it with and keep my head from being thrown and my jaw hurts and I try to focus myself on having finally said it, gotten it out, given it to her, the gift I gave her, and someone is shouting and I'm not sure if it's me or her, and then the bitter taste spills into my mouth from both sides, and I know I'm over the climax, this time I was let off easy, just another minute or two, it's almost comical to see how my shoulders and arms are spread out in little sections in all directions. Now it's more like break dancing than flamenco. You can even hear my teeth, which means my jaw has unlocked, and this time somehow it's all shorter than usual, I'm already doing the finale, including a curtain call with a grunting crescendo—

Now it's quiet, and kind of pleasant. The warmth slowly returns to all my limbs, and there are pins and needles, but they are very soft, gently licking different spots. It's an almost humorous thing that the body does—not great humor, perhaps, but at least you can see it's trying. What's new here is that I don't really care that she saw it. It's as if I suddenly realize that she's already guessed I have these numbers in my repertoire anyway, and that I haven't been inactive since the convulsions, the blueness, the fits and vomiting of ages five and fifteen, and that during my foreign sojourns I have even enhanced my methods. I examine myself again and find that no, I am not troubled by realizing that she must have known long ago—not all the details perhaps, but the essence; she must know about the creative blackness inside. Who am I kidding? I try to guess what else she knows, and think she is extraordinarily wise for not having said anything to me about it, ever. And now a narcotic calm descends upon me, as it always does afterward. Here and there I release another graceful flutter forgotten in the cellars, but the worst is behind me, and I sit there exhausted, drenched in sweat, like jelly, incapable of opening my eyes because my eyelids weigh a ton. I laugh to myself about how everything turns around and is eventually restored to its natural order: she is the healthy one and I am the sick one. She is health and I am sickness. She reaches out and gently caresses my hand up and down repeatedly, twenty, a hundred times, so gently and quietly, and so right that it somehow reaches me through all the trembling fortifications inside.

After she does her favorite back-opening exercise on him, he says, "Now I'll do it for you."

"Are you sure? I'm heavy."

"It'll be fine."

"I'm much heavier than you are."

He's already standing with his back to her, spreading his arms. She comes and stands behind him, back to back. His hair touches hers. They interlace their arms. His warm skin is on hers.

"Slowly," she says. She's afraid he'll be humiliated if he can't lift her.

The two of them, in silent coordination, strengthen the grip of their arms. He inhales calmly. Steadies his feet. He seems so mature to her at this moment. She glances back at his watch. In the country he's living in today, she guesses, it's lunchtime now. She smiles to herself. It's nice for her to be there with him, without his knowledge, a stowaway in his secret travels. In mid-thought he bends over and her feet are lifted off the floor, and a delightful sensation, mingled with slight panic, spreads through her. She is still cautious, wanting to be sure he can take it. He turns out to be stronger than she thought. Sometimes in strengthening exercises, even the moderate ones, she can see the hems of his shorts trembling from the effort, and her heart goes out to him.

"Is it hard for you?"

"No."

"Tell me when it is."

In response, he leans over a little more, lifting her higher. She allows herself to relax her body. Closes her eyes. She is amazed at his ability to find their shared balance, and at how wise his back is. She decides to give him another thirty seconds, for his self-respect, but then the room slowly fills with a silence disturbed only by their softly intertwining breaths. Without realizing it, she has become completely relaxed, unable to resist goodness when it comes. Her back cracks and opens up, her internal organs slowly release from the grasp of consciousness, flowing to the sides. His breaths fill her up. They are effortless. Her lower jaw drops. She sighs softly, thoughts slowly waft up inside her, disconnected. Soon it will be good, she knows, precious memories, beloved images. She relaxes her body, making space for the pleasure, but as usual, a moment before it becomes good, and much like anyone sailing away or taking off, she must pass the customs officer and pay the tax: the oven has been broken for six months and there's no money for repairs, the antique fridge she bought from some Russian widow is making her life a misery: if she doesn't defrost it for a week she has the entire Siberian wilderness in her kitchen. And where is she going to find the money to pay the repairmen, those sons-of-bitches, and what should she straighten first, Eden's teeth or Inbal's lazy eye—she could have at least bequeathed them good teeth and eyes. And the daily phone calls from the bank, and the long-reaching arms of the landlord, who is willing to make all sorts of arrangements with her, but that's not it, she explains to herself for the thousandth time with a kind of false assertiveness, as if she just needs to tell it to herself rationally and then she'll somehow be able to unravel the thicket. The cutbacks are the thing, and the way poverty is breaking her up into small change, that's the thing, and her paralyzing fear that perhaps she no longer even has a life of the soul. "Worry about making sure I have a pair of underwear without holes first," Rotem jabs at her, and Nili groans. Rotem again, Rotem from every direction. Stop, please, I don't have the strength to carry her on my back anymore. Rotem with her principles and her cold, twisted rationalism, finding the most painful way to take her revenge on me, with her bodily destruction, thickening and bloating herself—when did this happen? When did she slip through my fingers like this? But now she's hazy already, finally, the

208

tax is paid, relatively quickly. After all—she breathes a sigh of relief—there are some advantages to being like one of those Weeble toys. The thoughts descend, soon they'll disappear beneath words, the morphine of pleasure starts spreading through her veins, her breath becomes light as a feather. It's been years since she's been able to relax like this, in this pose. Her body is still and floating and entirely open. Underneath, somewhere down there, his back is supporting her, but without demanding a thing of her. He's there. She's here. They touch only at one tiny point, two people in the universe touching each other for a moment in goodness. You can go a whole lifetime without knowing this kind of touch. Usually you must go through a whole life in order to be able to give such a touch. She asks herself where he has this knowledge from. What age he has come to her from. She feels as if she is barely putting any weight on him. For a moment she can imagine them spinning around and around in the air, and now she is the one carrying him with that same ease. Silence. Breaths. Floating. Her soul fills, drop by drop, with the rare nectar of trust.

"Who are you studying with?" she asks tightly when I turn the page.

"What?" I perk up. "What?"

"Rotem," she says wearily.

I gulp. Consider carefully, decide there's no point. "I took a few classes."

"Did you at least find a good teacher?"

"Yes." I wonder how long she's known, from which moment in the story. "Someone Melanie recommended. He's Japanese."

"The Japanese are a bit dry," she declares, and shuts her eyes. "You told him about me?"

"Yes. A little."

"And what did he say?"

"Nothing. He listened. He heard. He usually doesn't say much."

I can feel her scanning inside my head. My thoughts leap inside and I close the door behind them in a split second. Once, in a nature movie, I saw tiny little fish swarming into a sea anemone to escape a preying fish, and I recognized their movement of evasion and the motion of the anemone itself—a fleshy, complex mind, rushing to hide them. My Japanese yoga teacher had listened to what I told him and said, "The woman you spoke of doesn't work right. She relies on her intuition too much, and she's not at that stage yet." Then, at the end of the class, he came up to me again and said, "That woman, she works like someone who doesn't have a teacher. If she had a teacher he would reprimand her."

"I wanted so badly," she says finally.

"I only took a few classes, it's really not—"

"And are you going to continue?"

"I don't know." And I forced a laugh. "It's easier for me to write it than do it."

"No, no," she sighs, "you should keep doing it, it's good, it will be good for you."

She just lies there. Completely still. Because of her condition she has the strange ability to be present without being. In the space that now opens up between my chair and her bed, I remember the nights when Melanie taught me how to sleep together. I don't know why that comes into my mind. She seems to be resuscitating me from far away as soon as I start to weaken. I close my eyes and see myself fleeing from the bed to the mattress on the floor, and from there to the couch, and the rug, and Melanie following me sleepily from one place to the next. I shout that I can't fall asleep within the magnetic field of another body, and she mumbles, half asleep, "Come on, try a little longer." And so for a few bleary-eyed, sleepwalking weeks—and as if having no knowledge of it the next morning—she gave me the nocturnal portion of a withdrawal treatment from loneliness: one night we spent a whole hour together, the next night two hours, then a week of regression and crisis as I tried to adapt to the horrific idea of a shared blanket. Until suddenly, out of utter exhaustion, I discovered that our bodies had already reached an agreement—even mine, the illiterate one, must have caught on, because one night I woke up from a deep sleep and realized how beautifully we turned over together in bed, embraced. Now, when I smile, Nili looks at me, and I can't escape in time.

But as if operating her immediate healing mechanism, she remembers something. "There's something you should add."

"Where?"

"When you say what my face is like, how my jaw drops, you know, when I'm on his back."

"What should I add?"

"Write that when I'm like that, I mean *she*, then she thinks to herself that that's how she'll look when she dies."

"No, no."

"And then write: And she thinks of how everyone will see then that she really was a complete idiot. Write it. Now."

His ignorance amazes her. When she tells him she lived in India for three years, he asks if it's true that everyone there is black. When they talk about vegetarianism, he suddenly claims, with a strange fervor and a kind of vexation, that elephants are carnivores. "Elephants?" She doesn't know where to start refuting such nonsense, but he refuses to be convinced by all evidence she provides, slams his face closed, and locks himself up to her: that's what he's decided, and that's that. What are they teaching them at that boarding school? she wonders. Then something else happens, something trivial, that depresses her for the rest of the day.

While they're doing breathing exercises, sitting across from one another, she presses three fingers below his navel, in the body's furnace, seemingly searching for something. She doesn't find it, and hesitates; a moment later, she intuitively pushes her thumb hard into his navel. "When I press here, exhale and push out at me with your breath."

But he turns pale with the first sign of pressure, depleted. "I think I'm going to pass out."

"Lie down, you're just dizzy," she says as she supports his back and calms him, contemplatively; she is surprised again at how quickly he melts and starts to whine, as if the entire complex, delicate structure that he maintains hidden inside himself collapses in an instant upon contact with danger, with fear. He moans, and she rubs his shoulders distractedly. "Don't tense up, relax, relax. It'll pass." But she senses something else, as if whatever secret he is hiding is there, very close to the surface of his skin, and the slightest touch might tear its outer layer. For the hundredth time she wonders how he came to cut himself like that, on his wrist, and why, what had caused him to go so far. She murmurs, "Don't fight, you're fighting. Just get into it, into this feeling, I'm here, I'm with you, protecting you." A pallor spreads beneath his brown complexion. Beads of sweat appear on his forehead. What's going on here? Nili wonders, tightly pressing a finger beneath his nose. We must have done something bad, or premature. Or maybe I frightened his tender stomach again. She tries to recall what had suddenly caused her to change the three-finger pressing and proceed with such certainty to his navel. His hand flutters like the wing of an injured bird. He keeps trying to remove her hand from his navel, even though it is no longer there. Nili stares at the strange, compulsive motion and feels his panic inflaming itself rapidly, like a little fire. He grunts, starts to choke, and Nili finally breaks free and wakes up, quickly lifting his feet onto a chair. She slaps his cheeks lightly, rubs his temples, calls out his name, shouting, "Kobi, Kobi." That seems to help, the color starts coming back to his face, his breath stabilizes, the muscle spasms let up gradually. She caresses his damp forehead and, vaguely guessing, starts to repeat his name over and over, gently, compassionately, smiling. She can see his eyes flutter every time she calls his name, eagerly pulsating against his tight eyelids, and she thinks how strange it is that she has hardly called him by his name until now.

When she tries to stand up, he reaches out blindly and feels for her hand, grasping it tightly, signaling for her to continue. She recites his name to him like a mantra, moaning, singing a little tune, but inside her something is already darting around the edges, grumbling and thorny. It's my fault this happened, it's unprofessional, the whole thing is unprofessional. I'm going too fast with him and doing too many experiments and forgetting that he's only a kid. I've really gone too far, seriously. She keeps rubbing his chest, trying not to infect him with her anger at herself or any other random angers, until she notices that his eyes are open with the damp sparkle of a smile: "You know you're talking to yourself the whole time?"

"I am?"

"Yeah, with your lips. You keep doing it."

She kneads his shoulders with threatening force. "Well, just don't tell anyone." But after a moment she can't resist: "So what do you know about me now?"

He sits up, delaying his exciting discovery for a while, then throws it at her: "You're going to buy something big."

"Me?" She bursts out laughing. "Yeah, right!"

"Yeah, a house or a car. Something awesome. A Mercedes?" He is unconvinced by her peals of laughter, enjoying his role as the all-knowing. "A ton of money. You were making calculations with your lips."

Her laughter breaks off at once. Her heart sinks and crashes. That's the end, really. If I'm bringing all that into my work now, even into my work with *him*. That's it. Give the keys back to the management, go and be a secretary, do telemarketing, clean houses, things you can handle. She gets up and walks over to sit in the corner. He stays on his mat, looking at her, not understanding what's going on. She lets her head drop back against the wall with her mouth open. Rotem and Einstein can both take a flying leap. She remembers how she once swore, years ago—yes, yes, when she was standing in the light—that as soon as the yoga became nothing more than a living, a craft, she'd get up and leave. "I'm not buying a house," she says to him, to her surprise, knowing that if she doesn't talk now she'll scream. "And I'm sure as hell not getting a Mercedes. I'm actually trying to figure out where I'll find the money to pay next month's rent."

She tells him about herself. About the expulsion from Jerusalem. Even about Inbal's father, who disappeared, leaving her with a huge debt she had guaranteed for him. She even tells him about the broken fridge, and that the stereo system doesn't work and they haven't had any music at home for a year. And then, because what difference does it make now, she also lets him in on the hostile suspicion she's developing toward the other appliances; she has a whole conspiracy theory about them and their allies, the repairmen, and every time she turns on an appliance, even a light switch, her heart skips a beat. Then she tells him about the girls. In detail or in abstract, probably in abstract—she knows she must maintain some separation, because here she belongs only to him. It's only the two of them.

The sun sets and a pleasant dimness settles in the room. He lies there, resting on his elbows and listening. It's clear to her that he thought she was in a completely different place in life, and that now he is trying to figure out what this means about her, and maybe about both of them. He may even be recalculating his own position in relation to her, on the chain. Nili gets up, goes over to the mirror, and prods her scalp and hair a little. She looks into her eyes. Have I made a mistake by telling him? She finds it hard to read an answer. Lately she doesn't trust herself even with smaller things than this. As if with every movement she makes in the world she is scattering breezes of hurt and damage and failing. Midas and his leaden touch.

She goes over and collapses on her mat, knowing that something bad is happening to her, as if somewhere along the way she has lost the most basic confidence, the most natural and primal sense. As if every choice she makes immediately becomes a mistake, just because she made it. Go figure out what's right and what isn't, she thinks with her head lowered, what you can say to someone and what you can't. Is it even permissible to give advice to someone? To guide them, God forbid, along some path? Not to mention the truly unbelievable accomplishment of bringing a human creature into the world. How did I dare? She suddenly panics and pulls back and straightens up. How did I do it? How did I have the audacity?

Her hand moves over the blanket until she touches my knee and holds on to it. She doesn't say anything, and I don't ask. I have a thousand questions, but I don't ask. You can't go backwards to fix things.

Later, when everything between them settles, she says in a very tired voice, "You still haven't said what you felt before."

"When?"

"When you weren't feeling well."

"I don't know, I don't know," he mutters, and she gets the feeling he is avoiding her, and it annoys her that she's so transparent to him, while he is able to conceal and compartmentalize.

"I don't know," he says. "Your finger, like . . . I thought it was going into my stomach, like making a hole in it."

He lies on his back, relaxed, quiet. It's so quiet in the room that she thinks she can hear his hearts beating. A minute goes by, then another, and his breathing becomes tranquil. Then hers does too. The darkness thickens. Nili hugs her knees. Her eyes, which have dulled a little, brighten. The panic that flooded her earlier begins to melt away. Her lungs expand and she spreads out her inner limbs. Every so often she looks at him and feels that now another knot has been tied between them, because they are both, in their own way, downtrodden. It's strange that she'd never thought of herself in that way before, and yet now, because of him, it actually moves her, gives her strength.

He asks sleepily, "Hey, I forgot how it goes—the umbilical cord, do they cut it off both of them at the belly button?"

"What do you mean, both of them?"

"The baby and her?"

"The mother, you mean?"

"Yeah."

"Are you serious?"

He lifts up on his elbows, surprised at her tone of voice, almost hurt. It takes her a minute to grasp, and then she sees with painful clarity the impression sketched inside him: a thread stretching from his navel to his mother's.

She falters briefly. He looks at her with penetrating eyes, and a sudden and decisive urgency darts between them. She smiles at him, her pros and cons get mixed up, and somehow, out of the smile, an answer escapes. She could never tell lies, but she was an expert at giving little gifts like this.

As I reach the last word, she sighs. I don't ask. I wait. It occurs to me that we've actually been living apart for longer than we lived together. You could say that for a long time we've known each other only in chapter headings. But how could that be? I mean, how could such a reduction occur between us? Or between her and anyone.

Reduction is not the right word, though. It's more as if over the years we've become two polite tour guides at a disaster site, but one that destroyed our lives. After the incident she retired. Stopped teaching. He was, in fact, her last student, and I think she also stopped doing yoga herself. I'm not sure about that; I've never been able to ask her, and now it's too late. She made a living doing odd jobs. She modeled for art classes. She was a salesclerk in a housewares store. Then she sold paintings for an old artist, going from door to door asking people to just take a look at the pictures. I left her on my seventeenth birthday, my gift to myself. Then I came back, or was sent back, with my tail between my legs. Then I left again, and the same thing all over again. She once said, with uncommon sobriety, "Our umbilical cord has shriveled up." Years later, during one of the disconnects, when I was already deep in my London life, I found out from a friend that she was ill. We developed a tolerable routine: one conversation a week. She would give me a sign with two rings, and if I felt like it, I'd call her back. Once I came to visit her, courtesy of Walter Tours. It wasn't a good visit. ("Cursed is the parent," she told me then, before I left in the middle of a horrible row, "who can be objective about his own child.") During those years, in my rare flashes of composure, I wrote the tourist stories and collected them into a book. I tried to dabble with cinema a little, and journalism, and I discovered my limitations, and mainly I learned that there was a price to pay for that childhood (it turns out there's no such thing as a free starvation), and that in the meantime the world had filled up with other children who hadn't wasted all their strength on just surviving but had simply grown and opened and deepened, and that only in her innocent eyes could I still be considered worth anything.

"Within every effort there has to be calm," she recites for him. "Always, in every pose, you have to stop just before the effort becomes pain."

"Sometimes I think . . . a bird, for example," he says.

"Yes, what about it?"

"To fly, it has to keep flapping its wings, right?"

"Definitely," she agrees gravely.

"I'm not talking about gliding," he says fussily, and her ear opens a little at the sound of the new word. "There are birds that glide without making any effort, but I'm talking about a bird that has to make an effort to fly up."

"Okay." Nili shrugs, wondering where he himself is flying with this.

"And a bird that lives, say, for a year? Two?"

"Let's say."

"And all that time it has to make an effort with its wings, otherwise it'll fall?"

"Definitely."

"But maybe once, like one time in its whole life, it happens that it can fly up high, the highest—for maybe a whole minute—without making any effort at all with its wings?"

She leans forward, shrinking the crease between her eyes, sensing something approaching. "And how exactly does that happen?"

He takes on a mysterious expression. "It gets it from the air."

"I don't get it."

"Like once in every bird's life, the air lets it fly up without making any effort."

She blinks. What is it with these aerodynamic theories all of a sudden?

But he's very serious and focused. "It's like . . ." He searches for an example, his fingers moving, pulling something from the air. "It's like, say . . . a holiday bonus, like the air is giving it a bonus. A discount. Once in a lifetime."

"Oh." Nili laughs with sudden comprehension. "And does it know, the bird? Does it understand?"

He falters. "That's what I keep wondering. 'Cause if it doesn't understand, then it's like the air's efforts are wasted on it, no?"

"I guess so," she answers, delighted.

"And if it does understand, then . . . No, that can't be . . . No. It *must* not understand, 'cause it's just a bird, with a bird brain. Sure." He gets excited; now that he's made up his mind, his face lights up. "It's something the air just does for fun!"

From the great relief on his face she guesses how long the question has preoccupied him.

"It doesn't even realize it at all! Just that suddenly it feels light, but it's the air that decides: Okay, now you. Now you. Playing with its birds, you see?"

Do I see? Nili wonders, looking at him contemplatively.

"And by the way," he adds gravely after a minute, "it's the same with the sea and the fishes."

"Okay," she sighs, "tell me about her."

I tell her. "She's huge, Melanie, tall and wide, even a little scary at first, but she is such a soul, and warm and honest and"—for some reason the word in Hebrew escapes me—"kind of tangible?"

She is surprised. It's not how she'd imagined Melanie. She refused to even look at a picture. So I tell her more. Little things, like her work at the rehab institute, and the way she rides her purple bike around the streets of London. And her simple, healthy self-confidence—if only I had a quarter of it—and her masses of energy, which, to me, are sometimes simply paralyzing. "That woman needs almost no sleep." I laugh. "And there is her absolute honesty toward any person—no one gets off easy. And sometimes, here and there, there's a toughness," I say, then add, "a kind of intransigence," surprised at how a little spray of betrayal has escaped me. "She has these definitive principles which sometimes, to be honest, can make life pretty complicated. Actually, Melanie could easily fit in with that gang of yours, the ones that collect birds at four in the morning."

Nili hears everything, including the crumple in the middle of my laugh. The intransigence and toughness—it flashes in my mind—of someone who has never yet broken down, not even cracked.

"And does she know what the story is about?"

"She knows everything that happens in my life."

I shouldn't have said that, certainly not that way, but I knew why I had to say it that way, to correct a mistake with an error. I could actually hear a little sound from within her, like a match snapping.

Now there is silence. Her feet are exposed at the bottom of the blanket. They are huge, swollen. Bluish yellow. I stare at them. The toes look joined into one mass.

"And what did she say?"

Her voice can't fool me. I want to change the subject, but I'm also not able to completely give up, pulled this way and that, feeling like a child of divorced parents forced to convey messages between them. "What did Melanie say? She said that I should have written it years ago." She said something else too, but I don't have the guts to convey that. She thought that if Nili had read this story years ago, maybe she wouldn't have gotten ill.

When her head sinks, her goiter looks huge, red, crisscrossed with veins. Tiny waves travel through it. What is she thinking now? Strange how difficult it is for me to guess her when I'm sitting right next to her.

Melanie was angry about me hiding from Nili that I was writing about her. In her lucid and balanced world there was no room for such miserable little acts of deception. Nor for my sense of relief at having managed again, with the help of a little disguise or a slight paring down of the facts, to protect my little piece of often-looted privacy. She could not understand why I keep up these concealments even now, why I need to. We never fought so much as during the months when I was writing about Nili. I never felt that she was so close to giving up on me and on my lousy personality. After every phone call to Israel I would hang up and curse myself, and let her know that she should chalk up another week of punishment for me on the list hanging on our fridge.

For a minute I steal a quick immersion into her. Melanie studying at night, her large body curled up on the rocking chair we found on the street. Or cooking lamb curry for us at five in the morning, wearing headphones and dancing. Or standing in front of a photograph in an exhibition from Kosovo, crying loudly with her mouth open and her nose streaming, until you literally had to drag her away. Or her irresistible motion when she rubs one of her lotions onto her hands before a massage. And her murderous workout every morning, with exercises that doctors would forbid me even to watch, and her pagan lunar worships—if I even dare smile at them, I'm dead. And the Tottenham soccer games she dragged me to week after week—me—until I was forced to admit that there was something about them, I couldn't say exactly what, maybe seeing Melanie roaring and going wild and cursing in Welsh. And the moments when you can't tell which of our stomachs is grumbling. And my place in the world, my home, a preserve meant for only one protected animal, me, in the indentation of her shoulder. And not to be taken lightly are also the salt and pepper shakers we bought on Portobello Road, and our antique claw-foot bathtub, which was the real reason we rented the apartment. And our sixty-seven CDs, and the copper tray, and the two big orange mugs we bought on our first anniversary—

When you look at it that way, I think to myself carefully, we really have our own little household.

As time runs out, hour by hour, he thaws. When she reminds him of how he walked into her room the first time, all hunched over, he jumps up and corrects her, showing her exactly how he held his shoulders and how his chest caved in. Nili is amazed. "Do you walk like that on purpose?"

He smiles proudly, as if he had been complimented on his acting. "I can walk however I want." And he shows her his imitations of an old man, a drunk, an important man, the school rabbi. In two or three movements, with talent as sharp as a knife, he cuts the whole character out of the air. He is especially cruel to his father, with his bombastic way of standing, his lazy eye, and his roosterlike expression.

Nili laughs wholeheartedly and senses again the discomfort he arouses in her sometimes; she would never think to fake a walk. "And how do *I* walk?"

"You?" He smiles calmly, deliberating with himself, maybe even enjoying how it unsettles her. Because there is that part of him, she senses, that can't resist the temptation to give someone a little pinch, and twist it around, supposedly in jest.

"Yes, me." She thrusts her chin out, prepared.

He walks around her for a few seconds with his hands behind his back, and she already regrets asking, afraid that something will be broken, but also childishly eager to see herself in his eyes. He takes his time, immersed, pulling her out of himself, and slowly he changes. She doesn't even understand exactly how and where, but she suddenly feels a chill, because he is different. His body rushes up from inside, fills up, rounds out. He lifts his head with a gesture she knows well and walks past her with suppleness, in her lioness stride. His toes are spread and they hug the floor, his face slowly takes on a complex and alarmingly precise expression, the face of the woman she is, with her smile, still innocent, offered generously, and with the permanent wrinkle of effort between her eyes, the wrinkle that is also the place where she shrinks inside, afraid that you can already see the rapid reduction, the hiding ruses, the ignorance, and here it is, revealed to all, everyone can see it, you can stop trying so hard.

Even so, despite everything, something about herself pleases her; she is definitely still alive, still bold and undefeated, with that walk, that flexibility. I would hit on me, she thinks, I'd give myself a look on the street. Even the strained, slightly frightened spot between her eyes, it too may disappear in time, when things get better. She applauds him and thanks him for presenting her to herself like that, mercilessly, even generously. "You're so talented," she says with wonder. "You could be an actor."

He recoils. "No, no, I'm gonna have that restaurant. And anyway, actors are fags."

"Really? Says who?"

"Everyone knows they are." He thinks for a minute. "The supervisors at school. And my dad."

"Oh yeah? And who else is a fag, according to your dad?"

"I dunno. Dancers, for sure."

"Who else?"

He smiles; wearing his father's character again, he spreads his feet and places his hands on his knees and leans forward as if crudely watching a soccer game. The slightly devious twinkle appears in his eyes. "Singers."

"And who else?" She also crouches down with her hands on her knees. "Who else?!"

222

"Lefties."

"And?"

"Hairdressers!"

She roars, laughing, her perfect white teeth sparkling. "And who else?"

"Waiters."

"And?"

"Noncombat soldiers! Professors! Ashkenazis! And Hapoel Tel-Aviv! And everyone is a fag!"

"So says your dad," she sums up, standing straight.

"So says my dad."

Silence.

"And what do you say?"

He slowly straightens up, flashing her a well-practiced, cartoonish smile. But it seems to her that in the depths of his eyes—perhaps just an illusion—she sees the flashing movement of a long, supple beast, slinking between dark trees, its lazy tail wrapped around a trunk for a minute, then pulled away and slowly disappearing.

"But who's looking out for us?" she asks on the second-to-last day, after interrogating him again so that she could be with him once more in that place of the air-and-birds game. "Who looks out for us poor human beings?"

He thinks for a long time, brooding and deliberating, but Nili knows he already has the answer—he's just deciding whether or not to let her in on it. "What looks out for people is . . ."

"The earth!" She jumps up, shooting her hand into the air like a good student.

He seems surprised. "Why the earth?"

"I thought . . ." She is embarrassed. "The air looks after its birds, and the sea . . ."

"With people"—he glances at her, inspecting, and she knows

she's about to enter into another of his mazes—"with people it's something totally different. With people it's talking."

"Talking?" She swallows. She's not sure she understands him, but she definitely feels a warm, slender finger touching the depths of her being for an instant.

He hesitantly presents his thoughts to her. "Every day, it's like there's one word—"

"And if I say it—"

"Then you win!" His black eyes glow in front of hers; for a second he is open to her, and she sees inside, into his darkness, and a tiny spot of gold flickers there.

"But what? What do I win?"

"I dunno." He laughs softly, insolently, and walks around the room with his arms outstretched to the sides. "How should I know? Maybe you win the lottery? That kind of thing, perks."

Or fall in love, Nili sighs deep inside. "But tell me, who's the person who knows what the winning word is on a given day?"

She should have guessed his response: he smiles mysteriously and keeps flying around the room. She almost bursts out laughing at the ridiculous, arrogant importance he puts on. But he is also so exposed and transparent at this moment that her heart goes out to him. "Cheapskate! At least tell me what today's word is."

"No."

"Then just tell me if during the days we've been here I've ever said the right word."

He remains mute, lifting his arms up high, delighting in the suppleness of his limbs. "I can't tell you, it's against the rules. But if you happen to say it today, then this evening I'll be allowed to tell you that you said it."

They shake hands ceremoniously, and as they look into each other's eyes, his coal-black wades into her green. But he never told her before he left. Maybe he forgot, or maybe she really didn't say the word.

She smiles. "All that, all that whole last bit, I don't know where you came up with it. It's a thousand percent unlike him."

That's how she says it, and I close my eyes, not in pain, but as if I can't go on seeing from the outside. And I don't want to either, because I can almost feel him in me. It finally happens, out of the blue. And it was her negation, her absolute certainty of what was unlike him, that did it. For a moment I feel him hovering in front of me and existing independently and almost without any connection to me. And so for the first time he is suddenly with us in the room, more alive than he had been in all the words I had written, all the thoughts I had imagined and tortured myself with. Out of negation comes affirmation, just because she is so sure of what is a thousand percent unlike him. Eighteen years later, she still knows him with such confidence.

It used to be that just that thought could have shattered me, but now I stand outside my pain for an entire minute, not even caring whether the other things I had imagined weren't like him either, and I even manage not to ask her about the rest of it, about the Chinese restaurant, for example. I think that's unlike him too—so what? I just sit and delight in how much it doesn't hurt, and I am even capable of thinking that everything I'd written and imagined isn't like him. That he was an utterly different kid. A thousand percent. That he was a macho kid, loud and boisterous and wild, for example, or dumb and dense, or even sly and conniving—a bastard who abused her the way they all did. An array of princes and jokers in his image fans out like a pack of cards, and with wonderful peace of mind I close the circle segment and choose one card with my eyes shut, and that is him, my kid—

I dare to breathe in the place that even the writing hadn't opened up for me. It had been sewn up with iron wires, and he—the boy, the kid—is in front of me, alive and sharp, and then, unhurriedly, he changes his shape as in a dream, and now he is a young bird at night, emerging from the darkness into the light of my window, curiously drawn to the light, and we both look at each other through the glass and see each other, and the bird gets scared first and disappears again, and I am left with my longings, but it doesn't kill me now, I don't know why not, it just doesn't kill me anymore.

"So should I take out that whole bit?" I ask in a voice struggling to be dry, and what comes out is a squeaky, choking sound, and I am also stung by a different kind of disappointment. "To tell you the truth, I also felt that it wasn't really him, the whole thing with the winning word, but I really don't want to give up that bit."

"God forbid, don't take anything out."

We both say nothing as we quiet ourselves. I've started getting used to these silences, and I even like them. They're so different from the noise we used to share. I also notice how quiet it is here. It's strange that you can't hear any sounds from the street. Exemplary Walter has done a wonderful job of sealing off his house. No world.

I moisten her lips. My eyes are very close to hers. I ask softly how she feels. She makes an effort to smile. "I wouldn't recommend it." She asks if it's hard for me. I say it isn't. It is. That it's really mixed up. I still can't tell her how it moves me, to be exposed to her like this, as if without my knowledge, and also somehow, without being able to prevent it, with a kind of self-anesthetization or self-abandon, to feel her finally reading my story.

"Listen, you don't happen to have any cigarettes in the house, do you?" And before I can apologize for the stupid question, she digs her hand beneath the mattress with a seductive smile and pulls out a crushed pack of Marlboros, not even Lights.

"Just open the window afterward. He mustn't find out or he'll kill me." She chokes down a giggle. "He might drown me in tears."

I light one for myself and one for her, and take a long drag. I haven't smoked for three months. It was part of the rehab I was asked to do, required to do, and I was hoping it was behind me, that I'd overcome it, but then suddenly this sucking urge came over me. I inhale and look at her. I watch the way her eyes shrink as she takes a drag, the sluttish pleasure of a huntress of delights lighting up in her. Her whole vitality is now contained in the cracked lips that pull on the reddish glow, and for an instant it's as if a curtain has been opened and I can see her as she is, as she should be, as would make her happy, probably, were she not trapped in my little dictatorship.

As always when we reach this juncture, I am struck by the thought that maybe I never really understood what I had been given in the blind lottery of life—what I had won. And again, as usual during these attacks of mental weakness, it's a short road from here to wallowing in the swamp of if-only: How did it happen that I am the only person on the face of this earth whom she is somehow incapable of completely reading? What rare misfortune placed me in her blind spot? And yet I know that even that is not completely accurate, because that is exactly how I wanted it, that's what I fought for, and was slaughtered for. To strengthen my failing soul, I remind myself of all her transgressions, and remember with horror that I have a fairly long list of them further on, a choice little minefield. I sigh and say, "Okay, well, don't tell Melanie either."

"She doesn't let you smoke?"

"Are you kidding!"

We both inhale with a strange delight, somewhat hysterically, filling the room with clouds of smoke and choking with laughter.

"When you were born, you were a little pint-size thing, and you were in the preemie ward for three weeks. I wouldn't let you stay there alone."

"Really?" Instinctively I straighten up in my chair, already hearing the impatient dryness in my voice. You're such a shit, I think to myself, why are you fighting her? Give her the pleasure now, gift-wrapped.

"And I plunked myself down there for three weeks, and the nurses yelled and the doctors threatened, but it didn't do any good, I got under their feet in there for twenty-one days, sunrise, sunset, drove them all mad. Well, that father of yours was always very busy, and I wouldn't have trusted him with something like that anyway."

The shadow of a smile filled with satisfaction, almost craftiness, passes over her face. That's how I should have taken a picture of her, assimilating the smoke and passing it through her corroded windpipe and bronchi, happily scorching them.

"At night I would sit among the incubators with the preemies and talk to you, and sing to you, and tell you about Siddhartha and Vishnu and Parvati. I told you all the stories I knew. They thought I was crazy. They weren't the only ones." She titters. "They said to me, What can a little thing like that understand? There was this one nurse there, Kurdish, I think, but a real sharp woman, and she said to me back then, Your girl will grow up, she'll be a writer."

"Oh, so now we know."

"I even gave you massages in there."

"Massages? But how . . . it's supposed to be sterile!"

"Well, you turned out all right, didn't you?" Her thick fingers stretch and move around of their own accord. "I would put my hands through the rubber circles on the sides. You were like a little chick, and you were a bit translucent too, I could see all your veins."

A warm fingerling darts through my stomach. Me? Translucent?

As he arches his back, she inquires again, matter-of-factly, whether his father asks about what he's doing here all these days. He laughs. "My dad can ask all he wants." She tries carefully to understand the nature of their relationship, tries to paint his world, to guess what might nourish him when he goes back there.

"What do you do, say, when you go home for Shabbat? Are there any friends that you—"

"No friends." He cuts her off and drops his pose, and Nili feels his heart chakra constricting in him with a quick spasm.

"Then what?"

"Nothing." He sits with his legs crossed, puts his head on his hand, and stares at the floor tiles. "We maybe go get lunch at the Burger Ranch, and that's about it. *He* sits in his room listening to the game, and I sit in mine, with headphones on so I won't hear."

"And you don't talk?"

"What do you want us to talk about?"

"Don't you have any—I don't know—topics of conversation?"

He stares at her intently. He has a kind of look, sometimes, as if he's peering at her over a thin glasses frame. You saw him, didn't you, his look says. Yes, she answers, I most definitely did. She tries delicately to explain to him, without explicitly using any cauliflower, that even our parents are somehow chosen by us. Meaning, we choose parents who will help us grow, gain strength, sometimes even overcome what they do to us.

"And do we choose our kids too?" he asks with bitter mockery.

She is confused until she realizes he means only his father and himself. She slowly absorbs his pain. "Yes, kids too." Then she assails him again: "But he loves you, you can't understand that yet, but when you have children . . ." She inflames herself, recalling his father's surprising tears of shame when he came to give her his proposal. Only now does she recognize the familiar combination, the mixture of immeasurable compassion and cruelty that only parenthood, it seems, can produce. "And just so you know, he may not know exactly how to say it to you, but I'm sure you are the most precious person in the world to him."

"He hates me, he hates me!" His voice rises and turns into a wail. "If he could make it so I would die, so I wouldn't ever shame him . . . You know what he calls me?"

She says nothing, remaining alert and tense. For a moment she can almost read his father's derogatory name for him in his eyes, but the word is quickly erased before she can get it—again that tail, the speckled one, wrapped around a tree, lingering, then disappearing.

He gets up, walks around, and lifts his T-shirt up. For the first time since they met she sees his bronzed, velvety back, ripped up and down and across with long stripes of strange scabbed pinkness. "He only stopped when I got taller than him."

As if he had been listening in on their conversation, his father comes to see her after their class. He slips inside the room. Her whole body is on edge. He stands with his rooster chest puffed up, a smile smeared on his indecent lips. When he sees her face he falters; he thought she'd be happy, that she'd tell him something about the kid. Still, he makes an attempt. "What's up? Since he's with you we don't see anything of him. He's a real handful, my son, hey?"

Her eyes dry up the words in his throat. "Get the hell out of here."

Absorbing the punch, he utters, "What the—?"

"You heard me. Go."

"But what's the matter with you? Did I say something wrong again?"

"Leave, or I'll . . ." She starts moving toward him.

He moves to the door in alarm.

Nili stumbles back in and slams the door. She leans over the little sink, her whole body shaking. I could have murdered him.

Her hands were always drawn to touch. If anyone's body made some gesture or expression of pain, her hand would instantly be drawn to massage, to melt. With everyone: strangers, acquaintances, a girl from my class who brought me my homework when I was sick, a lonely neighbor, a hairless dog racked with scoliosis who adopted her and became addicted to her massages. Her hands were a natural extension of her gaze, her talk. Once, she did it with my school principal: in the middle of a discipline talk in her office, the two of us were sitting there innocently when suddenly the Tyrant put her hand on the back of her neck and moved it around, sighing. Nili was behind her in a flash, at the ready with her ten fingers, while I measured the distance to the window and a redemptive leap. But then there was a strange struggle among the principal's facial features, and an unbelievable fraction of a minute during which Nili, alone, almost beat the entire system.

Time is running out; they both feel it and think of it, and he, almost eagerly, tells her more and more: the studies at the boarding school, the wild boys who live there with him, who've already been kicked out of every other institution, the friend he once had there—

"A friend?" She perks up. "Wait, you didn't tell me about him, who is he?"

But he ignores her—and the Arab who converted to Judaism and is now his roommate. And running away nights to go and play pool, and the punishments they endure, and the supervisors' beatings, each one with his own method, and the obligatory fasting days, the spiritual reinforcements, and the card games in the basement, where the loser has to give someone a blow job.

"And you take part in this?"

"Not in that." He looks straight at her, a look that is too horizontal and congealed.

She becomes alarmed. "But in what?"

He wants to tell her, but he resists it too. She can feel the pressure mounting at once between the joints of his fingers, in his shoulder muscles. "There's an old guy," he finally says, looking at her fearfully, "a little old midget of a guy, Iraqi, he's maybe fifty, lives near the market, and he pays."

"For what?"

He gets up and walks around the room quickly. Then he stops and stands in warrior pose, with his arms reaching out to the sides. "All kinds of stuff. He gives me clothes to wear, you know, girls' clothes. He doesn't touch. Just watches and jerks off."

"And you?"

"Nothing. I what?"

"Do you enjoy it?"

"Are you kidding? It's for money. Twenty shekels every time."

But she already knows the changing tones of his voice, and she senses the skin of her scalp stretching; her heart feels crushed. He shifts his weight to the other foot. His eyes are focused on his fingertips. She glances at him. Somehow it doesn't surprise her. She thinks about herself at his age. What did her father know of what she was going through? And what does she know now about what's really happening to Rotem? (If only, oh God, if only Rotem is hiding a stormy love story from me, if only the whole world knows about it but me. Not even stormy, as long as there is some love there, some affection, friendship, one single drop flowing beneath the layers of flesh, behind her antibiotic look.)

But she won't let him off this time, it's too late, and she goes back and insists: "And that friend you mentioned?"

"It's nothing." There is already a slight darkening in the shadow behind his eyes.

"A friend is good," she insists, and knows that he can sense every time her voice tries to conceal an ambiguity. "It's good to have someone to pour your heart out to, isn't it?"

"I'm hitting the showers," he says, and leaves her feeling as if her fingertips had touched a glowing ember.

Two hours later, they relax at the end of an exhausting class in which she seemed to be trying to polish and peel him. He is tired out and glistening with sweat, and she sits beside him and tries to direct herself to what he needs most (remembering that as a girl she was always surprised at how the medicine she swallowed knew exactly how to reach the hurting part of her body). If only he would tell her explicitly what he needs. But he is taking, she thinks, he is definitely taking something. It's not clear what, but something is being taken from her, her exhaustion today tells her that, a little like when she gets her period. And she thinks that since yesterday, since he mimicked her, he has really started consuming something from her, but in his own way, he is careful to keep his content a secret, incredibly trained, trained to conceal. Sometimes when she's with him, she feels like a big city, abundant and serene and innocent, and he is a stealthy guerrilla, emaciated and glowing, who slips into her every so often from his forest, grabs something he needs to survive, then disappears.

232

And maybe it has nothing to do with her yogi qualities, this thing that he is taking? She opens her eyes in wonder: What, then?

"Is there perhaps something you'd like to tell your body?" The question pops out of her mouth and surprises her, and he hardens a little. "You can say it now," she suggests, recalling how he had almost cried when she talked with him about his body two days earlier. Still, she feels something has opened up in him since then. "Say it silently or out loud. Tell it what the problem is." She sees a slight furrowing of his brow, and quiet. Then he lets out a very small smile.

She holds back, and the class goes on, but before he goes off for lunch, he stops at the door. "Know what I said before to . . . my body?"

"What?"

He laughs, kicking at the tiles. "Nothing really, I just asked if it was happy with me." She doesn't understand, but he eagerly explains: "I always thought of it the other way around, like whether I'm happy with it. But suddenly, when you said to ask it, I felt sorry for it, you know, that it had to be mine, like . . ."

She smiles with him and still doesn't comprehend. Such a beautiful body, refreshed, etched, and it responds to him with suppleness and harmony. For a minute—without even feeling it—she stretches out her healthy, gloriously beautiful body like a person taking a deep breath after leaving a sick friend's house.

Later, when she's alone again, she throws herself into her weekly room cleaning—her little display of freedom against the manager and the cleaning staff. Something disturbs her: the permanent, insulting thought that she is, in some way, not complicated enough. Apparently not messed up enough either. There are clubs, she knows, that wouldn't let her in; the people she feels closest to and loves most have whole areas she is forbidden to enter, and all her seeing skills aren't enough to even guess at what goes on in their twisted, sophisticated crevices. She will never know what they really think of her there, and she has always had a gnawing suspicion that those are the places where she is being betrayed. Now that she has come this far, her thoughts already know their own way home: maybe one day, years from now, the girls will finally appreciate her true value. They'll grow up—

"Rotem."

"What?" She alarms me when she stops me like that in mid-sentence.

"I have a request."

"I'm listening."

"Don't read now. Speak it to me."

"Speak what?"

"What you have written down."

I don't get it. "What—"

"Don't say 'she.' Say 'you.' Talk to me."

I shrug my shoulders and quickly scan the next lines with my eyes. I don't know where she got the idea, and I briefly consider objecting in the name of artistic freedom. I decide to give her the "you," but certainly not to compromise on the other protagonists. *"Maybe one day years from now"*—I read to her, hesitating a little at first, checking every stone before stepping on it, but then it starts to flow—*"the girls will finally appreciate your true value. They'll grow up, they'll be mothers too, their eyes will open . . .* Is it all right like that? Is this what you meant?"

"Yes." Her eyes are closed. "Go on."

You lean on the mop, dreaming up scenes from their future motherhood, conjuring up for them a quiet smiling man with broad shoulders, a Lego house with a red roof, and two or three kids, maybe even four, why not. There will be joyful moments on the playground and at the dinner table, and there will also be arguments over what to wear to kindergarten and when to go to bed, and then over what time to come home from parties, whether or not to smoke, and what to smoke, when to start having intercourse, and with whom, and then a new understanding will emerge in them, and they'll suddenly comprehend the gift of motherhood you bequeathed them. The internal liberation you gave them with your ostensible anarchy, and with the absolute equality that prevailed between mother and daughter in your home. You sigh quietly: it is true that sometimes, if you were to look at things unflatteringly, from an external and foreign point of view, it may seem as if you and they are in fact the same age, helpless and scared subjects of the arbitrary and misunderstood adult world . . .

"Yes," she murmurs, her eyes still closed, her lips moving along with mine.

But then, out of the murkiness of your blessed forgetting, you see a row of what look like humps—different-sized islands of memory, both the inconsequential and the critical: the lunchboxes taken to kindergarten and found to be empty at lunchtime, the puddles of urine gathering next to the front door when you were late getting home. The furious quarrels that erupted every time you tried to help them with their homework, and the boredom and suffocation that took hold of you when you were forced to sit with them for even ten minutes and study for an exam. Every minute seemed like an eternity to you. And the slap you once gave Rotem while she was struggling through the Pythagorean theorem. Your insistence on treating her only with homeopathic medicine, even when she had strep throat, and the horrible comment made by the doctor at the ER, who happened to be a former classmate of yours, giving you a broad perspective on your character—

I keep on reading the long and fairly tedious list. I enjoyed writing it, and I felt just and strong and full of self-pity, and I thought what fun it was that everything was behind me and I could be happily embittered over every episode as if it had just happened yesterday. But now my insides are shrinking with insipidness and shame as I realize that this is the hot air I've been existing on for thirty-five years. Even so, I keep on reading to her, setting off land mine after land mine in her face, but preserving the same voice and clean staccato I've been using all evening, not a single word emphasized, no blaming and no apologizing, no influencing and no bribery. I present her with my text without interfering, and I have lots of experience doing that, because in some sense, that has been the way we have talked in recent years, the method I developed so as not to flare up when she would invade me in mid-conversation and hover around my allergic areas with her criminal innocence. But when I have almost reached the end of the list, my mouth starts to grow dry and I glance feebly at the clock. It's ten now in London. Melanie gave me unequivocal instructions about the next few lines. She talked about the need for total honesty, even now, especially now; "It will purify," she said. "It will liberate you both." But I'm not Melanie, and I fix my gaze strongly on the dark corner of the lie, and pathetically skip to the beginning of the next section.

Nili, with her eyes closed, grasps my wrist with a strength she does not have and says, "All the way, Rotem, read until the last line."

. . . And men staying the night, trapped in front of torn childish eyes as they walk out of the shower naked, relaxed, staring in embarrassment; and the nights Rotem sobbed as she banged on your locked bedroom door, lashing out against everything that was stormily occurring inside it; and that cursed week, which should have been shoved into a place it could never emerge from in any therapy, when you stayed in the apartment getting high with two of them, two animals—oh God, what did you do to her?

Silence. She finally lets go of my hand, and I have shrunken to the size of a foundling. It scares me to see what she is capable of knowing if she only wants to. That's exactly how it was when, suddenly, in the middle of a normal phone conversation two months ago, she said, "You're writing that story, aren't you?" I choked and tried to squirm my way out of it, and she asked, "Why that of all things? Don't you have any other stories?" And I said I simply had to, and she asked, "Now?" And I said, "Yes," and I wanted to scream. How can you not understand that it's my last chance, while you're still with me a little. I won't be able to do it later. But all I could say, with a kind of embarrassing squeak, was "Please, Nili, just don't tell me not to." Melanie, making a salad behind me, stopped and didn't move; she understood from my voice what the conversation was about. Nili was quiet, then she took such a deep breath that she seemed to be inhaling me through the line, and said, "But afterward come to Israel and read it to me, as a farewell gift."

Now, with a voice that is quiet but tight, she admits, "It's good that you said it."

"Really?"

"When you started with that list, I was afraid you wouldn't say it."

I shrug my shoulders weakly. "Well, now I've said it."

"Thank you."

We both sit quietly and I think about Melanie. I touch her, refuel, and come back. Then suddenly, unrelated to anything, I think, That's enough. How long can you keep towing that childhood around? How long can you be enslaved to it? You have to move on, have to start somehow letting it go.

Nili says dryly, "And those two peas in a pod, your sisters in the story—you don't need them anymore."

"So you have nothing to worry about," she reassures Leora, who calls again at some impossible hour of the morning. "I'm not falling in love with him, and he's not exactly falling in love with me either; it's not at all about that, but I may help him love himself a little more." Leora doesn't answer, embarrassed for some reason; she swore to herself that she wouldn't phone again, and it's not clear to her how it happened that she did, or what is really happening to her, what has been unsettling her all these days that Nili has been there with him.

Nili forces herself to talk, to break the silence. "Maybe I need to try and influence him more, direct him a little, advise him maybe, I don't know. Maybe make him see that he needs to protect this gift God has given him. He should study yoga up there in the north, or find some dance or movement class—what do you think, Lilush?" She almost shouts, angry at herself for being frightened like a child because of Leora's ominous silence.

Leora finally comes around, lurching forward with a grimace of resentment. "You know, now that I think of it—why not? I mean, if you're going to create a human being, go all the way with it, play God all the way, don't even take Friday off."

"No, no," Nili says with utter seriousness and gravity, "I'm not creating him, he's the one who knows exactly what he needs all by himself. He's always driving at something. And look, even if he doesn't really know it now, even if he has to spend years making mistakes, and even if he forgets it all along the way, and forgets this week too—in the end he'll get to what he was supposed to be. You'll see."

"But what? What is he supposed to be? A yogi? A guru? Hare Krishna?"

"No. I think he's looking somewhere completely different. Somewhere even deeper than that."

"You—" Leora shakes her head and is suddenly flooded, to her complete surprise, with a burning sense of jealousy toward this foolish boy and his scandalously good luck. "You seem to be forgetting again that we're talking about a boy. He's fifteen!" (Nili, with her last remaining strength, manages to restrain herself from mumbling "and a half.") "And you attribute so much to him, and load him with tons of, of"—and for a minute Leora sees a picture of a hesitant, slender, hunched young man, and someone using a thick pipe to pour the entire content of Victoria Falls down his throat—"now, you listen to me and try to answer me honestly: don't you think you're making a little too much of him with all these—forgive me for saying this— but these inscrutable interpretations?"

There is a long pause. Leora repeats her question, now in a slightly feeble, almost trembling voice.

"No," Nili says eventually. For the millionth time, but somehow always the first time, she clearly grasps the huge effort she has to invest to keep Leora from *ever* penetrating her. "It's not at all something I can be wrong about," she says softly, cleanly, giving up any argumentativeness. "It's something that either I know completely, all the way, or I have no sense about at all. You know, that's how it is with me when I'm inseminated"—or at least, when I used to be, she silently rephrases—"and that's how it is when I'm in love, and then it's immediate, on the spot, bingo!"

A pause, then silence. Leora, at home, raises two well-plucked arches over her eyes, slender and ironic, and ticks silently like a tact-bomb.

"Okay, okay," Nili accedes, "so I've made some mistakes here and there—who hasn't?"

I haven't, Leora thinks sourly, and a horrible headache suddenly erupts on the edges of her skull and advances quickly, and a lump in her throat starts darting up and down like a little devil stomping his feet furiously. Me! I haven't!

"But I'm not making a mistake with him. And I'll tell you something else"—her eyes shine and her chest swells, and Leora knows how beautiful she is in her feverish state, in her sudden change of seasons, when all her emotions are portrayed on her face, her honesty, simple and innocent—"and you can laugh all you want, but I feel as if I had to go through all these twenty years of hard labor, and not a second less, so that I'd be completely prepared when he arrived."

She slowly turns her heavy head to face me. Her eyes are bloodshot, but her face is soft. I recall her response—three years ago? four?—when I first told her I was writing. "What do you want to be a writer for now, at your age?" she had asked innocently. "When you get old, like Agnon or Bialik, then you can write!" I had practically wailed, because of the vast distance, unbridgeable, lost. Because of the hunger of orphans. Now I tell her, with a relief uncommon in these lands, about the feeling I had during the last weeks of writing. "It was as if someone were grabbing me hard by my neck and taking off with me. Honestly, like they were actually forcing me to leap out of my skin and take off . . ."

Her eyes glimmer. "That's happiness, isn't it?"

"Yes," I admit. "It's the best."

For a minute she fills with light, you can really feel her spirit awakening and moving freely, illuminated within the impervious tissue of her flesh. I too open up inside, all my particles start to spin, and we get closer and pull back and are drawn into each other, and we can't look into one another's eyes, and my throat is gripped with the familiar burning pain, which once, in one of the *Tourist* stories, I called "the cry of a disillusioned infant."

"Rotem," she murmurs, "Rotem, Rotem." Motionless, we both are gathered and drawn to the same exact place, and I close my eyes, and we are briefly together, within a huge embrace that is the embrace of—insane as it may sound—Mother.

The mother we never had.

"And that friend of yours?" she asks as soon as they meet, willing to get slapped but absolutely needing to find him someone close, at least one person in the world with whom he can abate his loneliness a little.

His shoulders arch up instantly. His eyes grow dark, peering out at her from a cave. But this time, to her surprise, he answers, "He's not at boarding school anymore. He left."

"Why?"

"Why?" Again that smirk spreads over his face, revealing a foreign object, sharp and injuring, which is pinned inside him. " 'Cause they said I was no good for him. That I was doing him harm. That's why."

"What were you—?" It flashes through her: the speck of saliva that fell from him and dropped on her face. The way he leaped to wipe it off. "But why?"

"How should I know? Ask them."

"I'm asking you."

"I don't know. His parents came, took him away. That kind of stuff. He was also a little crazy."

"Also? What else was he?"

"No . . ." He laughs, embarrassed. "I meant I am too. Aren't I?"

"No, you're not. God forbid. You shouldn't have those kinds of thoughts. But where is he now?"

"I don't know. Maybe France. They didn't say. He has a sister in France, and some aunt in Canada. Maybe there. Maybe he's even here. What difference does it make?"

"Don't you have an address for him, a phone number, anything?"

He seems engrossed in his long fingers.

"And he didn't write to you, didn't leave any sign?"

"I . . ." Then he falls silent. Breathes rapidly. His lips turn pale. "They probably told him we weren't allowed to be in touch. I don't know, I think so." He shrugs his left shoulder in a round, gloomy way.

She suddenly feels a tremendous weight. She leans back against the door and looks at him, and he is imploring her to understand, to relieve him of the need to tell. With great effort, she makes her way through everything that's spinning around inside her and asks a question, already knowing the answer: "So tell me, when did it happen? When did he leave? When did they take him?"

"I don't know. A year ago maybe." He surreptitiously threads his arms together behind his back and sees her look, and puts them back in front submissively. She sees his unraveled flesh through the watch and the scar. Then he says softly, "Seven months. Plus a few days. Twenty maybe. Twenty-two."

Nili stands motionless. Dying to sit down. Collapsing under his pain, his insult, his longings. After a prolonged silence, she asks, "And what is his name?" Because she suddenly has a reckless, mad thought—Nili the savior, the all-powerful—that she'll find his friend for him. She'll investigate and detect and use all her connections, enlist all the freaks she's met during her travels, and she'll locate him, and respin the thread between them. She can already see how her broken mailbox becomes the secret nest for their encounter and their relationship.

But he hesitates. His eyes roll down.

Nili looks at him imploringly. "Well? Don't tell me his name is a secret too!"

"No, not a secret."

"Then?"

"Kobi."

She laughs. "He's also Kobi? Two Kobis?"

"No, he's Kobi."

"And you?" Now the laughter hangs emptily on her face.

"I'm not."

"Why . . . How can that be?"

"I'm Tzachi."

This is too much for her. She sits down on the floor. A strange nausea burns her throat, a roux of emotions undigested and regurgitated into her throat by a stubborn diaphragm. How could he be Tzachi? That name doesn't suit him at all. She remembers how he told her his name the first time. Remembers a second of hesitation.

Amazed at how, in the blink of an eye, he had decided to lie; she no longer understands anything, and doesn't wish to, and thinks how easily she is conned—what the hell is it about her that makes people take her for a fool? She curses the twisted crevices in which she is always betrayed, and remembers with some torn and final train of thought how he had impelled her to call him Kobi. The vague trembling around his eyes when she had said the name. "Listen, um . . ." She refuses to force the false name through her lips. "Maybe at least you'll tell me about him now?"

"Not now, maybe later." But he's alert to what is occurring within her, to her hurt face as it falls, and he gets up irritably and walks to the door. Just don't let him leave now, I can't be alone. He must sense her thoughts, because he stops and turns to the grunting air-conditioning unit and stands there playing with its buttons. Off and on. "I pissed you off."

"Well, do you think I like being—" Then she grumbles, "Why didn't you tell me at first?! Why did you have to cheat me like that?"

He half turns to her. "Should I tell you how we used to talk?"

"Go on." She wants to and yet doesn't. She already knows his tricks. The quick slalom moves of a liar as he pulls a rabbit out of his hat in mid-conversation, relying on her infantile curiosity.

"With questions. You're only allowed to use questions."

She relaxes her shoulders. What does he want from me now? Why can't he be direct? She can't be bothered with his riddles.

"Right from the start it was that way," he tells her, his excitement rising. "That's what we decided. Actually no, first it was his idea, he always has ideas, that one"—a yearned-for smile lights up the corners of his eyes—"and as soon as he saw me there in the yard? As soon as I first got there? And he was already there two years, he's older than me, I was ten when I came, and he right away started talking to me like that, with questions." His voice rose and became thin, and Nili also thought he was starting to talk in a different kind of dialect, from another place. "And I straightaway answered right, 'cause I read him in two seconds. Till I came along they thought he was crazy, and they none of them would answer him, just kept beating him up. But me, as soon as I got off the bus and he saw me, he came right over to me. Well, it doesn't matter." It does matter, she knows, hearing the exposed note of pride, and a large warm bubble bursts and drips down inside her. "I was only ten years old, and since then it was like that all the time, in our room too, and in class. And say when he was having one of his fits? He would fall down, he has that disease where you keep falling, and as soon as he'd come back? Again the same thing, a question from him, a question from me . . ." His eyes gleam, he runs his hand through his short hair, and Nili senses the tenderness of the touch, and with her seer's eyes she sees an image of a boy taller than him, thin and supple and restless, with a sharp face and a tortured, tense look, moving like a cheetah pacing around in its cage. "So that's how it was, always only with questions all the time. Questions, nothing else is allowed." He breathes rapidly and gives her a sad smile. "For maybe five years, we never tripped up."

"But how long can you talk like that? What can you say?" she asks, beginning to emerge from her tears, large and bright and yellow, with her innocent Weeble smile.

He suddenly gets excited. "Wanna try it?"

"Do you think I can?"

"Haven't you noticed you're already doing it?"

"Me?"

She smiles with cracked lips and looks at me, and her look says, Oh my, you're such an inventor. Then she says, "You really have a whole world in there." She gestures at my head with her bald eyebrows. Only then does she let out a deep sigh, and my first thought is that somehow by chance my story did touch her, kissing some dormant memory. I become alarmed, not wanting her to suffer from it too much.

"Look, I mean, we don't really know what motivated him, and sometimes you can die just from sudden abundance, like the survivors

244

from the camps." I explain to her (as if I need to): "There were survivors who gorged themselves to death after years of starvation. Or at least you can want to die." Like me, for example, I think. Like me, during my first period with Melanie, and even today, sometimes, at moments of mortal excitement, I really want to die, because how can you bear all this unfounded goodness, this scandal of goodness—

There is a heavy silence soaked with words, absolutely dripping with them. I sit there exposed, urgently needing to be grounded somehow. To one particular body.

Then she sighs again, a long, horrible sigh. She lies on her back, broken in two right in front of me, and I suddenly realize it's not only the sorrow, the grief, and the guilt—it's also that she has missed him all these years, simply missed a person who touched her life in a place no one else ever had.

Three days after she came home from the Dead Sea, he disappeared. He ran away from the boarding school on Monday evening through a hole in the fence, and that was it. They never saw him again. And now it comes back to me as in a nightmare, how she cried then, for weeks. She talked to herself, cried out in her sleep, slammed her head against the wall, on the table, on doors, dozens of times, impervious as a piston, and she sprayed out words like shavings. Then suddenly Leora and Dovik showed up, their debut appearance in Rishon, to figure out what had happened, and while they were there they held a field court-martial for her in the kitchen, for all her crimes, no statute of limitations. I hung around downstairs outside the building until I couldn't take it anymore, and then I burst inside and screamed at them to leave her alone and get the hell out of our house and our lives. Go back to civilization. And they really did, with an imposing air of offense like two righteous cardinals, and Nili sat fatigued in a corner of the kitchen and looked at me with boundless gratitude. She had no strength to speak, but I'll never forget that look.

Then came the journey, her private journey to search for him all over the country, hitchhiking. It was long after the official search was over. They had searched for him for three or four days, police and army and volunteers. Then they gave up, added him to the missing-person statistics—how much effort can you invest in a kid from that kind of boarding school, a kid who isn't worth anything? At that point she finally woke up out of her shock and decided that everyone was wrong, because they didn't know him, and that he hadn't fallen into a pit or jumped off a cliff, he hadn't been kidnapped and he hadn't drowned. He had gone underground, she determined with a crazed kind of self-persuasion, and her eyes glistened with wonder at his resourcefulness. "He's hiding behind a different identity," she explained, as if she had free access to his center of consciousness. "That kid has an immense talent for camouflage and acting. He just disappeared himself, and when he feels like coming back, he will." And with a secretive Moneypenny look in her eyes, she determined that if he happened to see her anywhere, he would come to her. To her, he would come.

Then she surpassed herself by coming up with the brilliant idea that I should go with her to look for him. Me—with her—for him. Of course, I laughed in her face and turned my back on her, and when she realized there was no chance, she begged me to at least help her pack, because I was always a champion packer (no one can outdo me at stuffing an infinite number of things into a tiny space). I was so psychotic that I went and packed her a bunch of scarves. I pulled out all her dozens of scarves and shawls from the closet and stuffed them into a tattered backpack, not even a single pair of underwear or a bra or a dress, or toiletries. I fastened the backpack and shoved it at her: "Now go." When she came back a week later, in the middle of the night, I woke up immediately. I could smell her on the stairs, the whole space was flooded, she'd never had such a scent, an almost inhuman smell, the smell of an animal grasping that this time it has really made the mistake of its life. She didn't have the strength to even make it to the bath or to bed. She collapsed on the orange couch and slept for twenty hours straight. Every so often she would mumble something in her sleep about how they had tossed her from one place to another, laughed at her, treated her like a madwoman. Over the next few days she didn't talk, as if she were dried up. All the juice had run out of her. She even became practical and tried to throw herself into home-improvement projects. She cleaned out years' worth of dirt, tidied closets, clothes, kitchen utensils. If I could have allowed myself to feel anything then, if it weren't so beyond my capabilities, I might have felt sorry for her, because even I could see how much she was suffering through her exercises in acquired motherhood. But we stopped talking completely. There were no words for her story with him, and later not for all the rest either, and then I left. I couldn't go on living within the mourning for her catastrophe—it had nothing to do with me, and I wanted nothing to do with it.

We've never spoken of it since, even during the last two months, when she knew I was writing the story, and when I begged her to give me a hint, something, she claimed she had erased it all, that from her point of view it was over. She, who was incapable of keeping a secret for a second, never betrayed that secret, his and hers. So all I have is fragments, no more, the normal fragments of mosaic from which children somehow piece together the mystery of their parents' lives. "But that's it, it's over," I tell her, and then I say it again, as if one of us is not completely convinced. "Enough, it's enough, it's over, and just think what price you paid." Maybe even the illness too—this I don't say, of course, but I'm certain it's gone through her mind too—because how could one conceive that *she*, of all people, and at such a young age . . .

On the last evening she gets an idea—what an idiot for only thinking of it now—to suggest to him that they work at night too. He rejoices—yes! And he dances around her. She's never seen him this way. She asks if he's not tired, and he laughs—he'll keep going all night, right up until he leaves.

The spa area is locked at night, so she invites him to come to her room. She nervously tidies it in anticipation, until she hears a soft knock at the door, and he comes in hesitantly. As he did when he first

247

entered the yoga room, he takes a few sliding steps until he is standing exactly in the right place for her, in the solar plexus of her round straw mat. He stands there for a moment absorbing, unconsciously, and only then he suddenly wakes up and is surprised to find her room so small—it doesn't look anything like a hotel room, with her Indian fabrics hanging on the walls, which suddenly look pathetic to her: the mattress on the floor, the plastic bags bursting with all kinds of foods he doesn't recognize—her seeds—and the spice jars arranged on the bureau. He walks around slowly inspecting. By all means, let him look, it's all part of learning. He even peeks in her ashtray and finds the cigarette butt from lunchtime. He looks at her slightly shocked. "Are cigarettes allowed in yoga?"

She shrugs her shoulders. "What can I do? Don't tell on me. I only have one a day. But when I do, I want the smoke to fill every single cell of my lungs!"

They work enthusiastically and with a kind of pre-separation euphoria. They repeat things she taught him and she finds that he hasn't forgotten any of the poses, not even the more complex ones, and that his body seems to have recorded every nuance: when to breathe and when to hold the breath, where the foot points when the fingers of the opposite hand are stretched out. And she thinks, not for the first time, that perhaps she did not teach him anything, just blew some dust off an ancient manuscript lying inside him.

An hour goes by, then another. They move quietly, almost in silence. They feel as if they are the beating heart of the huge, unfeeling hotel. Every so often they rest, talk a little, sink into relaxation, tell each other that it's all right if they fall asleep for a few minutes, and after the relaxation their bodies start moving again of their own accord, pulled from one pose to the next, choosing their favorite asanas. Nili asks him not to try too hard. He has a long day of traveling ahead of him. He says again that he's willing to go all night like this, and in fact she is too. She wants to equip him with as much as possible, with the richest supplies, with her royal jelly, and she can already see that she won't have time to even touch the tip of the iceberg, and she is sorry for that, and consoles herself, and is happy and sad and a little drunk.

During one of their sleepy nocturnal conversations, he tells her that every week he sends a letter to a different country, in alphabetical order, with the name of his friend but no address, just the country name. Then he waits. He knows there's no chance—but maybe there is? Sometimes miracles happen, don't they? She says nothing, glancing at his watch, imagining to herself his secret, persistent wanderings among the countries, and now she sees in her mind's eye a completely different boy—short, with brown curly hair, a refined and slightly lost boy with a birdlike face, huge eyes, and lips that always seem poised to question.

He suddenly fills up with freshness and even becomes garrulous, and he tells her about the restaurant he's going to open. He'll build it in the most remote place in the world, on a cliff in the desert, or even in Eilat, as long as there aren't a lot of people there. "But there are people in Eilat, loads of people," she is forced to point out. "No," he says firmly, "what do you mean? There aren't any people there at all, Eilat is a wilderness." "That's not true," she retorts, "what are you talking about?" He is quiet for a minute as he lies on his back, holding his left arm straight up in the air. That's how he likes to think. He can even fall asleep that way. At boarding school they're used to it now, but at home, with his dad, it really gets on his nerves, and he always goes into his room and knocks his arm down. "Then more remote than Eilat," he finally gives in, "on Mount Sinai even. Or on Venus." But there aren't any people at all on Venus, she thinks, but doesn't say it. "There are people," he says argumentatively, as if she had tried to refute him; "they sent spaceships there and now there are people." She listens to his voice and wonders what she's hearing now, and if she should perhaps save him a little from embarrassing ignorance—who better than her to know how embarrassing. But suddenly, in a moment of illumination, she blurts out: "Of course there are people on Venus, how could I forget? They sent a spaceship there from India." That's just it, he says, and she hears him making an effort to turn off any hint of a smile in his voice. "And the Indians are all black," he continues the thread she has given him, "because Venus is close to the sun." "Assuming, of course, that the elephants don't eat them," she cheerfully summarizes, and senses his hidden laughter, like a boy squirming beneath a blanket. She trembles in delight at the little discovery he has allowed her about his secret life, his underground, his anarchic struggle against dry, hateful facts—

"Why did you stop?"

"I thought you were asleep."

"Why did you stop?"

"Because . . ." My eyes suddenly well up.

She looks at me and understands. "It wasn't really like that." She sighs. I sense she is being cautious with me now, and that's even more painful. "You're the one who invented the whole business with the spaceship and the elephants and the facts," she explains to me as if to a child, trying to console, to go backwards and correct.

"Yes, of course. I don't know." I stand up and sit down again, fighting with all my power against an idiotic sob that has suddenly erupted in my nose, completely out of season. "Just the fact that you laughed with him there, it doesn't matter over what, but you must have laughed at something together, that's the most—"

"Yes," she says quietly, looking at me as if she is photographing something and taking it with her for the road. She closes her eyes, tightens her large face, and I don't know where she is; perhaps she is seeing my side of the story for a moment, perhaps for once she sees only my side. What do I know? What can you know about another person, even if they're your mother? Ultimately, the umbilical cord is cut off or shrivels up and a glacial loneliness surrounds you. This immersion of hers goes on for a long time, and I suddenly get scared that now is the moment the illness will really defeat her, all of a sudden, and I say, "Stop, Nili, Mom, let's go on."

"So who's going to come to your restaurant?" she asks with a smile, and he sits up on his elbows.

"See, that's the thing. I don't care if only one person comes once a year, but when he does, I'll lay out a twenty-foot table for him and give him the feast of his life, with all the dishes made just for him, and all the sides and the sorbets. I'll put out the whole menu for him."

"Wait, but what will you do the rest of the time?"

He ponders. She thinks the dream is a little vague for him. "It's not like that. You don't get it. I make him the meal every day. Every single day. But he only comes one day a year."

"And what about the other days?" She still doesn't comprehend.

"The other days I wait for him."

She is quiet, thinks that if she's lucky, she may happen upon his restaurant one day and be rewarded with the meal of her life. She deliberates again, thinking maybe she should give him her phone number, but again she decides not to, and reminds herself of her great talent, the art of separation, and her heart aches with the pain of giving up. I mustn't, she recites to herself. He has such a clear and unique destiny, and just like he found me, he'll keep going and find his path. Because it is clear to her now that that is his great talent: finding his true path, listening inside and knowing. She sighs loudly, and he asks what happened, and she says, "Nothing, you know," and looks at him, and knows she was only a station on his long journey, and that she must bless her good fortune and not expect anything more; an evil voice hisses inside her, "As always." And a very un-yogi-like prod of simple and raw hostility passes through her toward everyone who will meet him later on, as he continues on his way.

"Hey," he drawls, and turns his back to her. "Is yoga also massage?"

"What?" She opens her eyes. "What did you say?" She raises her arms to hug her body. She suddenly feels cold.

He says nothing.

"Yes. With me at least, in my yoga."

Silence.

"So . . . you know how to?"

"Yes. In Jerusalem I did it all the time. In hospitals too, when I was working. And for my students." It seems strange to her for him to be closing the circle his father had opened. She knows she will consent to anything he asks. He sits down. His eyes don't look at her. "Do you . . . Have you ever had a massage?"

"No."

"Because you didn't want to, or it never worked out?"

"Both."

"It can be very nice."

"Is it like in . . . you know, in those clubs?"

"There are all kinds. Are you talking about clubs with girls?"

"There's one in the neighborhood. A massage parlor. Some guys went to check it out."

"Did you?"

"No. But listen"—he quickly runs his tongue over his upper lip—"No. Never mind."

"What, what did you want?"

"I was just thinking." He looks closely at the tips of his fingers and the air around him thickens. "I dunno, is there a difference between how you give a massage to a man and a woman?"

She giggles, embarrassed, unsure of whether she's understanding him correctly. "Of course there's a difference, but it's hard to put into words." She can feel she's getting a little entangled. "Look, I never really give a massage 'to a man' or 'to a woman,' I just give it to the particular person who . . ." She stops, and starts drifting away, and he gives her a longing and frightened look, which slowly steadies in front of her and becomes clear. Then he nods once, almost imperceptibly, like a spy signaling from a dark forest.

252

"Lie down," she says as she stands up. "Lie on the mattress and take your clothes off, just leave on what you're comfortable with. I'll be right back."

She goes into the bathroom and chooses some bottles from her collection of oils, and leans heavily for a moment, with two fists, on the marble shelf below the mirror. She asks herself what has really happened to him with her these past few days, and what it was that her yoga massaged and softened and released in him so that he is now capable of asking her these questions, voicing them. And she thinks, Oh God, how far he's come—much further than I imagined, much more yogi than I thought. She tilts her head to the room, but there is no sound coming from there. I wish I knew what I've given him, she thinks, suddenly tired; maybe I could give some of it to myself. She fills her lungs with air and looks in the mirror, which her breath has fogged over, and for a minute she sees nothing.

When she comes back from the bathroom with her massage bag, he is still sitting as she left him. She asks if he's changed his mind, and he says no. She arranges the bottles of oil on a chair, the jars of creams and lotions, and two clean towels. Then she turns away and messes with the bottles for a while, so as not to embarrass him, and lights some incense sticks and a few vanilla-scented candles, which she places in different corners of the room. When she turns back to him, he's already lying on his stomach, wearing only his shorts, with his forehead resting on his hands.

.

"Rotem."

"Yes."

"If it's hard for you, you don't have to."

"It is hard for me, and I do have to."

We're both slightly short of breath, but she still has the strength to give me a little smile, of encouragement, I think. I look at her again before diving into the final pages. Her hands are folded over her chest. Her face, beneath the fringes of white hair, is calm and almost beautiful now, the Simone Signoret face she used to have. I wonder if this is the time to tell her things I never have. Not dark secrets, just little things that may comfort her, ease her, or even make her laugh. For example, that I'm far more similar to her than she imagines, and that the similarities are actually in areas I always tormented her over. That I'm not much smarter than her, for example. That my brain is also weak, that I forget a lot, maybe even more than she did at my age. Maybe it's because of the pills during my tourist season, or maybe I'm also lacking the protein that ties fact molecules together. Maybe this is the time to tell her that my legendary strength, which she was so afraid of, and my infamous determination are now like melted butter. Just so she knows that time is equalizing us.

"Rotem?" she asks gently, extracting me.

I rearrange my pages, and that motion organizes me, and suddenly I am washed over by a wave of happiness for it, for my little story, because it is a place, a home even, and I can go back to it from wherever I am. That is the reality—she herself said so when I asked before. "That's exactly the reality I want to hear." My reality. Firsthand.

She sits down beside him and touches the back of his neck, and feels him shudder. For several minutes she slowly runs her hands over his body, balancing the chakras and reading with her eyes closed. Then she pours some thick oil in her palm and rubs her hands together to warm the oil a little, so it won't chill him, and starts slowly rubbing the sides of his neck.

"What kind of lotion is that?"

"It's grape-seed oil, feel it." She lets him smell her palm. "It's not a very strong scent, is it? I didn't want the scent to be too strong in here, what with the candles, so it won't distract us."

She concentrates on his back, on the place where he hunches, pressing and kneading first, then switching to more gentle motions, squeezing his flesh between her fingers, gathering up knots of toughness and anger and protest, and giving them back to him soft, appeased. Then with her knuckles, she prods the flesh on both sides of his spine, from top to bottom and back again, and for a long while she tries to soften the stubborn muscles around his neck. Only after making friends with his back does she dare to touch its scars, oiling them and rubbing in circles; she can't understand what his father used to beat him with, and she wonders what his dad knows about him and what he guesses.

His spine is like a thread, and she moves away from it to the outer areas of his body and rolls out his flesh to the sides with her palms, enjoying the way it springs back and swells and turns red and dark. She makes notes of the spots where the muscles are tense, and can't understand how he's capable of such flexibility with the mess he has in there, between his shoulder blades, where the scaffolding of his hunchback costume twists and turns like tendrils. As she works, his body becomes more awake and alert, unlike other people who sometimes drift off the moment she touches them and spend the rest of the massage floating in and out of sleep. Now she thinks she can sense his question about men and women throbbing along his body, and she hesitates a little over which one to start with. She grasps his shoulders and starts kneading hard, one shoulder after the other, pulling them up and back until it almost hurts, crushing and pushing with all her strength. Then she slowly fills them with broadness and power, and digs with her demanding fingers beneath his shoulder blades and muscles, and bends his arms back, and with her elbows she presses the lumps of tension and melts them into his flesh. She stops for a minute to wipe the sweat off her forehead with the back of her hand—she, who never perspires during a massage, and yet as soon as she started with him there was concentrated, sharp sweat. She smiles inside, because it occurs to her that men, if she's not powerful enough, don't feel they're getting their money's worth. A moment later she's unsure of whether that had been only a thought or whether she had said it out loud, because with his mouth flattened against the mattress he grunts at her to rub hard, but looking at the other side of his face, she can immediately see a thin smile, mocking, directed at them or at himself, she doesn't know. She fills with cheer and new energy, and blows on his neck: "Get ready, here it comes," and she showers his back and shoulders with a hail of rapid punches, sideways and lengthwise. His muscles tense at her, surprised, and deep from his throat comes a moan of desire and permission, and she feels he is responding to her strength, to the galloping intensity of her hands. He moans dimly beneath her, squirming and stretching and rounding, and wants her to hurt him, to dig into him, to bring something up out of him. She grows stronger and more vigorous by the minute, her stomach muscles rising and falling; she bares her teeth from the effort, and for several minutes she works like that, without a break, at times barely distinguishing his body from her own. Everything in her is overflowing, and she moans rhythmically, hoarse and sweaty, and with fingers that seemed to have suddenly become thicker and rougher, she carves out the biceps on his forearms and the long braids of muscle along his back, and shapes the tendons on his neck and arms, take, take—

Until she feels his body relaxing, as if he has disconnected from something, and for a minute or two he sprawls under her, breathing heavily, and she holds her hands up over him without touching, waiting to know his desire. He slowly calms down; he does not move, but he is unstill, because when she places her hands on his back he flows smoothly between her fingers, arching and streaming in waves beneath his skin, and her hands inquire, spreading over his skin questioningly: What do you want now? What are you telling me? His body clings and twists into her hands and begins rubbing against them, and his skin is made of a thousand little mouths, trembling and leaping toward her with the desperate eagerness of fledglings who hear their mother's wings. "But what do you really want?" she murmurs. "Tell me, you're telling me all sorts of things, and I don't want to get it wrong."

He stops at once and buries his face in the mattress, and she suspects he already knows the answer but wants to hear it from her, that he needs her to guess his innermost yearnings without having to tell her. A familiar fear awakens inside her, the life-or-death fear, because who better than she knows how deep you can reach with a touch, all the way to the places that are completely helpless and that don't even have names or words to protect them, to insulate them or blur the roads that lead to them. Perhaps, she thinks suddenly, perhaps that is why Rotem has always resisted and recoiled and never allowed me all these years. She weakens briefly, looks at the boy lying there, and knows that he too is one of those people created by touch. She is afraid that if she makes the smallest mistake now, if she makes the wrong choice out of all her options, she will lose him, and this moment of grace will also be lost—and he may not have any more of them in the places he goes to.

She gathers up her body and closes her eyes, trying to think, but the thoughts scatter and her body lifts itself up and carries her to the window. She stands and stares at the red lights marking the shoreline, and breathes quietly for a few minutes, summoning all her ancient strengths to return, if only for one final time, to be with her here. When she turns around, she sees that he has taken his shorts off and now he is lying on his stomach, his buttocks like a beautiful, heart-shaped bright spot on his body. She stops and looks, despite herself, at the delicate way his ankles are crossed, at the silky quality flowing on his skin. Her gaze slides over him and she reads in him sign after sign of loneliness and longing, and his protest, so fragile, transparent, and brave. Then he slowly turns over and lies with his eyes closed, his body taut and his slim member folded in a plume of hair, and now he looks so young to her, so soft and helpless.

She sits by his head with her legs on either side of his shoulders, and his head is heavy and dense in her hands. She gently rubs his scalp and massages his ears, the fetus image folded inside them; she presses and rubs them until they become warm, and feels the heat flowing from them to his entire body. She softly caresses his face, his eyes, and knows that in his quiet, mysterious way, he has managed to seep into her, into the place from which her strengths emanate, and that he is taking from them boundlessly; she can feel them dwindling, but she cannot keep them from him, because someone that brave or desperate, reaching that far, is entitled to everything. She lays her hand on his high forehead, full of thoughts and secrets and innocence and schemes, and makes circles around the third eye between his eyes, the one that watches the universe, the eye that in my body, she thinks, is becoming covered with cataracts. But even so, I was capable of seeing you. His cheeks are smooth to her touch, and his lips, which she now touches for the first time, are two rolls of velvet. She has never touched lips so exposed in a man or a boy, and the thought passes through her that his mouth is already prepared, and she is happy, as if something has gone right for her, easily, and now the road is open. She bends over him and rubs her short hair against his, gently at first, then forcefully, wildly, growling like an animal rubbing its body against its pup, to infuse it with the essence of its knowledge. When she moves her face away from his, she finds in his eyes the look she saw after he came down from his first handstand. Her heart leaps, and she already knows what she must do, and she knows that this time she is not wrong.

She never forgot, despite her sieve brain, and for years afterward, in good and in bad moments, mainly in bad, she would recall the flash of emotions and scenes: the neck, for example, how she slid it between her fingers over and over, up and down along its stem, lengthening and refining it, touching its artery every so often with fluttering touches like drops of perfume. Then his chest, the dark brilliance of his chest, how she circled the mounds of his boyish breasts with a thousand patient movements and leavened them and molded and cupped them to each other, and the flesh was now soft and supple and responded to her hungrily, with the happiness of an innocent creature. Then she turned him over and massaged and

258

spread his flexed buttocks, and enlivened the tight hills around the two beauty spots he had there, on his cheeks, until they acquiesced and melted at her touch. And in between, she sculpted his hips, arching them further and further, smoothed the glistening, violin-shaped plots of flesh with smooth, slow movements. She thought of the hands that would hold him there one day, and prayed that they would be good and right, and thought of the men who had held her like that, and of women whose hips she had known. Without any difficulty she remembered—she has a wonderful memory for this—the touch of beloved bodies, their smell and warmth and the music of their movement in her body, and sweet dizzying pleasure poured into her, and with all her might she emptied herself into him and diluted his body with a thousand lovers, of all colors, all languages and continents and sexes, as if wanting to alleviate his going out into the world, and the pain of translating his unique body into all the clichés of flesh he would encounter. Then she rubbed her favorite jasmine oil into her hands, the most pleasurable and profound of all the oils, and asked him to turn around again. He turned over slowly, and she went down to his feet and drew again, precisely, his thin ankles, and in her heart she blessed each and every toe and rubbed them with oil and rolled them between her joints, and powerfully rubbed his hard heels and his tensed arches, and wished for those feet that they would walk in beautiful places and dance with cherished souls. She smoothed his thin, youthful calves with quick, uplifting motions, rubbed his childish knees a little, and prayed for them that they never kneel or bow, and that they have the strength to proudly and bravely bear their wonderful, unique person.

With two strong hands she rubbed and rounded and leavened his narrow thighs, and was glad that he was giving his body to her completely, as if having emptied out all his desires and knowledge and slyness and secrets, with immense relief, as if he had retreated into the roots of his innocent being. Inside her, a fullness began to form, as if she were filling up with milk, and it occurred to her that she had never done anything like this for anyone. A fragment of a sensational image sparked in her, of her and Rotem this way, her giving Rotem a massage like this, carving out of Rotem the girl she used to be and finally liberating the young woman from within her, the woman she was meant to be. Because maybe it's not too late yet, she thought, to try and direct the vessel that she is, that grumbling little stomach which always seems to strike just next to the correct note—why not save her from a few bad years of unhappiness and loneliness and wandering, why not fight for her, goddammit, force her to give herself over to her, for once overcome her infantile fear; after all, she is nothing but a hardened little kitten, yearning, lost. She wondered how that had never happened.

Then she repelled the thought immediately, knowing that now she must be only with him, fight only for him, with her entire being, and she swiftly erased the image from within her, and with a brief motion she ironed out her body with both hands, from top to bottom, finally wrapping her fingers around her toes. She felt warm, madly warm, and for a moment she almost took her clothes off, but she remembered what she had sworn on the first day: give him only what he needs. She stopped and cooled herself off and let it sink in, as he lay on his back, fantasizing, dreamy, murmuring word fragments to himself. She ran her hands over his stomach, which no longer flinched at her touch but spread out for her like a taut little valley, waiting for its own blessing. She touched it and her fingers were light and became excited at once, and he started mumbling, "Good, good, good." She listened with wonder. This wasn't like the moans she had heard from thousands of others, but like someone suddenly recognizing something they had previously only heard about, like a boy who sees an airplane in the sky for the first time, not in a storybook, and he stands and cries out: Airplane, airplane! When she looked at him, a sigh escaped her. He was so beautiful at that moment, as if a boy and a girl were twisting inside him like two ropes or braids, intertwined, like something you see only in dreams, she thought, or in the Indian shrines, and even there it's not like this, not this pure and whole and glowing. She whispered to him eagerly,

"You can do everything, you'll see, nothing will stand in the way of your courage." She saw that he was moving his lips, repeating her words, moving in hallucinatory slow motion, with closed eyes; he looked as if he were swimming inside a bubble or a large drop. And she, spontaneously (because that may be the best way for me to give to him, she thought), talked to him within herself, perhaps also saying things out loud: "Never mind man, never mind woman, never mind what they told you, what they laughed or mocked, never mind what your dad calls you, what names, and why he hits you, and why they took Kobi away from you, they don't understand anything, they're just on the outside, they're in the noise, they can't hear what you can, and you can hear wonderfully, I want you to know that I haven't met many people who can hear like you do, just don't give up, don't give in to them." Then she became alarmed. What non-sense am I saying? What gives me the right? "You'll have a difficult path, very difficult, I hope you make it, you have to be as strong as Hercules to get out of there, to escape all that and remain who you are." And when she said it to him like that, she felt something occurring within him. His body began to squirm and spasm at her touch, his face twisted in strange, tormented labor pains, and she removed her hand and saw him massage within himself, painfully and passionately, the hidden, covered pit that she had sensed in their first class, which now seemed to be swelling by the minute, heating up and ripening and becoming golden and bursting and finally erupting with a bitter, broken sigh that passed through his body like a chilling furrow from head to toe. Her fingers were drawn after the sigh, strumming up and down with rapid touches to his body, as if she wanted to replay the new tune to him as it sounded outside his body. She saw a glimpse of the boarding school's filthy showers again, with their strange rust stains dripping on the floor, and his father's stupid, covetous face, asking her to make him a man.

She wailed with the fury of a beast: "Forget about them, it's all you, only you"—and she went on talking deliriously, massaging his entire body, but almost without touching him now, with fragments of thoughts, with heat waves that erupted from her, and only after several minutes was she able to calm down and sit at his side, large and stormy and breathless. She realized that he was already lying completely still, with his knees pulled into his chest, and his eyes were open and looking at her with a focused and slightly amazed look, as if he had only just finally grasped something that had been hidden from him, that had never been so revealed and clarified for him, like a promised land, or perhaps a verdict. There was no way to tell what was going on inside him, in his dark shell; maybe he was only thinking dully: The road home will be so long, and tomorrow it's Shabbat, and me and him alone at his place, and then I have to go back to boarding school. Nili smiled at him happily, compassionately, and took his limp, long-fingered hand and placed it on her blouse for a moment, on her left breast, which she thought of as the prettier one, the one that gave more milk when she breast-fed, so he would feel the touch and the warmth and the power. "Touch," she whispered, "see how sweet our body is, how much happiness it can give us."

Then she lay down beside him on the floor. She was so exhausted, so full and engorged, that she couldn't open her eyes to take in one more image. He got up and dressed with an odd, panicked speed. Then he lingered by the door for a long time, as if he already knew something and was afraid to step outside the place where everything was possible. She was surprised that he said nothing to her, and thought vaguely that perhaps he needed to be alone with himself for a while. She heard the door click shut behind him and smiled, and told herself with her seer's certainty that he'd be back soon, and then they'd say goodbye properly. And although she didn't have a drop of imagination, she fantasized about how they would stand facing each other, how they would be so embarrassed that they'd almost shake hands, and then she'd grasp him in her arms and they would embrace, and she'd feel the flutter of his lips against her neck for an instant.

That was what she thought, that was what she hallucinated and dreamed, and that was what she tormented herself with later, during all the years to come—the years of aridity, of longing, in a world which perhaps did not contain another boy like him. When she opened her eyes, she found the hotel already bustling with its daily noise; the quarry workers from the north had gone on their way long ago. She lay on her back for several more minutes, extremely quiet, and lamented something very transparent and rare that had passed her by, hovered for a moment, and disappeared.

I put down the last page. My neck and shoulders are hard as stone. Only after several breaths do I dare look up. Her lips are pursed. She's focused on something.

"You and Melanie," she says finally, shocking me by being completely unpredictable. "You're happy together."

She doesn't ask. She asserts. I find it difficult to talk, so I nod my head.

"You and she, you're good for each other." She looks up at the ceiling with her eyes wide open, and I am completely shaken: How is it that she doesn't talk about him? Or about him and her? How can she not say a single word about the ending I gave her and him? As if it has no importance to her, as if that is not the story now.

"I felt it so intensely all of a sudden when you were reading," she sighs, "in the massage, at the end. I felt so strongly what you have between you."

"Really?"

We are both quiet. Each submerged in herself. My heart suddenly flutters twice. A skip ahead and a skip back.

"Tell her to take care of you. Tell her from me."

"I will."

She reaches out. I put my face close to her. She runs her finger over my forehead. My eyes, my nose. My mouth.

"That mouth." She smiles.

Which is slightly swollen with bitterness, I quote myself. Her hand climbs up. I put my head down. She draws wavy lines on the back of my skull. With her last remaining strength, she presses my throbbing painful spots. Even now her finger is smarter than my whole brain. Then, for an eternal length of time, roughly my whole childhood, I just sit there bent over, inhaling her touch. Her finger traverses with angelic gentleness, walking over the winding crevices of my brain, in the cold and sad regions, in the places that were always closed off to her, the places where—as she always knew, without resentment and without bearing grudges—she was betrayed.

"I'm so glad we finally talked," she says.

June 2001

A NOTE ON THE AUTHOR

David Grossman is the author of seven novels (which
include *See Under:Love* and most recently, *Be My Knife*
and *Someone to Run With*), three books of journalism and
numerous stories for children. He has won many prizes
internationally and was made Chevalier de l'Ordre des Artes
et des Lettres. David Grossman lives in Jerusalem.

A NOTE ON THE TRANSLATOR

Jessica Cohen is a translator based in Seattle. Born in
England and raised in Jerusalem, she has translated several
contemporary Israeli novels as well as Hebrew poetry
and works of non-fiction.